By Kaylea Prime

By Kaylea Prime

TⓌF

Tears of Flame

<u>Novels</u>
A Spark From Embers

<u>Novellas</u>
A Ballad of Hate and Hope

KAYLEA PRIME

A SPARK FROM EMBERS

TEARS OF FLAME

Cover design by Fantastical Ink

Interior Design by Kaylea Prime

First edition: February 2024

ISBN 978-1-7380885-2-2 (hardcover)

ISBN 978-1-7380885-3-9 (paperback)

ISBN 978-1-7380885-4-6 (ebook)

www.kayleaprime.com

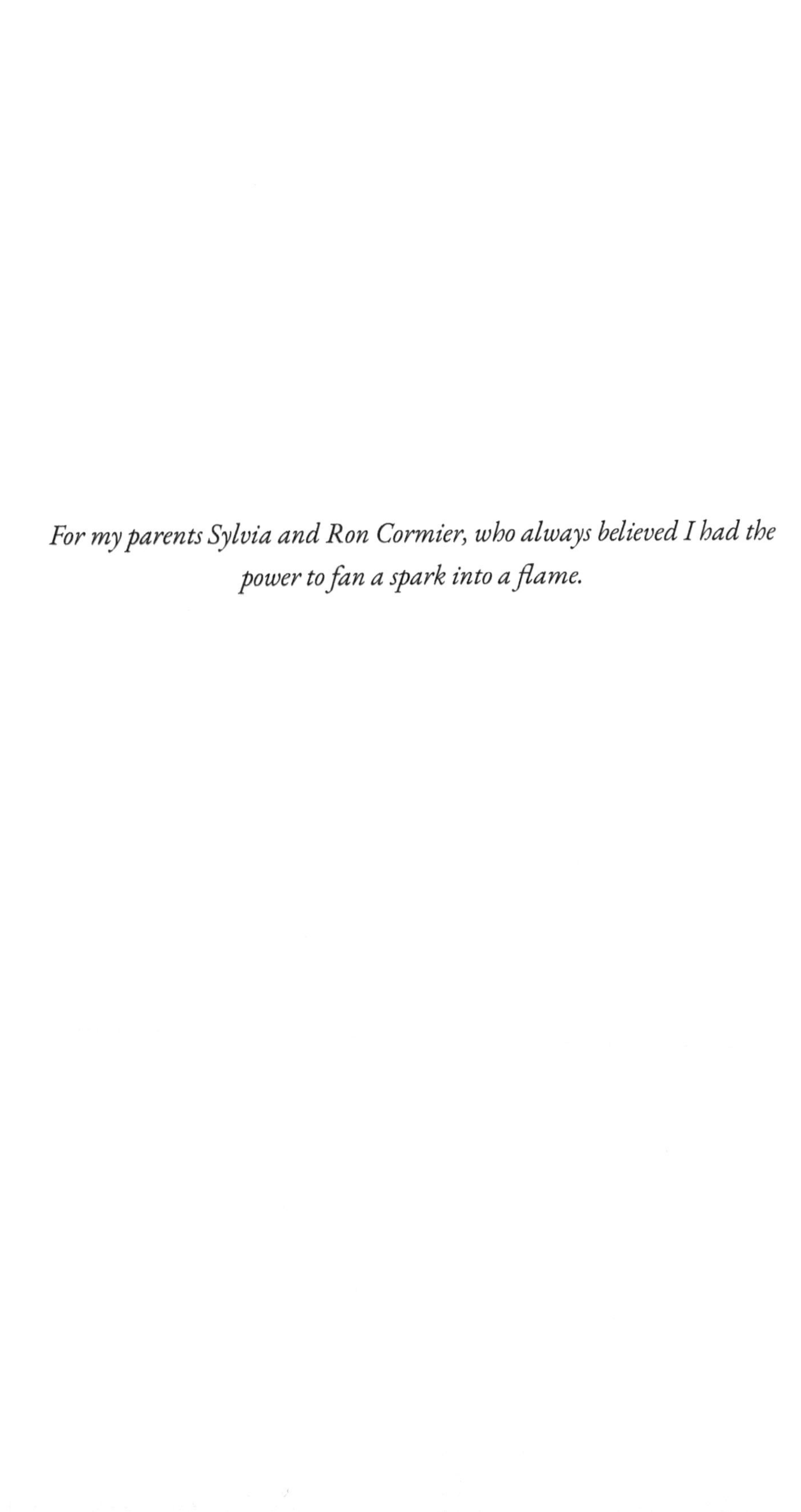

For my parents Sylvia and Ron Cormier, who always believed I had the power to fan a spark into a flame.

NORTH WESTERN
HEMISPHERE OF ARWÉ
NIROSULA
CARMELLE

CENTRAL CARMELLE
Tulandí
BELLAND
Carenthia
Steepleton
E
CARENTH-HILD
Yena Aisis
Voita Woods
Aganeni
MELLOTH
Edgewater
Athatair
Helgur
Calessar
GAP OF TALARÍ
FIRNETH LOMIN
Tariq
TOLOTANTEAU
LOTHILYA
Velleneni
CAR
Aspengrove Island
C
Dharma

ÉALOTH
Evírn Aisis
Evírr
NANDO
ORINLOTH
DÉLUREN
Seforu River
Tor Niro
Nironení
ení
Tor Yena
Keleb-Sola
TOR
STELLA
LALÍTÉ
TANTEAU NÍR
ELLE
VASMORLOTH
Norance Dunes

Contents

Darkness gnaws at a dying fire's embers
Like the void between stars, a space forsaken.
But within every fading ember a spark smolders,
waiting
ready,
to reawaken.

From obscurity's black hollow, a light ignites.
Filling empty hearts with a hope most keen.
Flames shedding shadows of shattered dreams,
waiting,
ready,
to finally feel seen.

—Performed by Storyteller Nensola. 913, F.A.

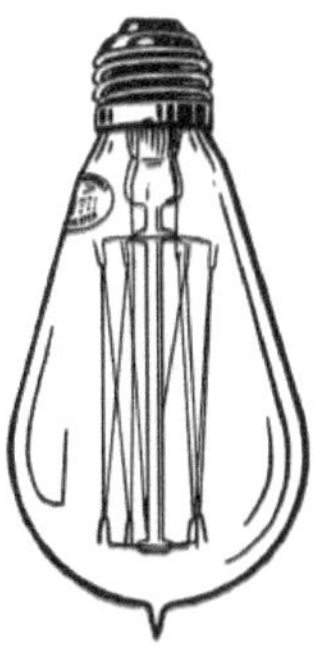

Prologue

When Worlds Collide

June 13, 1886. Vancouver, British Columbia

His time was almost up.

Therius touched the pendant resting on his knobby sternum, a metal flame encompassing a clear, diamond-like stone. The stone glowed softly at his touch, a bright light in the dim curtained cabin, and the man sprawled on the peeling wooden floor writhed and screamed. After a few seconds, he let go. Just a reminder. A taste to motivate the man to speak.

"Tell me," he hissed. His voice sounded faded and hoarse even to his own ears, like chalk scraped across jagged rock. "Tell me where to find Curie. I know he's a friend of yours, Thomas. You cannot hide the truth from me."

Thomas moaned and lifted his bruised face to focus on a framed photograph perched on a cedar desk, featuring a family with a baby. "I'm sorry," he whispered at the family. A single tear carved a path through the streaks of blood painting his cheek. Never taking his eyes off the photograph, his voice held a bit more strength when he told Therius, "I don't know what possible interest you and your heinous Master could have in his research, but I do know if you find what you seek, both Earth and Arwé will suffer for it. I will never help you."

Therius studied the stubborn set of Thomas' jaw. "No, I don't believe you will."

He stepped towards the desk, ignoring Thomas' widening eyes and futile attempts to drag his weakened body into Therius' path.

Layers of diagrams, pieces of metal wire, a variety of magnet—he tried to discern patterns but found none. Sketches of glass tubes with two wires connected to something inside and the names Woodward and Evans scribbled beneath were tucked under similar drawings with the name Edison attached. Letters signed by names like J. Henry snuggled up to telegrams saying someone named Tesla could not be reached, all pinned beneath a miniature wooden man joined by intricate metals. He didn't understand this collection of papers and objects, but his Master needed them to advance his plans, and they might contain a clue to Pierre Curie's invention. An invention that could allow his Master to finally exact his revenge—and give Therius the power he had always dreamed of.

Wrinkled fingers scrabbled at the hem of his robe, but Therius stomped on them viciously. He had expected someone who had fought in the Harthoné Orin War to hold up better under... *persuasive...* interrogation, but time had clearly been cruel to Thomas just as it had to Therius.

Well, not *just* as it had to Therius. His hand tingled, and he looked down to see fresh dark spots and lines weaving across his dried skin like thin strands of a spider's web. Sweat beaded on his forehead, though the pendant's magic should have prevented his body from reacting to sweltering heat.

He didn't have time for this. The pendant's power waned, and his body deteriorated more with every passing second. Gritting his teeth, he kicked Thomas' face, eliciting a sickening crunch and knocking him unconscious.

Touching the clear stone again, he closed his eyes and beheld flames burning the brush and grasses a few miles away, a few men monitoring it from the peripheries.

He smirked and squeezed the pendant.

A strong gust of wind caught the flames, swirling them in a flurry of sparks and blowing them into the trees like a dragon breathing fire. The men shouted, panicked, and ran for their lives. The wildfire grew quickly, consuming the dry trees and grasses voraciously. It would soon reach the city, and this cabin.

He stuffed everything from the desk into a satchel hidden under his robes and strode out of the house. With another squeeze of the pendant, he sealed all exits behind him. Then, without pausing, he touched the clear stone one last time and the cabin burst into flames.

He was out of time, but the city would burn for the information he had been unable to obtain.

And Thomas Sheldon, trapped in the flame-drenched cabin, would be the first to burn.

Chapter One

Daydream Believer

July 1914. Vancouver, British Columbia

Balancing on the narrow precipice between life and death was always a challenge, but Sadie feared her mother's ambitions far more than a fatal rooftop fall. At least she might feel a momentary glimmer of weightless freedom if she pretended falling was flying like Peter Pan.

Gripping the dark green spine of her book between her teeth, she clung to the white iron railing of the widow's walk and shimmied the hem of her lace-trimmed skirt up to her knees so she could swing her legs over.

As soon as she found her footing, the white pearl hanging low in the inky sky tugged threads deep inside her like the moon pulling the tide to the nearby coast. Reading by its soft silver light should help erase an early dinner of bubbling shame with a side of disappointment before the next course of dashed hopes was inevitability served at the ball this evening.

She reached the stone bench fastened to the centre of the widow's walk and flopped down with a sigh. Unfortunately, from this perch she could still see and hear her parents arguing through the slightly ajar dining room window. Her father clutched a snifter of brandy like a shield between him and his wife's wildly gesticulating arms, warding off her demands to find a suitor for his errant youngest daughter—Sadie. Her mother thought marriage would tame her nearly nineteen-year-old daughter, but

Sadie wouldn't let it. Becoming the passive, submissive crown jewel of her husband's empire was a path for her older, perfect sister, Tanaya, not her.

Sadie traced the gold filigree letters of *The Iliad* tenderly with her fingertip and opened it to her ribbon-marked spot but paused as her parents' shouts devolved to seething whispers.

"And what if the book I saw Connor tuck into his jacket pocket is *his*?" her mother hissed, coating the pronoun with ominous venom. "What if Sadie sees it?"

Goosebumps pimpled Sadie's arms. She stayed as still as possible, barely breathing.

His? She didn't think her mother referred to her younger brother Connor, but then, who?

Tanaya's mocking smile at dinner resurfaced in Sadie's mind, a sneer born from their mother's comment claiming she wouldn't have to worry about money if she knew she wouldn't have to support Sadie for the rest of her life. Her father had pinched the bridge of his nose, wilting under his wife's tired accusations. Sadie had scraped back her chair and fled the dining room.

Shaking her head to dispel the raw memories, Sadie swallowed the jagged edges of the words she regretted not saying, the retort lodged in the back of her throat she should have thrown at her mother instead of running away. She longed to emulate the courageous characters in her favourite stories, so why was her defiance so inconsistent?

Tucking her regrets into a back pocket of her mind, Sadie strained to hear more of her parents' conversation, but the drawing room window no longer framed their silhouettes. Sadie shrugged and immersed herself into Homer's epic of bloodlust and revenge. She battled alongside Hector and Odysseus, toppling those denying her freedoms with her sword instead of letting others dictate her chance at happiness. She wanted to be Achilles, not Helen of Troy.

A grandfather clock from inside the mansion chimed the hour. Heart stuttering, she snapped her book shut. She could delay getting ready for the ball no longer. The spell of words had worked its magic, allowing her to escape the multiplying steel bars closing in around her.

Sadie used to think magic was real. Had even thought *she* could do magic. That her imagination could be fanned into sparks of tangible magic if she concentrated hard enough.

Now, she knew the truth. Magic wasn't real. Heroes could not slay their own dragons.

But Sadie Sheldon could not stop dreaming that someday magic would save her life.

With Homer's descriptions of blood-tainted honour and fatal deceptions still rattling in her head, Sadie opened the trap door behind the bench and descended the short ladder and steep, narrow, winding staircase. When she reached the landing, she peered cautiously around the corner like a villager fleeing Troy, heart pounding to the foreboding rhythm of her mother's clicking heels. The empty hall mocked her paranoia, but Sadie still padded softly into her room across from the widow's walk stairway. No need to hand her mother more ammunition.

The cloying scent of lavender layered with vanilla assaulted Sadie's nostrils, alerting her to Margaret's presence before she even spotted her maid laying a pair of Sadie's black satin gloves out on her vanity. Stealing a spritz of just one of her mother's perfumes never satisfied Margaret—she always dabbed on a second. Why her mother indulged Margaret's audacity mystified Sadie, but she suspected her maid emulating her tastes flattered Victoria's vanity too much to be reprimanded.

"You'll have to hurry, Miss Sheldon, I was sent here twenty minutes ago, there's only half an hour till the ball starts, I don't see how—"

Margaret never hesitated to reprimand Sadie. Subtle criticism layered beneath propriety was an art form Margaret had learned from Victoria Sheldon. How Tanaya's rehearsal dinner for her wedding had evolved into a ball Sadie still didn't know, but somehow her mother had justified the extravagance of dancing instead of a shared meal. Margaret must be in a tizzy.

Without a word, Sadie presented her back to Margaret and allowed her to start unbuttoning her dark green dress. She stared at her reflection in the gilded full-length mirror beside her vanity, barely registering her blotted red cheeks and errant auburn curls escaping her stiffly coiffed bun before finding sanctuary in her dark green eyes. When she fixated on the silver lines streaking across her nebulous irises, or counted every silver fleck dotting her pine forest orbs, she could lose herself imagining Norse gods battled with minuscule bolts of silver lightning against a tumultuous sky, or tiny silver fairies flitted amongst the evergreen boughs of an enchanted forest. She could tune out the menial chatter of her maid as she laced her corset and forget the hideous floral design papering the walls of her prison.

"Miss, your book, I can't get the sleeve over it—"

Sadie snapped her eyes to *The Iliad* still clutched in her hand.

Switching the book to her other hand, Sadie let her dress slide the rest of the way off her wrist and handed it to Margaret to hang up. She pulled reflexively at the corset binding her waist over her shift, then crossed over to her nightstand.

"I forgot, I'll just put it away—"

But as her fingers brushed the Sheldon family crest carved onto the drawer's knob, her room faded until she stood in a line of soldiers defending a castle at dawn.

She'd been here before, in another unfinished daydream.

She peered at the horizon, where the deep golds and brilliant oranges of dawn sparked the tips of the opposing army's lances and bathed their armour in molten flames. Through her spyglass, she could see the soldiers' hardened expressions, and imagined they clenched their jaws and locked their joints against their rattling armour just as she and her comrades did. Biting back the bile that rose in their stomachs and constricted their throats.

Perhaps they too felt lost to the needs of the many, suffocating under the pressures of honour and fealty, expectations they could never fulfill. Both sides made furtive attempts to catch the eyes of the soldiers next to them, desperate to feel humour again, to connect with the cause, remember why death was imminent. Cast out for the lifeline of a smile, an understanding nod, maybe a wave of mercy—but there was no mercy.

Mercy did not exist today.

Maybe it never did.

It was always the same story.

But people never learned.

The bard standing beside her had taught her this, a truth he had learned after singing of countless battles, voicing the joys and sorrows of the people around him, archiving the rise and fall of their cyclical errors and triumphs.

There was no such thing as an original story, he had told her one night after regaling the troops with an epic song of love and war. Maybe even no such thing as original people.

It was a truth Sadie was starting to realize.

Dry and cracked, the craggy parched plain boasted deep chasms and rivers of dark shadows contrasting with the caked yellow soil. A low, whistling wind wailed across the plain, stirring pebbles and churning up golden dust before blowing across the chained drawbridge of the castle where she waited.

The wind caressed Sadie's cheek, her back against a knotted wooden flagpole, one hand resting on the hilt of her sword at her waist, the other pressed against the cool stone teeth of the tower's rim. Even if all battles were the same, Sadie still exulted in the anticipation of them. Nothing made her feel more alive than the imminent possibility of death. When she fought for her life—protecting the people and world she loved so much they made her chest and stomach ache—she could not be accused of passivity towards life. She never wanted to be guilty of that.

But the narrative of people's lives never changed. People gambled, hoping the outcome would be different, that the dice would be cast a different way.

Yet there was always something to regret.

The barren wasteland tremored, rattling the pebbles like a thousand rolling dice as the enemy army marched towards Sadie. When the army was just out of arrow range, they came to an abrupt, uniform halt.

The pebbles stopped rolling.

The dice had been cast.

Whether they won or lost the battle today, the gamble had still been lost.

Because the story was always the same.

"Miss Sheldon, are you quite well? We must hurry, or you'll be late for the ball!"

Margaret's impatient whine shattered Sadie's daydream and she squinted at her, refocusing on the wisps of her thin greying chestnut hair. Her throbbing heart pounded so erratically she had trouble reconciling it with her breathing. She was prone to daydreams, but this one had felt so *real*. She touched her cheek, still warm from the wind's heated caress, and swallowed what little moisture lingered in her mouth down through the crags of her dry throat. The soldiers' thudding footsteps still reverberated in her ears.

"Oh, she's well, she's just daydreaming instead of focusing on her future. *Again.*"

Sadie's fingers burned like fire thawing near-frostbitten skin. Dropping *The Iliad* in her drawer as though it scalded her, she whipped around to face her mother, heart still pounding beneath the swirling fragments of her dizzying daydream. She forced herself to take a deep, even breath.

"Mother, you don't have to worry, I'll be ready on time." Sadie positioned herself in front of the full-length mirror again. Her voice shook through gritted teeth, and even she couldn't tell if the tremors were aggravated exasperation or anxiety that her mother could somehow see her daydream reflected in her wide eyes.

"Margaret, please leave us." Dressed in a bright floral gown of jungle green and daffodil yellow with a tiny tiara perched amidst her tumbling curls, her mother epitomized a leopard poised to pounce on its prey.

Margaret bobbed her head obediently and exited the room, closing the door behind her.

With each stalking step that brought Victoria Sheldon's reflection closer in the mirror, Sadie added another brick to the wall of defiance building in her mind. She could not allow her mother's words to pull on threads of doubt, or she would unravel.

"When are these foolish daydreams going to stop?" Victoria hissed without preamble.

"When are you going to accept that I'm not Tanaya?" Sadie countered.

Her mother yanked on Sadie's corset strings, but Sadie refused to wince. Instead, she grabbed her mother's wrist and simply said, "Don't."

Though her grip was light, her steady, immovable tone stilled her mother's fingers. The flash of her silver-flecked eyes as she pierced her mother's gaze in the mirror was a steel-edged promise her mother dared not challenge.

"Fine, look like a wilted flower if you wish," jibed Victoria, adopting her usual pattern of sidestepping the moments Sadie dared to challenge her instead of admitting defeat. "But you *are* still a flower in the prized Sheldon garden, and I will not allow you to be weeded or infect the others. You and your father can think what you want, but I am trying to protect this family, and allowing you to stray too far from your inevitable path will help no one."

"Father thinks I don't need to marry as well?"

"No, your father does not want to think, period. Not about household affairs. He wants things to run smoothly at home, but he does not want to think about the *how*. His stubbornness regarding your future is the manifestation of his desire to avoid conflict. Like me, he does not understand why you do not want to marry, but he thinks your future will magically sort itself out. Rather like you, I suppose."

The sour curving down of the corner of her mother's mouth told Sadie the irony tasted bitter.

"Well, I'm sorry I'm not more like Tanaya, Mother," said Sadie softly, sarcasm mingling with exhausted truth. This tired apology had been repeated so often it had become a refrain. "I don't have anything against the institution of marriage, but if I marry one day it will be for love, and not to further myself in the high society life I loathe, or to gain independence. And I'm not ready for marriage. I haven't seen any of the world yet. I haven't had any adventures. I haven't had the chance to just be me, no strings attached. If I marry now, I'll fade away. Become invisible."

"What a naïve thing to say, Sadie," chided her mother. "There are *always* strings attached in life, always rules to follow, steps that need to be taken for survival. Nobody's life is entirely their own, otherwise how would society function if everyone was just looking out for themselves?"

"I'm sorry," repeated Sadie, "but I can't change who I am."

"Of course you can! We can all change who we are. Change is the one constant in life, and one of the few things us women have control over. *That* is what I have been trying to tell you Sadie, what you need to understand. If we can't change who we are, if we can't adapt our dreams to create the best lives for ourselves in the limited ways that are possible for us, then we have *nothing*. We become powerless."

Sadie blinked rapidly, trying to bring the gleam of her mother's triumphant eyes back into focus. Her tense lips slackened and her hands dropped to her sides, creating the perfect opportunity for her mother to slip Sadie's evening gown for the ball over her head.

Is my mother right?

No. Her stomach clenched, halting the sinking weight.

"Change *is* a constant, Mother, but you're wrong that women need to change to meet society's expectations. It's society's expectations of women that need to change, and if we don't stand up for that change *then* we are powerless."

Back still turned to her mother, Sadie watched Victoria's eyes in the mirror flicker from Sadie's clenched fists to her lifted chin and flushed cheeks. But instead of tensing and bristling, Victoria's whole posture slackened and slumped, as though the burden of battling her children for their well-being had become too heavy to bear.

"If only that were true," her mother whispered through a bitter smile, slipping the last button on Sadie's dress through the loophole.

The words lingered in the space between them, weighted with the words Victoria didn't say.

"We will say no more on the subject now," said her mother, retreating towards the door, away from the unspoken truths suspended between them. "Guests will be arriving soon, and I must check on the servers to make sure they have recovered from your brother's immature prank. He's almost as impossible as you."

Sadie hoped her scowl branded the back of Victoria's neck as she swept out of the room.

Almost, almost, almost.

The word echoed through her mind as though shouted in her ear, a ringing accusation that heated her neck and clutched her chest.

Connor caused far more trouble than her, but his harmless misdemeanours and often reckless adventures never threatened to publicly shame the family. He accepted the mantle of heir to the Sheldon family business and fortune, and always knew where to draw the line.

But Sadie's life could be summarized in that one word: *almost.*

She was *almost* a sister worthy of Tanaya's time.

Almost tame enough to not stray too far over the line between adventure and reality like her brother.

Almost clever enough to find a path allowing her to stand up for herself *and* make her mother and family proud, thus earning her father's begrudging respect.

Almost the daughter her mother wished she had.

Almost strong enough to pack a bag and leave this house, her family, and that loathsome word behind.

Almost.

But not quite.

Her eyes strayed to the nightstand and the memory of a craggy, sun-drenched plain, but she forced them to snap back to the mirror and her reflected eyes.

Survive the night. That's all she had to do. Wade through the menial chatter and discussions of her future without her limbs icing and heart burning between squeezed lungs. She rolled her shoulders back and straightened her spine, inhaling deeply.

Connor leaned against the door frame of Sadie's room, frowning at her glazed eyes as she stared at her reflection. Embroidered black roses trailing down her burgundy bodice glinted in the soft golden light from an oil lamp, black gems winking at the lacy straps draped across her narrow shoulders. But Connor knew his sister well enough to know she took in none of these details. He knew the deep breaths rattling her beaded bodice were the pieces of armour she strapped on before social functions to brace herself against verbal blows. And her glazed eyes signalled her retreat behind the fortified barrier in her mind, though Connor was never sure if that wall was to stop barbed words from flying in or to prevent her own serrated emotions from firing out.

Unfortunately, Connor never knew what to say to ease her dread and render the mental armour unnecessary. He had proven this again tonight at dinner, trying to catch Sadie's eye and calm her with meaningful looks instead of standing up for her and calling his mother's scapegoating out himself. He cringed every time unwarranted vitriol was thrown Sadie's way, but he never voiced his disappointment to his parents. He could lighten the mood and scheme meaningless quests that might temporarily satiate her lust for adventure, but when it came to real actions to better her situation, he had no ideas. He was a white knight with no horse or sword or map.

"You know what happens when you look in the mirror too long, don't you? You'll become obsessed with your own reflection like that man from Greek legends." Connor's empty words carved a hollow in the pit of his stomach, but he tried not to wince at the pain of his inadequacies. His sister needed him to soak up her insecurities like a sponge, not wallow in his own. He forced his mouth to hook up at the corner, his trademark crooked smile.

Whirling around, Sadie scowled at him.

"Stop creeping up on me like that!"

"What, and sacrifice that hilarious little jump you do when you're scared? Over my dead body."

"That can be arranged," muttered Sadie darkly. "And I am *not* Narcissus."

"To the contrary. You have been staring in the mirror for the past five minutes. You do look nice though," he added.

"How charming of you to notice." Sadie surveyed Connor, and he glanced at his own reflection in the mirror. Crisp black vest, trousers, and tailcoat with a black bow tie knotted expertly at his throat, and the short waves of his warm chocolate brown hair slicked back. His sapphire eyes twinkled as though teasing an elaborate inside joke. Little did Sadie know, that joke was him.

Begrudgingly, Sadie admitted, "You look nice too."

"It is a difficult burden to bear, but we must try not to outshine the bride-to-be at her own ball. Speaking of the bride, how are preparations for Tanaya's wedding coming?"

"Just dandy, Connor," Sadie quipped. "This last ball before the wedding is right on course to sail down the same river of dull insignificant small talk, mundane chatter, and false flattery. The wings of pretentious affluence will still flutter and waft the same stale dreary air over everyone."

"Sounds like I'm about to develop an allergy," Connor remarked.

Sadie snorted. "Why do you think a rash breaks out every time I'm stuffed into one of these opulent dresses and forced to stay in one conversation for too long?"

"The heady scent of dozens of clashing perfumes?"

"Well yes, that too," Sadie laughed. "What ridiculous prank did you pull this time?"

"Not a good one, I assure you. I strategically spilled soapy water so a servant would slip and cause a distraction for me to escape the library unnoticed with this."

Reaching dramatically into a deep pocket on the inside of his tailcoat, Connor pulled out a book and handed it to Sadie with a theatrical flourish. Connor bit down on the smile quivering his lips and held his breath as he watched Sadie stroke the embossed spine in awe before flipping the burgundy leather cover open to peruse the thick bronzed caramel pages of parchment.

"This book is beautiful Connor," she breathed.

"Yeah." Connor shrugged, not really understanding how a book could be beautiful. It was something his father might have said in deference to the tree the paper had been cut from, but Connor had never quite emulated Roger's admiration for the lumber industry that had built the Sheldon fortune. His father had been far more successful instilling that passion in Sadie, but she wouldn't be the one to inherit. He would. "But that's not why I wanted you to see it."

Connor turned the book over in Sadie's hands. Gold lettering stamped across the cover read:

Adventures in Carmelle
Thomas Sheldon

Butterfly wings brushed Connor's stomach as he observed Sadie's eyes widening in recognition.

Sadie had heard the name Thomas Sheldon whispered furiously behind closed doors after their mother had caught her defying the family rule of never touching the paintings. Ten years ago, eight-year-old Sadie had come to Connor in tears and explained the whole story. Unable to quell her insatiable curiosity about why thick dust coated one of the paintings when all the others were kept immaculately clean, Sadie had swiped her finger across the canvas. She had glimpsed dancing green eyes before their mother swooped down, whirled her around and yelled, "What do you think you're doing, child?"

When Sadie had emerged from her room after supper, she discovered the portrait had been taken down. No one had seen it since. But Connor understood Sadie's fear at their mother's irate, unhinged reaction, and the name Victoria had whisper-yelled at their father before she'd been sent to her room, must have lingered in the dusty corners of Sadie's mind. And there had been moments when both Connor and Sadie had sworn they'd heard Thomas' name whispered behind the shielding hands of their high society acquaintances.

"I know," said Connor, swallowing an uncomfortable lump in his throat at the memory of Sadie's round tear-stained cheeks. "I couldn't believe it either."

"Where did you find this?" Sadie breathed.

"In the library, I found it earlier today when I was hiding out from Mom after I—well, that part's not important," said Connor, waving away his misdemeanour. Every bone and tendon had felt like it had been vibrating in anticipation of the right opportunity to show Sadie this book.

"What's it about?" Sadie asked, scanning the pages. "If it's written by Thomas Sheldon..."

She trailed off, letting the sentence and its implied scandal hang between them. They didn't know what Thomas Sheldon had done to be ostracized from his family, but maybe this book held the answer. Even the title would have sparked controversy. Sheldons didn't go on adventures, even imaginary ones. And they certainly didn't write books about them.

Connor fumbled through the pages, heart racing, until he found the correct page and swivelled the book back to Sadie.

"*This* is why I wanted to show you this book."

On the left-hand page a short paragraph was written in careful calligraphy, the black ink gleaming wetly as if by magic. But Sadie's eyes flicked to the painting of a battle on the right-hand page first.

In the foreground, humans fought on a lush green battlefield against the most bizarre creatures Connor had ever seen. Hideous and foul, they were blacker than the yawning darkness behind the moon, with sharp fangs and claws and sleek slimy bodies. Their bloodshot or eerie yellow eyes glared at the humans with such intense loathing Connor's heart skipped. Beyond these creatures another strange race stood in a line with bows raised and arrows nocked. Antlers of varying heights sprouted from heads of luxurious hair, and feathered wings as tall as their bodies unfolded from tan and warm copper skin. Some had both antlers and wings, but most had only one—or neither. A noble, dignified air radiated from them as they glared in contempt at their foes.

"Who are *they*?" Sadie whispered, pointing to a group on a small hill with a shaky finger. Connor cocked his head at the shock in Sadie's dilated pupils.

A large host of long-robed men and women stood with arms thrust high above their heads. Lightning leapt from the pewter grey, purple, and black clouds above them, the chaotic storm in the sky reflecting the chaos taking place below. A dark-skinned woman stood near the front of the host, and Connor noticed Sadie's eyes lingering on her hands and the magical blue light emanating from them. Far in the distance, beyond the endless lines of armies, loomed a massive castle. Its winding stone turrets and towers were tipped with flags flapping in the turbulent storm.

Sadie shook her head as though trying to shake off a mosquito.

"Is something wrong?" Connor asked.

"Of course not, just in awe."

"I get that, I was too," he empathized. His eyes lingered on a man Sadie hadn't seemed to notice, though he had drawn Connor's gaze to him like a magnet. Hair and eyebrows so pale blond the colour seemed to be leeched out of them, wrinkles around his eyes and brow line, and thin spidery fingers steepled below his chin raised the hairs on Connor's neck. The man's eyes radiated quiet menace as he observed the battle unfolding from the vantage point of a small hill at the edge of the painting.

Sadie turned her attention to the left-hand page, unaware of Connor's prickling stomach. He circled behind her, peering over her shoulder to read the inscription again with her.

This painting was done by Varis Vanyë, an amazing artist of Lothilya, as a favour to me. The image is of course a portrayal of Harthoné Orin, the War of the Wizards. The original is a massive painting covering an entire wall in a palace of Lothilya. This war is especially important to me as the first war I ever fought in. It spurred my military career forward. Varis was even kind enough to paint me into this version; I am there fighting among the soldiers of Carenthia, my bright red hair sticking out. Thomas Sheldon, in a famous painting! I never would have imagined it in those days.

Sadie spotted a man with flaming hair a shade lighter than hers, savagely cleaving one of the beasts in two. Her eyes widened further.

"Is that...?"

"Yes. I think we can assume that is Thomas Sheldon," said Connor softly. "The family resemblance is uncanny. This book reads like a journal, but it must be fictional... right?"

His heart pulsed in his throat waiting for Sadie's answer. If there was even the slightest possibility this book wasn't fictional, it would mean Connor might have finally offered Sadie a life preserver in the stormy seas she swam so hard against just to keep her head above water. This could be tangible hope, proof that life beyond this manor could exist for a Sheldon, and Thomas' book might outline the steps Sadie needed to follow to get there. He could finally feel useful to his sister.

Sadie's sparkling eyes punctuated her wide grin. "I don't know, but I'm going to find out."

Chapter Two

The Ball

Veins vibrating to the beat of her racing heart, Sadie glanced at the mantel clock resting above the lit fireplace in her room and moaned. Connor followed her gaze and cursed. Thomas' book had delayed them, and they were now five minutes late for the ball. But not even her mother's impending wrath could puncture the hopeful balloon swelling in Sadie's chest. After ten years, the enigma of Thomas Sheldon had resurfaced in her life, and the timing seemed too fortuitous to ignore. Adventures in a magical world with fantastical creatures seemed absurd outside of a fairy tale, and yet... didn't seemingly impossible things happen all the time? Horseless carriages powered by gasoline, moving pictures that captured stories through nickelodeons, airplanes to carry humans across the sky like birds, and mechanical humans. Maybe Thomas had discovered the secret to unlocking magic in their mundane world, and she could too, if only she could discover the key.

Tucking Thomas' book into her nightstand drawer on top of *The Iliad*, Sadie bounced to the door on her toes, about to follow Connor out of the room—and then returned to her vanity, inspired by the image of women using magic in battle that lingered in her mind. Opening the bottom drawer, she pried open the false bottom, retrieving a folded piece of paper. Tucking it into the elbow of her long ebony gloves, she followed Connor down to the main hallway on the second floor. She may not have ever attended a women's rights meeting in the city like the poster tucked into her glove advertised, but she hoped carrying it with her might lend her the courage she needed to make it through the night. Like carrying her dreams around in her pocket.

Dreams of sailing across the Pacific Ocean or the Caribbean Sea, wind whipping through her tangled, sun-streaked hair, the tang of salty sea spray kissing her lips as she gazed at a horizon of endless possibilities. Weaving through the trees in a Madagascar rainforest, searching for undiscovered species. Exploring the secrets of Arctic glaciers under the dancing indigo and emerald lights of the Aurora Borealis. Climbing Mayan pyramids, searching the ruins for ancient artifacts.

Or maybe, just maybe, wielding a sword or magic like heroes of ancient legends—or the women of Carmelle, apparently.

Dreams that involved *something* other than the menial repetition of a high society woman's life of social gatherings, refined fine arts, and protecting her reputation.

At the top of the grand staircase, she paused.

A collage of colours burst before her eyes as women swirled around the front foyer, flitting from group to group, gracefully juxtaposed against the mass of black that was the men. Feathers and flowers and lace caps adorned most of the ladies' heads, and all wore broad grins as they greeted each other cordially, heading into the ballroom.

A hand tapped her shoulder and she turned to find Connor offering her his arm.

"My fair lady," he said with a slight nod. "May I have the pleasure of escorting you to your doom?"

"Why certainly, my brave sir. But I must warn you, those who associate themselves with me inevitably meet their doom soon after."

"Ah, here they are," Victoria announced as they reached the bottom of the stairs. "My daughter, Sadie, and my son, Connor," she informed the couple she had been chatting with.

Sadie and Connor pasted fake smiles on their faces as their mother paraded them around the foyer in a circuit of polite introductions. A few subtle smirks and raised eyebrows accompanied the smiles, as though the guests guessed Victoria would be trying to pair her next daughter with a suitor tonight, now Tanaya would soon be wed, and they were judging her worthiness of their sons or nephews or neighbours. Sadie shifted her shoulders uncomfortably under their scrutinizing glances.

Enticing music from the ballroom wound about her feet like a cat demanding attention, and she longed to let it sweep away her growing self-consciousness. Why did they think it acceptable to assess her worth, or claim a right to her heart?

Stifling air wrapped around her head like a scarf, and Sadie wished she'd brought her fan down. Where had the cool breeze drifting through the open front doors gone? The warm heavy air weighed on her, pressing on her chest and gripping her lungs until she feared she might suffocate. She gasped but refrained from clawing at her chest, her breathing rapid and ragged as though she had sprinted around their whole property.

Connor's hand gripped her arm.

"Mother, we're going to go dance now," he announced in a clear, confident voice. "Sadie promised me the first dance."

Victoria shooed them away with a flick of her wrist. She hadn't noticed Sadie's pain. She never did.

Connor dragged her through the mass of dancing guests and into a little deserted side chamber off the ballroom.

"What in the name of Thomas Sheldon are we doing here?" Sadie demanded. "And get your hand off my arm, you're hurting me!"

"Sorry," he apologized, releasing her arm, but the intensity in his gaze did not waver as he locked eyes with her. "But if you think I wouldn't notice when my sister starts hyperventilating... What the hell is going on? Are you all right?"

A warm haze wrapped her heart at his touching observations, but it couldn't temper the heat from her chest pains. She felt weak, like a woman who should carry smelling salts, not wield a sword.

"I'm fine Connor, really. I guess the combined heat and mundane speech became a bit too much when my mind is still consumed by the discovery of Thomas' book. Every time someone looks at me knowingly, like it's my turn to get married next, I feel my future narrowing, my dreams slipping further away. My one goal for the night was to get through it without having a physical reaction to the pressure I knew I'd feel, and I've already failed."

"If you don't like the way this ball is going Sadie," said Connor after a pause, "might I suggest doing something about it?"

Mischief sparked in Connor's eyes, and Sadie knew he meant stirring up mayhem for their parents, but his words ignited a better idea in Sadie's mind.

"Ready to venture out into the sea of swirling sanity?"

Connor rolled his eyes. "When the invitation includes alliteration, how could I refuse?"

Dancing wasn't his favourite past time, but Connor had been forced to attend so many balls the steps came as easily as breathing. He could let his mind and eyes wander as his feet fell into rhythm, leading Sadie in a weaving pattern across the ballroom.

He spotted Tanaya dancing with her fiancé Henry a few paces away and choked on his saliva.

"What's wrong?" Sadie asked, eyebrows drawing together at his splutters and coughs.

Connor pointed towards their sister and Sadie snorted, her hand flying to cover her guffaw.

Henry's ungainly feet kept stepping on Tanaya's satin heels, and Connor couldn't help but laugh at his oldest sister's winces through her pasted smile. He felt bad for her at first, until he observed Henry's fumbling antics endeared him to the onlookers more. Indulgent whispers such as, "So sweet, look at him trying so hard for his future wife", or "He must be so nervous for the wedding, the poor man" circled the party. With her royal blue gown winking with tiny silver diamonds and a long train attached to a silver bracelet on her wrist, Tanaya looked like a celestial goddess, and not even a clumsy fiancé could tarnish her status as the belle of the ball.

Warmth trickled along his chest at Tanaya's good fortune. He and Sadie poked fun at their sister's obedience and need to please their parents, but he had observed the pride and adoration in her eyes when she looked at Henry. The secret smiles she couldn't quite hide when someone mentioned his name. If she had found genuine love and a match that pleased their parents, then he was happy for her.

"You know I—" Connor began, but he broke off as someone else caught his attention. Someone he had never seen before. A young woman with loose blond hair and a genuine smile, laughing without restraint as her partner twirled her around the ballroom.

"You what?" Sadie repeated, but Connor didn't answer. Trying to keep her in sight, he steered Sadie towards her, and when the song ended, he excused himself hastily and sidestepped through the bustling bodies to reach her.

Wiping his sweaty palms on his trousers, Connor cleared his throat and said, "Excuse me, may I have this dance?"

Though he could feel the burning glare from the man she had just been dancing with boring into the side of his head, Connor's eyes locked on the girl's sage ones, directing the question to her alone. When she nodded her permission, Connor extended his hand.

Warmth tickled his palm as her fingers slid into his, and his heart thudded so loudly he felt the heat rise in his cheeks.

"I'm Connor," he said into the awkward silence, partly to cover up the cacophony of his pounding heart and shaky breaths. "What's your name?"

"Nice to meet you Connor, I'm Mabel," she replied. Her measured voice projected confidence without arrogance, and her bright smile matched her sunny yellow dress. It was an infectious smile, one Connor couldn't help mirroring.

"How come I haven't seen you at these functions before?" Connor asked.

"My family just moved here from California," replied Mabel. "My great-uncle found gold there during the 1850s and became rich, and he recently passed and bequeathed his fortune to my dad. We came to British Columbia to invest in the Canadian Pacific Railway, and hopefully find more gold."

Connor gaped at Mabel. He wasn't used to people discussing their wealth and monetary ambitions so openly. He admired her for it.

"And what do *you* hope for?" Connor asked.

"Languid days by the ocean with someone who sees past the money."

Connor laughed. "Good luck finding that here."

"Oh, I don't know," Mabel mused. "Panning for gold is hard, but I feel my luck turning already."

Her smile as she winked at him set his heart fluttering.

"Really, I just want to help my family however I can," Mabel continued. "I like helping people, and my parents have no idea what they're doing in high society, so I hope we can all find a way to fit in and be happy."

"I guess that's all any of us can ask for," agreed Connor.

Catching sight of Sadie over Mabel's shoulder, Connor slowed a little. One arm crossed her body, clutching her elbow, and her mouth hung open slightly, frozen exactly where Connor had left her. His chest tightened. He hadn't intended on abandoning her so quickly. He really was the worst white knight.

Mabel followed his gaze, and twin roses bloomed on her cheeks.

"That's your sister, right? Sadie?"

Shoulders slumping, Connor bowed his head towards his sinking heart. Mabel knew he was a Sheldon. Duty to the host had probably compelled her to dance with him.

"Yes," Connor affirmed quietly. "I fear I may have offended her. Maybe I should make sure she's all right."

"It's very noble of you to want to ensure she is happy," said Mabel, a low note of disappointment plucking at her words.

Uncertainty clawed at Connor's lungs, but then Sadie waved at him and grinned. Exhaling the breath he hadn't realized he was holding, Connor grinned sheepishly back at his sister before turning back to Mabel.

"She wants you to be happy," said Mabel. "What you want matters too."

Breath catching in his swelling chest, warmth swirling in his stomach, heart racing—Connor couldn't pinpoint the emotions coursing through his body as he squeezed Mabel's hand. He just felt *seen*.

Sadie's gaze lingered on Connor and the girl for a moment longer, pushing down the swell of loneliness rising inside her. She was genuinely happy for her brother and loathed the idea of her own insecurities marring his happiness, so she left them to enjoy each other's company and inched along the wall in search of her father. She needed answers about Thomas Sheldon, and the ball provided the perfect opportunity while her mother was distracted to corner her father and discover what he knew.

Spotting Roger Sheldon by the refreshment table, Sadie weaved through a few dancers and joined him as he lifted a canapé to his mouth.

"Avoiding Mother again?"

Her father fumbled the canapé and nearly dropped it, guilt and embarrassment warring beneath the twitches of his moustache.

"What? Of course not! Why would I avoid your mother? I just got hungry. Damn balls always disrupt regular meals. Why aren't you off dancing with some nice gentleman? Isn't that what a young woman's goal should be at these things? Finding a partner and all that?"

Sadie snorted. "Maybe *some* women, but we're not all Tanaya."

"Tanaya does what is expected of her as the eldest child, and there's nothing wrong with wanting to find someone to be by your side for the rest of your life, Sadie. She may not always show it when she is trying to impress your mother, but she cares about you. She wants you to be happy. So does your mother for that matter, though I know the way she shows it can seem more... *critical* than caring."

"Critical is one way to put it," muttered Sadie, raising an eyebrow. But the bile of guilt burned her tongue. She knew she was being unfair to her older sister, and maybe even her mother. Though Tanaya could be cold and derisive towards Sadie, echoing their mother in her chastisement of Sadie's wild imagination and immaturity, Sadie knew Tanaya was trying to help, in her own way. Her sense of duty and practicality in securing the best future for herself and her sister through what limited factors she could control showed a kind of strength Sadie admired, and even envied a little. Armed with her allotted weapons of charm, beauty, and wealth, she took charge of her life and forged a path to happiness.

Sadie wished the same path could be enough to fill her heart instead of draining it.

"Yes. Well. She does take things too far sometimes..." Roger trailed off, tapping the outside of his leg and averting his eyes.

"What," he continued after an awkward pause, "does a woman with a mind of her own do at balls then?"

"Take the opportunity to have conversations of value. For example, what do you know of our ancestor Thomas Sheldon?"

This time Roger *did* drop the half-eaten canapé. He stared at Sadie instead of retrieving it, eyes wide and mouth gaping like a hooked fish.

"I know it's his portrait missing in the hall of past Sheldons," Sadie pushed recklessly, reeling him in. "I overheard Mother mention his name ten years ago. Why was it taken down?"

Mouth opening and closing uncertainly, her father spluttered, "I don't know what you're talking about. Your mother would not like—I do not even know the full story! Your great-grandfather shamed our family—"

"Great-grandfather?" Sadie interjected, her skittering heartbeat leaping to her throat.

An erratic tic pulsed below Roger's eye. "We should not discuss..."

Sadie exhaled through her nose, forcing herself to stay calm.

"Of course not, why discuss something so obviously important to our family's history? Fine, if you can't talk about Thomas Sheldon without invoking Mother's wrath, then let's move on to a safer topic. Did you ever hear tales as a boy about magical doorways, or secret hidden passageways, or anything strange and unusual in the Sheldon manor?"

Roger's expression darkened from panicked, to suspicious, to stern.

"Sadie, is this one of your foolish fantasies again? I do not know what possible interest you could have in a secret passageway except indulging some fantasy you read about in a book, which leads me to believe that maybe your mother is right. You are more concerned with fantasy than reality, and that is not healthy. Would it be so bad to find a suitor and plan a future with him? Get married in a few years and start a family of your own like your sister and mother?"

Repulsion laced with doubt bubbled and churned inside her stomach.

"Yes, Father, it would be. I don't intend to become invisible."

Turning on her heel, Sadie stormed away.

A short young man stepped in her path, his wavy brown hair ruffled, and the glasses perched on his pencil-thin nose sliding down as he asked, "Would you like to dance?"

She hesitated, but her heart pounding in her ears convinced her the exertion might help let off steam. "I would love to, sir."

They stomped about the room in time to the music, and a smile flitted across Sadie's face.

"My name is Derek Spencer," the man informed her. "What's yours?"

Her stomach swooped like a flock of startled starlings. Most men only wanted to dance with her because they knew she was the daughter of the man who owned the oldest and wealthiest lumber company in Vancouver. Could Derek possibly have asked her to dance because he was interested in *her*, not the Sheldon name? "Hello Mr. Spencer. My name's Sadie Sheldon."

"Oh, so then this is your house!" Derek said in surprise. "It's very lovely."

"Thank you, Mr. Spencer."

"I'm sorry if I seem a bit forward," he added, misreading her raised eyebrows, "but the moment I saw you I was stunned by your beauty and just had to ask you to dance."

"How sweet of you, Mr. Spencer. I'm truly flattered."

The reply was automatic, a response drilled into her by her mother in her lessons of etiquette, but her mouth tasted bitter.

As they danced, Sadie learned Derek was twenty years old, worked for his father's publishing company, and loved to read. This fact raised Sadie's spirits, and for a while they discussed the finer points of *Beowulf*, *The Wanderer*, and other Anglo-Saxon works for which they shared a mutual passion.

"You seem well-read, Mr. Spencer. I wonder, have you ever heard of a book called *The Adventures of Thomas Sheldon*?"

Derek's eyebrows raised in surprise. "No, I haven't. Sheldon, you say? Not related to you, is he?"

"He is indeed, though I don't know much about him. I only recently discovered his book."

"Maybe I could borrow it sometime!" exclaimed Derek, seemingly eager to prove his interest in her and her family.

"Perhaps, Mr. Spencer."

Sadie hadn't really expected Derek to know of Thomas' book, but she couldn't help the sinking feeling of disappointment plummeting to her stomach—a feeling that intensified when she noticed her mother watching them, with a smile of barely suppressed glee, out of the corner of her eye.

"What do you think of Mary Kingsley's writings of West Africa, Mr. Spencer?" Sadie asked on a reckless whim inspired by her mother's approving gaze. She studied his face closely for a reaction.

Derek cocked his head to the side and raised an eyebrow, a half-smile tugging at his lips as if unsure whether Sadie teased him or asked in earnest. "Well, I think she was very brave, undertaking so many adventures in a strange and dangerous country alone, but I'm not sure I agree with her defences of some of the Africans' barbaric practices and suggestions that the British should not try to change them. And of course, while her pursuit of scientific knowledge was honourable, I'm not sure how feminine it was, despite her insistence she was not a New Woman. Maybe that's why she never married."

The knot of disappointment plummeted to Sadie's toes, but she forced a thin-lipped smile.

"Maybe Ms. Kingsley believed, as I do, that so much of history is just perception, and is therefore worth questioning."

"Oh... er... quite right," Derek said awkwardly.

Sadie had met very few men who could praise Mary's travel writings without adding a derisive comment about her lack of femininity or, conversely, her feminine sensitivities that allowed her to empathize with foreign customs they viewed as abhorrent. She was not surprised at Derek's words, but they stained him with the same brush as so many other high society men.

When the musicians struck up a slower song, Sadie and Derek adjusted their rhythm and grew silent. As they glided near the open French doors leading out onto the veranda, a cool breeze played across Sadie's face, and she longed to escape from the stifling ballroom. Glancing back at Derek, she noticed his eyes averted from her face for the first time since they started dancing. He watched a group of young men huddled in a tight-knit circle. Their urgent whispers were low, but Sadie caught a few words.

"Yes, yes that's what I heard. He was killed by a Black Hand terrorist named Gavrilo Princip. His country demanded war with Serbia, but Serbia refused and went to Russia for aid."

"Yes, and then Austria-Hungary went to Germany asking for the same."

Sadie frowned. Though she took an earnest interest in these rumours, she had mixed feelings about the possibility of full-scale warfare in Europe. She did not fear it as others seemed to, but she would not be allowed to fight as a woman, and it was difficult to say how it would affect the home front.

Derek kept steering her around so he could keep the group in view.

Turning to face her again, he said, "Sorry, they're discussing something I'm greatly interested in, but it probably wouldn't be of much interest to you. Thank you for the dances, Miss Sheldon. I hope I shall see you again before the night is over."

Sadie could do no more than nod as Derek hurried off to join the war-talkers.

Whirling around, she stormed off, pushing her way through the dancers as she headed towards the veranda. A cool breeze greeted her, and she paused in the doorway, taking a deep calming breath as she drank in the night air.

That damned Derek Spencer! The news about the assassination had occupied everyone's minds lately, even her mother's, but to assume she had no interest in it because she was a woman...

Sadie's hands clenched into fists.

As everyone knew, the man whom they referred to was Archduke Franz Ferdinand of Austria-Hungary, and he had been shot near the end of June. It was now the middle of July and nothing had happened—but tensions were boiling over, and the threat of war loomed.

Sadie slipped the square paper out of her glove and unfolded the poster, re-reading the bold lettering crying out for women's rights for the umpteenth time. Her mother had always forbidden her to attend a women's civil rights meeting. Though she had contemplated sneaking out to attend one against her mother's wishes, the Sheldon manor was in the countryside thirty kilometres outside of Vancouver, and it wasn't easy getting to downtown Vancouver alone.

War brought change, but she doubted much would change for women. She still lived in a man's world, and until men recognized women as equal humans with rights instead of passive invisible figures, how could women begin to discover their potential or a sense of self outside of societal norms?

Sighing, she stared gloomily out into the shadowy lawn, watching the moonlight dapple the dark green blades of gently swaying grass with silver before the woods swallowed them up. Stars winked and the sliver of pearly white moon grinned indulgently at her.

I would give anything to fly away from here, Sadie thought desperately.

A black shadow flitted in the corners of her peripheral vision, and she caught her breath, twisting around to see what it was—but nothing was there.

Frowning, Sadie peered into the gloom. The trees were so thick and close together it was impossible to discern anything amidst all the black. Deciding it had been a figment of her imagination, Sadie was about to turn and head back to the ballroom in search of Connor when it appeared again.

A shadow peered out from behind a tree, a deeper black among the black of night. It vaguely resembled the outline of a man. As Sadie watched, it flitted to another tree closer to the edge of the lawn. Her heart pounded against its prison. Who would be wandering in the woods so inconspicuously at this hour?

A moonbeam illuminated his face, and Sadie's heart fluttered at eyes crinkled in warm mirth, not malice. Stars reflected in his eyes like they held the promise of otherworldly wonders and magic. Like Peter Pan flitting to the window of the Darlings' nursery, ready for a story and adventure without grownups interfering. Was he a party guest involved in an elaborate prank?

Raucous laughter erupted from the ballroom, and Sadie's focus fractured. Cursing, she tried to find the strange figure again, but it had vanished, melding into the trees. Sadie continued to search the trees in vain and did not notice someone silently join her at the railing.

"It's a beautiful night, isn't it?"

Sadie jumped, and the suffrage movement poster slipped from her hand, fluttering to the ground a few feet away from the veranda, carried on the light breeze.

"Mr. Spencer, you frightened me!" Sadie exclaimed, pressing a demure hand to her heart.

"Shall we go back indoors?"

He offered her his arm, and though his earlier assumptions about her interests and intellect still stung, she took it.

As the wave of noise and loud music swept over her again, Sadie glanced past the fallen women's rights poster one last time, looking back at the woods.

They were empty.

Chapter Three

Victoria's Revenge

Sadie ran her fingers over the ivory keys of the family's grand piano, savouring the smoothness of their surfaces. Poising her fingers over a selection of keys, she paused before striking them with the first few notes of her song. It was a slow, sorrowful song, mixing deep mournful tremors and high tinkling chords like falling stars. It was Sadie's favourite, and she knew the entire piece off by heart, leaving her mind free to wander.

The mystery man from last night flitted across Sadie's mind, and she wondered about his surreptitious behaviour. If he had been spying on someone at the ball, she could not imagine who, but she could not stop thinking about him. Whether his intentions were honourable or not, the mystery of him was far more intriguing than Tanaya's upcoming nuptials, and his shadow hovered in her mind.

But the mystery man's shadow did not loom nearly as large as Thomas Sheldon's. Though her feet and arms had throbbed and ached when she collapsed on her bed after the ball, Sadie's mind had still raced. Lighting the candle in the chamberstick on her nightstand, she had read Thomas Sheldon's book by candlelight until the sky peeking between her delicate lace curtains had lightened to the pale grey preceding dawn.

With each turn of the page, a hollow ache grew in Sadie's chest where memories of her great-grandfather should have been. He seemed a decent man, with a strong moral compass guiding his decisions, and a curious mind eager to soak up knowledge of customs, rituals, geography, and scientific principles different from the ones he knew. His book was full of detailed accounts and diagrams of the peoples and lands he came across in Carmelle, chronicling his findings as though conducting a field study. Several times he emphasized his admiration for the equality of roles between men and women across all fields, and the leadership many women in Carmelle assumed with no objection from men. Sadie couldn't help but reflect sadly that Thomas probably would have been an ally for her and supported her dreams. Maybe he would have even taken her to a rally. She had already woken up determined that she would sneak out to a meeting, no matter what it took.

When Sadie read a line about Thomas being excited to tell his grandchildren of the existence of giant Lightning Birds that could summon thunder and lightning with their wings, she stopped reading for a moment to wipe away an errant tear. He had envisioned having a family to share his stories with. And the Sheldons had denied him of that. Sadie's parents had created a canyon too wide to cross by keeping Thomas' existence secret.

The discovery that had hooked her imagination and taken root in her mind more than any other, though, was that Thomas had entered Carmelle through a mirror he stumbled across in the forest bordering the Sheldon manor.

Glancing out the drawing room French doors leading onto the veranda, Sadie contemplated the line of trees bordering their property. So much of her childhood had been spent playing in those woods and walking among the trees with her father as he pointed out their virtues, instilling an intrinsic love and respect for the resource that sustained his empire. Had that canopy of evergreens been harbouring the gateway to her freedom all along?

The notes of her song grew a bit too staccato and cheery, so Sadie forced her fingers to slow, waltzing across the checkered ivory and ebony floor, singing of a sorrow this world could not contain.

Her brother's rapt expression as he danced with the blond girl last night flashed before her eyes. They had danced together nearly every song, a feat she had not thought possible for her brother who normally bored of balls faster than she did. Sadie had to meet the person who ensnared Connor's attention so thoroughly, so she had waylaid them at the refreshment table to introduce herself. A mask of practiced polite charm had greeted her when the girl introduced herself as Mabel Brown, but the spark in her eyes and quirk of her lips belied the mask and conveyed genuine affection and a hint of defiance. Though Sadie's first impression of Mabel had been positive, it hadn't stopped her stomach from clenching or the feeling of water rushing through her ears when she noticed Connor's fingers reaching out to subtly brush Mabel's during their conversation. Connor was Sadie's anchor in a stormy sea. If her anchor was hoisted, what would stop the swelling waves from crushing her and carrying her away?

Spots marred Sadie's vision and her finger slipped, hitting a wrong note, jarring the song.

"Curses and 'cantations!" she mumbled.

Her own romantic excursion last night, if one could even call it that, had been abysmal. Sadie could not make herself feel any attraction for Derek. His reaction to Mary Kingsley's writings and his dismissal of her interest in foreign affairs proved he wore the mask society demanded of him without protest, just like all the others.

"Sadie, a package has arrived for you!"

Her mother's shrill voice from the doorway marred the beauty in her sad song and Sadie paused, fingers still suspended over the keys. She glanced at a small white box clutched in her mother's hands.

"Did you order something for me?"

"Certainly not. I do not know who sent it, but there is only one way to find out."

Sadie blinked. She hardly ever received mail, let alone anonymously.

Sliding it free of her mother's prying fingers, Sadie handled the box gingerly as though it might explode. It was unremarkable—save for a white wax seal marked with a leaf, balanced between the tips of a crescent moon pressed upon the opening. Familiarity stirred in her mind like a guard aroused by a disturbance, but she couldn't place the symbol. Stomach fluttering, she broke the seal and pried the lid open to reveal a bracelet.

Her heart stuttered, appreciative goosebumps rising on her skin.

Crystal beads shaped like aspen leaves separated crystalline stages of the moon cycle, linked with a delicate silver chain. When she picked it up, a tiny rolled up piece of paper toppled off the navy velvet cushion into her palm. Unrolling it, she read:

A token in honour of our mutual affinity for adventure books of historical importance.

Sadie frowned.

"Who is it from?" Victoria demanded.

"It doesn't say, but based on the description I assume Mr. Spencer. He and I discussed our mutual love of Anglo-Saxon literature last night. That must be what the note's referencing."

"That's wonderful, Sadie! I guess you must not have been as rude to him as I thought."

Sadie stabbed her nails into her palm. "What do you mean?"

"You were so cold towards him. I am surprised he did not turn to ice at your touch."

Gritting her teeth, Sadie forced words past her dry, swelling tongue. "Ever one for hyperbole, aren't you, Mother?"

"Do not speak to me like that!" Her mother balled her hands into fists, cheeks reddening.

"You're right, I wouldn't want you to overexert yourself." The heat scalding the back of Sadie's neck and burning her cheeks warned her to take a deep breath, to calm the anger searing rational thought from her mind, but Sadie couldn't quell it. Rage at the unfairness of the world that it would demand her mother to teach her daughter that her worth lay in her ability to attract a husband blazed in her heart, and all she wanted in that moment was to incense her mother with cool mannerisms and empty words. If her mother insisted on treating her like a wayward, uncouth child with a never-ending list of failings just because she yearned for something more, then she needn't censor herself.

"The only thing putting me under strain is *you*. All your life you have deliberately tried to provoke me with your foolish imagination, but it is time to come back to reality. You are almost nineteen and you must act properly! You must accept your future and stop embarrassing yourself and this family. Stop being so selfish and realize family and loved ones are the most important thing in life. It is time to accept who you are!"

"Selfish?" Sadie hissed, her voice a strained whisper of suppressed rage. "*I'm* selfish? You want me to lead a life I despise so *you* don't look bad! All I want is to be myself, to find a *purpose*, a reason for existing beyond an endless parade of meaningless social gatherings. Is that too much to ask?"

"Yes, Sadie, it is! We live in a world where propriety is our only ticket to happiness."

"And whose happiness would that be, Mother? Mine, or yours?"

"Yours! Sadie, this is a woman's way of life. If you want to be successful, you must abide by the unwritten laws of social etiquette."

"And by successful you mean rich."

"Of course."

"Then maybe I don't *want* to be rich!" Sadie screamed. "It doesn't seem to have done you any favours! Your whole life is an illusion. You play the social game and pretend you have power, but you're powerless. What did you tell Tanaya again? 'Women are like marionette puppeteers, pulling the strings from behind the curtain while maintaining the illusion that men control the performance'? But *that* is the illusion, Mother. This lie that women run the high society show. It may make you feel better to think so, and you might be able to manipulate and coerce Father for the trivial stuff that doesn't matter, but I've seen you cower under his chastisement. Seen you bend to his will like a frail reed in a light wind whenever you cross a line or fail to fade into the background and remain decorative and unobtrusive."

"How *dare* you—" Victoria began, but Sadie cut her off, desperate to shed the weight of impossible expectations and make her mother understand.

"Until I was five, I thought you had an illness restricting your ability to speak, because I hardly ever heard your voice unless it was behind closed doors. You have always feared losing your privilege, so you surrender control of your own life and exert power in the only way you can: controlling your children's lives. But I can't surrender control of my own life, Mother. I *refuse* to become you!"

Victoria recoiled, Sadie's words a vicious slap. Sadie swallowed against the claws raking her throat and squeezing her lungs, trying to take back the harsh words. She couldn't look away from her mother's watery eyes. Maybe Sadie was wrong. Deep down, she knew her mother cared and wanted the best for her. She had needed her mother to understand how she felt, but she already regretted the delivery of impassioned anger instead of calm compassion.

"You *will* behave yourself, Sadie Sheldon," her mother said, her voice impressively measured. "Your childish tirade means nothing. You live in our house and we are still your parents. You talk of an illusion I'm under, but your delusions are far more fanciful. At least my feet are grounded in reality. Your father and I have indulged your silly fantasies of exploring dangerous parts of the world unaccompanied like a man—but that ends now. You will be a proper lady and take pride in your family. You will choose a respectable husband of proper lineage, or you will find yourself caught in an arranged marriage. You have nothing without us. No money to travel the world, no companions to offer lodgings or assistance, no job prospects for an unskilled upper-class woman. You have no choices, and you know it. Your *only* choice is to make this easy or difficult, but either way you *will* take your place in high society."

Her chest swelled as she opened her mouth to unleash a scathing retort—and then deflated as Sadie noticed herself reflected in the glossy sheen of her mother's unshed tears. Pressure squeezed her pounding heart at the lace on her lavender day dress, the pearl earrings dangling below her curled hair. The cameo brooch at her throat.

A brooch like the one her mother wore when Sadie was four and had charged at her with Connor's toy wooden sword while they played on the lawn under a spring sun. Power had surged through her tiny body as she revelled in the feeling of control over her actions, deliberately stopping just short of her mother's chest, sword tip pointed at the brooch pinned to her lace-trimmed throat. The brooch Sadie had thought locked her mother's voice. The lock she hoped would never cage hers.

Now Sadie's reflection in her mother's watery eyes did not show her a hero. Sadie's hopes and dreams entangled with the teary illusion clinging to her mother's eyelashes. Stripped bare of her fantasies, Sadie was just a scared young woman, unsure how to navigate a world in which she did not belong.

The fire inside of Sadie snuffed out. Only a tiny ember, a pitiful single flame remained. Her mother was right. This wasn't a Lewis Carroll novel. There was no magical looking-glass waiting for her to crawl through and discover a world of whimsy. No deeper meaning to her life's purpose. She was just *this*. A superfluous trinket like her mother had always made her feel, destined to become obsolete.

Other women may have poked holes in the mould of societal expectations in the past, but Sadie wanted to shatter it. And maybe that wasn't possible. Maybe all the stories she read *had* filled her mind with impossible ideas. Bowing her head in defeat, she pressed her hand over the hollow ache in her chest.

"Now," whispered her mother, seeing Sadie's obvious signs of submission, "you will come with me and help Tanaya with her last-minute wedding plans. She is getting married in two days and I want everything perfect. Perhaps it would do you well to take a leaf out of your sister's book."

Following her mother silently out of the drawing room, Sadie's numbness consumed her, drowning her in a grey pool that would never change hue. The cruel reality of her life had begun, leaving surrealism behind—forever.

Chapter Four

The Man with Brown Eyes

Colour leeched from the world with every slow, heavy step Sadie took across the lawn towards the forest. A smoky sun shone on pewter leaves and charcoal grass. A light breeze tickled the sweeping ashen branches of her favourite willow tree under a steel grey sky. Even Connor appeared monochromatic walking beside her, matching her slow, despondent pace. It was as though she walked through a still photograph of her life rather than a moving colour reality.

Her dragging feet snagged the uneven grass and she wobbled, throwing out her hands to steady herself.

"Sadie, what's wrong with you?" Connor blurted.

Sadie opened her mouth, but no words spilled from her constricted throat. Swallowing her gummy saliva, she cleared her throat and tried again.

"I'm fine."

"Oh, come on, those were the most emotionless two words I have ever heard you utter."

Sadie bit her lip. That's not what she had even meant to say. In truth, she had asked Connor to join her for a walk in the woods today so she could tell him her decision to stop pretending. It wouldn't feel real until Connor knew, and she needed to embrace her new reality so she didn't sink into a well of despair she couldn't climb out of again.

"It's just... I never thought I'd say this, but I think Mother's right. I always thought I could be the exception to the rule. That because I wanted something different, I must be destined for a different path than other high society women. But Mother and I fought yesterday, and even though I accused her of being selfish and living a lie, I realized she's right about one thing: my lie is bigger. I don't agree with her on so many points, but the truth is I'm not a hero. I'm not a revolutionary who can change the world through sheer will power. I'm just a privileged young woman living a child's fantasy."

Her voice sounded distant and detached even to her own ears. Connor's eyes had narrowed with every word.

"Sadie those are just Mother's barbed words poisoning your ears again. You have never let them get you down before, so why now? Why are you submissive instead of mad?"

Sadie pondered the question. "Did you know that Thomas Sheldon is our great-grandfather? And he supposedly entered Carmelle through a mirror he stumbled across in this forest?" She gestured around them. "For a moment, I actually believed the gateway to my freedom, to the adventurous, heroic life I always dreamed of, was right in my backyard."

A soft, hollow chuckle sounded deep in Sadie's throat.

"When Mother labelled my fantasies as foolish attempts to escape inevitable reality, it felt like my stomach hollowed out. Thomas wrote a fantasy book to escape the dull realities of his life. But wishing something to be true, even if we feel it in our bones, doesn't make it a reality. There's no entrance to another world hidden in the forest. No magical destiny awaiting me."

Sadie recoiled a little at the shock and disappointment in Connor's wide, pitying eyes.

"I don't entirely understand how someone so full of life could suddenly give up," admitted Connor. "What about sailing in the Caribbean or

Mediterranean? Finding treasure or ancient relics in exotic places? Those dreams don't have to end."

"Thomas was rewarded for his audacity to imagine a different life by being ostracized from his family," said Sadie. "I don't want that to be me, Connor. I don't want to be the outcast, the rogue family member that's spoken of in hushed whispers, all memories of me erased. My dreams matter, but I also want to matter to people. I don't see that happening when I'm a penniless wanderer sailing the Caribbean as a stowaway. And that would be a far crueller type of invisibility."

Connor's hand twitched as though he wanted to reach out to Sadie, but he shoved it in his trouser pocket instead and averted his gaze.

"How's Mabel?" Sadie inquired, changing the subject.

Connor raised an eyebrow at her and answered slowly, watching her face. "She's fine, or she was when I saw her yesterday. Why do you ask?"

"Can't a sister ask her brother about the object of his affection?"

"She can if she's sincere, but I know you don't like her."

"And what makes you think I don't like her?"

"The forced cheeriness in your expression when you met her. I'm not ignorant."

Sadie opened her mouth to respond, hesitated, then asked a different question. "Why do you like her, Connor?"

Connor cocked his head in consideration, and a small smile curled up towards the twinkle in his eye as he replied simply, "With her, I feel seen."

Halting, Sadie faced her brother squarely. His eyes lit up with youthful glee and blissful freedom despite the pressures their father imposed on him to shoulder the responsibility of the family business. Sadie would not deprive him of that.

"I'm happy for you, Connor."

He smiled sheepishly at her, and she couldn't help but smile feebly in response. Some things, like smiles, are too infectious not to be shared.

They walked in silence for a while, content in each other's company, the thickly intertwined net of leaves shading them from the hot sun.

Connor stiffened. It took Sadie a few seconds to realize he stood immobile, staring at a spot to his left.

"What is it?"

He waved a hand impatiently in her direction and held a finger to his lips. Frowning, Sadie peered closer. The bushes convulsed and shook slightly.

Two deep brown eyes blinked from a gap in the tangled twigs.

Sadie's heart fluttered at the first real colour she had seen today.

"Who are you?" Connor demanded, his voice menacing despite the fear in his wide eyes. "I know you're there, I see you!"

But those eyes fixed on Sadie, gazing unblinkingly into her own. Though a voice in the back of her mind insisted she should feel fear, Sadie did not look away.

Seeing the direction of the stranger's gaze, Connor scowled and shouted, "Show yourself! You've been seen by us both and this is our land. I—"

The eyes disappeared.

Whoever it was had slunk back into the cover of thick trees and bramble, vanishing.

Loss mingled with hope bubbled in her chest like champagne.

As the bushes settled, Sadie noticed a narrow tan tube tied with a twine bow against a yellow-green leaf. A tiny roll of parchment.

Stomach clenching, Sadie bit her tongue hard so she wouldn't cry out and alert Connor. She didn't know why, but every instinct in her body screamed to keep this information to herself. This note was meant for her alone.

Pity returned to Connor's face when he noticed Sadie's distant stare.

"Come on, we better get back. I should tell Father about that man. Strange men sneaking suspiciously in our forest without permission is a matter he should be aware of."

Sadie opened her mouth to request Connor not involve their father but changed her mind. Telling their father would not change the contents of the note, and maybe prudence was wise. Trust should not be given blindly.

"Tell Father if you wish," Sadie said instead, "but for what it's worth, I don't think he means harm. His behaviour was suspicious but not, I think, harmful. Caution is not a crime, and that's the only behaviour he has exhibited thus far. First impressions aren't always as they seem."

Connor scoffed but said no more as they trudged back to the mansion. As they passed the man's hiding place, Sadie snagged the roll of parchment and tucked it up her sleeve.

When she reached the privacy of her room, Sadie unrolled the parchment. Two short sentences were written in calligraphy above a hastily drawn map:

The gateway is real. If you choose, this map will lead you there.

Heart pounding, Sadie felt more alive than she had her entire life.

"Here she comes!" whispered a lady in the pew behind Sadie.

Twisting around in her seat, Sadie watched her sister glide down the aisle like a queen ascending her throne. Sadie had to admit her sister looked gorgeous in her wedding gown. Draped in the finest lace imported from France, Tanaya wore a beautiful fitted white gown with an immense train held up by two young girls in frilly dresses. A small smile peeked through a filmy white veil, and as she passed Sadie in the front pew and ascended the steps towards her future husband, Sadie deemed her the epitome of a perfect bride.

Despite their differences, Sadie felt happy for her sister. She seemed to be marrying for love, a rare gift for a woman in these times. *Far too rare,* Sadie thought bitterly. She glanced at Derek Spencer, who sat on her left. He watched Tanaya and Henry with a smile. He had been invited to the wedding by her mother and given a special place of honour beside Sadie. To Sadie, that meant he was to appear as her beau, or perhaps her fiancé, though no such arrangement had been made—yet. The smug look Derek exchanged with her mother suggested a proposal might not be far off.

Sadie fingered the anonymously gifted crystal moon and leaf bracelet she had decided to wear to the wedding. Derek hadn't acknowledged it, but she could think of no one else who would send her jewellery. She felt like it symbolized her new life.

Her mother watched the ceremony with a broad smile beneath watery eyes. Though the prospect of her favourite daughter marrying a respectable, rich man filled her mother with unbridled joy, Sadie couldn't help but question the authenticity of the tears. She felt guilty for thinking so cynically about her mother, but she knew Victoria's mind was always partly playing the social game.

"Do you, Tanaya, take Henry Lestron to be your lawfully wedded husband," droned the priest in a monotonous voice. "To have and to hold, for better or for worse, for richer, for poorer, in sickness and in health, to love, honour and cherish, from this day forward until death do you part?"

"I do," replied Tanaya without hesitation.

"And do you..." the priest began asking Henry, but Sadie stopped listening. She knew what his answer would be and didn't need to hear it. Her heart ached, squeezed tight as though pinched. She clutched a bead stitched to her mint green dress and rolled it between her thumb and forefinger.

"You may now kiss the bride." Her sister kissed her new husband proudly. Everyone in the church clapped, her mother let tears spill freely down her cheeks and then dabbed at them hastily as if only now remembering she held a handkerchief, and the priest announced loudly to the crowd, "I now pronounce you husband and wife."

A crescendo of clapping crested, and a few whistles chimed in.

Sadie remained silent and still, watching the joyous scene unfold as if through a glass window, able to see but feel none of the others' joy. She was alone. Alone and trapped.

The reception that followed passed in a blur, the exuberant faces of those Sadie talked to melding together. She might have been talking to the wall; the talk was that mindless.

The reception took place outside the Sheldon mansion on the vast expanse of land around their house. Little round tables placed at strategic intervals were covered with white tablecloths embroidered with little wedding bells, and four finely crafted chairs painted white with pale pink cushions were grouped around each table. People sat in assigned seats, happily sipping tea beneath the warm afternoon sun as they discussed the wedding and raved over the new couple. One long rectangular table presided over the others, where the newlyweds sat with their immediate family members, including Sadie. Again, her mother sat on her right, but this time Connor sandwiched her on her left.

He wolfed down food as if he had never eaten before and kept stealing glances at Mabel, who sat at a table nearby. Sadie would have thought the sight of someone staring at you with food dribbling down his chin would be grotesque, but Mabel returned Connor's gaze fondly. The sight made Sadie sick, and she turned away only to narrowly miss being clubbed on the side of the head by her mother's giant hat. Wide as the wheel of an automobile, it spanned across the little space between them, frequently bumping Sadie's own smaller hat.

"Cheer up, Sadie, maybe a bird will mistake the feathers of Mother's hat for a nest and she'll have to abandon it," Tanaya joked, noticing Sadie's struggles to avoid an errant feather poking her in the eye.

Sadie snorted and shared a rare wickedly delighted grin with her sister. She could count the number of times Tanaya had poked fun at their mother on one hand. That was usually an endeavour only she and Connor shared. Tanaya must be in a good mood.

Unfortunately, Victoria ruined the moment.

"Oh, Tanaya," she chuckled. "You're so witty."

Picking up her fork, Sadie stabbed at her slice of cake. When Sadie poked fun at her mother she was chastised, but when Tanaya did it she was witty. Averting her eyes from her mother, Sadie surveyed the crowd again. It did not improve her mood. Whether fake or not, every single person wore a smile. Why could everyone else at least pretend to be happy with their lives while she could not stop feeling trapped? *I want out*, she felt like screaming. *I want out!*

Sadie's whole life stretched before her, flashing across her vision like a Nickelodeon, one image slipping into another. Just like now, everyone would munch over the same chatter, chew over useless gossip, and spit out deadly reputation-squashing rumours. She would have to attend an endless parade of balls, teas, and cocktails, always surrounded by the same array of dull women and bland, predictable men. Connor would get married and abandon his keenness for adventure and practical jokes. She would marry and have children, and never taste the freedom of adventure on the open seas. But she would always want more, and the fire burning within her would grow until she could stand her imprisoned life no longer. It would either explode into a shower of fiery sparks, burning those around her with her rage—or consume her.

Faster and faster the images flashed—and then ceased altogether with an ominous finality.

Gasping, she gripped her fork until her knuckles turned white. No one noticed. The din of the crowd thrummed painfully against Sadie's ears, pounding with merciless fists. Pain exploded in her chest, boiling in her bloodstream, and lancing her lungs as her muscles tightened, squeezing.

She couldn't breathe. Ragged gasps erupted from her sandpaper throat, catching in her chalky mouth.

Panting, she looked at the guests with blurry, watery eyes.

She couldn't be here anymore.

"Excuse me," she mumbled incoherently, and without glancing to see if anyone heard, she jumped up, lurching past her usual sanctuary beneath the cascading curtain of the willow tree towards the woods, away from the wedding reception, away from her family, away from her life.

Sadie didn't know how long she ran. Her throat erupted in sobs as she threw her arms over her head like a shield against reality. Crashing through the trees, she barely noticed the sharp branches slashing her face and tearing her dress. She tripped over her feet and slammed into the ground. For a few minutes she lay immobile, her hiccupping sobs the only sound. Slowly her crying ebbed to only the occasional tear trickling down her face. She pressed her cheek against the cool earth, eyes closed.

When her breathing slowed, she pushed herself to her knees and stood. Leaning against a nearby tree, she wiped the tears from her cheeks and stared at a stream of golden sap sliding down the bark of a cedar tree.

She wasn't going back. She *couldn't* go back. She would not succumb.

Her fingers no longer shook as she pulled the tiny map out of a clandestine pocket in her beaded dress.

Unrolling it, she peered at the forest bordering the Sheldon mansion and tried to orient herself. According to the map, the gateway was in a clearing nestled in the heart of the forest, just beyond a sharp bend in a creek marked by two giant firs.

It was difficult not to feel suspicion instead of validation. She had roamed these woods with Connor hundreds of times throughout their childhood. Wouldn't she have stumbled upon the glen before?

But then, how would a stranger know what she sought and be able to make a map of its exact location if it wasn't real? If it was a trick, it was a far more elaborate one than she could fathom, and her instincts told her otherwise. She didn't know how the man had found out about Thomas Sheldon's mirror and her desire to find it, but he had given her the tools to find it herself and make her own choice.

Heading northwest, Sadie held the map in front of her, wending her way through fallen trees dripping with shaggy lichen and thin reedy pines tangled in towering cedars.

She promised herself that *if* she found the glen she would *not* approach a mirror if the man who had left her this map awaited her there. She would turn and run to alert her father, just in case her instincts were wrong and he meant her harm.

As twenty minutes of following the map turned into thirty, and then forty, that quiet *if* became a vociferous bellow.

She should have found the glen by now.

Just as she was about to give up, she passed between two towering fir trees and into a small clearing.

Walled in by a circle of tall evergreens, lush grass carpeted the glen, shining a glossy unnatural green. Purple-and-yellow flowers gleamed like gems. Branches did not hang into the clearing, as if an invisible barrier protected it. The glen opened to a clear blue sky devoid of clouds.

There was no one else there.

Just a mirror.

Hope bloomed inside her heart's garden.

Looming more than eight feet, the mirror gleamed pure gold. Despite its residence in the middle of the forest, it did not bear a single scratch. Ancient runes etched the frame beside two spiralled poles. The top arched in a half circle, and a massive ornamental sigil emblazoned the centre. Shaped like a sunburst, the sigil contained a leaf within the sun's braided core. The leaf's stem split in two near the bottom and curled up. At the bottom of the mirror a golden vine wrapped around the frame, adorned with golden leaves and a flower with eight petals. On the left side of the frame a keyhole protruded onto the clean glass, and in that keyhole sat a large golden key.

Thomas Sheldon's mirror. She had found Thomas Sheldon's mirror.

Chills raised the hairs on her arms and prickling tingles electrified her veins.

It's real.

This was her Looking Glass to Wonderland.

She didn't know what would happen if she turned that key—if a land called Carmelle would be waiting for her or not.

But she had to find out.

Slowly, Sadie stepped into the clearing, ensuring the man was nowhere in sight, then reached out to touch it.

It was warm, a warmth that spread through her, lending her strength.

She turned the key.

Nothing happened at first. Then the mirror shimmered, and an image took shape. Deep purple-and-golden-yellow flowers winked into view, studding long locks of lustrous grass. For a moment Sadie thought she still looked at the reflection of the clearing where she stood. But as more of the image came into focus, Sadie noticed the differences. A bright sun shone against an azure sky, but there was no forest, no trees bordering the grassy knoll. Instead, endless rolling hills and a snow-capped mountain range jutted up in a tiny line against the horizon.

A surge of excitement bubbled through Sadie, then fizzled out like flattened soda water as an image of Connor's crestfallen face rippled across her mind. Could she face this new adventure without him? Would he ever forgive her for going to Carmelle alone and abandoning him? But no... she wasn't abandoning him, not really. He wasn't alone in the same way. He was *her* anchor, but she had never felt like she was *his*. And he had Mabel now. If he really wanted to, he could follow her. He knew about Thomas' book and the mirror—and she would return. This wasn't goodbye forever. Thomas had returned, so she must be able to as well.

A twinge of guilt twanged her heartstrings as she thought of her father's disappointed frown, and Tanaya's sad eyes. Maybe her mother would miss her, once she recovered from her fury at the audacity of Sadie leaving. But she had no doubt they would all carry on with their lives. If she left, her family might experience heartache. But if she stayed, her heart would *break*.

And no one would pick up the broken pieces.

Her bracelet burned against her wrist, and she gripped the full moon crystal, holding it away from her skin.

Something flickered in the corner of the mirror's image. A wall of flames roared along the crest of one of the hills, hazy smoke billowing into the air. And fleeing from the flames, his hair matching the fire that pursued him—

Sadie's heart leapt to her throat and stopped beating.

It can't be.

He couldn't be alive. And in Carmelle, needing her help.

Could he?

For a dramatic moment, her fingers paused mere centimetres from the mirror's surface.

She could stay and make her parents and siblings happy. Or she could take a chance on a world that respected women, where exciting adventures full of magic and heroism would make her feel alive every day.

And maybe she could save her great-grandfather, and right some of the wrongs her family had committed.

Determination sparked the smouldering embers in Sadie's chest. Her heart had made this decision from her first glimpse of Thomas Sheldon's book. It was time she heeded it.

She brushed a violet petal on the closest hillside in the mirror's image with a deliberate, steady fingertip.

Purple mist swirled about Sadie, and the glen vanished. Suspended in the cool mist, floating between worlds as though caught in a nebula above a black void between stars, Sadie reached towards the rolling hills and snow-capped mountain peaks still hovering before her—but an invisible force yanked her in a different direction, towards sleek obsidian dunes with jagged peaks, waterfalls of flame, and rivers of magma.

No.

She needed to get to Thomas.

Pulling against the invisible force, Sadie concentrated all her energy on reaching those rolling hills and blue sky and breaking free of the force trying to dictate her future.

This was *her* adventure. *Her* choice.

Pressure squeezed her temples, trying to break her determination, but Sadie fought back, clenching the sudden queasiness in her core as she took a step toward the hills. And another.

With a final roar of effort, Sadie heaved herself away from the fiery land and broke free of the invisible force, stumbling into the mirror's image and falling onto a hard surface with a dull thud.

Chapter Five

The Mirror of Carmelle

Something prickly tickled her face. She breathed in the sweet fresh scent of the first spring rainfall or morning dew—but the grass was not wet. Lifting her head, she glanced at her wrist. The bracelet had cooled, but the irritated skin beneath still itched.

Thomas.

Heart pounding in her ears, Sadie rolled on her side and pushed herself up, panting and cursing her corset under her breath. Squinting against the bright sunlight, she peered at her surroundings. She stood in the middle of a field of grass crowning the top of a hill. Identical rolling hills rose in every direction, dotted with the same tiny purple-and-yellow flowers that had studded the grass in the glen. Shaped like six-pointed stars, they were stitched into the rich grass gown that blanketed the hills.

Shading her eyes with her hand, she watched a few fluffy white clouds float lazily across a vivid azure sky. There was no sign of a fire. Or Thomas.

Sadie spun in a circle, searching frantically among the hills for a glimpse of Thomas or flames or billowing smoke. Should she have gone to the fiery land the force pulled her towards instead? She clutched her midriff, hoping to assuage the queer prickling sensation in her stomach.

But she had done it. She had walked through a *mirror*.

Her chest swelled, heart fluttering lightly as though tethered by a thin string.

Lifting her chin, she threw her arms out and spun in a slow circle, breathing deeply. Revelling in the thrumming adrenaline pumping one phrase through her veins over and over: *I'm free!*

Her dream had come true. She had *made* it come true. She laughed, a freeing laugh that lifted the weight of her mother's expectations off her shoulders and eased the tension of potentially having to marry Derek Spencer from her neck.

But...

Slowing her spinning, she scanned the mountain range on the horizon again and bit her lip. What did you do when your dream came true?

She could start by finding Thomas in a land humming with magic...

Humming.

She whipped around to ascertain the source of a droning hum. Shimmering purple mist spiralled in the mirror. Seconds later, someone toppled out and landed on the grass beside her.

Sadie froze warily as the person unfolded himself and peered at her with intense dark brown eyes.

It was the man from the forest.

His licorice green tunic, brown breeches, and dark chestnut brown hair tied with a black ribbon at the base of his neck immediately explained why he had been able to blend into the forest so well. Though the hard planes of his cheekbones and jawline suggested the innocence of youth had long been left behind, Sadie guessed he was still in his twenties.

He broke the silence first.

"Our hard landings appear to have damaged the sacred grass of Calessar," he observed with a wry quirk to his thin lips. "Never quite understood why there's a portal here."

Sadie narrowed her eyes at his nonchalance.

"Who *are* you?"

Chuckling softly, the man answered, "My name is Tristan West."

Sadie's stomach knotted and she angled her body away from Tristan. "And what trickery have you been playing at, Mr. West? Why did you hide in the woods and give me a map?"

"To aid the princess in her quest to escape one privileged existence for another."

Sadie scowled so deeply it hurt her cheeks. "You don't know anything about me or my life, so watch your tone. But *why* try to help me? What's in it for you?"

"Not much," replied Tristan, "but it's my duty as a soldier to complete the tasks Alldían, Lord of Caris Nando, sets for me. And he assigned me the task of escorting you to Caris Nando once you arrived in Carmelle."

Sadie raised an eyebrow. "And you're a dutiful man, are you?"

"To a fault."

Sadie clenched her jaw, biting the inside of her cheek.

"Then I'm afraid we're at an impasse, Mr. West. I've no intention of letting a man leash me the moment I break free of my last tether. I'm not a marionette."

"No," Tristan mused, his tone soft. "I can see that. But I'm not trying to take away your freedom. And I think you will find it difficult to navigate a world you know nothing about without a guide you can trust."

A twitter of nervous laughter bubbled from Sadie's throat. "*Trust*, Mr. West? Why would I trust you? Skulking around a mansion in the shadows like a thief is hardly trustworthy behaviour. Giving me the map speaks nothing of your intentions, or your Lord's. How would he even know who I am, and why would he want me to come to Carmelle?"

"Alldían has many ways of seeing things near and far, most of which you would not understand—"

"Why, because I'm an unintelligent woman?"

"No, because you're a hot-headed stranger to this world with no concept of its unique magical properties," continued Tristan through gritted teeth.

"Though Alldían obviously saw your worth, because he said it was in Carmelle's best interest for us to help guide you here."

Muscles seizing, Sadie tried to think past the whooshing in her ears.

"W-well what of the fire?" she stammered, latching onto her last bruise of indignation as her brain attempted to process the weight of Tristan's words. "Did you create that deceit too?"

Tristan's eyes widened. His gaze flitted across the rolling hills. "Fire? What are you talking about?"

"The fire in the mirror, the one the man was running fr-"

But Sadie stopped mid-word. The mirror no longer stood behind Tristan.

It had vanished.

"*Where's the mirror?*" Sadie demanded, voice cracking. Dizziness blurred her vision. Sweat beaded on her forehead. She gripped her arms, panting.

Her way home had vanished.

Was she stuck in Carmelle?

"I don't..." Tristan trailed off as he stared wide-eyed at the spot the mirror had been a second before, a deep frown furrowing the angular lines of his jaw. "I'm sorry, I don't know where... this has never happened before."

Sadie hadn't expected him to become flustered, or falter. She had witnessed a lot of fake confusion from people trying to protect their reputation, but the bob of his throat as he visibly swallowed, and the tick of his clenched jaw, suggested attempts to mask genuine vulnerability.

She believed he didn't know the answers. Whatever he had planned, this wasn't it.

A jarring screech echoed across the hills. A bright flash of deep orange blazed across the sky in the distance behind Tristan. Sadie could make out a dark flying shape against the azure sky, weaving through plumes of thick grey smoke rising from the ground.

The fire. Thomas must be there.

Tristan whipped around and swore. His hand twitched toward his hip as though about to grip something there but retracted quickly as it closed on air.

Sadie started to run past Tristan towards the fire, but he threw out a hand to stop her.

"Stay here!" he ordered and sprinted off in the direction of the smoke and flames.

"Like hell I'm staying here!" Sadie yelled. "That's the fire I came here for!"

Cursing her restrictive corset and undergarments again, she sprinted after him.

Tristan stuck to the folds of the hills, rounding bend after bend but always keeping as straight a line as possible, eyes fixed on the flying shape in the sky. Sadie focused on that shape too, foreboding billowing inside her. Though she had only ever seen drawings of them in fairy tales, the huge body, long neck, and giant wingspan were unmistakable: dragon.

They ran for ten minutes, the acrid smell of smoke becoming more pungent with every step. Distracted by the sound of screams mingled with roars, Sadie didn't notice Tristan halt abruptly as they rounded yet another bend, and she ricocheted off his back like a coiled spring. She opened her mouth to berate him for his sudden stop, but the words dried on her tongue.

Small charred and broken clay homes littered the only street of a tiny village about two hundred metres away, their thatched roofs ablaze, flames dancing out of open windows and doors. Debris and bodies intermingled in the street, fanning out like mangled weeds in a riverbed. Smoke billowed from every orifice, cloudy grey rivers rising to meet the thick swells of a charcoal ocean sky. The putrid stench of burnt flesh, fresh blood, and heavy smoke wafted towards them. But more horrifying than any of the sights and smells assaulting her were the sounds. The roar of the flames, the screeches of the fell beast swooping low over the village, and above all, the blood-curdling, terrified screams of people who knew their death and the death of all they loved was nigh.

She did not see Thomas Sheldon anywhere.

"What is this place?" she whispered to Tristan.

"This is Helgur, one of the small villages that borders the Sacred Lands. They are a peaceful community with no weapons, situated here in reverence to Calessar, not to guard it. There has never been a dragon here. Never violence. They—" Tristan swallowed hard, his lips pressing tightly together. "They know no malice."

"Where are the villagers? I hear screams."

Tristan pointed towards the largest building at the end of the street. Rubble littered the ground around an altar-like monument by the door and its clay walls, carved with patterns of waving grass studded with flowers, but its smoking wooden roof was still mostly intact.

"They have probably taken refuge in there."

Sure enough, as Sadie watched, a man and woman burst out of a burning home, carrying an infant and a toddler in their arms. They sprinted towards the larger building, ducking behind fallen debris and overturned carts as they ran to shelter from the dragon. A woman sprinted down the middle of the street, shielding her head with her arms from the burning thatch bundles peppering the street around her.

The dragon swooped down on the lone woman, extended the talons of its hind legs, and scooped her up in its claws. Transferring her to its fore claws, the dragon bent its long scaly neck and impaled her in its jaws, silencing her feral shriek.

Sadie turned away. Her stomach bubbled so violently she thought she might be ill.

Out of the corner of her eye, she noticed Tristan studying her face. She could see the indecision warring in his eyes. Helping the villagers would be suicidal and would not protect her, but he couldn't do nothing. And neither could she.

"We need to help them," she said firmly.

Without waiting for a response, Sadie sprinted to the closest house and pressed herself against the back wall, keeping low so the dragon wouldn't see her. Peering into a back window, she determined no one remained in the house before racing to the next one and ducking in the front door.

"We mustn't linger too long in any of the houses," said Tristan, joining her as she scanned one of two bedrooms for any villagers who might be hiding.

"I know, I just want to make sure..." she trailed off as a small sob punctuated her panting.

Dropping to her knees, Sadie peeked beneath a bed. A young boy had pressed himself against the wall in the furthest corner, his arms wrapped around his shaking body.

"We're here to help. Take my hand, we'll get you to safety," Sadie told the boy.

He cowered, shrinking further into himself.

"He doesn't speak English, he can't understand you," said Tristan. Crouching down, Tristan reached a hand out to the boy. *"D'ashani."*

Slowly, the boy reached out and gripped Tristan's fingers.

Scooping him up, Tristan trotted out of the house, Sadie right on his heels.

A thunderous *crack* echoed from across the street, raining down chunks of clay. The dragon whacked a house with its tail, reducing it to rubble.

Luckily no scream escaped the boy's open mouth. Running along the back sides of the houses, they reached the large building at the end of the street unscathed. Inside, a dozen villagers huddled in the corner furthest away from the smoking roof.

At the sight of the boy, a dark-skinned man let out a strangled sob and fell to his knees, arms open wide. Tristan released the boy and he ran to his father, burying his head in his shoulder as his father stroked his hair.

"We can't stay here," said Tristan without preamble, addressing the villagers. Some of them looked at him blankly, but a few nodded their heads to show they understood. "Are more people trapped?"

"I don't think so," said a woman with a long, grey-flecked braid. "The rest of the surviving villagers have already taken refuge in the tunnels of Athatair, but we returned to attempt a rescue for Ahmeric here and help others if we could. Thank you for saving him."

"We need to reach the tunnels then. This building will not withstand the dragon's attack," said Tristan. "I'll distract the dragon while everyone runs to the tunnels. Where is the nearest entrance?"

"On the north side of the second hill south of the town," replied the woman solemnly.

"Good. Wait a minute or two after I leave, then head to the tunnel as quickly and surreptitiously as possible."

Sadie started to follow Tristan out the door, but he shook his head.

"Go with them to the tunnels," he instructed. "Help the injured, let them lean on you for support. They need your help. I'll meet you there."

Sadie didn't argue. She helped the villagers to their feet, looping the arm of a young teenager with a gash in his upper thigh around her shoulders.

With bated breath, they listened to the dragon's roars as Tristan started distracting it. She couldn't imagine whatever tactics he used would last long, so after a minute Sadie motioned for the villagers to follow her out of the building. She needed to get them to safety before Tristan got himself killed.

The woman with the braid took the lead, heading towards the hills in the vague direction from which Sadie and Tristan had come, keeping to the shadows of the destroyed homes. Sadie glimpsed Tristan dodging a blow from the dragon's spiked tail and diving for a broken door, which he held before him like a shield as the dragon turned to snap at him.

Wincing, Sadie turned away and concentrated on closing the open distance between the last house and the nearest hill.

As they rounded the bend of the first hill, a terrified, high-pitched scream tore through the air, and she whipped around. Ahmeric had found his voice.

And the dragon had heard.

Its head swivelled in their direction, and the bellow it emitted chilled Sadie's bones and raised the hair on the back of her neck. Launching into the air, it flapped its enormous wings and swooped towards them.

Sadie could see the tunnel entrance now, carved into the side of the hill and barricaded with a heavy stone door that stood slightly ajar. Waiting for them.

But they wouldn't make it in time. The dragon was too close, the door too far. Sadie could see Tristan sprinting after the dragon, but there was nothing he could do.

Ahmeric's father tried to pry the boy's arms off his neck, trying to hand him off to the woman with the braid. But Ahmeric clung to his father desperately, crying hysterically at the prospect of being separated from him.

The woman's face hardened. She shook her head at Ahmeric's father and said something to him in a language Sadie did not understand. Ahmeric's father hesitated, then ran past her towards the tunnel, hugging Ahmeric tighter. The woman squared her shoulders, then stepped towards the dragon.

Sadie's mouth fell open, but she couldn't stop. She still supported the teenage boy, his shaking leg barely supporting his weight. They hobbled to the door, Sadie craning her neck to look back over her shoulder.

The dragon's enormous wings whooshed its ascent to a halt, beating the air hard to stop its progress and hover over the brave woman walking out to meet it. Sadie could hear the rumbles of the wind from its wings echoing like thunder.

For a moment the woman stood her ground, chin lifted to meet the dragon's soulless eyes defiantly. She closed her eyes—and the dragon lunged at her.

Sadie looked away, but she couldn't block out the screams.

Helping the injured youth into the tunnel, Sadie started to enter after him, but turned to see the dragon approaching once more. Not every villager was in the tunnel yet, including Ahmeric and his father. Even if they made it inside, what then? Would the dragon smash down the door to reach them? And what about Tristan?

Though the sound of her racing heart thrashed erratically in her ears, Sadie changed direction and ran away from the tunnel entrance, screaming at the dragon to follow her.

At first the dragon hesitated, but when Tristan changed direction to reunite with Sadie and started yelling at the dragon too, it followed them both.

Sadie's legs burned, her searing lungs heaved, and bile rose in her throat. Never had she run this long or this fast in her life. But though her dizzy brain screamed at her to stop, she ran another step. And another. She could hear the dragon's massive wings beating, feel the heat of its rotten, fiery breath, the rumble in its chest before it roared again. A dark shadow passed overhead and then the dragon was in front of them, landing with a thud that shook the earth.

Tristan and Sadie halted, panting.

The dragon's bright red scales blazed with bolts of silver shooting across its hide like lightning, and its long-fanged snout snarled at them. Sharp spikes lined its back and marched down the tail, ending with three larger spikes in a triangular formation at its tip.

The dragon lunged at Sadie, its mouth wide open. She screamed. Covering her head with her hands, she waited to feel its fangs pierce her body, but she was knocked off her feet as Tristan barrelled into her. Sadie barely registered the dragon's head hitting the ground where she had just been with a tremendous thud, before she rolled down the hill, jabbing her elbow into the ground. Pain lanced up her arm.

The dragon shrieked with a fresh surge of fury as Tristan landed beside her and dragged her beneath a stone outcropping of the hill's shoulder, just large enough to crouch under and confuse the dragon. The earth trembled beneath Sadie's feet as the dragon's enormous paws pounded the ground, crushing the flowers. A burst of flames billowed towards them and Tristan dove again, yanking Sadie down with him. The blazing heat of the flames narrowly missed them, though the smell of singed hair permeated Sadie's nostrils.

Scraping stone grated behind her where Tristan had landed, but she couldn't look.

She couldn't rise again. Her limp legs wouldn't support her weight.

Gasping for air with her cheek still pressed to the earth, she inhaled dirt and coughed. Pebbles bounced and vibrated among the grass as the dragon approached.

She lay immobile, waiting for her dreams to kill her.

Gentle but firm hands rolled her like a barrel—and she plummeted down a dark hole.

All air vacated Sadie's lungs as she slammed into a thick coating of dirt. Every bone and muscle ached. Roars of fury echoed far above her as boots landed beside her with a heavy *thud* and hands dragged her out of the sunlight. The dragon's shadow paused over the opening, casting them into deep darkness.

She was sure her pounding heart would give away their position.

The enormous snout thrust through the opening, snorting puffs of steam down upon them.

Sadie screamed. The dragon roared triumphantly.

A hand yanked Sadie aside as a burst of flame bloomed where she had been standing.

Tristan bent to pick something up then hauled her further into the darkness. Dimly she could hear the dragon emit one last scream of fury before the dull pounding of its huge feet thundering across the grass signalled its departure. She released a small sigh of relief, incapable of speaking. Her chest heaved, her limbs shook weakly, and the screams of the woman with the braid echoed in her head...

After a few minutes, when they were far enough from the entrance, Tristan paused. Light flared in her face, and she shielded her eyes from the sudden brightness of a lit lantern.

"Are you okay?" he asked Sadie.

Sadie didn't know how to answer that. She wasn't, but she didn't know how vulnerable to be with Tristan. Instead of answering, she asked, "Do you think the villagers of Helgur are all right? Do you think they made it safely into the tunnels?"

"I do," replied Tristan gravely. He met her eyes, holding her gaze. "You were very brave, leading the dragon away from them. You saved their lives."

Sadie's cheeks burned. "*You* saved them. That woman saved them. I just—I couldn't let that dragon get Ahmeric. Too many sacrifices had already been made."

"Sacrifices are always made when disagreements escalate into conflict. And it's usually the innocent who sacrifice the most."

Sadie scrutinized Tristan's pinched eyebrows. "Did the villagers have a disagreement with the dragon? Or are you referring to something bigger happening?"

Tristan sighed. "I have my theories, though only time can prove them correct. But I don't think this was a random dragon attack. Dragons don't normally come this far west, and never to the Sacred Lands. At least not the dragons from Vasmorloth, the only ones who attack people. This was calculated and purposeful. My guess is the Redpath sent the dragon. They disagree with another faction called the Ilyance over how the people of Carmelle should live, and tensions have been rising."

A knot tightened in Sadie's stomach and the hairs on her forearms stood erect as the calculated assassination of Archduke Franz Ferdinand skittered across her mind.

"At least we should be safe in these tunnels," continued Tristan. "Spells ward the place from evil. We'll travel through the Athatair to a different entrance further west from the dragon, and hopefully avoid meeting it again."

"The Athatair?" Sadie repeated.

"Yes, Athatair means Caves of Learning in the Lantian tongue. The Athatair is part of the Melloth, the Sacred Land. At the turn of the Age a band of wizards warded these tunnels with powerful charms to keep evil at bay and preserve its recorded contents."

He held the lit lamp aloft, casting its glow on the walls.

The walls were made of a deep yellow stone that glittered like gold in the lamplight and arched into a red brick ceiling. Strange symbols and ancient runes covered the walls in organized sections from ceiling to floor, like a manuscript contributed to by different hands over time. Some had drawings or diagrams etched below their scrolls. By the light of the lantern, she could see Tristan's familiarity with at least one of the alphabets, as he studied the carving closely, his pupils sparkling with interest.

"This is why recorded history is so fascinating," commented Tristan, eyes still glued to the carving. "It says here that the Battle of Dhírnin was won due to an unforeseen numbers advantage, but it wasn't. I was there. The Dharmaelian King's son won the battle for his kingdom through the element of surprise and a secret advantageous lookout point. But I'm sure to the inexperienced army of Dern it seemed impossible for one man to vanquish as many enemies as he did. So much of history is just perception."

"I have often said the same thing myself," remarked Sadie slowly.

Tristan's eyes flicked to hers, widened surprise melting into amused approval. "I guess Alldían knows what he's doing after all... I never did get your name, what is it?"

"No way," Sadie protested, shaking her head. "I give you my name when you answer my questions."

His eyes searched for a crack in her obstinance. He was about to be disappointed.

Sighing, Tristan broke eye contact and muttered, "All right, ask away. But I must warn you that I don't have all the answers. Or I might be prohibited from revealing them. I won't lie, however." Branded by her searing glare, he added, "I'm sorry, I promise to answer as best I can. I have my own rules and restrictions I must follow."

Before Sadie could ask her first question, Tristan sat down on the soft earth and indicated she should do the same. Placing the lantern on the ground between them, he studied the light of the flickering flame, casting eerie dancing shadows on the planes of his face.

"Was sitting for this necessary?" Sadie asked, though her burning feet shouted a weary *thank you* to Tristan.

"You seem like you can talk a lot. This felt easier than trying to bully our tired brains into walking and talking at the same time."

"Is that a task you normally find difficult?"

"Is that your first question? My mistake, it was technically your second. Perhaps I should put a number limit on questions."

"Fine, I'll get to the point. Why did Alldían send *you* to find me?"

"I didn't want to, you can be assured of that," Tristan answered quickly. "In fact, I would have refused if Alldían had not forced me. I don't care for your world much."

"Why not?" Sadie demanded.

"Let's just say I have been there before and have seen and heard enough to justify my dislike. But that's why he chose me, I suppose, because I am at least familiar with it—and we have a close bond. I am his godson."

"And how exactly did he know to bring me here? You weren't very clear on that before."

"I cannot share all of my godfather's secrets, but he has a few different ways of seeing what is happening in other worlds, and prophetic visions, both of which he used to discover the importance of guiding you to our world, Arwé."

"I thought we were in Carmelle?"

"We are, but Carmelle is only part of Arwé. Carmelle stretches from the northern ice fields of Froríz to the southern isles of Kai-Nalu…"

Tristan trailed off and stared at her wrist.

Sadie looked down at her bracelet. She wrinkled her brow, confused. "What's wrong?"

"Where did you get that?"

"I don't actually know," Sadie admitted. "It was a gift, but I don't know who sent it."

"When did you receive it?"

"A few days ago. Why?"

Tristan's eyebrows were so furrowed they practically touched at the bridge of his nose.

"That's Alldían's symbol. The moonleaf."

Butterflies swooped in Sadie's stomach, and chills skittered up her arms to her neck.

"Alldían sent this to me?"

"Maybe? But I don't know why. Does it… do anything?"

Sadie's skin prickled. "It's a bracelet. What would it *do*?"

"Things are not always as they first appear in Arwé. Trinkets are rarely just trinkets. If it was from Alldían—well, the possibilities of what it could *do* are endless."

Sadie fingered the full moon crystal, her wrist tingling with the memory of the bracelet burning her skin right before entering the mirror.

"It did burn a little, right before I came through the mirror. And then I saw—someone in the mirror, and a fire..." Sadie faltered, avoiding Tristan's eyes. She had been so sure the man fleeing the fire in the mirror had been Thomas Sheldon, but doubt gnawed at her resolve now. She hadn't found him. Maybe it had been an illusion.

"That's right, you mentioned something about a fire when we arrived. And you wanted to help someone fleeing it? Is that why you chose to go through the mirror?"

Tristan's tone held begrudging admiration, but Sadie didn't feel she deserved admiration for being gullible.

"Partially," admitted Sadie, "but not entirely. I made the choice for me. But if it wasn't real—if the man and the fire were an illusion created by the bracelet, designed to provide extra motivation for me to go through the mirror—then my choice was still tainted with deception. It wasn't my own."

Tristan tugged on the tip of his long nose. "The symbols on the bracelet do remind me of Alldían, I just don't know how he would have even sent it to you, or why he would have deemed the extra motivation necessary. He told me you were needed here more than on Earth, but that you must not be forced to come. That I was to guide you to the mirror only, but it had to be your choice to walk through. But I do agree that creating an illusion to lure you here compromises your choice. If that's the case—if Alldían sent this to you, if he used deceit to sway your decision—I am sorry. If I had known about the bracelet, I would have told you. I would never want to lure someone into a life-changing decision under false pretenses."

Confusion coated her tongue at this slew of information. She fought down the burning bile in her throat, the angry words she had been ready to scald him with. He had apologized. She had no reason to believe his apology, no reason to think he wouldn't have known about his godfather's deceit, but the men in her life didn't apologize to her very often. Most of the time, they didn't feel like they owed women an explanation for the actions they took in service of their own agendas.

But Tristan had looked her in the eye and had apologized with unblinking sincerity.

And she believed him.

"Thank you, Mr. West. I still don't quite understand how you knew I was the one Alldían sent you to look for, though. Or why he thought I was needed here more than in my own world. Why *me*? I'm nothing special. What is it he thinks I can do for Carmelle?"

"Alldían described you as having fiery red hair, misted green eyes, and a stubborn yet sad air about you that I wouldn't be able to miss. That I wouldn't have to go far, and I would *know* when I saw you." Tristan shook his head slightly. "I thought he was crazy at first too, that a *feeling* was no reliable way to identify someone—but to my surprise, he was right. I saw you pull back the curtain of a willow tree, and I knew.

"I don't even know if Alldían has an exact idea of what you can do for Carmelle," admitted Tristan heavily. "All I know is tension has been brewing in Carmelle for some time now, between alliances whose viewpoints no longer align, between ancient foes extending the long arms of their shadows once more to threaten the peace of this world. Alldían became worried and turned to the tools that might help fortify us against impending darkness, and they showed him you. Like recorded history, 'special' is a term steeped in perception. You may not think you're special, but the portents of Arwé do. I guess only time will dictate which perception is correct."

"You think I should follow you blindly to this Alldían and trust he has my best interest at heart?"

"I think stubborn determination can only take you so far," Tristan replied smoothly. "You are woefully unprepared for a solo adventure in a foreign world you know nothing about. No one is saying you must comply with Alldían's plan. I'm not even sure if Alldían *has* a plan. But what he can offer you at the very least is food, shelter, and a place to get your bearings and learn more about Carmelle before you make your own decisions about how to spend your time here."

Rubbing her nails anxiously as she contemplated an etching of a dwarf perched on a giant's shoulder, Sadie had to admit Tristan was right. She knew nothing about Carmelle, and her privileged upbringing hadn't exactly taught her wilderness survival skills. She needed a guide, at least for now. She was still in control. She would allow no one to take away her freedom and choose her path for her in this world, not even a lord. She needed a purpose, a reason to stop being a passive observer in her own life, and she wasn't going to find it wandering aimlessly around the countryside.

"Prove I can trust you," Sadie demanded, gripping her knees as she held Tristan's eyes and did not back down. "You say you didn't know of the bracelet, that Alldían instructed you to guide me to the mirror but not force my decision to walk through. How did you do that?"

"I started by letting you glimpse me that night when you were on the veranda. Tried to show you in that quick moment you saw my face that I was a friend, not a threat. That day when you walked in the forest my first thought was to introduce myself and be honest about why I was there and what awaited through the mirror, in the hopes your sense of adventure would be enough to inspire you to take the leap, but I couldn't let the boy know what was going on. Already he was suspicious of me enough to want to tell his father, and if he was unsuccessful in persuading you to stay, what if he decided to come with you? What if him knowing about the mirror proved a liability?"

"And what made you think *I* wouldn't report you to my father, even if Connor—my brother—didn't? Why leave me the map? You reference my sense of adventure, but you don't know me."

"It was a risk, I'll admit, but I didn't have a lot of options with your brother there. I guessed you must have a bit of adventure-lust in you if

Alldían thought you were more needed in our world than yours. Plus, I saw you walking on the rooftop, climbing over the railing, and reading by moonlight. I'm no expert, but I'm guessing the average high society woman in your world does not do that. I left the map hoping you would find the right opportunity to use it."

Sadie memorized the pattern of dirt on her broken shoe, digesting everything. She didn't know how to feel about Tristan's role in influencing her decision to activate the mirror and come to Carmelle. Another question nagged at her.

"How do I get home? Where did the mirror go, and when will it come back?"

"I don't know," admitted Tristan, an uneasy edge to his voice that disturbed Sadie. "The mirror has never vanished before, at least not that I have seen. Portals are supposed to work both ways. The only explanation I can think of is that it has closed. I know they can do that in times of great need, when a serious threat is posed to one or both worlds, but beyond that, we shall have to ask those more learned in these matters, like Alldían."

Sadie refrained from asking how portals could sense danger. Obviously he didn't know. Hugging her knees, she fought back the tears threatening to well up. The disappearance of the mirror and the shocking cruelty of the dragon had joggled her senses and struck fear in place of courage and excitement. The screams of the villagers still echoed in her head.

"I know this is overwhelming," Tristan continued gently, "but you are not alone. I will guide you through Carmelle to Caris Nando to see Alldían."

"How long will it take to reach Alldían?"

"That's a good question. We can no longer take the direct route," answered Tristan, his brow furrowing. He tugged on his nose thoughtfully. "The dragon has changed everything. Do you remember the Redpath organization I mentioned earlier? They must have sent the dragon to guard the Melbeth, the Sacred Gate that leads through the Gap of Talarí to the farmlands beyond. Dragons do not wander the lands preying on small villages that hold nothing of value. Of course, it might not be the Redpath who sent the dragon. Many evil things in this world would want to guard the Gap. Either way, my plan to turn east over the farmlands of Tamarack following the line of the Talarí river and then crossing the Toloneni into the lands of Caris Nando are ruined."

"Couldn't we look for the mirror?" Sadie blurted.

"It would be a fruitless search. The mirror does not simply get up and move to a different spot. It would take a strong spell few wizards today are capable of casting to move the mirror. I believe something strange and serious has happened either in this world or your own. You will not be able to return to your world until the mirror returns, and there's no way of knowing when that will be, so you may as well come to Caris Nando and find real answers from Alldían."

"How are we going to get there? I thought you said the way was blocked?"

"I said the way I was *going* to take was blocked. That does not mean other paths don't exist. But that is a matter I must sleep on."

He lay down, back against the wall and eyes closed.

"You're sleeping *now*?" asked Sadie.

"I am attempting to, yes," Tristan grumbled, eyes still closed. "I advise you to do the same. We will have a big day ahead of us tomorrow."

"Sleep here? On the ground?"

Tristan huffed; Sadie could feel his eyes rolling beneath closed lids.

"I suppose you have never slept on anything other than a fluffy bed before."

It was true. Her parents were furious any time she got dirty, even as a child.

"Tonight can be your first experience sleeping on dirt. You'll have to do it for most of the journey to Caris Nando. Don't worry, it won't bite."

Sadie scowled but slid down against the wall, the laces and boning of her longer corset digging into her skin after so much jostling exertion. Cursing under her breath, Sadie yanked her tattered dress up in exasperation and warned Tristan in a dire voice, "Don't you dare open those eyes, Mr. West, unless you want me to gouge them out for you. I need to take this damn corset off."

"Fine by me, I'd rather not witness that anyway." Tristan's eyes remained firmly closed as he rolled over and faced the wall.

After a few moments of profuse grunts and vehement cursing, Sadie managed to extricate herself from her corset without fully taking her dress off, and flung it into the darkness. Instantly she felt freer, released from both bodily constrictions and the societal constraints of her past.

Tristan's chest already rose and fell in the shallow rhythmic pattern of sleep.

"By the way, my name is Sadie. Sadie Sheldon," she said into the silence.

There was no reply.

Sadie sighed, then shuddered as the cool dirt chilled her bare arms. She tossed and turned, trying to find a spot where the earth contoured to her body, but finally gave up and curled up into a tiny ball like a cat.

Lying on the ground, wrapped in a blanket of shock, she could hardly make herself believe she had been transported to another world. It was absurd, illogical, impossible—and yet true. Sadie had fantasized about this, dreamed of being swept into a magical world full of unexpected adventures and romanticized fantastical creatures, but never had she believed they would come true. She was stuck in Carmelle, a place she had only learned about not even a full week ago, with no hope of getting back to her own world anytime soon.

Flipping over, she eyed Tristan suspiciously. His elusive and mildly abrasive demeanour reminded her of a rock amid a swirling stormy sea, battering him without breaking him. A long and arduous journey together did not enthrall her.

Chapter Six

The Road

"Curses and 'cantations!" Sadie cursed as blended vermilion and gold light pierced her eyes. She batted the lantern away and refracted light danced across the clay walls, a fiery sunrise shimmering through hazy heat. "Did you have to shine the light right in my eyes?"

"What did you say?" Tristan asked, amused.

"You heard me. I said did you have to shine the lantern right in my face? Are you *trying* to make my life more miserable?"

"No, I mean that little curse of yours."

"Oh... uh... c-curses and 'cantations." She blushed, ducking her face out of the light.

Tristan didn't say anything, but his smirk broadened.

"It's not my fault, it just bursts out of my mouth at random intervals, it has since I was ten, I have no control over it!"

"I didn't say anything."

Sadie glared at him and then yawned, stretching her sore limbs, and wincing as they refused to yield.

A cloak slithered down her waist and pooled at her feet in a puddle of midnight blue like a stream at night reflecting the moon. Looking up, she found Tristan staring at the cloak in her lap with embarrassment.

"Is this yours?" she asked.

"I had to give it to you last night, you were shivering violently, and I thought you were going to catch pneumonia. Alldían would be furious with me if I let you die, and his wrath can be terrible. I did not want to give him a reason to unleash it upon me."

"How thoughtful of you," said Sadie. She meant the words, but a sarcastic edge serrated them at his implication that he had only been kind out of self-preservation. Taking charge of her life would mean choosing to interact with genuine people uninterested in imposing their own agendas on others, so if self-serving kindness was all he could offer, he could keep it. She meant to start taking charge of her life *today*. Tossing the cloak to him she added, "You can have your cloak back. I can take care of myself."

"I doubt that," Tristan retorted, catching the cloak easily and settling it about his shoulders in one fluid motion, "but I'll take it back anyway. Wouldn't want anything happening to this reward from Lord Eberon of Lothilya for doing him a favour."

"A selfless favour? Or just trying to avoid someone's wrath again?"

"I know waking up with a lantern in your face probably didn't make you feel warm and fuzzy inside, and for that I apologize, but did it also sever your sarcasm detector?"

"Oh." Sadie shook the lingering sleep from her head. "I guess it did, sorry. I just... I'm more used to people helping me to buoy their own circumstances, so I guess I hear what I expect. I'm just tired of hearing it. Why did you wake me, anyway? It's still dark."

"Of course it is, princess."

Evidently, he hadn't forgiven her rudeness. Sadie scowled.

"Don't call me princess, it makes me want to vomit."

"You're right, I wouldn't want to upset you further. Tellurian."

Sadie narrowed her eyes at the tiny smirk tugging at the corner of Tristan's lips.

"Tellurian? An inhabitant of Earth? Is that supposed to be some kind of insult because you don't like Earth? Or are you trying to banter with me? Because I must warn you, I am a champion. I have years and years of practice with—"

But Sadie choked on the last words and averted her eyes to the dirt floor. *Connor.* Her chest ached, and she wondered if she would ever see him again. Connor had always supported her dreams of seeking adventure among the ruins of Pompeii or searching for the lost city of Troy away from high society, and Sadie had assumed her brother would one day seek the adventure he yearned for as well. Or they would embark on their adventure together. But he had never voiced his own personal dreams. Would he be devastated that in the moment of choosing adventure, her choice hadn't included him? Or had he never really planned on shirking his Sheldon duties?

Whether he felt betrayed by her or not, she needed to make amends for forgetting him. He needed to know she hadn't meant to hurt him.

Noticing Tristan watching her from the corner of her eye, Sadie knew she would have to figure out whether she could trust him soon. She would need help to reunite with her brother, and she hoped Tristan could be counted on to help her.

"Never mind. Why is the tunnel always dark, Mr. West?"

Tristan studied her face, and she tried to hide her melancholy desperation behind determined resolve. "Call me Tristan," he said after a moment. "We're not at a fancy soiree. In the days of its prime, the Halls of Learning were lit brightly with everlasting torches enchanted by the wizards that would burn like captured flames of the sun, but the flames died after the tunnels were defiled in the last major war in Carmelle—over seventy years ago now. Scholars still come here to add inscriptions in the walls and record new events, but now they must bring light with them. The torch brackets are still here, however."

Holding up the lantern, he let its light fall on an ebony torch bracket etched with carvings.

"Why don't we start finding our way out of here," Tristan suggested. "Follow me, Miss Sheldon."

Sadie's eyes snapped up at the mention of her name. Apparently he hadn't been asleep. Tristan offered her a small but warm smile. She couldn't help but smile back.

As they set off through the tunnels of Athatair, Sadie noticed a new script carved into the yellow rock every few feet, sometimes with large gaps separating them, and in other places huge paintings depicted scenes of battles, or nobles being crowned.

"So much happened after coming through the mirror yesterday I forgot to ask," began Sadie. "How is it some of the people here, including you and that woman in Helgur, know how to speak English? I wouldn't have thought anyone in a different world could speak the same language as me—and none of these scripts are in the English alphabet."

"Some of them are in English, we just haven't come across them yet. English is not a native language of Arwé, but people from Earth have been coming through portals for years, and some of them have spoken English," explained Tristan. "It wasn't until a man named Thomas Sheldon came to Arwé, however, that many Carmellians learned the English language."

Sadie's heart beat so fast she stopped and swayed where she stood, reeling with dizziness.

"What's wrong?" Tristan asked, noticing she had stopped.

"Thomas Sheldon is my great-grandfather."

Tristan puffed his cheeks and released a slow, loud blast of air. "I suspected the connection when I heard your name last night, but I'd assumed Alldían would have told me if you were related. I don't know why he didn't."

"Seems to be a lot of things Alldían chooses not to share," noted Sadie dryly. "How did Thomas teach people across Carmelle English? Why?"

"During Thomas' time in Arwé, Carmelle was at war against a formidable foe. He joined the Carenthian army, a nation whose language already shared similarities with English, so he taught it to a lot of Carenthians to start with and learned their language in return. But as the war progressed and more nations needed to band together to defeat the same foe, Thomas saw a need for a common language to unite them and increase effectiveness of communication. English even became a sort of code language to use around the opposing armies—only their highest-ranking enemies knew it. After the war, English's popularity spread even more because of the fame Thomas' exceptional deeds earned him. Not everyone speaks English of course, but enough people across different nations and races in Carmelle learned, so now you can find people who speak English in almost every major city you visit, especially among the leaders. Carenthians have adopted it as a second language, and it is most common there."

Sadie shrugged to dislodge the discomfort icing the nape of her neck. Tristan spoke like Carmellians had embraced English as a language they admired and wanted to learn, and Sadie hoped that was true, but she promised herself she would try to learn Carmellian languages too.

Another thought needled the doubts shadowing Sadie's mind. "If Arwé has had so many visitors from my world that Earth's existence is common knowledge in this world, why is Arwé's existence not common knowledge in Earth? Have Carmellians not visited Earth as often?"

"Unfortunately, the same door does not always provide equal access to everyone," Tristan replied, one corner of his tight lips twisting up in a sad smile bordering on a grimace. "Carmellians have indeed passed through portals to Earth, but they are not always met with a warm reception. Magic is not a natural resource on Earth like it is in Arwé. Here it is imbibed in all elements of the natural world, infused at the deepest level from particles formed during the world's inception. Magic is expected here, as normal as breathing. But magic is not inherent to Earth; it is not a fact of life. People must choose to believe in magic, but everyone fears what they don't know, so it is a rare choice. Portals are not common knowledge on Earth. Disappearances through portals are labelled as tragic accidents or mythic anomalies. Attempts at scientific explanations are dismissed as childish fantasies or maladies of the mind."

Sadie thought of Thomas' book, and the fear his attempts at informing Earth of Arwé had engendered, to the point of ostracization.

"When someone from Carmelle comes to Earth, especially if they are obviously different in abilities or appearances like a Lantíé, they are typically revered as a God—or feared as a threatening demon. Neither the Carmellian nor the people of Earth benefit from such reactions, at least not long term. Some stay on Earth and assimilate, usually humans with little or no magic. But there is less incentive for the people of Arwé to seek visits to Earth. Would you want to go to a different world if you knew you'd face more prejudice than in your own world?"

"No." Though the way people on Earth reacted to magic wasn't her fault, she could still taste the bitterness of shame.

"Alldían can tell you more about parallel worlds when we get to Caris Nando," Tristan added, perhaps sensing her discomfort. "He's the expert, not me."

Swallowing the sharp tang on her tongue past the lump in her throat, Sadie nodded and fell silent.

A couple of times Tristan had to choose between different paths as they continued walking, but always chose the one on the left. Eventually they emerged into a wider tunnel with walls of deep red brick, several doors with arched tops branching off the tunnel. Sadie marvelled at the size of the Caves of Learning.

Taking his first right turn through one of the doors, Tristan led her up a slightly sloping passage to a stone door.

"And we're sure the dragon won't be waiting for us out there?" Sadie asked.

"Reasonably," replied Tristan, which wasn't quite the reassuring answer she was looking for. "Whoever sent the dragon wouldn't want it pursuing us this far from the Gap, Helgur was probably already too far. The dragon was wearing a *vulnek*, a collar designed to track and deliver increasing levels of pain the further it gets from its master. It must have been in agony during the fight at Helgur. Probably the only reason we escaped with our lives."

He reached for the door, but Sadie shot her hand out to snatch the iron ring before him. He raised an eyebrow but gestured for her to continue.

Sadie pulled on the iron ring triumphantly, fresh determination surging through her at opening the door to the next step of her new life—but nothing happened. She pulled again, digging in her heels, but the door didn't budge an inch.

"Is it locked?" she asked Tristan.

He smirked. "Nope."

"Great, so what you're telling me is that I came through a mirror to prove my worth, only to be thwarted by a door?"

"Only if you let it."

"What do you mean? I'm obviously too weak to open it."

"Are you too weak to ask for help?"

"But that's not strength, getting a man to do the hard work for me!" Sadie protested, balling her fists.

"I disagree," replied Tristan, his voice still calm and smooth. "It might not show physical strength, but strength comes in many different forms. Strength of character and strength of mind are far more important than physical strength. Learn to recognize your different strengths, and apply the right one to the right situation. Asking for help means your mind is strong enough to adopt humility in place of arrogance. Shelving your ego shows great strength."

Sadie studied the indents on the iron ring. Tristan's words seemed wise, but also like something a man would say to appease a woman, and not necessarily mean it in earnest. Once again she felt like she had no choice, this time because of her own inadequacies.

"All right," Sadie conceded, gritting her teeth. "Might you help me open this door, Tristan?"

"It would be my pleasure," he replied.

Ignoring the iron ring, he put his hand on the door—and pushed.

The door swung open.

Sadie gaped at Tristan as he burst out laughing, outrage roiling with the laugh bubbling up in her stomach.

"Oh, you're going to pay for that," Sadie promised darkly as she stalked past him.

Weak dawn light blinded Sadie after the constant darkness of Athatair. A rim of short pale green grass greeted her, sloping a few feet ahead of her at a steep angle and curving into the roundness of a bowl. Bare patches of grey rock poked through the grass and the yellow light of dawn filled the bowl to the brim, spilling over the top like sparkling golden soup.

"Is it supposed to look like a bowl?" Sadie asked uncertainly.

Tristan closed his eyes and heaved a deep sigh as though steeling himself for a long day of tedious questions. "Yes. Maeldré, it's called. The Golden Bowl. It marks the last of the Sacred Lands. Once it was an enormous well, filled with a clear liquid boasting a hint of sweetness, like spiced mints. It's a Lantian creation known for its reviving qualities, one they still make today, though few mortals have tasted it."

"How do you know what it tastes like then? Are you immortal?"

"No, but my godfather is an immortal Lantíé, so I am one of the lucky few mortal humans who have tasted it. The drink is called *yenalin*, meaning 'star water.'"

"Are many races immortal in Arwé?" Sadie asked.

"Only two in Carmelle," replied Tristan, crossing his arms and shuffling his feet. "The Lantíés and the Armindís. Though the Armindís are kindred of the Lantíés, they evolved from lightning birds, while Lantíés evolved from perytons, so their rules of immortality are slightly different. Perytons were creatures like deer with eagle's wings. Some Lantíés still have antlers or wings, or both."

Sadie remembered the beings with antlers and wings in the painting from Thomas Sheldon's book, surprised the person wanting her in Carmelle was one of them. For some reason she assumed it would have been one of the magic-wielders.

"What happened to the bowl? Where did the *yenalin* go?"

Tristan looked into her eyes, all traces of even a mocking smile gone. "Vashi."

Sadie paused, caught in the net of his solemnity.

"Who's Vashi?"

Tristan locked his eyes on the Golden Bowl. For a moment Sadie thought he would refuse to answer, but then he said softly, as if it pained him, "Vashi is the ruler of Vasmorloth. He is very powerful and perilous. You will learn about him soon enough, far sooner than you'd like I suspect, for he's the enemy of all good people of Carmelle, and his evil name is known to all. He's the formidable foe I told you Thomas Sheldon helped fight."

A sharp gleam like the edge of a sword flashed across his deep brown orbs.

"The bowl was drained by the foul creatures of Vashi at the end of the First Age when they attempted to destroy the elements of the Sacred Lands, and it was never filled again," Tristan continued before Sadie could think what to say. "Its original name, Teardhí, meaning the Seeker's Well, was changed to its current name, given for this golden light that fills it every morning. We are lucky to be able to see it at this time of day in its full splendour. But we can't tarry. We have many miles to cover before the sun sets."

Tristan's abrupt end to their enjoyment of the Maeldré and dictating of their travel schedule irked Sadie, but she dug her fingernails into her palms to quell the rising heat in her cheeks. He knew this world, she did not. She needed to pick her battles.

The beginning of an overgrown path met them at the far side of the bowl, so worn and trampled and weedy that Sadie found it remarkable something so rutty could begin at the foot of such beauty.

"This is the Road. It winds its way northwest, leading to a small town called Edgewater, and then to the coast of the Tolotanteau beyond. We will travel on this road for many days, so you'd best make yourself acquainted with it," Tristan advised.

Sadie thought she knew the answer to her next question since she didn't see any towns or cities on the horizon but didn't want to make assumptions. "And we couldn't... you know... hire transportation of some sort instead of walking the whole way?"

Tristan's smirk returned.

"Sorry to disappoint you, tellurian, but you'll find none of your father's fancy carriages in these parts of Carmelle," said Tristan, smirking. "You'll have to rely on your own two feet to carry you most of the way to Caris Nando."

"I wasn't expecting a carriage, thank you very much," retorted Sadie hotly. "I'm an independent twentieth-century woman using my strengths and assessing all possibilities before making a decision."

Heat burned her cheeks and throbbed in her fingertips at his mockery—and at having to defend herself—but she coaxed her pounding heart into steely resolve. It was time to start acting like the heroic, independent woman she knew she could be. She may need a guide, but she would not be ordered around or let Tristan mock her inexperience. And she would *not* let Tristan steal all her significant moments marking her new freedom and resolve, even if those moments seemed insignificant to him. This was her adventure, her new life, and she would choose when to take the first step down her new path.

Shading her eyes with her hand, she made a point of looking around, taking in the golden light creeping up the bowl as the sunlight shifted. Rolling hills devoid of dragons and mirrors hid the secrets of the Athatair behind her, and a treeless plain stretched out before her, stark and intimidating in its bareness. This was it. She would step onto the Road, and there would be nowhere to hide. No shield to protect her from the perils of an unknown world, but no cage to hold her back either.

Squaring her shoulders and tossing back her braid, Sadie stepped confidently onto the Road, leading the way to Edgewater.

On the third night since Sadie first entered Carmelle, she lay on her back under the stars, watching them wink at her knowingly. A meteor shot across the sky, and her first instinct was to make a wish. But she didn't know what to wish for. What did you wish for when your only wish since you were five had come true? And what did it mean when your dream left you feeling hollow?

Her stomach rumbled, and she glanced down at it with a frown. For the past three days she had eaten nothing but dry biscuits and berries. This morning, Tristan had looked in his pouch and frowned. Not a good sign. She had asked Tristan if he could hunt, and he had said yes but there was no game until they got to the forests near Edgewater.

She had known adventures would be difficult, but she hadn't expected the monotony. The awkward, minimal conversation with a stubbornly recluse travel companion, the repetitive landscape, the lack of new people or cities or creatures or *anything* to add excitement and spark conversation.

She refused to give credence to the doubt gnawing at her resolve, though. To believe that the bravest thing she had ever done in her life could be a mistake.

Sighing deeply, she returned her gaze to the stars and wondered if they were the same stars dotting the sky in her world. Was Connor looking at them too? Was it even night there? Sadie didn't know. Everything had become so jumbled since arriving in Carmelle.

Connor had been excited about Thomas' book as well, eager to embark on an adventure. Guilt and sorrow burrowed into every crevice of Sadie's body. She missed him. He was her best and only friend, the only person she could talk to, the only person truly there for her. The person whose love she could be sure of. And she had thrown that gift away for an adventure. A chance to be a hero. What kind of hero sacrificed their brother?

A single tear trickled down Sadie's face. She let it fall.

Lying beside Tristan, watching the ebony void weep pearly tears, Sadie wondered if Connor missed her. If anyone did.

Had they noticed her absence?

Connor would, she reasoned. Maybe her parents and Tanaya, too. Tristan was right. Strength came in all kinds of forms, and Sadie was beginning to think she might have underestimated her mother and sister's strengths. She wished she could tell them that.

Would they look for her?

Staring up at the moon, Sadie vowed to do everything in her power to return to him and support his dreams, even if it meant giving up the magical reality of hers. Her brother deserved a happy ending too, and she would not be the one to take that from him.

Chapter Seven

The Sputtering of the Flame

Connor stared at the moon, eyes dry but raw, throat constricted as he held back the sobs fighting to break free. He would not cry. Hope was not lost yet. Not while things were so uncertain. Until they found her body...

Connor gripped the rail of the veranda, knuckles turning white. He could not think like that. Those thoughts would only pull him further away from hope, make him despair at last. And he could *not* despair, not when there was still hope left. He had promised her he would always look for hope. Always.

Yet she herself had lost hope. She had given up hope of ever leading the life she truly desired. She had stopped fighting, had stopped deliberately disobeying their parents' rules, had stopped defying the culture of the rich. She had sunken into depression and adopted silent submission. He had been mortified by the abrupt change. *Why* had she suddenly lost all hope? *Why* had she dropped everything she stood for? *Why* reverberated in his mind, but the answer eluded him, even when she had tried to explain.

Doubt folded into the spaces between facts in his mind. What if he could have helped her? What if the despair went deeper than he knew, deeper than she could climb out of alone?

Stop, he instructed himself firmly. She is *not* dead.

But he couldn't stop the doubt. It seeped through him like poison, bleeding through his veins and spattering an image on his heart, an image he knew would haunt him for the rest of his life. Her eyes the last time he had looked at them. Haunted and hollow, the green irises shrouded by a grey veil, a silver mist masking pain and vulnerability.

Connor glanced back at the moon. It shone innocently at him, unaware of his pain and doubt, ignorant of the possibility he might never see his sister again.

Sadie had been missing for the past nine hours.

Earlier that afternoon, Connor had seen her abruptly leave the table without any explanation. He had not missed her wide, watery eyes, but hadn't been sure if he should follow. Maybe the painful small talk had jolted her out of her submissive stupor and these emotions were the catalyst for her fiery tempestuous nature to resurface and shake the iron bars of her prison. Or maybe she had an epiphany about how to be happy within the confines of strict high society life, so her future could be safe and secure but still adventurous and fulfilling. Connor wasn't sure which one he hoped for, because although he understood and supported her desire for a more just world for women, he also knew breaking free of that life without completely alienating herself and becoming destitute would be much more difficult than she allowed. He had not gone after his sister, giving her the chance to sort through her emotions alone. He had believed he was doing the right thing.

Now, he wasn't so sure.

Guilt wrenched his heart. He could have been there for her, could have saved her.

Propping his elbows up on the railing, he cradled his head in his hands.

A hand gripped his shoulder gently, and he whipped around to meet Mabel's eyes. Though they brimmed with sympathy, Connor derived no comfort from them. She had entered his life when Sadie needed him most, distracting him when he should have been more attentive to his sister. If she hadn't been at Tanaya's wedding, maybe he would have gone after Sadie.

Turning away, he stared back at the moonlight. He could feel Mabel studying him, her round eyes boring into the back of his head as though trying to read his mind. She removed her hand from his shoulder, slowly. He could tell she was unsure of the gesture now, but he did nothing to reassure her. Anger pricked his fingertips and gripped his throat.

"Don't blame yourself," she said softly.

"How'd you—" he began hoarsely.

"It's written all over your face," she replied quietly. "Your face is an open book. You don't hide your emotions very well." It wasn't an insult or accusation, merely a stated fact.

Connor gawked at her. Sadie had said the exact same thing to him numerous times.

"It wasn't your fault. It's not your responsibility to look after her. You were there for her before today, and you understood her when she needed you the most. There was nothing you could do."

"I could have followed her," Connor argued. "I could have helped her deal with her emotions. She was vulnerable in that state, and I should have been there. It *is* my responsibility when I'm the only one who knows her, who truly cares about her. Do you know what it feels like to have the one person who meant something to you in this stupid goddamn world suddenly disappear? She could be *dead*, Mabel."

An awkward silence expanded between them while Connor seethed in self-loathing and Mabel stood with a downcast head. Whether penitent from his words or hurt by them he didn't know, and he found that he didn't care.

Finally, Mabel said in a meek voice, "I don't pretend to know what you're going through Connor—"

"That's right, you don't know!" he exploded.

Mabel persisted, unperturbed. "But I do know you can't let what could have been hold you back from what could be. I don't know Sadie well—we haven't had the chance to talk to each other much yet—but what I do know, I have learned from you. You told me she is determined and stubborn, has a fiery temper and thrives in the unexpected and unknown. Maybe she's lost, and if that's the case I bet she's having a grand adventure. Or maybe she's purposefully staying away, postponing the moment when she must come back and face the world, and nothing has happened to her at all. We don't know that she's dead yet."

Connor was quiet for a moment. Mabel's words made sense, but guilt still nagged at him.

"I still could have gone after her," he murmured softly.

"You know she would have just told you to go away anyway," Mabel replied smoothly.

Connor stared at his feet. Mabel was right. He couldn't control Sadie. That was what she was running away from. She wouldn't have thanked him for trying to control her emotions and prove her independence couldn't be trusted. There *was* still hope. He had needed someone else to echo that hope.

"Thank you," he murmured at last, looking up and meeting Mabel's eyes, "and sorry for snapping at you. You didn't deserve it."

In response, Mabel wrapped her arms around his waist in a warm embrace. They stayed like that for a long time; Connor clinging to her like a child, Mabel providing stable support and comfort, stroking his back in soothing circles. Connor held back sobs, but he let a few tears wet his eyes and trickle down his cheeks.

After a while, Connor pulled back a bit and asked, "How did you get so smart, anyway?"

Mabel smiled innocently and replied, "Woman's intuition."

Despite his heartache, Connor groaned. "I hate when women say that."

Mabel smiled, and the tight bands around his chest loosened slightly. She could never make up for the loss of Sadie, but maybe he could let her in a little.

"Have I mentioned how amazing you are?"

His eyes slid from the starlight reflected in her sage irises to the curve of her lips.

She shook her head. "Not for hours now."

"What an inexcusable failing on my part. You are amazing, far superior in every way to this miserable wretch before you."

Mabel laughed, a tinkling sound like the high notes of a piano plunking ballads of hope through his heart, and their laced fingers cupped moonbeams in their own little pocket of light.

Connor watched the search party stumble back up the veranda steps around dawn, their weary faces drawn, their slack jaws renouncing hope.

They had been sent out by Roger Sheldon two hours after Sadie had first left the table, armed with guns, and the wedding reception had come to an abrupt and confused end. Turmoil reigned, everyone panicking in their shock and confusion. Sadie would have been proud of the chaos she caused when Connor had lurched to his feet and shouted, "Where's Sadie?"

Immediately Connor had told his father he had seen Sadie run into the woods, and with astonishing speed Roger had gathered a small band of men together, including Connor and Derek. Together they had left to go search the forest for Sadie, still dressed in their best tailcoats. The search had been slow and careful, making sure they didn't miss any tracks or signs of where she might have disappeared to. Although they kept their eyes peeled and studied the ground and searched all the bushes, the fact remained there weren't any trackers or even good hunters in the pack, and they may have missed clues. A fact that worried Connor, but there was nothing he could do about it.

A few fruitless hours passed, and the sun began to set. It was then that his father had announced they needed to go back to the mansion, grab a bite to eat and some lanterns, and then go back out to search. When they had reached the house, his father told him he must stay behind.

"It's not because I don't trust your ability to track in the dark," he had reassured him, "but I need someone to look after your mother. I was not thinking before, but your mother must be devastated. She will need comforting. Also, I think it best that a man of the Sheldon family should stay here in case… in case something happens."

Connor had protested at first, but eventually agreed to stay behind and look after his mother. Of course when he tried to comfort her, Victoria brushed him aside, shielding her face as though the sight of him pained her. Maybe she wasn't ready to let him see her tears. Only Tanaya was allowed to join her seclusion. Tanaya had spent her wedding night consoling her mother while her new husband joined the search party. Since the search party had already departed and it was pointless for him to try and go after them now, Connor had taken up a post on the veranda, watching the forest and waiting.

Mabel had gone home around midnight with her father, but Connor had remained on the veranda, watching the black night fade into the pale grey morning of dawn.

He thought of Sadie.

About how she would have loved a morning like this, where the thick grey mist hung low about the mansion, weaving between the trees and hovering above the grass, its toes brushing the tips of the blades delicately as it floated past. She would have said it was mysterious and beautiful, the perfect atmosphere for the start of a grand adventure. Magical.

As the last of the search party trudged past him, offering nothing but vague nods, his father's grave voice came from the doorway.

"Connor."

He turned, heart eager and full of hope, but his father's pained eyes told him they had not found Sadie. Embracing the stabbing pain in his tight chest, Connor turned back to the rail and fixed his blurry gaze on the forest beyond. His father joined him.

They were silent for a moment, watching the swirling mists, until Roger said, "We're going to find her, Connor."

Connor just nodded; his father said it more to reassure himself than his son.

"When do you start looking again?"

"Right after breakfast." Stroking his moustache, he stared at the mist without really seeing it. "You know, I don't think Sadie was very happy with her life here."

Connor couldn't believe those words had just come out of his father's mouth. Did he not know his own daughter at all? The answer slapped him cruelly in the face—no. His father *didn't* know her. He didn't know any of them, not really. He knew Connor better than Tanaya and Sadie, but that was only because Connor was a boy, his only son.

"She wasn't," he replied bluntly. "She hated it here."

"Ah," said Roger awkwardly. "I suspected as much, at least lately. She wasn't made for this quiet life. I always knew it, yet I never did anything about it. I thought she would find a way to fit in. If I'd been able to get through to her, and help her find a way to be happier in her role, she might still be here."

Yeah, she might, Connor thought bitterly, but he kept his thoughts to himself.

Silence reigned for a moment, and then Roger added, "Times are changing now, too. There's rumour of war in Europe, and war always means change. I bet she would have fit in fine with the new changes."

Connor doubted this, but again he kept quiet. No matter what the future held, he couldn't imagine it including a freer world for women.

Unless the rules of propriety lessened for them, Sadie would never fit in. She was not a follower, and never would be. She was a born leader, a governor of her own principles, and she needed to be in a place where people would allow that.

"I hope we find her," Roger said sincerely. "She always had the most interesting perspective on our walks through the woods together, and... there's so much left to say."

Glancing at his father, Connor noticed a single tear trickling down his face.

So much left to say.

"Father?"

"Yes, Son?"

"Can I come with you after breakfast?"

"Of course, Connor." He opened his mouth to say more, snapped it shut again, opened it hesitantly once more, and held that position for a full minute. Connor watched curiously as his father struggled. After a few more seconds, he managed to mumble, "I love you, Son. You know that, don't you?"

Connor nodded. "I know."

A week passed. Still no sign of Sadie. Everyone had lost hope she still lived—except Connor. He clung desperately to the tiniest shred of hope, despite the whispers behind his back that he was in denial. Every day he went out with the slowly dwindling search party, and every day he came home without even the smallest hint of where his sister had gone. It was as if she had simply vanished. He kept telling himself he would find some trace of her fate soon, but he never did. Soon he had searched not only the forest bordering their mansion but much of the surrounding countryside as well.

On the seventh day since Sadie had gone missing, his father approached him again, this time with a purposeful, brisk stride that caught Connor's attention.

"What is it?"

"Connor, we've been searching for Sadie for seven days now and there's still no sign of her," Roger said. "We'll never know anything if we keep going on this way. I must ask you if you had seen anything... unusual before Sadie disappeared. Anything at all."

Connor racked his brains for anything he would label unusual. Everything before her disappearance had become a blur, a vague outline difficult to sift through.

"Well... we found a book the day of the ball, and she told me two days later about a mirror that might be in our forest..." Connor started slowly.

"A book?" his father repeated. "Sadie mentioned a book to me the day of the ball as well, and she was asking about... well, about—"

"Thomas Sheldon?" Connor guessed.

"Yes. Him. I didn't have any information for her, but I also became annoyed that she was even asking when she knows how much her mother loathes the topic and she had some foolish fantastical notion about it..." Roger trailed off, averting his gaze and scratching his chin in uncomfortable guilt.

"I think she wanted to find the mirror," Connor said, "but then her and Mother fought and she seemed to give up the idea... but maybe she changed her mind at the wedding and tried to find it again? Unless—"

A pair of deep brown eyes peering from between leaves flashed across his mind. Eyes staring with eerie intensity at his sister that day she had told him about the mirror in the forest...

"My God," Connor whispered.

The funeral took place on August 1ˢᵗ, exactly eight days after Sadie had gone missing. Connor was in a state of shock. He couldn't believe his sister was dead. Irretrievably, forever gone. He would never see those fiery eyes burning with excitement or flaring up in defiance. Never prowl about their mansion with her or seek adventure in the woods. He would never see her face again. Ever.

And it was partly his fault. He had forgotten to tell his father about the man in the woods that day, distracted by the wedding bustle, and Mabel, and the mystery of Thomas Sheldon lurking in the back of his mind. If he had, Sadie would not have been allowed to go in there. She would not have been killed.

For that was what they all thought now. Sadie had entered the forest, maybe to try and find Thomas' elusive mirror, and been murdered by that madman. Connor could have prevented that, could have saved her from suffering.

His father had immediately notified the police of the man in the forest, though he mentioned nothing of Thomas Sheldon to the police or Victoria. Connor wasn't sure if embarrassment kept Roger from mentioning fantastical mirrors and estranged relatives, or fear of upsetting his wife. But Connor followed his father's lead in keeping that detail between them. The police found no body and assumed she must have been abducted before being killed, so he didn't leave any evidence behind. There was no question in anyone's minds, however, including Connor's, that Sadie Sheldon was dead.

As he carried the coffin towards the grave, an unbearable sadness weighed Connor down, but he could not shed a single tear. His eyes had dried up, his throat constricted. No body rested in the coffin. It was merely a symbol of Sadie's life. Connor had insisted on picking an ebony casket with gold trimmings around the edges. Upon the closed lid Connor had laid a single red rose. He had also insisted Sadie not be buried in the graveyard behind their church, as his mother wanted, but beneath her favourite willow tree in their own yard instead. His mother had finally agreed, after much coaxing from her husband.

A fierce wind whipped black dresses and suits, the first real wind of the summer. Connor's own black jacket slapped the side of the coffin as he slowly lowered it into the grave, and his untamed hair buffeted about his face. He could hear people sobbing in the background, their voices caught in the wind, but to him the sound was dim, like a soft echo of previous losses or a foreshadowing cry of losses to come. Out of the corner of his eye he could see the wispy branches of the willow swaying, their fingers drooping in sadness, their green leaves dulled to a grey-green like the colour of Sadie's eyes. Even the wind rustling the leaves sighed mournfully. Thick pewter clouds crowded the sky, their swollen ducts ready to weep tears for Sadie.

Connor lowered the coffin into the grave and then stepped back to join the crowd with the other pallbearers. Together they melded into one solid mass of black, contrasting with the white tombstone. As the priest began his sermon, Connor stared at the tombstone, blocking out his words. Carved into the marble was the inscription:

Sadie Sheldon

1896 – 1914

"May her soul find adventure in the Other World"

Connor had written the epitaph himself. She had been so young... and it wasn't even as if her last days had at least been happy ones. They had been the worst of her life.

Connor remained silent throughout the entire funeral, standing a little apart from everyone else. He watched numbly as his mother and father wept, clinging to each other, immersed in grief. Connor hadn't spoken to his mother since Sadie had first gone missing. Other than himself, he felt his mother was the most to blame. If she hadn't been so disregarding of Sadie's feelings, then Sadie wouldn't have run into the forest, would not have felt so depressed and trapped. He could see their last argument weighing on his mother's shoulders as she shook with sobs. Her haunted eyes, the quiver of her chin, and the way she muttered to herself distractedly as she gripped her forearm and dug her fingernails in reflected her guilt mingled with grief. He had caught her sitting on Sadie's bed, clutching a wooden sword she used to play with as a child in one hand and the brooch at her throat in the other, a faraway look in her hollow eyes.

He might be able to forgive his mother one day. But not yet.

Tanaya cried too, clutching her new husband for support. Red had ringed his sister's perpetually wet eyes since Sadie's disappearance. Though Connor empathized with Tanaya's grief, he wished she had empathized with her sister a little more while she was alive.

Long after the other mourners departed, Connor remained by his sister's grave. He knelt before the tombstone and traced his fingers over Sadie's name. Rushing incessantly in his ears, the wind howled with grief, and Connor finally howled with it. Cradling his head in his hands he rocked back and forth, letting his loud sobs rent the silence.

When his raw eyes burned and he could finally breathe normally again, he relinquished his face from his stiff hands and looked at the name on the tombstone. His sister was gone forever. The flame had sputtered out. No matter what anyone said, part of the blame would always lay on him.

Closing his eyes, he saw her smiling radiantly like dancing fire. This was how he would remember her, always.

Goodbye, Sadie.

Chapter Eight

Nightmares and Nuisances

Sadie ran her fingers over the smooth log home she leaned against, heart aching as she closed her eyes and breathed in the familiar scent of shaved pine. Of all the emotions she expected to feel upon entering the first town not decimated by a dragon in Carmelle, nostalgia was not one of them. Yet as she waited for Tristan to finish haggling with a woman selling healing salve from a cart, watching a lamplighter light candles in intricately carved wooden tree-lampposts along the ring of Edgewater's circular town, all she could think of was home. The abundant forests of pine and cedar and the log cabins on the outskirts of Vancouver—cabins her father had always so proudly pointed out as an example of what could be built with the similar logs his lumber company cut down.

She needed to find a spark of magic to remind her why she came to Carmelle. A purpose to guide her actions. Without one, the familiarity left her feeling hollow and adrift.

"This should do it!" announced Tristan as he rejoined her, a small round tin in his palm. "There's no real Healer in town, so the townsfolk have perfected their own tinctures and salves to treat minor wounds and illnesses. It will at least keep your cut from becoming infected."

"Thanks," Sadie mumbled.

She touched the stinging cut by her eye and glanced at her finger. Dry. The bleeding had stopped, at least. Not a wound from their encounter with the dragon or some other adventurous feat, but from her own absentmindedness. She had let her mind wander as they trekked the forest path to Edgewater and had walked straight into the jagged edge of a broken, low-hanging tree branch.

"Here, let's put some on before we go inside," said Tristan, twisting open the lid and dipping his finger in a balm that smelled of honey and pine.

He reached for her cut, his hand curved as though about to cup her cheek, and Sadie recoiled slightly, heart leaping to her throat. Their eyes met. Sadie's cheeks burned at his closeness. The gesture felt... intimate.

Tristan's eyes widened and he took a step back, dropping his hand.

"Sorry," he apologized, wiping the majority of the salve on his finger against the inner rim of the tin so as not to waste it, and the rest on his pants. "You can apply your own salve, of course."

"It *is* a fairly simple task," Sadie agreed, playing along with his assumption she was upset at him treating her like a helpless woman, when his help applying salve to a wound she couldn't see would have been appreciated. Her heart slid back down to her chest, but still thumped erratically. Did fear keep her from trusting him?

Dipping her finger in the salve, she patted the soothing ointment across her cut awkwardly and twisted the lid back on with a confident flourish.

"There! Now, which building is the inn?"

"The biggest one, naturally," Tristan replied, pointing to a two-storey cedar log building across the square. "It's the only inn in Edgewater, but it's one of my favourites in Carmelle."

Sadie raised an eyebrow at Tristan. "High praise, for a small-town inn."

"Well, you're used to extravagance, so it might not be *your* favourite, but I like a more homely atmosphere, and you couldn't find a homelier one."

"You may not believe it Mr. West, but so do I," retorted Sadie. Marching across the square, she led the way past an eight-foot wooden carving of a bear with a salmon in its mouth.

A faint welcoming chatter drifted out of the open windows, and a sign swinging above the door showed an endearing fluffy white cloud blowing at the olive-green lettering of *The Whispering Wind Inn*.

Sadie grabbed the door handle, but Tristan's low, sharp voice stilled her hand.

"Wait!" he urged. "Before we go in there, remember you must not tell anyone where you are from. It's not a crime to come to Arwé from another world, but it happens so rarely that the knowledge of you being here before we have seen Alldían could prove deadly in the wrong hands. I know this is a small town, but small-town gossip catches like wildfire, and it only needs to leak to one wrong pair of ears for us to be in a whole lot of trouble. For now, you are a survivor from the attack on Helgur, and you're travelling with me to Carenthia as a witness to report the dragon to the king, and then I am helping you start a new life since your family and livelihood were destroyed. Can you remember that?"

"Shouldn't be too hard, most of it is true anyway," said Sadie, nodding.

"The best lies are always half-truths," agreed Tristan. He gestured for her to resume opening the door. She pulled the handle, butterflies swooping in her stomach.

Chatter crescendoed as the door swung open, and the earthy scent of roasted lamb assailed her nose. Saliva immediately pooled at the corner of her mouth, and she discreetly wiped it away with her thumb, hoping none of the heads turning in their direction noticed. A couple of dozen people dressed in simple, plain attire suitable for working in the woods sat at long wooden tables, candlelight centrepieces illuminating forks hovering halfway to their mouths or bulging cheeks paused mid-chew.

"Why are they staring?" Sadie muttered under her breath.

"Because we're clearly outsiders," he remarked as he led her between the rows of tables towards a door across from them, "and Edgewater is kind of out of the way, so they don't get a lot of folk passing through. But some of them know me."

He nodded to a few people who waved and nodded back, but none moved from their benches or gestured for Sadie and Tristan to join them. A small empty stage bookended the common room on one side, a brick fireplace with an empty grate bookending the other. A wooden staircase against the back wall led to the rooms on the second floor, and beside the staircase the door they walked towards opened and a woman bustled out, muttering to herself and drying her hands on the apron tied over a cotton sage dress.

When she spotted Tristan, her frown transformed into a warm, welcoming grin.

"Tristan!" she exclaimed. "Tristan West, I can't believe it! I haven't seen you since you stopped by here on your way to sort out that bragûl infestation on the borders of Voita."

"Yes, it has been a few years, it's nice to see you again, Nina! Those bragûl haven't given you anymore trouble, have they?"

"We haven't seen any here, though I can't speak to what's happening in Voita. No one ventures in there. What brings you here now?"

"Trouble near the Gap of Talarí, unfortunately. My acquaintance Sadie and I are travelling to Carenthia to report it to the king."

The frown returned to Nina's tanned face, and she put a hand on her ample hips. "What sort of trouble?"

Tristan glanced around. Most folks had returned to their meals and loud conversations, but some still glanced at them periodically between bites and guffaws.

"Do you have somewhere we can talk?" Tristan asked.

"Of course. This way," Nina directed, leading them out of the common room through the door she had just come through.

When they stepped into the clean but cramped kitchen, Sadie expected to see at least two or three kitchen maids or cooks busy preparing food, but only one other person stood chopping a long, green vegetable at a scrubbed wooden table. She was a few years younger than Sadie, her ruddy red cheeks beneath blond ringlets splotched as though she had been crying. Her hand shook slightly as she attempted to chop the vegetable evenly.

"All right, Dinah, don't hurt yourself, the world isn't ending," chided Nina, making the girl jump and nick her finger with the knife. "Go take a break and compose yourself, you'll do better when you've had a chance to take some deep breaths."

Dinah dropped the knife gratefully and hustled out the kitchen's back door.

"Is she okay?" Sadie asked uncertainly.

"She'll be fine," Nina assured her, taking up the knife Dinah had dropped and chopping the vegetable with such quick efficiency Sadie's mouth gaped open. "She's James' daughter, the man who owns this inn, and he wants to train her up to take over my job as Cook one day since I don't plan on working here forever, but she's just not a cook, plain and simple. James refuses to accept she can't be taught, but you can't teach a skill that requires passion to someone completely uninterested. What James should do is train the girl to take over for him one day, she has a much better head for business, but of course James' ego won't allow him to see that."

Nina dumped the chopped vegetables into a bowl of egg yolks, tossed them around until they were completely coated in the runny eggs, then emptied them into another bowl of breadcrumbs and herbs.

"I'm Marianina Ellwood, by the way, but everyone calls me Nina. Tristan's a fine man, but introductions aren't really his strong point," Nina continued with a wink. Tristan's jaw clenched, and Sadie's lips twitched as she tried to fight a gleeful smile at his chastisement. "And you're Sadie?"

"Yes, Sadie Sheldon. I'm travelling with Tristan to Carenthia. My town was decimated by a dragon."

"Oh, my dear, I'm so sorry." Nina's hands fell away from the breaded vegetables she had been spreading out on a pan. They hung limply at her sides as she looked from Sadie to Tristan, eyes wide in horror. "Did you... did you lose family?"

Sadie didn't even have to act. The pang in her chest was all too real. "Yes."

Nina came around the table and wrapped Sadie in her arms.

Sadie's breath hitched in her chest, and she stiffened. She had never experienced such a warm, tight embrace. And Nina didn't even know her. Sadie melted into the soft hug. A blurry Tristan hovered awkwardly in the periphery of her watery eyes, but she avoided looking at him.

Why couldn't her parents have hugged her like this?

After a minute, Sadie drew back and whispered, "Thanks."

"Any time, dear," said Nina, patting her cheek sympathetically. "Now I understand better why you are here, though I'm not sure what a dragon was doing by the Gap. Do you know?"

She turned to Tristan, and he shook his head. "I have theories only I'm afraid. I wish I could share more, but what I can say is that I don't think it was one of Vashi's. And I don't think it will venture to Edgewater. My guess is it has been tasked to guard the Gap and will not stray far from there."

"That's some relief at least," replied Nina, grabbing a few squat, red vegetables from a wooden bowl on the table and beginning to slice them into thin strips. "I expect you'll need supplies? Looks like that dress has been through the mill, Sadie, and I expect you'll need food and other provisions."

"You guess right," said Tristan. "We can't stay long; I hope to get back on the road tomorrow, but I would appreciate any help you can give us."

"Consider it done," replied Nina with a dismissive wave of her knife. "My whole family is coming to the inn tonight for a special Enchanter performance, so they'll be able to help source supplies for you. I'll get Maddie to bring a spare dress and boots for Sadie, Davin can bring dried meat, and Ethan's apples are ripening—I'll get him to pick some of the ripest for you. Where's your sword?"

Nina's eyes had landed on Tristan's hip. Tristan's hand twitched to where the pommel of a sword girded at his belt would rest, the same involuntary twitch Sadie had witnessed before they sprinted towards the dragon.

"Ah. That's a long story," replied Tristan evasively.

"I bet it is," commented Nina, eyebrow raised. "If you need one, Igino can talk to the blacksmith, I know she always has a few made ready to sell."

"I would be happy to pay for one," Tristan assured her, a hint of longing tinging his quick response. Sadie narrowed her eyes at the desperation in that longing. "And I'll pay for all the supplies."

"We'll sort all that out later," said Nina, waving her hand again. She gathered an array of vegetables, herbs, and oils from cupboards around the kitchen and brought them all to the table.

"Thanks Nina, your family is far too kind to me," said Tristan sincerely. He paused and then asked, "So this Enchanter... where are they from?"

Sadie narrowed her eyes at Tristan. His casual tone belied his blatant interest in the answer, but Nina responded as though his tone held no suspicion. "He's from Tulandí, I think. Which seems like a pretty small town for an Enchanter to come from if you ask me, but he says he travels all over Carmelle and hasn't even been back to the Belland region since his training in Orinloth. They say his magic tricks are a sight to behold."

Sadie's stomach lurched and her heart pounded against her ribs.

Magic?

She studied Tristan's face, but it remained impassive; she couldn't tell what he thought about this information.

"I should hope so, for the amount they charge," muttered Tristan.

Nina chuckled. "It's not my money, so if James wasted his on a scammer I'll enjoy the entertainment either way."

Putting down the knife and wiping her hands on her apron, Nina ushered them out of the kitchen, saying, "Come, I'll show you to your rooms so you can get settled. I'll let Igino know to gather supplies, he'll be passing through town soon on his way home from logging. Lucky for you, most of the folks coming to see the Enchanter tonight are local, so we still have rooms available. Then you can come down and try my corzco salad!"

When they came back down to the common room for dinner, Nina loaded their plates not only with her freshly made corzco salad, but the breaded green vegetable, roasted root vegetables, and a large cut of juicy meat. Sadie inhaled the hearty food, intent on nothing else but satiating her ravenous stomach for a while—until the Enchanter arrived.

Garbed in a deep violet and teal cape that he flourished with pomp as he sauntered to the stage, the Enchanter carried no bag of tricks or wand or any of the Robert-Houdin-esque accoutrements Sadie had come to associate with magicians in her world. Yet his confident lounge on the stool James brought to the stage, the deep vibrant colours of his garb, and the twinkle in his eyes all oozed magic and enchantment, and had the crowded inn holding their collective breath in anticipation.

Without a word to his audience, the Enchanter flourished his hands. The candlelight dimmed, and a single flame appeared cupped above the Enchanter's palm.

The crowd gasped. Sadie clutched her stomach against a sudden onslaught of nausea.

She eyed her nearly empty plate. Maybe she'd eaten something bad.

The flame became a lily bud that bloomed in his palm.

Sadie's stomach clenched.

She pushed her plate away.

"Finally full? I thought you'd be asking for a third helping," remarked Tristan, his lips quirked in amusement.

"Guess I'm not a bottomless pit after all."

"Pity. Nina's desserts are fit for deities. But I guess that means more for me! They'll be far easier to stomach than this Enchanter, even after all the food I ate."

"What do you have against magic?" Sadie asked.

"Nothing at all," replied Tristan, eyes widening in surprise.

"So, it's just Enchanters you don't like?"

"It's not that I don't like them, exactly. It's just that Enchanters are people who have a spark of real magical ability, but not enough to become a full-fledged wizard. They train in Orinloth, but only long enough to learn to control their limited magic, and then they become Enchanters—entertainers at inns and taverns, or if they're really lucky, royal courts. I don't begrudge them making a living off their magic. They have talents most of us don't, so why not use them? I guess I have seen enough wizard-magic to know Enchanters charge exorbitant amounts for the talents they have to offer. I think it gives people who haven't seen a wizard's magic a false sense of what wizards are capable of."

"Seems pretty elitist to me," commented Sadie.

"That's ironic, coming from you."

"And what's that supposed to mean?" Fire burned in her racing heart, and she gripped the table hard until her knuckles turned white.

"I'm sure your high society family never stooped to hiring street performers for their fancy functions. Their entertainment was always of the highest quality, am I right? Did you ever question their elitist taste, or ask them to hire someone who wasn't classically trained?"

"If you think I would have been able to persuade my mother to come down off her high horse—"

"I'm just saying that stigmas go both ways," interjected Tristan. "Enchanters may not be held in high regard among all societies in Carmelle, though the same can be said of wizards. Once, that wasn't true, but wizards have fallen in the eyes of many people in Carmelle due to associations with dark magic and circumstances outside of their control, and Enchanters haven't helped that perception—and I don't think that's fair either."

Sadie opened her mouth but was saved formulating an uncertain response when a girl around her age unceremoniously plopped down beside her. A wide grin plastered her freckled cheeks framed by two dirty blond braids, and she presented a pair of sturdy black laced-boots and a dark forest-green dress like a prize.

"You must be Sadie, Mom said you'd be with Tristan," the girl said cheerily. "I'm Maddie, I brought you some clothes!"

"Oh, thanks, I—"

"Don't scare the poor girl, Maddie, she's been through enough," a man with short, dark chestnut brown hair covering only half his head said in deep, honeyed tones as he drew level with their table. "Here, Tristan. I know it's not the type of sword you're used to, but—"

"It will do nicely, thanks Igino," interrupted Tristan, reaching for the basic, unadorned broadsword Igino held out to him.

When Tristan grasped the hilt, Sadie could have sworn his chest relaxed in relief.

"Isn't the Enchanter amazing?" asked Maddie, gazing at the levitating balls of different coloured light he had conjured. With a wave of his hand, they assembled into a circle and started spinning. Another wave of his hand turned them all from yellow to a sapphire blue.

Sadie grimaced, reminded of the twinge in her stomach.

"Yes, he's quite wonderful..."

Sadie trailed off as the Enchanter's eyes snapped to hers and narrowed.

Sadie tried to swallow the sudden dryness in her mouth. His eyes searched hers, but Sadie had no idea what he looked for.

The furrow in his eyebrows deepened and the balls wobbled—but then he looked away, concentrating on his magic. Sadie stared at him for a minute, but he did not look her way again.

Nobody else seemed to have noticed the way he looked at her. Tristan chatted with Igino while Maddie clapped and cheered for the Enchanter.

Sadie looked down at her plate. Maybe she was overreacting. Imagining things again, like her mother had always accused her of.

After thirty more minutes of entrancing magical entertainment, the Enchanter stood up.

"I have been Enchanter Arcturius Mauve, and I will return for a second act in twenty minutes," he announced. He sauntered off the stage, cape billowing behind him, and disappeared into the kitchen without another glance at Sadie.

But the memory of his calculating gaze followed her up to bed that night.

Sadie stood near a willow tree amidst a small crowd of people holding black umbrellas. She watched their hair whip across their faces, mesmerized by the way it streamed out in wispy banners, buffeted by a wind she couldn't feel. Touch and sound were barred from Sadie, blocked by an invisible shield. Grief-stricken faces cried out as an ebony coffin was lowered into the earth, rain bouncing off its sleek surface, and cloaks billowed in the wind, yet her garments and hair remained still. Faces contorted in pain and sadness, mouths open wide as their sorrowful wails rent the air, but Sadie heard nothing. Rain streamed down umbrellas in small rivulets, yet Sadie remained dry.

Why did her senses fail her? Where was she? It looked like a funeral, but whose? She squinted to identify clear features, to recognize someone—but the faces remained hazy and unfocused, washed away with the rain.

Slowly she weaved through the crowd, peering into blurred faces, trying to make sense of her surroundings. An inexplicable force pulled her towards the pallbearers and the black coffin. As she drew nearer, Sadie caught a glimpse of soft brown hair sticking up at odd angles from the wind, the colour of hot chocolate diluted with milk. A colour that had filled Sadie's vision as a child, as an enthusiastic boy followed her around...

The world around her changed like the switching of a film reel and sound flooded back into her ears, drowning her senses with a tidal wave scream. Yelling hoarsely herself, she clamped her hands over her ears, but the screaming didn't stop.

And then she spotted him.

Kneeling on the ground before her, his face buried in his hands was her brother, Connor. From him the scream escaped as he sobbed uncontrollably. Sadie could see the lines of pain carved deeply into his stricken face as tears flowed down his cheeks and leaked through his shaking hands.

Sadie stared at him, ice spreading through her core and numbing her weak muscles. The world was spinning, spinning, swirling in a blood-red sea as their two voices rose and melded together into one long, bone-chilling shriek that froze her blood and stilled her heart, until—

Silence. The screaming stopped, the world stopped spinning, the rushing in her ears ceased. Sadie did not remember closing her eyes, but they were closed now.

She snapped them open. White light blinded her. Panicking, she closed them again. Ever so slowly, she opened one eye a slit. White light inundated her vision again, only this time it was paler and dotted with little silver sparkles like tiny jewels. Sadie opened her eye a crack wider.

She was looking at her lap. The white light belonged to her white dress, embroidered with tiny silver gems, sparkling like clusters of shimmering stars nestled on a pearly white sky, or a swath of silver fairy dust. Pulling her hair over her shoulder, she could see it flowed to her midriff in wavy curls.

As she looked down at her bare toes peeking from beneath her hem, she discovered another startling fact. She was sitting on top of a white marble tombstone. Looking behind her, she gaped at the ten-foot-long train spilling across the immaculate green lawn like a shimmering river. A wedding dress, Sadie had thought at first. Now, with a tombstone beneath her, she deemed an angel's dress more accurate.

But why was she dressed like an angel?

It was then she noticed Connor kneeling before her, silent now, a peaceful expression replacing his mask of pain. He stared at the words inscribed on the tombstone below her. Sadie looked too.

Nothing was written on it.

Sadie frowned.

She glanced back at Connor to find him staring back at her.

"Connor!" she exclaimed. "Oh, Connor I was so worried, you were in so much pain, what's wrong, who died? I'm trying to get back to you, I'm so sorry I left, I didn't mean to leave you behind with no way to return—I'll find another open portal, Connor, I swear!"

But he paid no heed to her ramblings. He continued to stare at her with the same blank expression, a slight look of awe glistening in his eyes. Or was it tears?

"Why are you crying, Connor?"

Connor whispered softly, "Goodbye, Sadie."

Goodbye?

And then it hit Sadie so hard she toppled off the tombstone. The mourners, the black coffin, the pain, Connor's tears—*she* was the one who died. This was her funeral, Connor was grieving for her, and this was her tombstone...

As these realizations invoked a wave of nausea, she plunged into darkness, falling as cold hands slapped her face...

"Miss Sheldon!" a cool voice yelled in her ear. "Miss Sheldon, wake up! Wake up!"

A low moan escaped her lips, but she did not open her eyes. Grogginess gummed her eyelashes and rocked her disoriented mind. She lay flat on her back, her soft bed cushioning her... and yet her spinning mind felt incapable of bringing her floating body under control and away from the stars, back to earth.

"Miss Sheldon!" came the voice more urgently now, tinged with panic. "Miss Sheldon, you *must* wake up!"

Her plummeting mind caught up with her prone body, releasing her from her numb prison.

Her eyes flew open.

Bending over her closely, terror tangled with relief in his dilated pupils, was Tristan West.

"Finally!" he muttered, lines of worry quickly replaced with his usual annoyed grimace.

"And what do you think you're doing?" Sadie asked, raising an eyebrow at his closeness while she lay in bed.

Realizing what Sadie insinuated, Tristan scowled and took a few hasty steps backwards, away from her bed.

"No need to get excited, tellurian. I would never dream of *that*."

"Right," Sadie mumbled, sitting up and throwing back her covers. "Right," she repeated, slipping on her boots without doing the laces up and wrapping a cloak around her. Sadie stormed out the door, letting her frustration guide her feet away from Tristan.

Unfortunately, he didn't get the message. He cursed as she swept down the hallway, and a second later the whisper of his light footsteps followed her.

"Sadie!" he whisper-shouted, but she ignored him and hurried down the stairs, through the empty kitchen and out the back door.

Millions of stars embroidering the silky black sky greeted her, and she stopped to gape at them, hardly daring to breathe. Her heart continued to pound, but no longer in anger. Her chest expanded, making room for the wonder her mind alone could not contain.

In that moment, she felt as though nothing lay between her and the universe.

"Did you have a nightmare? About your brother?"

She tensed at Tristan's voice behind her, heart stuttering against her chest.

"Why would you think it was about my brother?" she asked without taking her eyes off the stars.

"You said his name in your sleep."

"That is none of your business. Leave me alone."

She didn't want to face him, didn't want to answer anymore questions about Connor. Didn't want to face the realization that she might have made the biggest mistake of her life when she walked through that mirror. She had feared becoming obsolete, so she chose a path of heroism, but in following her dreams she had written herself out of her family's story entirely.

She didn't know if her dream was a vision or just a dream... but it felt like her daydream before the ball at home, the one she'd had after discovering Thomas' book. All her senses had been engaged, the emotions raw, not muted.

Sadie's chin quivered and bumps raised on her arms beneath her cloak. Vision might not be the correct term, but her disappearance had probably caused her family to assume she had died. They probably *did* mourn her death.

Right now, her chosen path didn't feel freeing. Instead, it gutted a hole in her chest; soon she would become no more than a hazy memory to the one person who mattered to her the most.

"If you really want me to leave you alone, I'll leave," Tristan said after a moment, "but I want you to know that you don't have to be alone. I'm here."

"Why?" challenged Sadie, turning to face him. Tristan's hands were in his pockets, his shoulders hunched. "Why would you even care about me? I'm no one to you. Just a pawn, a package to be delivered to your lord. You're not getting paid to be my friend."

"I'm not getting paid at all," mumbled Tristan. He raked his hand through his hair, freeing strands from the ponytail at the base of his neck, and scuffed his boot across the starlit grass. "I know what it's like to feel alone in a new place. To be unsure if you belong."

"What do you mean?" Sadie asked sharply, heart racing. How did he know that even as they spoke her heart felt serrated, torn between family and her heart's desire, and the uncertainty of where she truly belonged?

Tristan hesitated then answered slowly as though choosing his words carefully. "When I went to live in Caris Nando with my godfather, I was the only mortal human among immortal Lantíés. I felt insignificant, inadequate, and utterly alone. Despite immediately being drawn to their lifestyle and traditions, it took me a long time to truly feel as though I belonged. That transition would have been a lot easier if I had someone other than my godfather to talk to. I don't expect you to fully trust me or confide in me yet, but if you need someone to talk to... I'm here."

When Tristan said those last words he met her gaze, and his deep chocolate eyes glistened with sincerity.

Tristan could never fill the hole in her heart, punctured by her separation from Connor, but maybe opening her heart to not feeling so alone in Carmelle could mend some of the cracks and fissures branching out from the hole.

"Yes," she admitted. "I had a nightmare about Connor."

"I'm sorry," Tristan replied. He offered her no cliched platitudes or false hope. He simply added, "Do you want to tell me more about the dream?"

Sadie considered sharing more, but her chest still ached from witnessing Connor's grief. If she recounted it, she would not be able to stop crying and she wasn't quite ready for that level of vulnerability with Tristan yet.

"No," she mused. "I don't think I will. I do appreciate the offer, Tristan; I think I'd rather contemplate the stars for a bit longer. With you by my side, if you're willing to stay."

A small smile tugged at Tristan's lips. "Of course."

They stood there together for a long time while Sadie balanced on the serrated edge of indecision. One foot planted in contented awe, one foot mired in unsettling regret.

But in a deep pocket of her heart, quiet and insistent, her heartbeat murmured of belonging.

Moments of Magic

Droplets of salty seawater sprayed Sadie's face as she splashed in the ocean, jumping and spinning, arms flapping for balance. The water reached her thighs, waves pounding against her legs as they rolled into the shore. White foam sprayed her face, the tangy salt kissing her lips playfully. She laughed and slapped the water with her hands.

"Oh sure, now you go in the water when it's nice and calm and there's no possible chance of drowning," Tristan teased from his position well back from the sandy beach. "Where was your enthusiasm for water-frolicking when we first approached the ocean two days ago? Waves too big for you, were they?"

"As a matter of fact, they were!" Sadie shouted, her voice carrying over the waves. She stopped playing to spin and glare at Tristan. "I'm not the best swimmer, and I didn't fancy trying out my skills on monstrous waves! Besides, I didn't see *you* so much as set a foot in the sand, let alone frolic with the man-crushing waves. What happened, courage run away?"

"I didn't want to take my boots off and have wet sand clinging between my toes," said Tristan, revulsion crumpling his features.

"How deeply pessimistic of you. Determined to steal the fun out of everything."

"That's my job."

Sadie rolled her eyes and resumed her frolicking, wading a little further so the water crept up to her waist. Thunderous roars echoed in her ears, followed by heavy crashes and a rushing that drowned out all other sound. As the waves broke and the zooming walls of water crumbled, she caught sight of calmer waters stretching on for miles until they kissed the tips of the horizon line. Her chest swelled as she breathed in the vastness of the ocean, bubbles expanding and popping in her stomach at the thrill of beholding something so much greater than herself. Stargazing elicited the same feeling. Sunlight streamed through the trees behind her, igniting the cerulean surface with sparkling diamonds. The dappled sunlight and soothing tide lapping against the shore bathed Sadie in a wave of tranquility.

"It's beautiful, isn't it?" Tristan called.

"It's gorgeous," Sadie said, sighing.

"I have always loved the ocean," Tristan mused. "I think a part of my heart will always reside here on the shore, riding with the waves."

Sadie's brow raised at his sudden optimism. When he allowed vulnerability to creep past his stony mask, she felt like maybe she could trust him. But his unreadable mask usually snapped back into place before she could decide for sure.

Their journey over the last two days had been pleasant enough. After saying goodbye to the Ellwoods and thanking them for all the supplies they had helped them acquire in such a short time, they had departed Edgewater, keeping to the coastline once they reached it. Unlike Tristan, Sadie enjoyed the feeling of sand slipping between her toes, and she made a point of walking barefoot through it as often as possible. The boots she had received from Maddie were sturdy but worn and a little too small, causing more pain than she had hoped.

Matching the foam of the waves, the white sand contrasted with the deep blue ocean. A few logs dotted the beach at random, and they would sit on them side by side, swinging their legs idly as they munched on apples, cheese, bread, dried meat, and other foods Nina had packed for them. Sometimes they engaged in small talk, but after the moment they had shared under the stars in Edgewater, a new-found understanding existed between them that did not always require speech.

Dunking her head underwater, Sadie let the cold wash over her, eyes closed as the soothing waves rocked her and billowed her shift around her. When she felt her lungs start to seize, she kicked hard upwards, and her head broke the surface. Taking a huge gulp of fresh air, Sadie inhaled the salty sea scent and shook her hair out of her face.

That was when she noticed Tristan. Not only had he set foot in the sand, but he had ventured as far as the edge of the ocean, the water lapping over his boots. It may have been her imagination, but Sadie thought he looked faintly embarrassed.

"Changed your mind after all?" she called to him over the rumble of waves.

"Hardly," Tristan replied as though the idea was ludicrous. "I merely came closer to see if you were dead yet. You were under for a long time."

"I'm not dead. Disappointed?"

"More than you know."

Sucking air in through her teeth, Sadie quirked a playful brow and waded to shore. "Right, for that comment you have earned a big wet hug."

"You do and you die," Tristan warned her.

"I thought that's what you wanted."

"Yes, but not at the hands of me. Murder of Alldían's precious new recruit is not exactly the best way to gain his favour," Tristan explained. "However, if it were to look like an accident..."

"Ah, so it's to be a well-disguised murder, with no way to trace it back to you," said Sadie with a comprehending nod as she padded onto the soft dry sand a few feet from Tristan. "How clever."

"I rather thought so, yes," Tristan agreed, eyeing the puddles dripping off her shift warily.

Plopping down on the log, she pulled an apple and a chunk of cheese out of the satchel they had purchased to carry their supplies. Stretching languorously, she let the hot sun dry her shift as she took alternating bites between the apple and cheese, savouring the sour and sweet pairing on her tongue.

Tristan joined her and pulled a loaf of hard-crusted bread from the satchel, breaking a chunk off and popping it in his mouth.

"We're making good time," he commented, staring out at the ocean. "This is our third day of travelling from Edgewater, and if I'm not mistaken we have another two before we reach Carenthia. Five days from Edgewater to Carenthia is not bad."

"So you're saying I'm not as weak as you thought. How sweet of you."

"I said no such thing," Tristan denied. "Although, I'm glad you're not holding us up too much; I must admit I thought you'd be complaining more, you know, with your background..."

The implied offence of her privileged upbringing hung between them.

"To tell you the truth, my feet *are* hurting me. I used to walk in the woods at home, but that's not the same thing. I have a feeling these boots are going to fall apart on me before we even reach Carenthia."

A sudden twinge assailed her middle region, and she rubbed it as though trying to soothe a stomach ache.

Tristan noticed. "What's wrong?"

"Nothing," Sadie lied. "I think part of that apple went down the wrong tube." She grimaced for effect.

Tristan nodded and returned to his bread. Sadie didn't bother to hide her scowl, and her hand lingered on her stomach long after the fluttering subsided. She gazed out at the waves again to distract herself from the odd sensation in her middle, and calm content washed over her once more. If she opened all her senses to it, the ocean swept her away on watery wings to exciting new worlds.

"Is it magic, the way the ocean can ensnare minds?" Sadie asked a bit shyly. She knew it sounded ludicrous and Tristan would most likely laugh at her, but she was genuinely curious. So much enchantment existed in Carmelle. Why couldn't the ocean possess magic?

But Tristan did not laugh. His mouth crooked slightly as he pondered the question. After a moment he replied, "No, I do not believe the Tolotanteau is enchanted with a spell. It's not easy to use magic on any form of nature, let alone something as vast as an ocean. Nature is a powerful force in all worlds, and casting a spell on something so powerful is not easy. I'm not saying it can't be done, but from my understanding, magic comes from the forces of nature itself, and so using magic against the originator can be difficult. I'm by no means a magical expert. Perhaps Alldían will be able to explain better."

"Does Alldían have magic?"

"No, he does not. That is, he cannot conjure spells or cast enchantments. His specialty lies with matters of the head and heart, with the ability to dispense excellent advice, and exert influence over people's decisions. Some would call this magic, but technically it's not.

"The Tolotanteau is not magical either, not technically. It does, however, have great powers. Someone once told me the ocean forces you to dream. He was right, but it's not because of an enchantment. Its vast beauty possesses natural powers to inspire. Never underestimate the powers of nature, Sadie."

Sadie shook her head to insinuate she wouldn't, but remained silent, staring out at the ocean. She couldn't help wondering if a portal existed in these mysterious, magical waters. She wondered if she could find one on her own, or if she needed to have magic... The idea of finding a way to see Connor again using a path she carved herself felt right, and the slumbering embers in her chest sparked.

"I've always said the Tolotanteau seemed to sparkle with its own magic," Tristan continued after a moment, "but there are many different forms of magic. Magic can be spells and potions, but it can also be the way we perceive things. Extreme happiness and contentment, the feeling of being alive—these things are also magic. That is what the ocean has always represented to me, and so in a way, it is magical."

Sadie stared at Tristan without bothering to hide her shock, distracted from her deliberation of portals. He didn't seem to notice the change in his tone. He continued talking, eyes transfixed on the ocean.

"Tolotanteau means the Great Sea in Tavé, the ancient language used by the Lantíés. It borders the entire west coast of Carmelle and spans thousands of miles across to Nirosula, the Land of the Keepers. Naturally, many great tales have been told about this ocean. Tales of heroes sailing the seas on grand ships worthy of their own songs, tales of explorers, huge fleets massing for the King of Carenthia, even tales of pirates. But there's one that has always been my favourite..."

Tristan began to sing. Sadie's heart fluttered and her mouth gaped open in astonishment. His voice was deep and strong and filled Sadie with both sorrow and longing. Though sung in a language Sadie did not know, his captivating voice transported her across the ocean on the notes of melodious waves.

É tanteau, kí etra eth talar
Ilya talarí on caris loth
Ce épelë on Tolotanteau
Cor han avë Carmelle
Anu Nirosula anu Arwé

Her eyes locked on his still lips, softened by song, parted by the hook of an unfinished story.

He remained immobile, ensnared by the ocean's spell. Silence pillowed the air between them, smothering her senses and enunciating the awkwardness of her fluttering stomach and skittering heartbeat.

"What... was that?" Sadie whispered.

"It was part of a long epic about the Tolotanteau," Tristan replied, eyes locked on the tumultuous waves. "It goes on to describe some of the more popular past adventures on its waters and the effects of the ocean on people."

"Do you speak the language?" Sadie asked. "Tavé, you called it?"

"Yes, I speak Tavé, English, and know a small amount of a few other dialects spoken in the northwest regions of Carmelle, most of which are derived from the root language of Tavé."

"And the Keepers you mentioned... they're another group of people?"

"If you can call four a group," replied Tristan with a wry chuckle. "They're the most ancient and respected beings in Arwé, imbibed at their core with the strongest levels of Elemental magic."

Sadie smoothed the raised hairs on her arms, suppressing the tingles of awe pricking her skin.

"And, er—" Sadie hesitated, nerves tightening her throat. "Where did you—that is to say your voice is so... how did you learn—"

Tristan's shoulders slumped, his stony mask sliding back into place. "I think it's time we got moving again. I still want to cover a lot of ground before we make camp tonight."

The content bubble swelling in Sadie's chest punctured, her lungs and throat constricting. She almost flinched at the abrupt dismissal but managed to control her face. Her heart had been opening to Tristan, their mutual passion for the ocean like a bridge connecting their two worlds and differing experiences. But he had slammed the door to his heart, severing the connection. Did he think she judged him? Was he ashamed of his voice? She wanted to let him know she admired it, but his expressionless mask radiated warnings to not push the subject.

For the rest of that day's march they walked in silence, swimming in their own ocean of thoughts. Sadie could not get the sound of Tristan's voice out of her head. The melodious waves and cries of seabirds rolled across her mind, a song of sorrow and hope woven with the crushing weight of the unknown.

Uncertainty dominated her horizon. Uncertainty about her travelling companion, uncertainty about her future in Carmelle, uncertainty about the queasiness plaguing her stomach, and uncertainty about whether she would ever see her brother again.

Uncertainty that she even wanted to return to her world.

That night they made camp just inside the forest so the overhanging branches provided shelter but the ocean remained in view. As soon as they deposited their gear on the ground, Tristan slipped silently into the shadows and vanished, his cloak hiding him in seconds. This had become a routine of theirs. Every night Tristan vanished into the woods to hunt for dinner, and every night Sadie stayed behind to start a fire. The first time she tried to start a fire with a flint purchased in Edgewater, she did not produce a single spark before Tristan returned from hunting and showed her how. Now, on the third night, she felt slightly more confident, though it would still take her a while to get the spark to catch and grow big enough.

When Tristan came back less than an hour later with a pair of rabbits, Sadie had a small fire going, though it wasn't quite hot enough to cook on yet. As Tristan started preparing the meat for spitting, Sadie stoked the fire awkwardly. She didn't know what to say to Tristan anymore. His singing and the abrupt return of his stony mask had rattled her. She couldn't think why he would be ashamed of his talent, so he must have regretted sharing it with *her*. Regretted his offer to be someone she could talk to.

After they had finished eating, Tristan had disposed of the carcasses and cleaned his knife, and Sadie had washed her hair in the ocean, a familiar lurch assailed her stomach, so strong this time she gasped.

"What is it?" Tristan asked.

It was a good question, but Sadie had no answers. The feeling was neither nauseous nor painful. It prickled like jagged butterfly wings brushing the inside of her stomach. At first Sadie had thought it a side effect of the mirror and entering another world, but the sensation had increased in regularity and power the longer she was in Carmelle. She wasn't ready to share her concerns with Tristan though, especially after he'd shut her out after his singing.

"What? Oh nothing," Sadie lied. "Hiccups. Hey, can I go on first watch?"

Tristan's piercing gaze seared through the lie. "If you wish."

"I do." Abandoning her blanket, she let her senses guide her to the ocean, caught up in the maelstrom of her mind. She found a large lone rock overlooking the ocean and sat on it, drawing her knees up to her chest protectively. Waves crashed against the shore, more powerful than earlier in the day, and for a while Sadie just listened.

The first time Sadie had kept watch, Tristan had crept up behind her and scared her half to death. After he'd finished mocking her lacking observational powers and she'd stopped cursing at him, he'd shown her how to *see*. She must hear every whisper, feel every breath of wind, see every swish of a tail, sort through every scent on the air, even taste every flavour of the night. Only then could she be a decent watch.

But Sadie couldn't concentrate. She tasted salt in the air, felt a cool breeze play across her face, saw the twinkling stars reflected in the midnight blue waters—and then questioned the disconcerting sensation in her stomach again.

A hand gripped her shoulder. Sadie toppled off the rock, landing hard on her rear. She scrambled to her feet, spinning to face the imposter, eyes wildly searching the ground for a weapon—

"Tristan!" Sadie shrieked, heart racing. Relief transformed to anger, and she spat his name out again like a curse. "*Tristan!* How dare you sneak up on me like that, *again*! What if I had attacked you, what if you had gotten hurt—"

"You could not have hurt me if you tried."

"—What if I had gotten hurt," Sadie ploughed on, "you don't do things like that Tristan, curses and 'cantations!"

"Are you finished yet?" Tristan asked, arms folded lazily across his chest. "I'm the one who should be giving you a lecture, you're supposed to be on watch! How did you let me sneak up on you like that a second time? What if I'd been an imposter, I could've driven a blade right through you without you ever knowing I was there. What happened, tellurian, did you fall asleep?"

"No, I was fully awake, thank you very much," Sadie replied coolly, climbing back onto the rock as she tried to calm her pounding heart. "Just thinking."

"Ah, a painful process for you tellurian, I know. In future, try not to inflict yourself any extra pain while on duty, it's far too distracting for this type of job."

"Why are you out here, anyway? It's not your turn for another couple hours."

Tristan shrugged, joining her on the rock. "I couldn't sleep so I decided to engage in my favourite past time: torturing you. Besides you're too far away to keep an eye on dangers from within the forest and I didn't particularly fancy being clawed by a bear in my sleep."

Sadie opened her mouth to spit out an angry retort, but Tristan whispered, "Sorry, had to get that last one in. I'm here because I couldn't sleep, simple as that. What's wrong?"

"What do you mean?"

"Come on, Sadie, something's clearly wrong; you don't hide your emotions well. What were you thinking about?"

Sadie appraised him with a long, calculating look. She knew he liked to tease her, but he seemed genuine right now. They were not real friends, even though he had shown her a vulnerable side of himself earlier, despite possibly regretting it after. Maybe he would appreciate a gesture of reciprocal vulnerability.

Looking pointedly away from him, Sadie muttered, "I know this is going to sound crazy, but ever since I arrived in Carmelle I've had these weird... sensations in my stomach. I don't know how to describe it, except that I know it's not a sickness. It's just... there. Not all the time, it hits me suddenly, like a jolt of strong tingling sensations."

Even the ocean seemed to hold its breath in the silence that followed. The waves had gone silent. Or she had gone deaf. Why wasn't Tristan saying anything? Maybe he thought her insane. He would tell her strange symptoms were a sign of mental illness and she should be in a psychiatric ward, not on a potentially dangerous mission.

To both break the silence and thwart Tristan's teasing, Sadie blurted, "Look, I know you probably think I'm delusional, and maybe I am but—"

"No, that's not what I think! Sadie... I could be wrong, but I've been around enough people with it to detect its presence, and your description fits what I've heard. Sadie, I think you might have magic."

Sadie blinked. "What?"

"I think you have magic," Tristan repeated.

Sadie searched his face, sure he jested. When she could find no trace of mockery, she stated firmly, "I was wrong. I'm not delusional. *You* are."

"Sadie, I'm serious."

"So am I."

"Look I know what you must be thinking. You probably don't believe in magic. You've read about it, probably fantasized about possessing it all your life, but you never believed it truly existed. Am I right?"

Sadie didn't bother answering. Sometimes it disconcerted her how accurately he could read her mind.

"And ever since you've entered Carmelle, you've had to start accepting magic does exist, and your old fantasies are not unrealistic. Part of you, however small, has started imagining yourself with magical abilities. Now your fantasies have become reality, it's understandable you're finding it hard to believe. You're scared, and you have every right to feel that way. Leaving behind innocence is a scary thought."

Sadie tried to remain calm as a new fear stained her heart, spreading like poison through her veins. Having magic might tie her more to Carmelle. How would she return to her brother if magic bound her to another world? Her voice shook as she demanded, "Your highly disconcerting telepathy aside, how are you so sure I possess m-magic?"

"I'm not sure. But would I bring this up, raise your hopes, if I thought I could be wrong?"

"I wouldn't put it past you," Sadie muttered.

"That's a bit disappointing. I thought we had grown closer today, that I might have earned your trust. Clearly I was wrong."

Guilt weighed on her lungs, but she could not believe him. It was impossible.

"I trust you, or at least more than I once did, but I'm sorry, I don't believe it."

"Sadie, I've seen people in the same position before. Just because there is magic in Carmelle, doesn't mean everyone possesses it. The majority are normal people like me, dreaming of wielding magic like you. For some, those dreams come true. They complain of sensations exactly like yours and then a wizard fetches them to learn how to deal with their abilities. Usually, they're detected at a young age, but since you were born in a world of no magic... Sadie, it makes sense. Everything fits."

"Except I *can't do magic*!"

"And how could you? You've never been exposed to it before, never been taught," Tristan reasoned. "How would you even know how to begin? Come on, you must admit it's possible."

"Possible, yes," Sadie conceded reluctantly. "Just highly improbable."

"I thought improbabilities were your specialty."

Sadie didn't answer.

"Look," Tristan continued in a much gentler voice. "I know you don't believe me or trust me, but think about this: Alldían wants you for a reason. Maybe this is it. Maybe he knew you had magic and that's why he needed to get you to Carmelle. I can't offer you proof, but at least consider the possibility."

"I'm tired, I'm going to bed," Sadie muttered, sliding off the rock. "If you're so awake then you can take your watch now."

"Sadie—"

"I'm tired!" she shouted, and without a backward glance she sprinted away from the rock, stumbling in the dark. When she reached the camp she cast herself unceremoniously on the ground, pulled her blanket up to her chin, and slammed her eyes shut. She endeavoured to block out Tristan's words, but they kept popping to the fore of her mind.

And that sensation in her stomach...

Sadie did not sleep that night.

Chapter Ten

Sunset Sentiments

Over the next two days Sadie could think of nothing but magic. The sensation in her middle region acted up more frequently as if trying to support Tristan's theory, but Sadie did her best to ignore it. She found it difficult to believe she was special when all her life she'd been told her only special traits were the wealth, privilege, and superficial comforts she loathed, instead of the heroic courage, warrior prowess, and justice for a good cause bigger than herself she craved. If she wasn't her mother's idea of special and she wasn't her own heroic idea of special—then who was she?

Another thought plagued Sadie: it couldn't be coincidence that two members of the Sheldon family had now entered Carmelle. Had Thomas possessed magic? More than ever, she wished she had completed reading his book before coming here.

On the morning of their fifth day from Edgewater, as they packed their blankets and prepared to embark on the day's march, she asked Tristan in what she hoped was a casual tone, "Other than him teaching English to Carmellians, what else do you know about Thomas Sheldon?"

"In other words, you were wondering if he possessed magic as well?"

"Did he?"

"Yes, after a fashion, although his abilities were limited. He earned his fame by rising quickly in the ranks and becoming captain of Carenthia's finest army, never losing a battle. His magic was limited to small basics like making fire and did not warrant further training than what he could teach himself. Other than a special Gift, the other prerequisite of coming to Carmelle is the person was meant to do great deeds here—they did not belong in their world, they never fit in, but that's because they were meant to belong here." Tristan paused. "No, belong is not the right word: stand out would better suffice. Great things are expected from people like you and Thomas."

Sadie flinched. It seemed no matter where she went, she could not escape the weight of expectations. Would these expectations be even more impossible to live up to than her mother's? Should she even try?

"Thomas lived up to his expectations," Tristan continued. "In addition to his battle skills and meagre magical powers, Thomas also possessed a rarer power, a gift that undoubtedly helped him win wars. He was a Colour Seer."

"What's a Colour Seer?" asked Sadie.

"When he looked at people he could see a colour aura that foretold their future emotions," replied Tristan. "He could see if an individual's future held sadness, happiness, excitement, anger, or even jealousy. It's an invaluable tool for accessing a person's story, maybe more than knowing the external events that might befall them. I could count on one hand the number of people who have ever possessed it."

Sadie wished she could share this information with Connor, but already the rift widened and fractured between them. For him, this information would be a lark to contrast with their mundane family members, a fleeting fact to wonder at and then move on. For her, it meant the familiar weight of pressure to prove her worthiness, this time in the higher stakes magical setting of Carmelle.

Had Thomas missed anyone on Earth? Or was she the only Sheldon to experience her heart tearing in two upon entering Carmelle?

"How did Thomas return to Earth? I know he went through the mirror portal as well... Was it always open to him, then? Waiting for when he wanted to return?"

"The portals did close for a time while Thomas was in Carmelle," Tristan said. "You'll remember I told you the portals only close when something strange or dangerous is happening in one or both worlds the portal connects to, potentially endangering the inhabitants of those worlds—Thomas got caught up in the war against Vashi, culminating in Harthoné Orin, the most catastrophic battle Carmelle has ever seen, and during that war, the portals closed. After Vashi's defeat, the portals opened again. I don't know how Thomas felt about the portals closing, but I do know he only returned to Earth after Vashi had been defeated and the portals reopened."

Sadie chewed on Tristan's words, rolling them across her tongue and volleying them between her cheeks. Thomas had not returned until the portals had reopened. Maybe he hadn't cared to try and reopen them. Maybe he had tried and failed. Either way, if she had magic, she owed it to her brother to at least try and find a way to open a portal.

For the rest of the day, Sadie found herself trying to do magic through sheer force of will.

"Are we there yet?"

"Sadie if you keep asking that question I will run you through with my dagger and leave you here to die."

Sadie walked several more paces along the forest path, glancing at the thick wall of pines and firs she'd been staring at for a full day. She missed the ocean.

"Are we there yet?" she repeated.

Tristan unsheathed his dagger.

"All right, all right, I'll stop," Sadie conceded, throwing her hands up. "I only do it to annoy you."

"Right, then I think it would be best if we kept our speech to friendly banter and left out the simply annoying because frankly, tellurian, I don't think our friendship or your heart could survive it," said Tristan.

"My heart?" repeated Sadie, raising an eyebrow.

"It's hard for a heart to keep beating once a blade is driven through it."

"Oh, I see." Sadie stopped to consider Tristan's face. "Did you mean it? The friendship part. Are we actually...friends now?"

Tristan stopped too. "Yeah. I guess we are."

An awkward silence billowed between them.

"I've never had a friend before..." Sadie admitted.

"Really?" Tristan asked, his expression disbelieving.

"Yes," said Sadie, shuffling her feet and avoiding Tristan's eyes. "The only person I've ever liked is my brother Connor. Besides, don't you know anything about the rich? They're polite to each other on the surface, but no one's truly friends. Do you have friends?"

Tristan snorted. "Does it look like I have real friends?"

"How would I know that from looking at you?"

"Even I can admit my demeanour doesn't exactly invite friends. I'm polite, but I have a hard time letting people in. I've had acquaintances, but no lasting friendships of significance."

"I think that might be the first thing we have in common," Sadie observed.

"Besides our mutual love for bantering and bickering you mean," Tristan corrected her.

"Well that too," Sadie agreed with a grin.

Late in the afternoon, Sadie noticed the trees thinning and sprinted through a gap into the open, longing to taste salty air again.

"Curses and 'cantations!" Sadie swore, throwing her arms up to protect her eyes.

"See, that's why you never run amok into the open," Tristan told her wisely. "You never know what might be ready to permanently disable you. Like blinding sunlight."

"Oh, shut up," snapped Sadie. Her breath caught in her chest as she soaked in the view.

Below her the bay glittered gold, sparkling in the setting sun, waves crashing against the jutting rock of the cliff. Tiny sailboats dotted the bay, their white sails bathed in gold, and anchored in the harbour, its tall masts and furled sails gleaming in the sunlight, was an impressive ship. Beyond the lush green carpeted cliffs the bay joined the Tolotanteau, its glossy mirror-surface reflecting the ice blue sky flecked with gold.

Tearing her eyes away from the captivating sea, Sadie looked to her right. A river flowed into the bay, sparkling like a gold-dusted ribbon, and at the mouth, situated on either side like faceless guards, were two immensely tall, pristine white towers, plain and smooth until their peaks opened to the sky. The setting sun bathed the closest one in a deep gold while the other remained white like a pinnacle of snow.

Beyond these towers, on the opposite side of the bay from where Sadie stood, the land formed a small hill. An enormous white palace stood tall and proud at its peak, its many turrets gleaming like pearls. Parts of the palace looked like a fortress, strong as the bones of the earth, while others were delicate glass-spun spires, twisting far above the others, their pointy tops flashing in the sun like crystals crowned with twinkling stars. In the centre of the palace curved a huge white dome.

If other portals existed, Sadie couldn't imagine a more fitting place to connect worlds.

"It's beautiful, isn't it?" whispered a voice beside her.

Sadie started as if waking from a dream. She had forgotten all about Tristan.

"Is this Caris Nando? Where Alldían lives?"

"No, we are nowhere near Caris Nando yet. It is a forested land, not a seaside city. That palace is called Nethilya, the Fair Crown. Its crown shape is vague, of course."

Sadie peered closer. She hadn't noticed it at first glance, but now she could see its resemblance to a crown with towers rising around the domed middle in a jagged circle.

"The city situated on the far side of the hill is Carenthia," Tristan told her. "It's designed to be shaped like a wheel, encased in a circular wall with eight connecting main streets leading to the centre like spokes branching off from the hub."

The streets and rooftops appeared fashioned from gold in the sunlight.

"It is the Sunset City, the core of the Sunset Lands," Tristan continued. "The tower furthest from us is Ilíta-onon, the White Tower. It is the only thing in these lands never stained with the colours of the setting sun. No one knows why. The tower closest to us is the Carenthonon, the Sunset Tower. Both towers serve as guards of the bay and the Tolonení, the Great River that flows between them. There are always guards in those towers, keeping watch. And this is Carenth-hild, the Sunset Bay."

"Why does everything have the word Sunset as part of its name? This is beautiful, but couldn't you see this anywhere—"

Sadie faltered at the look on Tristan's face.

"This is nothing," he assured her. "The sun has just begun its descent. Wait. You'll see."

Tristan paused for a moment, then added, "Carenthia is beautiful, but it does have its dangers. A shaky political foundation coupled with power-hungry members of the court and a public obsessed with political intrigue is a recipe for mischief and murder in and of itself, but the Redpath are also thrown into the mix."

Sadie's eyes widened. "The Redpath? They're in Carenthia?"

"Yes, and they are in favour with the Queen, so we must tread carefully. They hold great sway in Carenthia and show no love for members of the Ilyance like me. Not everyone is a Redpath ally though, and therein lies our hope of spreading word about the dragon and the Redpath's bolder, more drastic tactics. They wouldn't be pleased to discover you've come through a portal from Earth, so avoiding them as much as possible while here would be prudent."

"Why wouldn't they be happy I'm from Earth?"

"Some of them have petitioned to get the portals closed. They claim the portals pose a safety risk to Arwé because we can't control who passes through, and one day someone might come who destroys us all."

Sadie's fingertips numbed and she gripped her biceps, hugging herself against the prickle needling the back of her neck.

Destroy Arwé? She couldn't fathom someone wanting to intentionally destroy this magical, beautiful world, but even the unintentional could cause irrevocable damage. Her mother had frequently accused Sadie of ruining her life just by being herself—an accusation she hoped to avoid here.

"It's just an excuse though," Tristan continued. "The Redpath advocate for advancement and change, and keeping the gateways open to other worlds allows them to borrow ideas from worlds already more advanced than ours. Closing the portals wouldn't make sense for their group's mission. I think they want to control the portals for themselves, and they would be irked to know someone else sneaked in before they could take control. They might even seek to erase that person from Carmelle's narrative."

Tristan's pointed gaze pierced her heart and she gripped her upper arms tighter, unnerved.

⁂

Sadie stood at the edge of the cliff with her bare toes curled over the ledge like an eagle poised to take flight. She could feel Tristan's eyes boring into her back and see his tense body coiled like a spring in her peripheral vision as he perched on a rock sharpening his sword with a whetstone. Probably thinking her insanity would culminate in falling to her doom. Connor always said she seemed to derive a perverse pleasure from flirting with the line between bold and self-destructive. But the pleasure did not lay in flirting with that line. Sadie walked the narrow rooftop beam of the Sheldon manor and curled her toes over a cliff not to be bold, but to feel free. To feel on the cusp of weightlessness. To feel closer to her dreams.

The forest-green dress Maddie had given her flapped in the cool sea breeze, fanning out behind her and around her ankles, and her hair streamed out behind her like a banner. Sadie held her arms out like wings to balance against the breeze. Closing her eyes, she imagined she soared across the sea like an albatross, riding the wind without ever having to flap her wings.

A boot scraped across the gritty cliff beside her, and she jumped.

Her eyes flew open and her heart drummed a wild, erratic beat in her chest at the sight of roiling waves beneath her and nothing else. Waving her arms like a windmill, she tried to steady herself as her body tilted, one foot dangling unsupported in front of her.

Tristan grabbed her arm and pulled her back.

"Curses and 'cantations Tristan, you really are trying to kill me, aren't you?" she shouted, the accusation echoing off the cliff.

"Wha—of course not!"

She had raised her hand as though about to hit him, but quickly ran it through her hair instead. Her tensed chest relaxed as she took a deep breath, but a hollow ache replaced the tension as she remembered who else used to sneak up on her.

"Sorry," she apologized. She looked down at her feet.

"What's wrong?" Tristan asked.

"Nothing, just... my brother Connor used to do that to me all the time. Sneak up on me, I mean."

Tristan grimaced. "Sorry. I really didn't mean to scare you. I wanted to see what you were staring so intently at."

Sadie nodded and looked back at the horizon.

"You were right," she said. "The sunset *is* beautiful."

Gold had given way to deep orange, then steadily deepened to pink. Now all three colours were in the sky together, the horizon line brushed with gold blended with vermilion streaks, the fluffy clouds dotting the sky dipping their smoky tendrils in faint pink.

Sadie caught movement below one of the pink-tinged clouds. Squinting closer, she gasped and stumbled backwards, right into Tristan's chest.

Dragons.

"It's okay," Tristan assured her. The rumble in his chest when he spoke soothed her, and she released the breath she'd been holding. "They're called sun dragons. They're a different species than the one we encountered. They won't harm us."

Frolicking in and out of cloud wisps like playful serpents, they breathed colourful fire at the clouds, painting them in the same golds, oranges, and pinks of their scales. Their lithe bodies twisted and weaved across the sunset sky, enormous wings flapping the clouds into new shapes.

"Is that why the sunset is so beautiful here?" Sadie asked breathlessly. "It's enhanced by dragon fire?"

"Yes. The sun dragons are celestial creatures, inherently bound to the sun. They dwell in Nirosula but occasionally make the journey to the coast of Carmelle to paint the sunset in more brilliant hues. While Carenthians do enjoy the splendid sunsets, they view them with mixed emotions, some even staying indoors during sunset hours from superstitious fear. These dragons are connected to Celestial magic, after all, though the fact that the Keepers allow them to live on Nirosula helps persuade most folks that fear is unnecessary. They have never harmed a being while here, never even give them a second glance."

Slowly the gold faded, leaving deep orange on the horizon and fuchsia blushing the bellies of clouds. As the dragons flew further west, back to Nirosula, the clouds were drenched in swirls of pink and purple dabbed with blue. The sunset stained the lands in pink and purple, the walls of the Carenthonon and Nethilya blushing deeply. The sky seemed so vast from this vantage point, like she stood on the edge of the world with nothing before her but that painted sky.

"This is the most beautiful view I have ever seen," Sadie stated firmly.

"I know what you mean. I've been a lot of places and seen a lot of views, but this has always been my favourite."

A cozy blanket of silence warmed the air between them as they gazed at the sky in mirrored content.

Water droplets sprayed up from a spot near the cliffs below, and Sadie caught the glimmer of scales in the setting sun as a fluke-like iridescent tail splashed back under the waves.

"Was that—?" Sadie began, but her slack jaw could not finish forming words.

"A mermaid, yes," supplied Tristan with a grin. "They're probably taking shelter for the night. Mermaids have many natural enemies in the Tolotanteau, most of which hunt at night. The wyrms, dragons of the sea, ride the waves with their serpentine bodies, excreting an odourless and colourless oil from their mouths to paralyze their victims so they can feed on their fear, adrenaline, and life force. Once their victim is drained they turn them to stone with their formidable gaze, having no further need of their bodies. It is a mermaid's worst fear to be turned to stone and sink to the bottom of the ocean like a sunken ship, never to be seen again."

Sadie's eyes widened, but she didn't want to ask for more information about mermaids or wyrms in that moment. She turned to Tristan, mouth dry and stomach fluttering.

"Tristan, you know our conversation about friendship earlier?"

He nodded, and his fingers twitched at his sides.

"I know... I know you didn't like me very much at first, and you like being alone, so I just—I wondered if you're ready for friendship."

"I'm not sure," he joked. "You can have a terrible temper."

"I'm serious. You're my first friend, and I'd like to not mess that up. I'd like it to be something I get right for a change."

His eyes darted back and forth between hers, as though searching for the source of her insecurities. Whatever he found there elicited a small smile.

"Yes, Miss Sheldon," he assured her. "We are friends."

Her grin eclipsed his.

Chapter Eleven

The Redpath

A quick stopover, a resting and replenishing point, a chance to show Sadie one of the most renowned cities in Carmelle—that's what Carenthia meant to Tristan.

But to Sadie, Carenthia meant opportunity. A chance to taste that elusive purpose, search for a portal—or find more information to help her open one with magic—and not lose herself to the unknown.

A gate loomed above her, its dark green doors swung wide open in welcome, revealing the massive city beyond. Carvings had been etched deep into the thick doors, small statues of kings and queens with long sceptres and lofty crowns set into concave niches. Lookout towers sprang from the top of the impenetrable wall at strategic intervals.

Two guards with silver breastplates over leather jerkins and pleated leather skirts stood silently at the gates, watching people leave and enter the city. One of them caught Sadie's eye and she hastily looked away, though she wasn't sure why she should feel guilty. She wasn't supposed to reveal that she was from Earth yet, but she had done nothing wrong. Two large ornate pins decorated with a sunburst fastened their white capes to their armour and matched the sunburst in the centre of their breastplates, and their plumed helms of silver and white coupled with the swords girded at their sides and tall spears in their hands reminded Sadie of ancient Romans' attire. They could have been characters from the *Aeneid*.

With Aeneas' violent predetermined fate staining her mind like dried blood, Sadie approached the gates with a slight trepidation hitching her step.

Wagons and buggies laden with goods passed through the gates, and empty wagons trundled out. Some people tramped wearily on foot like Sadie and Tristan, often bearing packs strapped to their backs or full baskets at their hips. Others rode on horseback, and Sadie even glimpsed a colourful palanquin parading through the streets in the distance, carried by four men.

As she entered the city, the sudden upheaval of noise reminded Sadie why she avoided cities. She didn't do well with crowds, and the cities she'd visited all reeked of smog and pollutants. And sometimes human waste. To her, a city meant factories, machinery, and warehouses all squished together, mixed with the occasional clanging of a streetcar bell and rumblings of trains. Cities had always seemed dull and grey and dirty, a congregation of doomed and deadened souls.

But this city was different. No blackened buildings leered at her from behind shrouds of pewter smoke, no pungent smells assaulted her nose, and no machines clanked a cacophonous chorus in the background. Tall and narrow houses lined the relatively clean streets, brown beams nailed across white exteriors and roofs boasting red or brown shingles. Signs hung from windows and roofs, bearing names like "Damien's Daggers" and "Fiona's Fabrics". A massive market extended all the way to the end of this main street.

Striped tents lined both sides of the street, their goods overlapping each other. Glossy, colourful silks draped over long tables. Glass jars holding dyes and threads in a myriad of colours winked in the sunlight. Diamonds and gems sparkled on plump velvet pillows. A jumbled mix of savoury smells wafted towards them from a stand selling herbs and spices. Wooden toys carved into knights, jousters, archers, racers, swimmers, and other heroes of Carenthia's famous tournaments competed for attention at another stall. Sadie even caught a glimpse of caged hawks between the open flaps of a tent. A man stood just outside it, a hawk perched faithfully on his gloved forearm.

"Hawks here!" he shouted to the crowd. "Join the noble sport today with your own fine hunting hawk!"

Sadie couldn't stop gawking at all the strange and wonderful items on display. The vendors were keen to take advantage of her obvious interest: every one of them bombarded her with bargains, shouting hoarsely with frightening, desperate, urgency.

"A pretty necklace for a pretty lady!"

"Figs! Fresh figs!"

"Pies, girl, the finest in the city, won't find none better! Apple, blueberry, cranberry, take your pick! Get 'em while they're hot!"

"Would the lovely lady like a leather studded belt? Fit for the Queen Herself this is, of the finest genuine leather, take a whiff of that lovely leather smell! For you I give a special price, eh? Half price, miss, half price!"

One man rushed up to her brandishing a knife in his fist and crying, "*Hahk! Hahk na e ilya fila!*"

Sadie screamed, covering her face, but the man froze and looked at Tristan with wide, innocent eyes.

"It's okay, he's not trying to kill you," Tristan explained. "He sells knives. He was trying to sell one to you. Not everyone speaks English here. The man meant no harm. *Cor nûpar anín e hahk, ûnneth,*" he added to the confused salesman. The man nodded and retreated under his awning.

As they drew further away from the gates, the colourful market tents thinned and the vendors became less demanding. Gradually a collection of inns replaced the tents. Wooden signs branched out from the buildings, bearing names like "The Noble Knight", "The Jester's Juggle", and "The Savvy Seafarer". Each sign bore a little image painted next to the inn's name. A few inns had their doors thrown open in welcome, but since it was still before noon there was little activity inside.

Women dressed in plain dresses or wide slacks wandered the streets in chattering groups, woven baskets tucked in the crook of their arms. Ladies and gentlemen in bejewelled and embroidered ensembles of fine silk paraded proudly down the cobblestone streets, flanked by meek servants carrying parcels. Beggars slumped in alleyways, scrubby hats or dirty old mugs placed strategically in the road, hoping a coin would be tossed their way. Children clung to their mothers' skirts or chased each other around the streets, their laughter singing through the discordant deluge. Two women holding hands walked by, one planting an affectionate kiss on the other's cheek as she giggled. A smile crept over Sadie's face at a little boy and girl duelling with wooden sticks in an alley off the main street. An even smaller girl darted about them like an excited ferret, jabbing at the older duellers with her own stick. Maybe those girls *could* be in an army here. The thought made her smile.

When they reached the square at the heart of the city, Tristan strode toward a large snow-white inn with powder blue shutters and a sign swinging from underneath the wrap-around porch of the second floor with the words "The Crowned Sun" stamped across it in gold calligraphy. A picture of a gold crown resting on the brow of an orange and gold sunburst accompanied the name.

"We will be staying at this inn while in Carenthia," Tristan informed her, pausing just outside the double doors.

"Are you sure?" Sadie asked. "It looks sort of fancy. Wouldn't a smaller, simpler inn do?"

"No," said Tristan simply. Sadie rolled her eyes.

They entered the inn together, opening both doors wide to reveal a massive common room filled with carved wooden tables and benches. Deep burgundy velvet drapes framed a little stage. A staircase at the back of the inn led up to the second floor, and behind the stairs she could see doors leading off the common room. Straight across from them was another set of double doors, painted powder blue. Sadie guessed they led to the kitchen.

A short little man waddled towards them, wiping his hands on a dirty white apron as he came. He puffed and grunted like a winded elephant seal, and a fine sheen of sweat glistened on his forehead.

"What can I do for you kind folk?" he inquired, mopping his sweaty brow with the back of his hand.

"We'd like adjoining rooms for a few nights," Tristan informed him.

"Very good, sir," the innkeeper said, bobbing his head. "Right this way, Tristan. I have just the room for you and the young lady, I'm sure you'll be very comfortable there."

Tristan? Evidently Tristan stayed at this inn frequently enough to be on a first name basis with the innkeeper, but questions of why this inn, and what brought him to Carenthia, swirled in Sadie's mind.

The stairs creaked as they ascended, a sound Sadie found oddly comforting. The second floor featured two wide hallways with doors branching off into rooms. The innkeeper led them to a powder blue door at the end of one of the halls. Unclasping the ring of keys at his waist, he held them up to the light and picked out a little silver key, holding the unlocked door open for them to enter first.

"Here you are, sir. The other room is through that door by the dresser," he told them, pointing. "It's slightly smaller than this one but it's got a nice soft bed that'll feel mighty good after a long journey."

"Thank you, Phil," Tristan complimented the innkeeper. "It'll do grandly, I'm sure."

"If you need anything don't hesitate to give me or Muriel a shout or fetch one of the serving maids," Phil instructed them. "We're always willing to help and ready to serve. I expect you have things to do but I'll be talking to you later tonight, Tristan, to discuss business." Bowing reflexively, he backed out of the door with a routine swipe of his hand across his forehead.

"Business," Sadie repeated with a frown after Phil had closed the door. "What business did he mean? How does he know you?"

"I come here a lot," Tristan said evasively.

Sadie threw her hands up in exasperation.

Thrumming her fingers on one of the smooth, polished tables in the common room, Sadie glared at Tristan's back and huffed an exaggerated sigh.

Tristan's back stiffened, a muscle spasm throbbing in his neck. Without turning away from his conversation with Phil by the kitchen doors, he said, "Sadie, if you're that bored just wait for me outside in the square. I'll be a few more minutes here with Phil. There are sales carts you can browse, and sometimes entertainment."

Sadie leapt up from the bench and bolted to the front doors. That was all the permission she needed.

"*Stay in the square though, Sadie*!" Tristan shouted after her.

"Okay, *Mother*!"

Sadie didn't look back to see if he was offended. She burst into the afternoon sun heating the square and breathed in a bouquet of seaside scents. Sage, rosemary, seaweed, salty brine coating fresh fish and crabs. She slowed her steps, inhaling deeply as she wended through carts and tents selling seaside wares.

The air smelled like freedom.

When she reached the edge of the square, she hesitated. Tristan hadn't emerged from the inn yet. She could be obedient and sensible and stay in the square, as she would have at home.

But she wasn't at home. She wasn't under her mother's thumbnail anymore, and she was tired of waiting on Tristan's agenda. She kept wanting to ask him about portals, but every time she tried she snapped her mouth shut again. He would know she intended to return home through a portal if she told him she sought one, and since his whole mission was to bring her to Alldían so she could help Carmelle, she assumed he would try to stop her.

Unless she took the initiative, she would never find a portal.

Squaring her shoulders, she sidled between a juggler and a booth selling seashell art and strode purposefully down the nearest street branching off from the square. She didn't know what she looked for, exactly—a shimmer in the air like when Tristan had entered Carmelle through the mirror portal behind her perhaps, or maybe she would overhear someone talking about one—but she needed to try.

She passed buildings painted in a light palette of pale yellows and whites, some with slender balconies where people looked out over the city towards the Tolotanteau. Bright flowers in sunset colours studded vines spilling down corners of buildings.

When she rounded a bend onto a wider street, a group of people cloaked in smoky grey cloaks overlapping like a barricade of billowing fog caught her eye. A hammer crossed with a sword encircled by a black notched cog branded every piece of silver armour, including gauntlets and shin guards. Sadie's eyes narrowed at the cog. It evoked images of industrialization, of machines pumping thick columns of pewter smoke into the sky. Maybe it symbolized simple machines, and this group advocated for their use, but Sadie's stomach still swooped low. She wondered if Carmelle had experienced their own industrialization period, and if so... Could magic and mechanization coexist? If the lines between Earth and Arwé blurred so much, what tethered her to one world over the other?

People gave this group a wide berth, eyeing their tight grip on sword hilts wrapped in black cloth.

The soldiers halted in the shadows of an awning, huddled together around a man with black fur trimming his grey cloak. Glancing around covetously, he pulled something from beneath his cloak to show the others.

Inching closer, Sadie managed to catch a glimpse of the mysterious object between the shifting cloaks.

Her heart raced as she spotted small cogs and wheels and bands of metal bent into the vague shape of a human. She had seen objects like these on display before at fairs and exhibitions back home.

An automaton.

Sadie wasn't sure if it worked, but she still rubbed her fingers over her nails with a sudden anxiety she couldn't explain. These were recent inventions in her world.

"Hey, you, what are you snooping around us for?" one of them barked furiously. "Have some respect! We're members of the New Alliance!"

"The who?" Sadie blurted without thinking.

Sadie's regret hadn't quite frozen her entire body before she found herself in the middle of a half-circle formed by offended and armed soldiers. She gulped but stood her ground, raising her chin defiantly. She had done nothing wrong. The man with the black fur fringe stepped forward, peering at her with haughty suspicion.

"You don't know who we are?" he asked incredulously. "Or are you just being disruptive? 'Cause we have ways of dealing with deliberate trouble-makers." He fingered the hilt of his sword.

"I have no idea who you are," she replied. The leader's pompous attitude and his followers' exchanges of confused, disbelieving glances grated her nerves, but Tristan's voice in her head reminded her to stay out of trouble. "I'm visiting and was exploring the city. Sorry if I offended you. Can I please go?"

"We're members of the Redpath." Pride coated the man's tongue. He ignored Sadie's request.

Sadie managed to keep her face straight as the roar of a dragon echoed in her ears.

"There we go, knew we'd get there in the end," the Redpath leader exclaimed at her silence. "Though how you didn't recognize us or our name, I still don't understand. You must live in the middle of nowhere. Where are you from?"

This was crossing into dangerous territory. She had to answer, yet anything she said could be potentially fatal. These were Tristan's enemies. Her back stiffened.

"You're right, sir, I'm from a small town down south. There we get very little news of the rest of Carmelle, and what we do get is often muddled and no better than a flagrant rumour. I had heard of Redpaths down there, but—begging your pardon, sir—most of us didn't believe the rumours. Would you mind telling me who exactly the Redpath are and what you do? So I don't let my ignorance get me in trouble in the future."

Sadie did her best to relax her features into innocent curiosity despite the warning flags vying for attention in her head.

The leader studied her for a moment, then grunted and shrugged. "I suppose it's best you hear about us from me, so you can get your facts straight. I'm Commander Griswald, Leader of the Carenthian Company and the highest authority of the Redpath under Master Hargrim. We have many followers here in Carenthia, more than in any other city in Carmelle. We were patrolling the streets, looking for more recruits."

Sadie's stiff back muscles wilted at the prospect of them trying to recruit her loyalties.

"The Redpath was founded recently, only about five years ago now," Commander Griswald explained gruffly. "Our ultimate purpose is to bring change to Carmelle and further advance it. This world is too passive. There's a whole other world waiting for us out there, if only we can discover it. Folk here are too simple. They see only what's in front of them, keeping their minds closed and narrow, dreaming only of a tranquil, quiet life. But we dream of an easier way for all of us. We have a purpose in life, a dream bigger than ourselves that we know will change the world for the better. Wouldn't you like to not feel obsolete? To know that your life means something? It's so easy to get lost in this world. But with us, you will have a purpose."

A chill shuddered down Sadie's spine, icing her veins in congruence with the hope bubbling in her chest. All she'd ever wanted was to know her life meant something more than an endless string of garden parties and domestic security. To feel the hero of her own narrative. To feel part of something bigger than herself.

She forgot how to breathe.

With the Redpath, she could feel part of something bigger. She could have a *purpose*.

Her fear curled at the edges, shrinking in anticipation of the heat of her heart's desire.

Maybe Tristan was wrong. Maybe the Redpath weren't as bad as he claimed.

And then Griswald continued.

"Think what can be done with our resources, what advancements we could contrive if we only applied ourselves to the right kind of learning. Great power and wealth await us all, if only we have the gall to seize it. You say you're from the country? Imagine if an invention could do all the plowing and farm work for you. You'd like that, wouldn't you?"

Sadie clamped her tongue between her teeth to prevent any words from waggling off it against her volition. Power. Wealth. That's all he cared about. And she had not missed Griswald's allusion to another world, the tantalizing hint that someone from the Redpath had been to her world and seen the advancements there for themselves. Which would support Tristan's theory that the Redpath were interested in other worlds but wanted control of them, and therefore control of the portals—they would not be happy to learn she had come from one of the portals they sought to control, especially one leading to a world full of advanced discoveries they coveted. The hair rose on the back of her neck, but she steeled herself; she had to keep her temper in check.

Luckily, Griswald took her silence for meek acquiescence. "'Course you would. But there are some folk, believe it or not, who want to stick to the old, traditional ways. Lantíes, mostly, those decrepit old fools. Probably trying to weaken us so they can devour our souls," Griswald growled, spitting with contempt. "But you get nutters among mortals too. They blither on about preserving nature, leading the *simple life.* Complete and utter rubbish. The only thing simple about 'em are their minds. You can't have simplicity and purpose. It's an oxymoron. They're just cowards, too afraid of change in their precious lands that they're blind to the good in such a change. Fools."

The swelling force of Sadie's fiery rage surged past the clamp on her tongue.

"Only fools don't understand that the intention behind the change is everything, and intentions based in greed will never equate to change for the good. This isn't about advancements, this is about power, and if you seek to make change with power, all you'll create is death and destruction of the natural world. There will be mass production in factories and smokestacks blanketing the world in suffocating clouds of poisonous black air. How many people will you have to take advantage of to achieve these advancements? Everything will appear in masses, including deaths! You're the fool, commander," she spat, every word a scathing spark burning his skin, "and I hope you and the rest of your blind lapdogs will be the first to suffer at the hands of your *wonderful change*—because you will be consumed by it eventually. I guarantee it."

Ducking under the heavy blow Griswald aimed at her, she dodged around his soldiers and sprinted back the way she had come. She could hear them running after her, their distant curses and frantic shouts of *get her!* and *spy!* muffled by the crowd. Most people tried to move aside for the Redpath members, but it was impossible for them to spot the quick stealthy movements of one girl amid the throng. Soon the sounds of their pursuit failed, but Sadie did not stop running until she reached The Crowned Sun.

Tristan leaned against the wall by the entrance to the inn, his arms folded across his chest, a roiling storm cloud of anger and—could that be worry?—thundering in his eyes. Sadie skidded to a halt a few feet away from him, cowed by his tempestuous glare.

"Tristan," she panted, averting her gaze to the dusty street. "We need to talk in private. I fear I've made a terrible mistake."

"I suppose it was inevitable, wasn't it?" Tristan asked the empty, white-walled room at large, not looking at Sadie. "A run-in with these damnable Redpaths was bound to happen."

She perched on the edge of her bed, hands resting on the white quilted covers, supporting the rest of her unsteady weight. Tristan slumped at the foot of her bed. He kept running his hand through his hair, forgetting it was bound by a ribbon, then tugging his nose reflexively.

"And you never revealed your purpose in Carenthia or any hints of where you were staying?" Tristan shot at her for about the hundredth time.

"No," replied Sadie wearily.

"That's good, at least." He narrowed his eyes at her as though still unconvinced, then glanced away.

Guilt swirled in Sadie's stomach, nausea building at the thought of not living up to Tristan's expectations. Which was absurd, because she had never cared about his opinion of her before.

"There's nothing we can do about it but wait and hope the damage is minimal. There's no use brooding on it any longer," said Tristan.

"I do have one more question," said Sadie, pulling at a loose thread on the quilt. "Griswald mentioned something about the Lantíes wanting to weaken us to devour our souls. What did he mean?"

Tristan's eyes darkened and narrowed as his lips twisted in disgust. "He's referring to their evolution from perytons. A dark history haunts the Lantíés. Perytons were known for preying on humans from parallel worlds. Humans barely overlapped with perytons in Carmelle's evolutionary history, but the short time they did, coupled with stories humans from parallel worlds brought with them when they came through portals, was enough to instill a deep mistrust and prejudice against the Lantíés in some Carmellians. They believe the Lantíés still might kill humans in Carmelle even as evolved beings. Some parents still shield their children in fear every time a Lantíé walks past, examining their shadows warily. It's said when perytons consumed a soul, their shadow morphed into that human's likeness. Many believe Lantíés are immortal because of all the souls their ancestors harvested. Perytons were also known for their connections with Celestial magic so... You can see why many Carmellians still have a misplaced fear of Lantíés.

"It's infuriating though, especially when you see the way Lantíés with antlers or wings are often treated. No one should have to suffer for the sins of their ancestors. If you can even call natural instincts and inherited traits a sin. Alldían is my godfather, I grew up with the Lantíés, and I have never once seen them have any inclination to hunt a human. They're largely vegetarians now, and lead peaceful lives, often trying to help humans."

Sadie didn't know what to say. She wasn't sure she could even squeeze words past the lump in her throat. She knew how it felt to be different, to have people whisper as you passed.

"Look, I have to go down to the common room," Tristan said after a minute of silence. "I'll probably be down there until quite late. Just in case I don't see you before morning, tomorrow we're going up to Nethilya so I can warn the King about the dragon, so keep in mind we have an early start."

He left the room without further explanation. Sadie listened to his receding footsteps before leaping off the bed and hurrying out of the too-white room and into Tristan's. She felt calmer without a box of white enclosing her. Tristan had a point; there was no immediate reason to panic. Griswald and his soldiers probably thought she was an ignorant commoner with a big mouth. And she couldn't see how they could possibly find her again. Dwelling on it would not help.

Wandering over to the window, Sadie pressed her forehead against the cool frame. In the street below, a juggler tossed brightly coloured balls in the air while balancing a long thin stick on the tip of his nose. Beyond this street, various flat and slanting rooftops marched in scattered layers of light colours. Rising above these rooftops, its lush green slopes glowing in the light of the waning sun was the hill by the sea with the winding crystalline turrets of Nethilya crowned atop.

Sadie couldn't believe tomorrow she would be in that palace, meeting a king. Like she had walked into one of her favourite fairy tales, and now had a chance to uncover the next clue in her quest to find portals. Maybe Tristan's discussion with the king about the dragon would reveal another clue about the portals. If the Redpath sent the dragon and were also trying to control the portals, there might be a connection there that could unveil information to help her return home. Or perhaps she could sneak into the royal library if they had one, and there would be more information about portals there.

But that was the thing about fairy tales—they brimmed with false hopes and dark twists, and when you stood on the precipice of happily ever after, it became elusive.

Floating through the dark void of dreams, Sadie rode the notes of an unearthly song, an enchanting voice serenading the blackness. Her mind grew darker than folds of ebony satin, glossy and fluid like ink, blotting her dreamless sleep with the sweet, smooth lyrics of a beautiful lullaby.

Images began forming slowly on this canvas of black. Images at first simple and singular, like the vein of a leaf, but then expanded, lines branching off and curving in every direction. Leaves became trees, trees became forests, and forests became the shaggy coats of mountains, jutting sharply against a royal blue sky. And through it all laced that powerful voice, a collection of high notes casting colourful flower bursts, followed by a powerful rush of low notes as a waterfall came cascading down.

For a few minutes—a day, a year, a space outside of time, a glimpse of eternity—she floated in this enchanted world, this land of dreams. Then her eyes snapped open and Tristan's powder blue room swam into view. She was lying on his bed.

Yet that dream lingered around her still, the voice louder, drifting up from the common room below.

She wasn't aware of making the decision to bound down the stairs, but when she reached the bottom she leaned against the railing, gazing intently at the familiar figure on the stage without really seeing him. He sang of the ocean, detailing its many glittering hues, the sparkle of its surface in the sun, its powerful, frothing waves, and its vast possibilities. He sang of the sun and the moon, and they appeared, lighting the world with their gold and silver glows. He sang of roots, grass, birds, and beasts, and they all sprang to life.

And then words splashed into the pool of images like coins dropped in a fountain. She caught names like Bren and Lin and Ninaya and then—Vashi. As the song came to an end, Sadie identified the singer.

Tristan.

He sat in the centre of the stage, a small portable harp resting comfortably on his knees. His last note still hung in the air, a moonbeam suspended in a thicket of leaves. The common room erupted in applause, muffled to Sadie's ears. She had known he could sing, but his chorus at the ocean paled in comparison to what she had just heard.

Tristan's eyes locked with hers over the sea of heads, drawn to her disbelieving gaze like a moth to a flame. Something flickered in his eyes. Regret that she had heard? Fear? Or shame?

Sliding off the stool, he angled his way through the excited crowd, harp still in hand.

"Who *are* you?" she blurted when he stood before her.

Tristan sighed. "I'm a Storyteller, Sadie."

"A what?"

"A Storyteller," he repeated, searching her face for a reaction. "It will take some explaining, I know... I'll tell Phil I'm taking a break."

Tristan signalled to the innkeeper who nodded. Hopping up on stage, he clapped his hands to get the common room's attention and told the crowd Tristan was taking a break but would be back soon, so they should stay in the inn to not miss his next songs. Tristan led her to a secluded table in the corner of the room so they could talk privately.

"Storytellers are rare, especially these days," Tristan began without preamble. "At least, true Storytellers are. Most are Lantíes. I think there are only three mortals, including myself, in all of Carmelle that have the gift. The other two are from Dharmaelia. We recall stories of the past through song. We tell stories of Carmelle, Tolotanteau, Nirosula the Land of the Keepers, or Arwé as a whole. Sometimes we can recall stories from other worlds as well, but that is much rarer and more difficult."

"Can *you* recall stories from other worlds?" Sadie interrupted.

"Yes. Sometimes. I guess you could say we're like writers, only we recite our stories instead of writing them down. It's important to remember that we recall these stories, though. The skill of the Storyteller varies, of course, depending on their imagination and creativity in how they tell the stories they recall, but there can be no doubt about the truthfulness and realism."

Sadie rubbed her fingernails and studied a black scorch mark on the wooden table, frowning at the bitterness on her tongue. "An ironic word choice, truthfulness, given your evasion of the truth when I asked about the song you sang by the ocean, or why you chose this inn and what business you had with Phil."

Tristan grimaced and nodded. "I know I should have told you about being a Storyteller when I sang that day at the beach. I wanted to tell you then when you asked about my voice, and I have tried to tell you so many times since, knowing I would have to perform here to earn our keep, but I was scared."

"Of what? Being a Storyteller seems like an amazing gift that you should be proud of."

"I am proud to be a Storyteller, but... do you remember when I said I had been to your world before? And that I disliked the place? There are many reasons why, but one is that I was treated badly for my singing abilities. I was probably exposed to the wrong people with unenlightened views of masculinity, but I was young and didn't know how to defend myself, and was beaten pretty badly for it. I learned to keep it to myself around people from Earth. In Carmelle, Storytellers are respected, revered even by some, and I never feel shame. But you are from Earth, and though I knew in my heart you were different from the people who beat me, I couldn't stop the bad memories from resurfacing every time I tried to tell you. My brain fled those memories, and the doubt poured in. I usually don't care what people think of me, but I guess I do care what you think. I wasn't ready to risk our new friendship, so I took the coward's way out, knowing that you would hear me perform here and I could let the songs speak for me instead of having to find the words myself. I'm sorry."

Sadie bit her lip, stomach fluttering a little at Tristan's hunched shoulders and the way he rubbed the back of his neck self-consciously without breaking eye contact. Not trying to hide more truths from her, but genuinely anxious for her response.

"It's all right, Tristan, I get it," Sadie assured him. "I know what it's like not to be able to find the words. I wish you could have trusted me enough to know I would respect you, not deride you, for your abilities, but I get it."

Tristan's relieved grin warmed his chocolate brown eyes, and Sadie's heart swelled—then deflated.

She sought a way to return to Earth and her brother. Her budding friendship with Tristan would make leaving a world that already filled her soul with content that much more difficult. Maybe she shouldn't encourage building trust with someone she might never see again soon.

Tristan opened his mouth to say more, but Sadie cut him off. "You don't owe me any other explanations Tristan. I am curious though about the truthfulness of the stories you recall from the past. How do you know they're accurate? You said you don't have magic, but this sounds like magic."

A frown creased Tristan's brow, and he pinched the bridge of his nose. "You really challenge people's perceptions, don't you?"

His dry, sarcastic words held an undertone of admiration, and Sadie couldn't help her chest swelling with pride. There were worse things to be known for.

"I never thought of my gift as magic," Tristan continued. "To me, magic has always meant casting spells with Elemental or Celestial magic, or even the form of magic the Armindís use, more akin to witchcraft on Earth, and I have nothing like that. But I guess you're right; it could be perceived as magic. Sort of like Thomas Sheldon's Colour Seer gift. It's a singular ability with no applications outside of its intended purpose but it is a gift not everyone possesses, and one that requires channelling information across time. More than the accuracy of Storytellers' stories being verified by fossil dating and other evolutionary data, and aligning with other accounts of oral and written histories, there's the feeling of reaching across time. Of plucking events out of history as they're happening in real time and weaving them into song. A physical feeling accompanies these genuine images, a pressure in my head not relieved until the words have been sung. It's not a painful pressure, but still a physical manifestation I don't experience when it's just my imagination. Or when I am retelling a story from my repertoire I have already recalled from the past."

"There's no way to fake it, then?"

"Oh, people try. Some Carenthians have started claiming they possess the gift. A few can indeed recall certain events of the past, but their ability is limited and their imagination lacking. They use it for entertainment and fame only. Some have even taken to writing down story ideas and lines beforehand and memorizing them for their 'shows', which is proof they are not true Storytellers. True Storytellers only recall the past once they have started singing. They're not visions that come to us beforehand. They are channelled through song, and always relayed in Tavé, Carmelle's most ancient language."

"So, if you recalled something from the past about a portal, for example…"

Tristan's eyes sharpened, piercing through Sadie's attempts to keep her face nonchalant.

"You want me to help you open a portal?"

"I miss my brother," Sadie replied. "I abandoned him, and I need to make amends."

"You want to go back to Earth… forever?"

The muscles in Tristan's face had slackened, his lips curved down at the corners.

Sadie didn't answer, her words stuck in her throat. She had berated Tristan for not telling the truth. She couldn't lie to him now—and she felt like no matter what she said, it would be a lie. To herself, to him. To both.

"I see. What about everything you hated about your life on Earth? Those problems haven't vanished."

Sadie's chest and throat burned, and she blinked back tears. "I know."

Tristan ran his hand through his hair, tangling it in the black ribbon holding it back.

"I don't even know if anything I recall could help. I don't know how to direct it, I don't choose what I recall from the past, it chooses me, and even if I could, there's no guarantee you could apply it to your situation. I don't know enough about portals. I don't know if the same rules apply every time they close. I don't know if they have ever been opened before while closed. Even if I saw the creation of a new portal, it's unlikely you would be able to replicate that magic. No offence, Sadie, but while I do believe you have magic, you're not trained, you have no idea what you're doing—"

"I know," Sadie interjected, "but I have to try something."

Tristan eyed the determined set of her jaw. His own jaw clenched, his cheek spasming.

"I want to help you, Sadie, but I also have a duty to Alldían that I can't disobey. Can't you see him first and then figure out how to get home? He probably has the answers you seek about portals anyway, he could—"

"Forget it," Sadie snapped, standing up. "I know our short friendship pales in comparison to your relationship with your godfather. *I get it.* I'm not mad. But you'll understand that I also have a duty to salvage the relationship that matters more to me. With or without your help."

Stalking away from the table, Sadie ignored Tristan calling after her.

"Tristan!" Phil shouted from the stage. "Break's over!"

Sadie glanced over her shoulder when she reached the stairs to see Tristan slowly ascending the stairs to his harp on the stage, looking helplessly between it and Sadie.

She hurried upstairs before he could ensnare her with his voice.

Chapter Twelve

Earth, Water, Air, and Fire

Sadie squinted at the white-gold and silver bars wrought with a sunburst in the centre of the gates before her. Pointed tips like spears marched in a solid glittering line, sunlight reflecting off the sharp edges. Beyond these elaborate gates a palace of shimmering crystal-white surfaces touched with a glint of sunrise gold rose: Nethilya.

Glancing at Tristan, Sadie shifted her feet, a little wary in his presence after last night. She had meant what she said about understanding his predicament, but resentment still corroded her heart. For a moment after he apologized for hiding his Storytelling abilities, she had really thought he'd help her find a portal. Now she found herself questioning what other secrets lurked beneath his practised mask. Why did her instincts nudge her to trust him when he revealed his true self in calculated layers? She wasn't even sure if her heart sought his trust, or if the residual enchanting powers of Tristan's storytelling addled her mind.

Either way, she would have to figure out a way to open the portals on her own now. She would start with trying to sneak away to a library in Nethilya to find more information, and hope they had some manuscripts in English.

Tristan's eyes were fixed straight ahead, his long loping strides practised and casual as he approached the two heavily gilded guards standing stiffly before the gates. To Sadie's surprise, the guards barely even glanced at

Tristan. It was Sadie they peered at suspiciously. Tristan nodded to indicate Sadie's worthiness and they let them pass without a word. Torn between surprise and suspicion at his influence, Sadie settled for branding her heated gaze into Tristan's back like the heat of the sun concentrated through a magnifying glass.

Stepping onto a smooth cobblestone path, they passed through a courtyard bordered by a lush garden. Wreaths of yellow, red, and orange flowers like little sunbursts adorned tall trees bearing ripe pears. Sadie reached out to pick one before retracting her hand hastily, reminding herself she couldn't pick fruit from another person's garden, no matter how delectable it looked. Strings of silky white flowers hung above her, and magnolias and lilies clumped around her feet. Water spilled from basins of an enormous stone fountain in the main square of the garden, a statue of a little girl holding aloft a conch shell perched on top. Sadie trailed her fingers through the water of the lower basin before passing through an open set of carved ivory doors.

A peculiar ache hollowed Sadie's chest as she stepped into the palace, like her heart made room for a long-lost part of her soul. "It's beautiful," she said softly.

Speckled in white-and-pink marble, the glossy palace floor was patterned with a sunburst mosaic in the centre. A domed roof curved far overhead, its sloping sides painted with the golden rays of the sun, the translucent silhouette of an osprey with wings spread wide at the roof's peak. A twenty-foot-tall statue of a bearded man in long robes holding an unrolled scroll in his left hand and a long feather quill in his right dominated the spacious hall.

"Certainly, you could never accuse the Carenthian nobility of lacking opulence," remarked Tristan.

"Opulent seems too harsh a term," mused Sadie. "It's lavish, yes, but not ostentatiously so. Nothing is there just for gaudiness. There's a sophistication to the design that reflects the unique aspects of their city and peoples."

Tristan's eyebrows rose, appraising Sadie. "You spent a lot of time in museums and art exhibitions, didn't you?"

Sadie's cheeks flushed. "Far too much time. We frequented the City Museum in Vancouver. I know you're thinking my privilege is showing again and I sound snobby, and you may be right, but I do value art and history. Even though I had some of the paintings and displays memorized, I never tired of the glimpses into other people's lives. People who lived differently than me—who saw the world differently—and yet despite the differences, the commonalities were far greater. In the museum I felt less alone."

"You don't have to defend your affinity for art and history to me," Tristan assured her. "I didn't voice that observation as a comment on your privilege. I too was privileged enough to be raised among those who value art and history. It's nice to have another thing in common."

Sadie lowered the defensive jut of her chin and smiled. "Nice indeed."

Tristan crossed the entrance hall and climbed up one of two grand curving staircases, Sadie following more slowly as she drank in paintings depicting vivid azure ocean scenes like Renaissance paintings.

Winding spiral towers with sloping walkways instead of stairs surrounded the dome, rising to dizzying heights. Glass-spun bridges tinted a shiny blue connected the towers, their railings laced with metallic pink, and Sadie marvelled at how such a delicate feat of architecture could bear the weight of the people she could see walking across.

People passed them in the corridors, some glancing their way curiously or nodding in recognition to Tristan, but nobody stopped to talk or impede their business. Most people wore embroidered tunics or dresses of rich material, or the livery of palace servants, but some wore seafaring clothes with tricorn hats or garments woven from seaweed and palm fronds over blue skin. Sadie barely stopped her jaw from dropping the first time she beheld one of the blue-skinned people, and she averted her eyes quickly to avoid the impression of staring. She didn't want to draw attention to herself or offend anyone, but it took a few moments for her widened eyes to refocus, and when they did, it was to find a group of Redpath soldiers tramping through the hallways in a thick knot. She ducked behind Tristan.

With six floors, the dome was taller than all the towers on the west side of Nethilya—the side facing the ocean. As they walked, Tristan informed her that the first floor held the kitchens and the servants' quarters; the second was one great dining hall where the king, queen, nobles, and their guests ate; the third featured a huge ballroom for social events; the fourth was called the Judgment Hall where the public was allowed in once a week to have their problems settled by the king himself; the fifth provided sleeping quarters for members of the royal family; and the sixth was called the Window to the World.

"Why is it called the Window to the World?" Sadie asked.

"King Vindor and Queen Morgaine use it for certain state issues, esteemed visitors, and the personal matters that do not belong in the Judgment Hall," replied Tristan. "It's the view that gives the room its name. You'll see."

"Are there any libraries in this palace?" Sadie asked innocently, keeping her voice casual.

"Yes, but we don't have time to stop and read now," replied Tristan. Luckily he didn't bat an eye at her question, knowing how much she loved books since she frequently talked about reading. "Maybe after we relay our message to King Vindor about the dragon."

"You know, I don't have to go with you to relay the message. You could meet me in the library after," Sadie suggested.

Tristan stopped and stared at Sadie, eyes narrowed in suspicion. Sadie gulped.

"I thought you wanted to see the Window to the World and meet the rulers of Carenthia. Why would you change your mind now? What could possibly be more exciting at the library?"

"Nothing, I just thought it might be awkward," Sadie lied, wracking her brain for an excuse and coming up empty. "Never mind, we'll go to the library after."

They ascended a series of gradually sloping marble ramps with dusty-rose pink carpets running down the middle and speckled ivory railings. By the time they reached the heavy oak doors on the sixth floor, Sadie was faintly out of breath. When the door warden spotted Tristan, he bowed and let them through without interrogation.

A huge circular room carpeted in crimson greeted them, the short expanse of wall painted a rich cream colour. A silver dome arched over their heads in place of a ceiling. The most enormous window she had ever seen spanned most of the circumference of the room in place of walls. Through the glass the coast of Carenthia unfurled before her like a realistic tapestry.

The ocean stretched endlessly before her, a swirl of teal and azure. Beyond the waves crashing into the cliffs the sea dimpled from a light breeze. A few ships were anchored in the harbour, but most had set sail with the sunrise and were far out at sea.

The wharf swarmed with activity. Fishermen prepared to launch or hauled in the first catch of the day; vendors sold fish and seashells; a troupe of musicians serenaded the morning market bustle; and a few artists set up easels to paint the ocean. From this window, Sadie could see the Carenth-hild, the mouth of the Tolonení and its sentinels Ilí-ta-onon and Carenthonon, the edge of Voita Woods across the bay, and of course, the ocean. She glimpsed bits of the city in the peripheries, including a few oval arenas. Sadie now understood why it was called the Window to the World—to the king and queen and all their subjects this *was* the world.

Her stomach twisting from vertigo instigated by the immaculately clean glass, Sadie tore her eyes away from the jagged rocks below and focused on the centre of the room.

Sitting in identical silver chairs with high backs plastered in diamonds and pearls and upholstered with patterned ivory cushions were the king and queen.

Tristan bowed low before them and Sadie curtsied beside him.

The king's white velvet tunic covered in sunbursts bulged at his ample waist. His silver velvet breeches stretched tightly across his thick thighs, and on his shoulders sat a heavy white cloak trimmed with red, a massive sunburst on the back. His good-natured face boasted a ready smile unperturbed by facial hair, a mane of close-cropped black locks framing his warm umber skin, and turquoise eyes that sparkled like the sunlit ocean behind him. A golden crown perched at a jaunty angle atop his head. He beamed at Tristan.

But it was the queen's face that baited the wary hook in her mind and raised the hairs on her arms. Her pale skin appeared white like snow. Her silver-blue eyes glinted like frost, and her ebony hair fell thickly in a graceful tumble to her waist. A small, jagged silver crown perched upon her head, gleaming like bared steel. Her haughty glare radiated disdain, unimpressed with Tristan. She didn't even spare Sadie a glance.

"Welcome, Tristan!" boomed the king. "It is a joy to have you grace these halls again. How are you?"

"I'm doing fine, your highness, thank you," replied Tristan, inclining his head slightly.

"I cannot stand these formalities, let's be done with them," ordered King Vindor with a wave of his hand. "I don't call you Sir Tristan West, Swordmaster, Storyteller, and godson of Alldían the Wise, now do I?"

Sadie barely prevented her jaw from dropping. A rushing swell drowned her ears.

"No, sir, you don't, but you *are* a king," Tristan reminded him. "You have far more entitlement to be addressed formally than I."

"Nonsense," King Vindor snorted. "Who's the one out there fighting the evils of the world single-handedly like a hero while I sit here on a gilded throne locked away in a gaudy palace?"

"Mr. West is right," the queen interjected. The icy bite of her voice matched her appearance. "You are a king and should be treated as such by everybody. How else do you expect your subjects to respect you?"

"Nonsense," King Vindor repeated, glaring moodily at the queen.

"Allow me to refer to you as King Vindor, sire, and I shall spare you your other prestigious titles of Vindor the Valiant, best knight of the Order, and exceptional Swordmaster."

Sadie did not even attempt to hide her incredulous stare. This rambling, portly man was a *Swordmaster*?

"That's all in the past," the king dismissed, but a faint smile of pride tugged at his lips. "Now, who's this young lady here? You insist on courtly manners, and yet no introduction?"

"Sorry, majesty. This is Sadie. She is accompanying me on my journey to Caris Nando. My godfather wishes to meet her."

"What brings you to Carenthia then?" King Vindor asked.

Neither Tristan nor King Vindor paused to let Sadie speak. She scowled, the knot in her chest tightening.

"We were west of the Gap of Talarí and would have proceeded to Caris Nando through the Gap, but it was blocked," replied Tristan. "A dragon attacked Helgur, and we narrowly escaped through Athatair. We had no choice but to come to Caris Nando the long way. I suspect the Gap is heavily guarded and it would be too dangerous to attempt to gain passage through, or even go north immediately on the eastern edge of Voita following the line of the Dharlomin."

"But this is outrageous news!" roared the king indignantly. "My soldiers in Lenia need the Gap to journey here! There hasn't been a dragon west of the Gap in years. Who in Carmelle is arrogant enough to think they can control the Gap? You don't think..."

The king didn't have to finish.

"No, I do not think he is responsible," replied Tristan. "It is too bold a move, even for him. Only fools blind in their arrogance could have done this. I could be wrong of course, but my theory is that the Redpath are behind it."

Silence coated the Window to the World. The bitter taste of regretted words lingered on Sadie's tongue even though she had not been the one to utter them.

"That is a serious accusation," intoned Queen Morgaine, the shards of her icy tone barbed with warning.

King Vindor stroked his chin, glancing nervously between Tristan's locked jaw and his wife's frigid glare. "You want to be careful who you point your finger at Tristan. The Redpath are important to Carenthia. They hold great sway here. I'm not overly fond of them myself, but that's no reason to point fingers. 'A hasty accusation oft goes awry', as my father used to say."

"As I said, it's only a theory. I wasn't suggesting immediate action against them," Tristan assured him. "In any case I thought you should know about the dragon."

"Yes, thank you for the warning, to be sure," King Vindor rambled distractedly, still stroking his chin. "Will that be all? Only we have others to attend to before the session in the Judgment Hall later this afternoon... not that you're not welcome here of course..."

"That was everything of importance I had to say," Tristan affirmed.

"Then it has been a pleasure as always, Tristan," the king said with a sardonic smile. "Thanks for the news, I'll keep it in mind. When are you leaving?"

"Probably tomorrow. I must reach Caris Nando as soon as possible."

"What, so soon? There's to be a ball or party of some kind in a few days, I don't remember all the details, but there will be a feast and plenty of good wine. Won't you stay at least for that?"

"I'm sorry, your majesty, but I must make haste," said Tristan, not sounding sorry at all.

"I always miss the chance to show you off to all the noble snobs of this city, don't I?" King Vindor complained. "Sometimes I think you do it on purpose."

Tristan did not answer.

"All right go on, get out of here then. We'll have to catch up some other time. Give my regards to Alldían."

"Will do. Your majesties," Tristan intoned by way of farewell, and bowed once more before turning to leave. Sadie curtsied and murmured *your majesties* as well, but she suspected neither the king nor queen noticed.

When they were far enough down the ramp, Sadie bombarded Tristan with questions.

"I know I should be immune to surprises by now, but is there anything else I should know about you *Sir* Tristan? Are you the commander of an army? A world-renowned jester? A prince in disguise?"

"Don't be ridiculous," Tristan snapped.

"I don't think it's ridiculous to want to know the man guiding me to my future in Carmelle," Sadie retorted. "Am I just some pawn in a game to you?"

"No! I've never lied to you once since we met!"

"No, just evaded the truth. I don't know why I didn't see you were a lord before," said Sadie, shaking her head. "You're just like all the rich people I despised back home. You never show your true self to the world."

"Sadie, I promise, there's nothing else special about me, if you can even call what the king revealed special. You already knew I was Alldían's godson and a Storyteller. Just because I'm also referred to as 'sir' because of my Swordmaster title, doesn't mean I'm rich. I'm far from it. The person I was on the road is the real me, honestly."

"Cold and indifferent?"

"No, I mean… I don't know what I mean," Tristan faltered, looking more confused than Sadie.

"How am I supposed to know the truth of who you are if you don't even know?"

Sadie's throat burned and she clutched her roiling stomach guiltily, knowing her words were an unfair overreaction, but his inability to bring clarity to the situation infuriated her.

"Don't you think this is an inappropriate place to discuss this?"

"See, there you go proving my point! You don't want an argument to take place in such an important, public place—"

"I don't care about these people, I—" but he stopped abruptly, staring over Sadie's shoulder.

"Tristan?" came a voice of uncertain recognition from behind her. She whipped around to find a young man striding towards them with a smile on his face. "Is that really you?"

Tristan spared an awkward, apologetic glance for Sadie which fanned the flame in her chest higher before embracing the man like a brother and exclaiming, "Haldin!"

"It's been far too long," said Haldin. "You were a young boy last time I saw you, no more than sixteen. Now look at you! Long hair! And is that muscle I see in those lanky arms? Your face, however, is as dark and stormy as ever. Ah, but there is something new in the eyes. Can it be wisdom?"

Tristan laughed self-deprecatingly.

"I'm glad I ran into you," Haldin continued. "I feel too out of place here. The walls look like they'd shatter if I hit them hard enough, and everything's so white and bright…" Haldin shrugged uncomfortably.

He certainly looked out of place. His long, curly wheat-coloured hair hung like wilted straw. Rusty brown eyes in a hard-planed face matched the care-worn lines across his cheekbones despite his cheery nature and obvious youthful age. Short and stocky with well-muscled limbs, his battered armour over chain mail looked as if it had never been taken off. It was roan red with patterns of deep green and gold, reminding her of Celtic designs. In the crook of his arm he gripped a war helm, complete with nose guard and the symbolic feathers of his house gathered in a plume at the top. Everything about him spoke of a hard life and echoed faintly of war.

As he gazed uncomfortably at the marble, he noticed Sadie standing slightly behind Tristan. Seeing the surprise in Haldin's eyes, Tristan said, "This is Sadie Sheldon. She is joining me on my journey to Caris Nando. Sadie, this is Prince Haldin son of King Peladorn of Dharmaelia, and his little brother, Prince Airothane."

Sadie had not noticed the boy trailing behind Haldin. Short and skinny, he rocked on his feet like a frail reed swaying gently in the faintest of winds. His mane of wild tangled hair strayed down to his chin and mirrored his brother's wheat colour. Big, round, unnatural honeyed amber coloured eyes took up most of his small, narrow face and peered at her from beneath his untamed hair. He seemed unfazed by the grandeur of the palace and surveyed Sadie as if *she* were the child.

"Sadie…" Haldin repeated, testing the name on his tongue. "Your birth name sounds Dharmaelian, but your family name is certainly not. Would you mind me inquiring where you are from?"

"Oh, er," stammered Sadie. "You probably don't know it, it's a very small village…"

"I bet you I would," Airothane piped up. "I'm excellent at geography, I know all the places of Carmelle."

"Oh, well this is so remote, I'm not sure it's even on a map—"

"If it's in Carmelle, I'll know it," Airothane boasted.

Annoyance pricked Sadie's taut muscles. Why did this boy have to be so nosy? "And how do *you* know all the places of Carmelle? You can't be older than seven."

"I'm eleven, actually," retorted the boy haughtily. "I'm telling you, I'll know it."

Sadie bit her tongue to prevent it from saying 'Vancouver' just to stump him. Tristan would not thank her for risking exposure to the Redpath.

Haldin chuckled. "The scary part is, he probably will. He's a smart one, although not always the most polite. But never mind, the answer is not truly important. What brings you to Carenthia, my old friend?"

Tristan explained about the dragon. Haldin's eyes narrowed with every word.

"There's no way a dragon sent on Vashi's orders could have passed over the Zorlomin and through our lands without us noticing," insisted Haldin. "We always keep a close watch these days on activities in the east."

"Ah, but what if the dragon was not sent on Vashi's orders?" countered Tristan. "The dragon still would have had to come from the Black Mountains, but it could have been summoned by someone else."

"Impossible," said Haldin. "Dragons only answer to one man. Vashi. No one else could possibly, it's inconceivable..."

"Unless it was lured away by a promise of things Vashi could not provide," reasoned Tristan. "Things like the fresh meat of strong humans, not the tough stuff of Vashi's servants. It wouldn't have taken much, all the dragons of Zorlomin are blinded by their malice and greed. That coupled with unintelligent brains, and I'd say it would be quite easy to lure one out of hiding. They wouldn't have had to pass Dharmaelia at all, if they were careful, or they may have flown over your lands, high above the clouds so you wouldn't see them even if you knew they were there."

"Could it have been one from the Dharlomin?" Haldin asked desperately. Sadie could see he was obviously unwilling to believe his people failed to stop such an evil force before it reached the Gap of Talarí.

"It's possible of course, but I do not think so. Remember, the dragons of Dharlomin are few, and too intelligent to be tricked into leaving their hollows in the Red Mountains. Besides, those dragons are as morally good as dragons can be and could not be persuaded to guard a pass for the pleasure of instilling terror in others. Such a bribe would not tempt them.

In fact, it would insult them, and any person who proposed such an offer would be devoured on principle. No, it was a dragon of Zorlomin and there is only one group it could be serving."

"The Redpath," grunted Haldin with disgust, understanding at last. "You bear grave news, Tristan. Grave news indeed."

"Ill news has ever followed me like a shadow," agreed Tristan.

Sadie attempted a derisive guffaw, but it sounded more like a choking cough.

"You have something to say, Sadie?" Tristan asked, eyebrow raised.

"I just find that easy to believe," replied Sadie with a smirk.

Tristan grimaced as Haldin hid a chuckle behind is broad hand. "Yes, it is my curse, I suppose. What about you, Haldin? What brings you so far from the plains you love?"

"My purpose here is far more trivial than yours, I assure you," said Haldin bitterly. "My father needed a letter delivered to King Vindor and I offered to be messenger. I had some leisure time at home and Airothane wished to see the famed city of Carenthia and its champion king. Father encouraged the idea, thinking it would be a useful addition to the boy's ever-growing knowledge, but it seems I am needed at home now more than ever."

"Don't feel too guilty," said Tristan. "Even a hawk cannot see what will come to pass. I do not think your lands are in any immediate danger; the dragon will not stray far from its post at the Gap. I will let you deliver your message to the king now. We are staying at the Crowned Sun Inn, if you wish to visit and talk more, but we will be leaving tomorrow for Caris Nando. Oh, and Airothane," Tristan added as they began to leave, "don't judge King Vindor too harshly. He really was once as great as all the stories have claimed."

Sadie crossed her arms and raised both eyebrows. Vindor's flustered skirting of hard truths had not reflected the tough resolve and discipline of a skilled warrior.

"Farewell Tristan, Sadie. May the wings of time carry you to that happy eyrie at journey's end," said Haldin.

"And may you and yours forever fly among the clouds," replied Tristan.

They parted ways, Haldin and Airothane continuing their ascent to the Window to the World while Sadie and Tristan began their descent. However, they had gone no more than a dozen steps when a man lurking in the shadows like a panther stalked towards them. Ebony hair slicked back from a fair face into the smallest ponytail. A long black jacket trimmed with silver and dark green hung over a silky black blouse and black breeches, kissing the tips of his black leather boots.

"Lord Tacitus," Tristan acknowledged coldly as he passed.

The man barely inclined his head towards them and, never breaking stride, sneered contemptuously, "Tristan."

Then he vanished, slipping through a concealed doorway.

"Who was that?" Sadie demanded.

"Lord Tacitus," replied Tristan with obvious dislike. "He's the Loremaster of Carenthia, learned in all the ancient scrolls and recorded histories hoarded in the libraries of Nethilya. Some of those manuscripts date as far back as the early years of the First Age of Carmelle. He therefore plays the part of adviser to King Vindor and Queen Morgaine when matters of the past are in question. Sometimes I wonder where his loyalties truly lie."

"You just say that because of the way he looks," Sadie insisted.

Tristan sneered. "He'd be pleased you said that. I hope he didn't hear too much of our conversation with Haldin. He'd be very interested to know what we're up to."

A brief moment of silence stirred the waves of tension between them as Sadie contemplated which of their viewpoints was prejudiced. Maybe she was being naïve and if so, was it better to be naïve or too quick to judge? She opened her mouth to defend herself, but a voice interrupted her—

"Thought you'd try and escape Nethilya without talking to me, did you?"

"I wouldn't dream of it," said Tristan, turning around to greet the newcomer. Sadie sighed, irritated at another interruption, but Tristan looked like he expected at least this encounter. Though as soon as Sadie turned to face the man who'd spoken, she forgave him for the interruption.

"Prince Cassador."

"Tristan West."

Prince! He must be King Vindor and Queen Morgaine's son, Sadie thought.

He had inherited his mother's beauty, down to his raven hair and icy blue eyes—except his eyes glinted like a silver moon reflected in the soft blue hue of melted snow. His mother's frosty features looked congenial on him, like a cool pale morning in spring with the promise of warmth. The emblems of his house embroidered his white and silver clothes. His eyes held intelligence, compassion, and a jovial eagerness that mirrored his father's.

"I just had a little chat with my parents," Prince Cassador informed Tristan. "They told me about the dragon, but they did not tell me about this young lady with you."

He smiled politely at her, and before Tristan could speak for her again, she introduced herself. "I'm Sadie Sheldon. I too am travelling to Caris Nando, sir."

"Miss Sheldon, what a pleasure to meet you," Prince Cassador replied with a respectful incline of his head. "I hope you will forgive my rudeness, but I must discuss this dragon business with Tristan, and I have so little time—"

"You and everyone else," Sadie blurted bitterly.

She slapped a hand over her mouth in horror. "I'm so sorry, sir, my tongue wags on its own sometimes. Please continue your conversation. I understand it's of great importance."

"It is indeed important, but you need not worry about your wagging tongue," the prince assured her. "Mine is often out of control and has landed me in worse trouble than yours."

"I wouldn't bet on it," Sadie muttered.

"You know what this means, don't you?" Tristan asked, bringing the conversation back to dragons.

"Naturally," said Prince Cassador. "The Redpath have taken the first step in what I have long foreseen as an inevitable civil war. I am not as blind and naïve as my father—though to be fair, he is not blind. I think he knows it's the Redpath but doesn't want to admit it. He will be slow to act, which is what the Redpath predicted, no doubt. It will be a frustrating process trying to make my father see the right actions, especially since I do not know for sure myself."

"Methods of action can be decided later. What's important is making Vindor understand the truth of the Redpath's intentions," said Tristan.

"I agree."

Sadie pursed her lips. Did Tristan and Prince Cassador *know* the Redpath's intentions? Or were they projecting their own prejudices? Sadie loathed Griswald's obsession with wealth and power—it was what she couldn't stand about most high society folks on Earth, too—but she couldn't believe that was the entire intention behind all the Redpath's actions. Perhaps there were some members who just wanted to contribute to something greater than themselves in a meaningful way—like Sadie wanted to on Earth.

"I wish I could stay here myself, but I'm afraid I have pressing business in Caris Nando that cannot wait," said Tristan. The hint of a smile crooked at the corner of his lips as he added, "I guess it's up to you again to set things right, Cassador."

Cassador grinned like the strong sun after a flurry of snow. "What else are princes for? We will see each other again soon, Tristan, I am sure of it. I hope to see you again too, my lady."

Giving a short bow, he left, and Sadie stared after him until the sound of Tristan's emotionless voice telling her it was time to keep moving permeated her numb brain, so different from Cassador's sweet, silky tones. She snapped back to the present, her anger and frustration with Tristan rushing back.

"I don't suppose you're going to explain any of that to me," said Sadie testily.

Tristan sighed. "Come in here and we'll talk."

Due to their constant interruptions, they stood on the third floor of the dome where Tristan had said the ballroom was. He led her through an enormous set of elaborate mahogany doors inlaid with gold.

"All right, what do you want to know?"

But Sadie didn't answer. She had lost the ability to work her vocal chords.

Gold bedecked everything, including the walls and ceiling. Tall, standing candelabras lined the walls, illuminating the dark room with a soft glow. Layers of thick gold framed large inlaid paintings on the walls depicting different forms of entertainment including ballroom dancing, singing, orchestral performances, and a man with a harp who looked like a Storyteller. Women with colourful gowns and elegant gentlemen swept across the floor of a ballroom similar to this one. Above these, in a border separating the wall from the ceiling, a row of small square paintings of important looking people marched. Impressive and majestic creatures like whales, eagles, unicorns, and dragons completed this border.

The largest painting spanned across the ceiling, framed by ornate gold. Like most paintings in Nethilya, this one also featured an ocean, its massive waves rolling into the shores of a crescent moon-shaped island. Above this island, four people dominated the painting.

On the far left, a muscular man with a benevolent expression framed by his short, peppered grey hair and goatee held aloft a copper fox in one palm and a mature oak tree in the other. A patchwork cloak of green and golden leaves hung over a shirt and breeches the colour of rich soil, while a belt of bluebells snaked around his waist and a crown of autumn leaves encircled his head. Sandals of bark laced up around his calves with vines.

Next to him, a mermaid with golden hair like the sun's rays and eyes like the ocean smiled down at Sadie. Her tail shimmered with a rainbow of metallic colours, each scale sparkling with its own unique hue, and it ended in a pair of transparent silky white fins with silver veins. A purple starfish adorned her golden hair above her ear. She wielded a fish like a sword in one hand while mountainous waves spilled forth from the other.

Beside the mermaid some sort of metamorphosis took place. A great eagle, a winged horse, a tiny sparrow—all had the same human female face in place of their regular animal ones. Her features seemed more vague, as though the artist had been unsure of exactly what she looked like.

All three of these beings stood on the same level, conveying their equality, but the fourth was cast down to the furthest and lowest right-hand corner. His eyes locked on the three above him, burning with pure loathing. None returned his gaze, as though he was forgotten.

But the man did not forget them. His hateful gaze blazed eternal. The artist had smudged his clothes and physical traits with fire, but Sadie could see his billowing cloak of flames, red and orange tongues lashing out to taste the air greedily. Though his face looked like it could have been handsome once, it now appeared pale and sickly, his auburn hair tipped with black like the crisp burnt edges of flesh. The whites of his dark eyes were veined with red and sallow yellow. He held aloft a single flame in his palm, aimed at the man above him as if he longed to hurl it at him.

"Sadie?" Tristan repeated. Sadie continued to ignore him.

Click, click, click.

Her boots echoed off the polished wooden floor as she ventured slowly into the middle of the room.

Click, click, click.

Her footsteps became rhythmic, like the beats of a song.

Click, click, click.

She could see couples gliding across the floor like ice dancers and laughing people with glasses of champagne balanced in their hands peppered across the ballroom.

Click, click, click.

Sadie imagined herself dancing with them, gliding around the room gracefully, serenaded by a band of Carenthian musicians. Their music rode waves of opposites, rising in powerful, loud crescendos and falling in light, soft laps against the tidal shore. She danced like a wave herself, circling and dipping and turning, rising and rushing and then slowing in elegant, smooth turns.

Click, click, click.

She stopped in the middle of the floor and curtsied. In her mind she wore a glamorous gown with a huge skirt, and curtsied to a man who had asked her to dance. She could see the smile on his face, hear his deep voice strike a chord amidst the music, smell the wine on his breath. She extended her hand to him and let him sweep her across the floor.

She waltzed alone, arms raised to an imaginary partner, her boots beating out a faster rhythm in the cavernous hall.

The man twirled her.

She turned in a circle.

He twirled her over and over.

She started a series of consecutive twirls across the empty ballroom and laughed out loud.

The music stopped. The man let go of her.

She stood alone, in the middle of the yawning room. All that remained of those images, that dance, were the reverberations of the echoes. Until the echoes stilled too, and everything went quiet.

She could see Tristan's profile in her peripheral vision but dared not meet his gaze.

"Tristan?" Sadie asked the room at large, keeping her eyes on the painting above her.

A breathless silence. Then—

"Yes?" he whispered. His voice sounded hesitant. Stunned. Even a little timid.

"What is this room?"

"The ballroom of Nethilya," Tristan replied, his voice quiet as if afraid to disturb any remaining echoes. "It is very famous. Grand balls would occur almost weekly. Now they occur half a dozen times a year, if that. But it is kept in good condition. Sometimes it seems as if you can hear the music still echoing off the walls..."

Sadie whipped around to scrutinize him. His face held no trace of mockery, and his eyes scanned the walls as if he could hear the music. She released her held breath.

"What is this painting on the ceiling?"

"The Four Elemental Keepers of Arwé," Tristan informed her without looking at it. "Bren, Lin, Ninaya, and Vashi."

"Vashi?" Sadie repeated, her eyes flickering back to the man of flames with new understanding. A lump she could not explain knotted in her chest. "So that's Vashi, the evil man you spoke of."

"Yes. He was once the respected Keeper of Fire, but he was exiled from Nirosula, the Land of the Keepers, for his atrocities engendered by greed and envy a long time ago. He sought to rule the peoples of Carmelle. He still thinks it is his right as one of the first humans as we know them today in Arwé, but that is not the Keepers' role. They protect the elements that gave them their powers, but they are not Gods or royal leaders of all peoples. They are immortal, imbibed with stronger magic in the very essence of their being than any of us, but they are not invincible or privileged to dictate how the rest of Arwé's peoples live."

Sadie nodded, understanding why the other Keepers had to exile Vashi.

"Each Keeper represents one of the four elements," Tristan continued. "Bren is Earth, Lin is Water, and Ninaya is Air. They have been depicted here how they are remembered in stories and songs or from the rare glimpses Carmellians get of them when they visit here. They do not visit often, usually only in times of crisis or when one of the elements is abused, for they do not wish to meddle and are generally not interested in the politics and affairs of Carmelle. They care only for protecting the balance of Elemental magic and the creatures and beings formed by these anomalies. Ninaya is so skilled in transformative magic she rarely visits Carmelle in human form, adopting the form of an Air creature instead, so no one really knows what she looks like."

Sadie's eyes lingered on Vashi, but her mind returned to Tristan's deceptions and layered secrets. "I can't think of any good reason why you needed to keep so much of who you are from me. Prove you're worthy of my trust," she challenged, turning to him. "Answer my questions truthfully."

Tristan braced himself, adopting a ready stance. "Fire away, tellurian."

Sadie's lips quirked at his attempt to remind her of their bickering, which had always been honest.

"What exactly is a Swordmaster?"

"How dare you ask such a brazen question!" Tristan teased. "It's pretty much what the name implies. I am extremely skilled with a sword. It is a title bestowed upon few, with a vigorous testing process. There are only seven Swordmasters in Carmelle."

"And King Vindor's one of them?" Sadie inquired, raising an eyebrow.

"Technically, yes. King Vindor was the best knight in his day. Known for never losing a duel, always coming first in tournaments, and his amazing skill with the sword. Of course, opportunities to use his sword since becoming king have been few. I believe he still practices, but there is no doubt his skills must have waned. Still, he is one of the seven, a title people still respect for Vindor the Valiant of old."

"Of old? He didn't look that old to me."

"Vindor is seventy-eight."

"*What?*" Sadie's mouth dropped open.

"This is not like your world," Tristan reminded her. "Things are different here. Mortals usually live to around one hundred and fifty—well, not all mortals. Some have the life span of those in your world, but certainly those of the older nations like Carenthia and Dharmaelia. Vindor is at the prime of his life. Think of him as forty or so."

"And how old are you?"

Tristan hesitated then said, "Twenty-three."

Sadie exhaled in relief. If he had said sixty she didn't think she could have handled it, but he was younger than she had guessed.

"Vindor has been king of Carenthia for around thirty years now," Tristan continued. "He is one of the older Swordmasters, but still well respected."

"And you're no mere soldier."

"No."

"A lie, then," Sadie pointed out.

"An attenuated version of the truth. Technically, I am still a soldier of Alldían's, serving and fighting for him dutifully. I'm just also a Swordmaster. I've only been one for a year."

"Why don't you have a sword on you then?"

"It is forbidden to carry a weapon into another world, as it is considered an attempt to violate the peace between the two worlds." His voice hollowed, ringed with pain as he added, "You have no idea how hard it is to be parted from your personal sword. I left a sword hidden not too far from the mirror to regain upon my return so I wasn't defenceless on our journey back, but I couldn't retrieve it because of the dragon. At least I was able to obtain one in Edgewater. My own sword is being kept safely in Caris Nando until my return."

"Why is the king so hesitant to believe the Redpath are not innocent?"

Sadie couldn't shake this question from where it stuck in cobwebbed corners of her mind.

"He knows they're not innocent in his heart. He just doesn't want to blame them for anything. He's devoutly Ilyance, but his wife is not. Queen Morgaine supports the Redpath and she is powerful, with perhaps more sway in Carenthia than the king. Like Vindor said, the Redpath are important to Carenthia. They have many followers, and he knows it. He may be a bit flippant sometimes, but he's no fool. He knows most of his people have allegiances to the Redpath as well as to him, and he fears making them choose. Under the law they are bound to serve their king—he's just not sure everyone will. Especially since Morgaine is in favour of the Redpath; she is quite popular among her subjects."

Sadie struggled to process all these insights. "How do King Vindor and Queen Morgaine govern a kingdom when their fundamental values are so opposed? They would always have different resolutions for conflicts. It hardly seems like a just and fair way to lead, and honestly sounds like a mess."

"It is," Tristan agreed. "But Vindor and Morgaine did not marry for love. It was a political alliance, a marriage attempting to rectify the broken relationship of two feuding noble Carenthian families. They entered the marriage with optimism, hoping their opposing views would offer insight into the different opinions of their kingdom's inhabitants, and therefore allow them to make decisions that would benefit everyone as equally as possible. They don't always disagree. And to their credit, they have both shown infinite amounts of patience with each other, and usually try to find a compromise when their views on conflicts clash. But they are both stubborn, and to be honest, their decisions are not always in Carenthia's best interest. I'm afraid the responsibility will fall on Prince Cassador's shoulders once again to stop the Redpath."

Sadie nodded and started walking around the ballroom, studying the paintings on the walls. She had seen enough arranged marriages made for political and personal gain to understand King Vindor and Queen Morgaine's plight, and to even appreciate their efforts to make the best of their opposing views and compromise.

Tristan kept pace with her.

"How do you know Haldin?"

"When I was fifteen I lived in Dharmaelia for two years, staying in the house of King Peladorn," he explained. "Haldin is two years older than me, so we did everything together, including going to battle. He is a brave man and a skilled warrior. He's known as Haldin the Hawk among his people."

Sadie's eyes widened at the title and reputation he had earned at twenty-five, and yet it made perfect sense for a man who so fully embodied a warrior. She twisted her dress between her fingers and met Tristan's eyes.

"Will the people of Dharmaelia really be safe from the dragon?"

The edge to his wary eyes softened.

"Yes, I believe so. I sincerely believe the Redpath wouldn't dare attempt to extend their control past the Gap of Talarí yet. Even if the dragon escapes and flies to Dharmaelia, I don't think one dragon would do serious damage. Dharmaelia is well prepared for such attacks, living near the Zorlomin, for on the other side of the Black Mountains is Vasmorloth, the land of Vashi, and they are constantly plagued by his armies."

Sadie pressed a palm to her chest as her shoulders sagged in relief. The thought of Haldin and Airothane's home and people being destroyed like the town of Helgur had worried her.

"You spoke of other dragons to Haldin. Good dragons. Do they not all serve Vashi?"

"No, not all of them serve him. Before he created his own dragons, he persuaded already existing ones to fight for him, but they were too intelligent and resented Vashi's tyranny. They rebelled and left him to join his enemies who respected their freedom. Vashi created his own dragons after and was careful not to give them intelligence beyond necessary survival skills. Some of the original dragons remain and live in the Dharlomin passes."

Sadie massaged her temple. The amount of information Tristan imparted to her felt overwhelming, but she had one last pressing question.

"Tristan?"

"Yes?"

"Is there really going to be a civil war?"

Tristan shrugged. "There's no way to know for sure, but the Redpath are becoming too aggressive, and the Ilyance won't allow the changes they're talking about to take place. The Ilyance is not a real organization like the Redpath. There is no leader, no organized movement or army. Even the Redpath did not have an army in the beginning—but when people started vocalizing their concerns about the changes the Redpath were proposing and the means through which they planned to achieve these changes, the Redpath thought it necessary to defend their beliefs through physical force. That's when those who opposed their ideas started referring to themselves as the Ilyance, or "Fair Path" in Tavé, the ancient tongue. They are the antithesis of the Redpath.

"The Ilyance value the magic in this world. We see it ingrained in every element of nature, and the Redpath want to destroy magical sites for their changes. Most of the Redpath are innocent scientists and forward-thinkers desiring to make things easier for people in Carmelle, but too many of them crave advancements for power and personal gain, and they fail to understand that easier is not always better. The leaders will do whatever it takes to implement their vision, including brute force to impose changes where they are most beneficial to them, instead of advancing only where inhabitants share their vision. This business with the dragon proves how serious they are. I don't see how a civil war can be avoided."

A pronounced silence enunciated the doubts lurking in Sadie's mind. If she craved the same purpose as the Redpath leaders, did that make her morally corrupt? But she would never hurt people. She didn't want to fade into the background, but she wouldn't make herself seen at any cost.

"Come on, we better get going, it's getting late," Tristan said after a few minutes. "A public hearing in the Judgment Hall will be taking place soon and I'd like to avoid the crowds."

Sadie nodded and followed him out of the ballroom and out of Nethilya, deep in thought.

It wasn't until they had left Nethilya and were heading back to the inn that she realized the secrets revealed, people they met, and information she had been overwhelmed with had resulted in her completely forgetting about the library and her goal of finding out more about portals. Tristan had conveniently forgotten his promise to show her the library as well.

Chapter Thirteen

Fire, Flight, and Followers

Downstairs, the Crowned Sun buzzed with excitement in anticipation of hearing a Storyteller, but upstairs in Tristan's room,
Sadie sat cross-legged with her chin resting in her palms as she made
plans with Tristan and Haldin. The prince of Dharmaelia had arrived
at the inn with Airothane a few minutes prior.

"I've been thinking about the dragon all day, and I see no alternative," said Haldin. "I must go back to Dharmaelia by way of Caris
Nando, and I must leave immediately. Could Airothane and I go with
you tomorrow morning?"

Tristan raised his eyebrows at Sadie in question, waiting for her
confirmation. He kept saying her name and looking at her in the
conversation as if determined to make up for not including her as much
in Nethilya. Though Sadie felt a little reserved and guarded around him
still, she appreciated his efforts now. She inclined her head subtly in
consent. She had no problem with Airothane and Haldin joining them
in their journey. Maybe it would be good for both Tristan and Sadie to
have some company. At the very least, it would help keep some distance
between them so Sadie could focus on returning home to Connor.

"Of course, you may journey with us," Tristan told Haldin. "It would be a pleasure to have your company. Sadie and I have travelled alone together longer than may be considered healthy."

Sadie tried to ignore the sting of his words, even though they echoed her own thoughts.

"I've already arranged for horses for Sadie and me, but it shouldn't be a problem to speak to Phil and arrange for two more," Tristan continued. "He has many connections in this city."

"It's settled then," Haldin said, clapping his callused hands. "We will all leave with the sun's awakening."

"TRISTAN!" Phil bellowed from downstairs.

"I'd better get down there or we'll have nowhere to sleep tonight," said Tristan. "Haldin, you'd better come down with me to see what we can arrange in the way of a bed for you and Airothane."

"Can I come too?" Airothane asked, leaping off the bed. "I find Story-tellers fascinating!"

"Of course, anyone is welcome to come down and listen."

Though Haldin and Airothane followed Tristan out the door, Sadie remained in the room. Her heart twinged at the disappointment glistening in Tristan's eyes and hooking the corners of his mouth down, and she looked away.

Burying her face in her fluffy pillow, Sadie willed her body to fall asleep. Downstairs a fog of silence permeated the spectators, Tristan's lone voice the only sound. A voice still threatening to sweep her away if she lost control of her senses for even one moment. She would not succumb to vulnerability at the hands of Tristan West.

Eventually the soft echoes of Tristan's voice lulled her into the land of dreams.

A rough hand gripped her shoulder and shook her awake.

She bolted up in panic, heart pounding at the black silhouette hovering over her in the yawning darkness.

Sadie opened her mouth to scream but the callused hand smothered it. She clawed the hand with sharp fingernails to no avail; it did not budge.

A ray of moonlight slipped past a cloud and illuminated her attacker's face.

Tristan.

Sadie's surprised exclamation barely escaped her lips before it died in his palm. She raised an eyebrow. Tristan put a finger to his lips to signal silence, and Sadie nodded impatiently. Taking his hand off her mouth, he motioned for her to follow him. Attempting to lessen the creaking of bed springs and floorboards, Sadie joined him at the window and peered around the frame.

Creeping silently along the street below were several men in smoky cloaks, illuminated by moonlight and the bright orange flicker of their torches. They flitted from wall to wall like vague silhouettes beneath a black sea, heading towards the back door of the inn. Fear clutched Sadie's lungs. What were the Redpath doing here? Had they somehow discovered where she was staying? Surely they would not come after her in this manner, creeping to the inn in the middle of the night as if they meant to kill her...

Stomach flipping and heart racing, Sadie tried to breathe through the lump clogging her throat. This was absurd. They couldn't be here to kill her. She wasn't important enough.

"Me?" she mouthed at Tristan. He nodded grimly, confirming her fears.

Sinking slowly to the floor, Sadie didn't notice Tristan leave her side until he came back holding two packs. She took hers with trembling hands.

"We need to get Haldin and Airothane," Tristan whispered.

Though her weak knees protested, Sadie straightened her legs and shouldered her pack.

"No, I'll go ready the horses," Sadie insisted, shaking her head to replace fear with determination. "We need to get out of here fast, and I can help."

"Sadie, no, it's dangerous, you need to stay with me—"

"I'll be fine, I can be stealthy. My brother and I used to sneak around our manor all the time. You don't need to do everything, Tristan, I'm capable."

"I know you're capable but they're here for you, and—"

"Exactly!" Sadie snapped. "They're here for me, so let me do something to help the people putting themselves in danger for me. If you know I'm capable, then what's the problem?"

Without waiting for an answer, Sadie opened the door noiselessly and started creeping down the hall towards the inn's front doors.

"Do you even know how to ready the horses?" Tristan whispered hoarsely after her.

"I was taught proper equestrian skills from a young age, thank you very much," Sadie retorted. "Side-saddle mind you, but I can still ride." She neglected to mention she had never prepared a horse for riding herself though, having always had stable-hands preparing them for her, but she knew the basic principles so how hard could it be?

Sadie didn't give Tristan the chance to question her further. Turning her back on him, she padded softly across the hall and down the stairs, ignoring his quiet curse behind her.

When she reached the common room Sadie ran across it, fearing the open space. She had almost reached the door when a torch flared in her eyes.

"My, my, my," snarled Griswald, baring his teeth in a vindictive smile. Darkness inked half his face and a ghastly orange light stained the other half. "Sneaking out in the middle of the night, are we?"

Sadie didn't answer, lips and limbs frozen in terror. She kept her eyes locked on Griswald, but her mind raced, evaluating her situation. The high shuttered windows threatened injury even if she managed to open them before Griswald caught her. Dashing back for the stairs would trap her and her friends between Griswald and the Redpath coming up the back stairs. The adjoining kitchen was the only other way out of the common room.

She had never been in the kitchen here, but didn't kitchens often have their own back door? If not, at least there would be sharp knives.

She inched her way toward the kitchen under the pretense of intimidation, keeping her eyes locked warily on Griswald.

"Thought you were being clever, didn't you?" Griswald continued. A malicious glint flashed in his eyes. "Thought you could fool me with that innocent small-town girl story. I wonder how a commoner like yourself could afford such an expensive inn? Tell me who you're working for! Who's trying to stop us?"

"Why are you so certain I'm working for someone?" Sadie countered, stalling for time. "What if I'm the mastermind behind this supposed network trying to stop you?"

"Do you take me for a fool?" Griswald spat contemptuously. "No leader would be stupid enough to slip up in front of the Captain of the Redpath in Carenthia and accidentally reveal their intentions to destroy what we stand for. No, you're a spy for this 'mastermind', and a pitiful one. High in the ranks if you know so much about industrialization, which is why you're worth pursuing, but not the leader. It doesn't take a genius to figure it out."

"Clearly."

Griswald chuckled softly, a deep rasp grating his throat that raised the hairs on Sadie's arms. "There you go again, bold as you please. You may think you're courageous, talking back to me like that, but you're only setting yourself up for disaster."

He drew a sword.

Sadie stumbled back and clipped the back of her knee on the edge of a bench. Her knee buckled and she toppled backwards, landing hard on her tailbone. She scuttled back a few more feet like a crab, trying to scramble away from Griswald's advancing sword tip—and bumped against the stage. She twisted to try and jump to her feet and run, but Griswald thrust the sword under her chin and tickled her throat with the tip.

Sadie froze, afraid to move, afraid to even breathe. The point pricked her skin and she knew any sudden movement or attempt to cry out would produce blood—or a severed head. Red torchlight drenched the blade like a promise of spilled blood.

"You know, I never did catch your name," said Griswald conversationally.

Sadie said nothing.

Griswald pressed the blade harder against her throat and this time Sadie felt a warm trickle down her neck.

"I'm sorry, I didn't catch that," he whispered.

"Sadie," she croaked. She could have lied, could have made up a name, but fear clouded her brain.

"Was it worth it, Sadie?" Griswald asked. "Was it worth talking back to your enemies? Was it worth serving someone afraid of change? Was it worth dying for?"

With each word Griswald used the sword to turn her body back toward him, making sure she was trapped between him and the stage.

The icy fear in her stomach melted with the heat of indignation, and at its core she could feel a ball of fire growing steadily, feeding on her anger. What gave him the right to play with his captors and storm into an inn at night just to find a girl who had talked back to him? It didn't matter if he thought she was a spy. Where was his proof? She was innocent!

"The game is over now, Miss Sheldon," growled Griswald. "You will come with me where I *will* extract information from you by whatever means I must. If you survive I might let you go—but more likely you will die."

Sadie's anger flared beyond control, not because he threatened torture or promised death, but because he knew her last name. She had never told him her last name.

Which meant somebody else had. He had feigned ignorance for the pleasure of making her squirm.

Flames danced on Griswald's sleeve.

She had no idea how she did it yet knew somehow she had.

Waving his arm, he batted at the flames with his hand. His wild gesticulating ignited the stage curtains. The flames spread rapidly.

Taking advantage of Griswald's distracted state, Sadie dashed for the doors. She pulled one open as Griswald's torch dropped from his slackened grip. Flames licked the dry wooden planks greedily. Griswald's deafening bellows were bound to wake the whole inn, and the other Redpath members would come running to their captain's aid. She had precious little time if she hoped to escape.

Tearing her gaze away from the fire, Sadie sprinted into the cool night air. Her vision blurred as she ran alongside the inn to the stables diagonally behind it, heart thundering in her chest as she noticed the hulking shadows lurking outside.

The Redpath soldiers had not noticed her yet. She could hear them conversing in low voices but couldn't catch what they were saying. Had they abandoned their posts by the rear staircase to investigate the source of the screams and flames? Did that mean Tristan, Haldin, and Airothane had been able to escape and might already be in the stables?

The piercing screams rising above the roaring flames no longer belonged to Griswald. Nausea assailed Sadie's stomach at the thought of innocent guests trapped by the flames licking the shutters and windows and tasting the night air through billows of pewter smoke. People staggered out the front doors now, coughing and spluttering, but the screams intensified. Sadie twisted her fingers, forgetting her fear and anger as anxiety and guilt pummelled her stomach. Endangering hardened warriors like Tristan and Haldin just because they knew her was bad enough, but she couldn't bear endangering innocent bystanders who didn't know their suffering was because of her.

Making up her mind, Sadie sprinted back through the open front doors, throwing her arms up to shield her eyes from the smoke. Griswald was no longer in the common room. Flames erupted around her, but she found a path to the stairs and raced up them two at a time. Smoke hung thickly in the air on the second floor, blurring the guests being ushered down the stairs by Phil.

Haldin and Tristan hammered on doors or barrelled through them, helping people to the stairs and making sure no one was left behind. Airothane pounded on doors with his tiny fists, trying to help, but mostly people ignored him. Sadie didn't know why they were still in the inn, but their efforts to help hardened her own resolve.

Phil spotted Sadie standing at the top of the stairs. "You shouldn't be here!" he yelled, frantically shooing her away. "It's too dangerous! Go downstairs and get out of this inn before it's too late!"

"I want to help," said Sadie resolutely, standing her ground.

Sweat poured off Phil's round face, a leak even his apron couldn't stem. "Please Miss Sheldon, there's no need to panic, just turn around now—"

"I'm not panicking!" Sadie shouted. "I'm not leaving until everyone's safely out of this building."

"Sadie!" shouted Tristan hoarsely, hearing her voice. "Sadie, get outside—"

"No!"

Tristan paused, assessing her determination. "Fine, stay, but make yourself useful. Persuade these people to get down the stairs, they're scared of the fire below."

"Can't we use the back stairs too?" Sadie asked.

"We tried, but they've been barricaded…" Tristan trailed off, glancing at Phil, but he didn't have to finish. Sadie guessed the Redpath soldiers they had seen sneaking to the back doors had been instructed to barricade them so Sadie couldn't escape that way, forcing her to use the front doors and run into Griswald.

Sadie started pleading with people, pointing out she had just come up that way and was unscathed. Slowly the guests disappeared down the stairs, clutching the railings with white knuckles.

"Haldin get Airothane out of here!" ordered Tristan. "There's only a few left now, we can handle them!"

"I'm not scared, I can help!" Airothane said but Haldin scooped him up and hurtled down the weakening stairs as flames leapt to life on their floor now. Only two guests remained, and their hysterical shrieks mingled with tears, certain of their imminent death.

"Phil, go with them and get yourself out of this inn!" shouted Tristan. "Sadie and I will be right behind you."

Phil and the women were halfway down the stairs when a desperate shriek emanated from the bedroom at the end of the hall—Tristan and Sadie's room. Phil paused, but Tristan shouted, "Go Phil, we'll handle this!"

"Someone's trapped in there!" Sadie yelled in horror.

"But those were our rooms!"

"Maybe someone hid in there when the fire started!"

"But I triple-checked every room, there's no way—"

"Tristan, we must check! We must make sure!"

A thunderous crash boomed, and they spun around to find a stair railing had collapsed in a wall of flames.

The voice shrieked again.

"I'm going," Sadie told Tristan firmly, and she sprinted to the last door.

"Sadie, *no*!"

A staggering roar rattled the doorknobs as a wall of fire burst up through the floor right in the centre of the corridor, cutting Sadie off from Tristan and the stairs. She was trapped.

"NO!" The distress and terror in his voice embedded her own panic.

"Oh no, oh no, oh god, I don't want to die!" Sadie screamed as the flames roared and exploded in a shower of sparks. Heat blazed against her face, so hot she thought her skin would burn without the fire ever having to touch her.

"Don't panic, Sadie, you're not going to die!" Calm injected Tristan's voice again. "There must be a way out of there, we just have to think."

A narrow beam crashed to the floor on Tristan's side, wreathed in flame. He just managed to dodge it before it hit the floor, punching a splintered hole in the boards.

"You have to get out of here, it's too dangerous!" shouted Sadie through her tears.

"I'm not going to leave you there!"

"You have no choice!" Sadie spluttered, coughing. "There's no way out—AHHHHH!"

"*Sadie!*"

A figure hurtled out of the door behind her and pulled something rough and coarse over her head. Clawing at it frantically like a cat, Sadie tugged and pulled desperately at what she thought must be a sack, but her assassin held it in place, tightening it around her throat like a noose. Darkness assaulted her senses and her lungs rattled as she tried to gulp air down her constricted throat... she screamed, but it was muffled by the sack... she aimed a kick at her captor, but they held her at arm's length... she was running out of air and her fierce struggling consumed all her energy...

"Let go of her," Tristan demanded coldly.

"Cute, but we both know that knife is no threat to me," growled her captor. "Whether I kill her, or you do when I use her as a shield, either way she'll still die."

Sadie knew that voice.

Griswald.

Sadie gasped, desperately drinking in the remaining tiny pockets of air. As her vision became hazy, Sadie's anger flared up again. This was the second time she had come close to dying tonight at the hands of Griswald and she would not go this way, she would not let him kill her over nothing.

Using all her weight, she hurled herself backwards and stamped on his foot as hard as she could. His grip broke. In one swift motion Sadie flung the sack off her head and leapt through the fire, landing safely on the other side next to Tristan.

The fire hadn't even touched her. She was not burned, not even singed. It had felt more like a warm breeze.

Tristan gaped at her. For a second they stood there, Tristan marvelling at Sadie's unscathed body, Sadie filling her lungs with smoky air then coughing it out again. A deafening crumble erupted behind them and the floor where the wall of fire had flared collapsed, creating a chasm in the hallway too wide to jump across, Griswald now trapped as well.

"I think that's our cue to leave," said Sadie, and together they bounded down the stairs, leaving Griswald to his fate. As they reached the bottom, the steps completely collapsed.

Tristan grabbed her arm, pulling her away from the falling debris and across the common room. Bursting through the doorway now wreathed in flame, they staggered and stumbled out into the cool night air. Sadie inhaled deeply, drinking in the fresh air thirstily, then sank to her knees, unleashing a chain of hacking coughs as she rid her lungs of smoke.

"Are-you-all-right?" Tristan gasped breathlessly.

Sadie nodded, unable to form words.

"Tristan! Sadie!" Haldin shouted in relief. "You're alive!"

"'Course we're alive," Tristan replied. "It'd take more than a fire to kill us. You can't be rid of me that easily."

Haldin chuckled, an unnatural sound amidst the crying cloaking the air. Forcing herself to her feet, she surveyed the scene with horror.

A huge crowd had gathered around the inn, keeping a safe distance back. Guests and staff stood among folk from other inns and nearby houses who had seen the fire and heard the screams and came to investigate. Most still wore their nightgowns and bedclothes. When Sadie and Tristan, the last two guests of the inn, had emerged from the burning building some had cheered, but most seemed too shocked to speak. Sadie imagined they also felt like their nightmares had escaped their dreams to rattle reality.

She watched numbly as spouses clung to one another, sobbing children clung to parents, and families looked in horrified awe at the burning inn, now consumed by flames. An incredible guilt washed over her, drenching her fiery anger until her throat constricted and eyes watered.

It was her fault. People could have died in that fire, and it would have been because of her. She hadn't *meant* for a flame to issue from her, had acted in self-defence, but it didn't change the fact Griswald and the Redpath soldiers had come to the Crowned Sun Inn because of her.

And then Sadie spotted Phil and his wife, Muriel. They stood a little apart from everyone else, staring at their destroyed inn. Phil had his arm around his wife who shook shamelessly with loud sobs, as he stood there silently, eyes popping and mouth open. His whole life was ruined. The inn had been his business, his career. His home. And now it was gone, a pile of ashes in place of memories. What had she *done*?

Tears streamed down her face.

Sadie had never felt less like a hero.

"Sadie, we have to leave now," Tristan whispered gently. "The stables have been emptied, someone opened the stalls so the horses could run from the fire, so we have no horses, but we cannot linger and wait for them to come back. We'll need to walk."

A part of her brain dimly understood the imperative haste of their departure. It was too dangerous to stay. Everything was always too dangerous. She had to move. But she could not tear her eyes away from the fire.

Tristan turned her around, breaking her eye contact, and pulled her away from the crowd. Letting him lead her, Sadie trotted numbly in his wake, Haldin and Airothane alongside them. Soon the roar of the fire faded into the background, a distant hum as they hurried through a maze of streets, vanishing into the night. Her exhausted limbs lagged, begging for more sleep, but she didn't care. She never wanted to sleep again. She wanted to run and keep running, forever away, away...

She had to get as far from that fire as possible, away from her intolerable guilt.

The city gates were closed for the night, but Tristan remained calm and strolled up to one of the guards.

"Evening, Alessia," Tristan greeted the taller guard.

"Evening, Tristan," answered Alessia. "I heard the rumours a Storyteller was in Carenthia, but I wasn't sure if it was you. Leaving us so soon?"

"I wanted to stay until morning, but I received word from my godfather that he needs me to meet an associate of his sooner, so here I am. I was hoping for a few more hours of sleep, but duty calls."

Alessia chuckled bitterly. "I know what that's like. No one could ever accuse you of not being dutiful. Hope you catch a break soon, and that your meeting isn't far, if you're travelling on foot."

She frowned, suspicion starting to creep into her narrowing eyes, but Tristan shrugged and replied, "Phil was supposed to get us horses in the morning, but he didn't have enough ready now. It's all right, it's not far, and we don't mind walking."

Alessia's gaze lingered a little on Airothane's tiny legs, but she gestured to the other guard to open the gates and soon they had passed through, crossing into a blacker world. Wisps of cloud mingled with smoke choked the stars, the moon cowered behind a cloud, and Sadie couldn't discern between the shadows haunting her mind and lurking in the darkness.

A History Lesson

Amber light danced across the obituary in his hand, the crackling flames concordant with the crackling of the ancient newspapers and handwritten notes he rifled through. Though his armchair was cozy and the fireplace's glow created a warm ambience, Connor drew no comfort from them. He had read every paper from the stack of Sheldon death records on the circular oak table beside his chair, but there was no mention of Thomas Sheldon. No hint of his passing or fate. Connor knew Thomas had fallen out of favour and had been cast out of the family, viewed with shame and contempt by his descendants, but the merciless erasure of his existence chilled him.

What had he done to warrant such mutiny from his family? Was it just because he had dared to write a fantastical book? Had his family really been that derisive of his eccentricities? Sadie had been eccentric. Sadie had believed in fairy tales. Would the Sheldons try to erase her from history too?

I won't let them, Connor resolved. He had failed his sister in life. He would not fail her memory.

His father thought he lacked the strength needed to carry on the family business, and maybe he was right. Most of the time he didn't feel like he had the strength or courage to stomach the bureaucratic necessities of a businessman. But he would need a different kind of strength to protect Sadie's legacy. Maybe he could summon the courage to find it.

"Find what you were looking for?" came his father's voice from the doorway of the library's main entrance.

"No," Connor replied, pinching the bridge of his nose. He had asked his father where he might find the Sheldon family obituaries and death papers, though had not said why he needed them.

Roger sat in an armchair across from him and studied the flames flickering beneath the Sheldon family crest emblazoned on the marble fireplace where a mantle would normally be, face unreadable. His freshly pressed suit didn't even wrinkle as he tucked one leg under the other, and the sight of this high-class perfection grated Connor into speech.

"Do you know what happened to Thomas Sheldon, Father? Does anyone? Or did he vanish one day and no one cared to discover his fate, as long as he wasn't around to sully the Sheldon name?"

Roger released a long, rueful sigh as he leaned forward. "Connor, I'll be honest. I never gave Thomas Sheldon much thought. He was my grandfather, but when my father told me he had failed to uphold the standards of the Sheldon name and had been shunned, I accepted that and didn't think to probe further. I trusted my father. I'm starting to see now how wrong that was. I think Sadie saw it too. I never quite understood her interest in Thomas, but I've been thinking about it a lot since her death, and I think I see now why she became so invested in his mystery. She felt estranged from her own family, like she didn't belong, and maybe—like you—she felt that learning more about him would revive his place in Sheldon family history. Maybe she could avoid the same fate."

Connor almost dropped the obituary in his hand. Maybe he had underestimated his father.

"All I know for sure about Thomas is that he was last seen in the Sheldon household shortly after I was born. It was Thomas who built this house, you know. He left it to my father after it became clear he was no longer respected among his own family. He moved to the city, taking up residence on the outskirts somewhere; I think I heard my father mention a cabin at some point. After Sadie's death, I did a little digging. I found this letter in some documents my father left to me. After you asked about the Sheldon family death records, I thought you might want to see it."

Roger handed Connor a folded letter from his inside jacket pocket.

Dated in June of 1886, the letter read:

> *We regret to inform you that your relative Thomas Sheldon has been counted among those presumed dead in the Great Fire. His property has burned down, and he was reported missing with no trace of a body.*

Connor stopped reading, staring at the innocently swaying flames in the fireplace. The Great Fire. What a tragic way to die. Probably alone, with not even a body to mourn. The fire had happened a decade before Connor was born, but everyone knew how it had devastated the city of Vancouver.

"I'm sorry, Connor," whispered Roger solemnly. "He was your great-grandfather. I know you didn't know him, but this can't be easy to hear."

Connor dented the letter between the tight pinch of his fingers.

"Thank you for showing this to me, Father."

A bell trilled as he entered the little bookstore and closed the faded chestnut door behind him, shutting out the cacophony of city bustle. The smell of parchment and leather assaulted his nose, and Connor turned to make a snide remark about Sadie getting intoxicated off the fumes if she breathed too deeply—but Sadie wasn't beside him. Pushing down the tide of grief threatening to engulf him, Connor forced himself to return the shopkeeper's greeting as he passed the checkout counter and continued into the stacks.

Memories of Sadie prodded his mind, vying for attention as he trailed his finger along the books' spines, scanning the titles for any vague mention of recent Vancouver history or the Great Vancouver Fire. He doubted such a book even existed, but he couldn't get the fire out of his head and craved more information. Far too many pieces of the Thomas Sheldon puzzle were still missing, and he owed it to Sadie to continue her research and revive Thomas' story in their Sheldon family history.

Sheldon.

Connor froze mid-step and did a double take. There, two books before the spine his finger hovered over, was the name Sheldon. *Thomas* Sheldon.

Blinking rapidly, Connor pinched his arm to make sure he hadn't slipped into one of his grief-induced hallucinations. But the gold lettering was unmistakable against the burgundy leather cover: *Adventures in Carmelle.*

How could there be another copy in a bookstore? Connor had been under the impression the copy in the Sheldon library was the only printed copy. Something Thomas had spent money to print as a keepsake.

Cradling it as though the book might crumble to dust in his hands if he blinked at it wrong, Connor opened Thomas' book and found a handwritten inscription on the inside front cover:

Pierre,

This is the book we discussed. I'm afraid it's much more whimsical and fanciful than the Curie standard of scientific matter we usually discuss, but I hope you enjoy it all the same. Pay par-

ticularly close attention to the section on the Land of Crystals!
I think you'll find it of interest.

Sincerely,
Thomas

As Connor fiddled with the pages, wracking his brain for why he knew the name Pierre Curie, a thick wad of paper slipped out and fluttered to the floor. A newspaper clipping from the Daily News dated June 17, 1886.

Connor's heart accelerated and his lungs forgot to expand as he licked his suddenly dry lips.

With two words, the headline ensnared him: THE FIRE.

As he devoured the article like an insatiable wildfire, his eyes alighted on one line:

"It was about two o'clock in the afternoon that the breeze which had been blowing from the west BECAME A GALE, and flames surrounded a cabin near a large dwelling to the west of the part of the city solidly built up."

His father had mentioned something about Thomas living in a Vancouver cabin after moving out of the Sheldon mansion... Could this cabin have been Thomas'?

The hairs on Connor's forearms raised as his brain worked furiously. It was certainly possible the cabin at the heart of the fire had been Thomas'. After all, they never found a body, which suggested he had been so close to the inferno he had burned to ashes. But if so...

One thing he had learned since Sadie's death was the version of history that gets told is subjective and selective. What *doesn't* get told is no less important. It seemed an uncanny coincidence Thomas Sheldon had perished soon after his book started garnering more attention from embarrassed family members, scientists, and whoever else Thomas had decided to share it with... and Sadie had died soon after reading Thomas' book while probing for information and answers. Could the two deaths be linked?

And if so...

Would he be the next one to die by association with Thomas Sheldon and Carmelle?

Slamming too much money down on the counter but not pausing to stop for change, Connor tucked this copy of *Adventures in Carmelle* complete with the newspaper clipping in his coat and hurried down the street towards the post office.

He needed to send a telegram.

Chapter Fifteen

A Shadow in the Night

A silvery morning glow glistened on the rampaging rapids of the Tolonení running beside Sadie, sparkling against the bubbles of morning dew clinging to the blades of grass beneath her tired feet. Far in the distance, the tall spires of Nethilya flashed like flint sparking fire, but the palace would soon be out of sight. Sadie would miss Nethilya and the beautiful Tolotanteau, but her relief at leaving behind the guilt now tainting Carenthia for her outweighed the loss.

Exhaustion consumed her as they fled Carenthia, but they couldn't rest yet if they wanted to escape the Redpath. Tristan explained their imperative need for haste to Haldin and Airothane as they trudged on.

"I still don't understand why they attacked the inn," Haldin admitted.

"Frankly I don't either," agreed Tristan. "I'm surprised they went to so much trouble to find one insignificant girl."

"He thought I was a spy," said Sadie with a sigh.

They stopped walking. "A spy?" Tristan repeated.

Sadie nodded, head downcast.

"Right, this will obviously take time to explain," said Tristan. "Let's stop to rest our legs while we discuss it."

Sadie didn't really want to talk about it, but her thighs screamed to sit, so she plopped down without complaint. She told them about Griswald trapping her in the common room, how he accused her of being a spy and demanded to know who she worked for. She told them he used his sword to force her to comply and showed them the scab on her throat… and how she had been betrayed. Griswald had known her name.

Tristan's eyes glinted like a sharpened sword and a muscle spasm throbbed beneath his clenched jaw, but he remained silent.

"At least Griswald is gone now," Sadie pointed out, her voice hollow. "There's no way he could have escaped that fire."

"Yes, but that does not better our position much." Tristan sighed.

"What do you mean?" asked Haldin. "Surely with Griswald gone the Redpath will no longer be after you."

"Quite the contrary, actually," said Airothane unexpectedly. "The Redpath will think Sadie's at fault for killing their captain even if they started the fire with their torches. They're going to pursue her with more anger than ever."

Sadie winced.

"He's right," Tristan agreed. "The Redpath will want revenge. Sadie and her travelling companions are in danger."

Nausea assailed her swooping stomach, and Sadie pressed a hand against her pounding heart as a thought occurred to her. What if the Redpath pursuing her meant *anyone* associated with her was in danger, including her family on Earth? If she tried to open a portal and the Redpath members followed her, would her family be in danger as well?

Maybe finding a portal without help wasn't a great idea right now.

"I'm surprised they're not already pursuing us," Sadie admitted. She didn't point out she had inadvertently started the fire.

"They wouldn't be yet," said Airothane. "They'll want a proper burial for their former captain and then they'll have to pick out a new leader before setting out after us."

"Airothane's right again," said Tristan. "The Redpath value ceremonial processions and honour and glory. I have no doubt they will honour

Griswald with a funeral pyre. Whether they wait to consult Hargrim, the head of the Redpath organization, or set off collectively without a new captain depends on how angry they are about Griswald's death. From what I've heard, Griswald was admired by his contingent, so it's my guess they will pursue once the necessary funeral ceremonies are observed. We'll likely only have a day or two head-start over the Redpath."

Haldin and Airothane's clenched jaws and hollow eyes looked grim, but Sadie's guilt superseded her concern for personal safety. She couldn't stop thinking about Phil and his wife. Had they slept last night or simply stood there until the fire died down and the smoke cleared, revealing the heap of ashes and scattered fragments of their home? Were they sorting through the wreckage, pausing to pick up the remains of a favourite ornament or a charred scrap of the stage curtains where it had all started? Was Muriel still crying? Had Phil spoken yet? Did they too believe it was the Redpath's fault? Would they ever know?

"I wonder how Phil's doing," whispered Sadie.

"He loved that inn like a child," said Tristan. "He pampered it like one too."

"It was a beautiful inn," added Airothane solemnly as though he had seen many different inns in his short life.

"Phil is such a generous man," said Haldin, shaking his head. "It pains me to see him lose something so dear to him."

"I feel so guilty," Sadie confessed. Immediately she felt Tristan's eyes bore into her skull.

"You know it wasn't your fault, Sadie," Tristan stated firmly. "I know they came to the inn looking for you, but you were innocent. You're not a spy—and you did not start that fire."

Oh yes I did, Sadie thought despairingly.

When Sadie didn't answer him, Tristan persisted. "I know you feel responsible for Phil's loss, but buildings can be replaced. The Crowned

Sun was a prosperous inn; Phil has the money to rebuild. I'm sure he's just grateful no guests were hurt and nothing irreplaceable was lost."

"Except memories," muttered Sadie.

"The memories aren't lost, they're still imprinted in the minds of Phil and Muriel for them to peruse when nostalgia strikes," said Haldin.

"It wasn't your fault," Tristan repeated softly.

"I can still feel guilty about it," protested Sadie.

Tristan sighed. "I suppose that's natural. Just do me a favour and don't dwell on your guilt too much. What you should be more worried about is what will happen if the Redpath catch us. Now *there's* a depressing thought."

"You always know how to bring someone down further!" Haldin laughed, slapping Tristan genially on the back.

The sun's first rays illuminated the land with a weak light, chasing away the grey. As they prepared for the day's journey, Tristan led Sadie away from the others for a bit of privacy.

"Are you all right?" he whispered. "You've been so quiet."

Sadie didn't answer, looking at her toes.

"Please don't tell me you truly blame yourself for what happened. It was an *accident*, Sadie," he insisted. "It could have happened even if the Redpath hadn't come looking for you. Fire is a dangerous thing."

"You're telling me," Sadie muttered. Tristan arched an eyebrow. She'd have to tell him.

"Tristan, I—I started the fire."

"How many times do I have to tell you the fire wasn't your fault!"

"*No.* I literally started it. It was not because of a torch. Well, the torch probably exacerbated it when it fell from Griswald's hand, but... it was me who started the fire. I lost control, I didn't know what I was doing, it just happened! I was angry and desperate. He was going to kill me! Torture me and kill me!"

Lowering her panicked high-pitched voice, Sadie recounted her indignation at being betrayed and cornered, and how a flame had shot out of her and alighted on Griswald's sleeve, which then spread to the curtains.

"I still don't know how it happened," Sadie finished. "I don't even remember thinking about fire. It just... appeared."

She chanced a glance at Tristan. He tugged on his nose, clearly deep in thought. After a moment he said, "You know what this means, don't you?"

Sadie nodded, caught in the whirlpool of doubt and disappointment swirling in her stomach. "Yes. It means I really do have magic."

"That's how you jumped through the fire without being burned," mused Tristan. "I had been wondering."

"Yes, I suppose it was," acknowledged Sadie irritably, thinking the point irrelevant. "But don't you see what a problem this is? The first time I used my magic I burned down a building, endangering dozens of lives!"

"So your magic is as temperamental as its mistress," joked Tristan, lips quirking.

"That's not funny!"

"I beg to differ."

"Can we please be serious here?" she hissed, fully aware of Haldin and Airothane standing just out of earshot. "The first time I used it my magic caused significant damage! I wasn't a hero. I wasn't even a villain. I had no control, just like at home."

"I'm sure if you asked any wizard they'd say the same about their first experiences. Don't blame yourself so much. Think why you did magic in the first place. Think of the results."

"An incinerated inn and a dead man," summed up Sadie. "Yes you're right, those were positive results."

"No, Sadie. The first time you used magic, it saved you."

Cold seeped through Sadie's veins like the shaky chill after a fever. The hairs on the back of her neck and forearms prickled.

She had always wanted magic to save her life.

So why did she feel uneasy instead of thrilled?

Though she would have to deal with her magical abilities sooner or later, Sadie hoped to put it off until later—like when they reached Caris Nando and Alldían. She both feared what her magic might inadvertently do and didn't want to share this secret with Haldin and Airothane until she understood it better herself. She respected Haldin, but Airothane she found annoying.

The kid had an opinion about everything. All subjects warranted a remark, from a king's running of their city and the serious flaws of the Redpath, to what route they should take and when they should rest. He seemed to enjoy imposing his opinion on Sadie mostly, following her everywhere and rambling in her ear, oblivious to Sadie's clenched fists. Most kids didn't speak with such superiority or expansive diction, talking down to her like *she* was the eleven-year-old.

"Why don't you go talk to your brother or Tristan for a change?" Sadie asked him after several long hours of his endless babble. She tried to exude politeness through gritted teeth.

"I don't want to," he shrugged.

"*I* want you to."

"Why? Are you incapable of intelligent speech?"

"I'm far more intelligent than you!" retorted Sadie childishly.

Airothane folded his scrawny arms across his chest and raised his eyebrows. "Prove it."

Sadie faltered for a moment, then spat, "I don't need to prove anything to you."

"In other words, you are incapable of accepting my challenge," confirmed Airothane. "But just because I'm smarter than you, doesn't mean we can't talk."

"*We're* not talking!" Sadie shouted. "*You* are! And I'm sick of it. Leave me alone!"

But of course, Airothane did nothing of the sort and Sadie continued to stomp along dejectedly, her face burning with embarrassment as Tristan and Haldin tried to hide their chuckles.

Haldin, however, had many fascinating stories about Dharmaelia and its customs. He spoke of the heroic deeds of his forefathers, the endless battles with the foul creatures of Zorlomin and the King's grand mead hall.

"I have so many fond memories of the mead hall," Haldin reminisced. "It is the custom of our people to feast and celebrate there after a victory abroad. The golden goblet is passed around to the brave soldiers of Dharmaelia. These days it is kept at hand instead of locked away as of old, for the battles are so close together there is scarcely time to put it away before the next victory is nigh. In Dharmaelia, a soldier's life is a hard one full of death and evils, but it all seems worth it in the mead hall when you are celebrating with your dearest friends. There's nothing better than good friends and a good mug of mead."

"Haldin's being modest again, of course," piped up Airothane who trotted in the wake of his brother's long strides. "He never gives himself enough credit, always pretending everyone did just as much as he in battle. But my brother's a hero to his people. Haldin the Hawk they call him at home, Wielder of Ilígon, Slasher, the double-bladed axe."

Sadie glanced at the axe poking over Haldin's shoulder. Carefully crafted by a skilled blacksmith, the two massive blades boasted edges sharpened to a fine tip. The face of each blade bore the same symbol emblazoned into Haldin's armour: an eagle with its wings spread wide as if about to take flight. Strange symbols marked the haft of the axe.

"Even the mention of his nickname or his weapon will strike fear in enemies' hearts," continued Airothane dramatically. "He's referred to as the Hawk because of the way he rides his horse like the wind, blowing his enemies about like leaves in a high gale as he descends upon them with his axe like talons. His hawk-eyes can spot an enemy miles away or hone in on them amidst the chaos of battle. Once he identifies them as prey, nobody stands a chance. They would have to betray or deceive him to defeat him."

"Oh, Airothane, don't exaggerate so much," Haldin reprimanded. "I can be killed in battle like everyone else. I'm not even the greatest warrior in Dharmaelia, let alone a hero. I am lucky to have survived as many battles as I have. Many of my friends who were no worse fighters than I have not. I am not immortal, Airothane, and it is unwise to suggest it. Only the Lantíés can make such a claim. You may be wise beyond your years, little brother, but you still have much to learn of life."

But despite Haldin's modesty, Sadie's respect and reverence for him couldn't help but increase. Airothane might tend toward the dramatic and theatrical, but his hyperboles were rooted in truth. Maybe Haldin wasn't quite the warrior Airothane claimed, but his people—and his brother—obviously regarded him as a hero.

"Is that the sigil of Dharmaelia?" Sadie asked, indicating both his axe and armour.

"Yes," Haldin replied proudly. "The eagle is the animal of our people. Our flag is a bronze eagle on a burgundy field. They often fly over our lands and warn us of approaching enemies. They're magnificent creatures, majestic and noble."

A wistful look clouded Haldin's eyes. "It is the greatest wish of my people to fly like an eagle." Sadie noticed the same dreamy expression entrance Airothane. Closing her eyes, Sadie imagined herself soaring over vast plains and mountains and rivers with the wind in her hair and the land steadily shrinking below. Her grin stretched wider than Airothane's.

On the first night out from Carenthia, Haldin took first watch to give Sadie and Tristan much needed rest. But Sadie couldn't sleep. She tossed and turned, visions of fiery inns and flaming Griswalds dancing to the tune of bloodcurdling shrieks in the darkness. On the second night, though her eyes itched with tiredness, she volunteered for watch duty. She could at least make herself useful if she wasn't going to sleep.

Perched on the grassy ledge of the Tolonení, she let the sights, sounds and feelings of nature infiltrate her mind. A chorus of crickets struck up a melody nearby, and overhead a disgruntled owl trilled a series of spontaneous hoots. The stars hid behind an opaque veil of clouds. A cool breeze fluttered her hair and she drew her cloak closer. Legs hanging over the ledge, Sadie let the icy numbness of the river mask the pain of her sore, tired feet.

When she could no longer feel her feet, Sadie deemed it time to pry them from the river's icy clutches. As she laced up her boots, movement flickered in the trees bordering the bank. Stiffening, she kept still as she stared into the trees. Just as she started thinking her imagination played tricks on her, a twig snapped. Before she had time to react, the figure of a tall man cloaked in black emerged, stepping out from behind a tree.

Crying out in alarm, Sadie jumped to her feet and shook her companions awake.

"Tristan, Haldin, Airothane, everyone get up, *get* up!" she shouted desperately. "Somebody's here!"

Tristan sprung to his feet at her cry as if he had never been asleep. Haldin and Airothane were quick to follow.

"Where Sadie, where?" shouted Tristan, eyes darting in every direction.

"There in the trees! Can't you see that—that..."

But she trailed off. The figure had vanished.

"It was here a second ago, I swear!"

Haldin frowned. "What was it?"

"A man," replied Sadie confidently. "A tall man with a long black cloak. He had his hood up; I couldn't see his face."

The grim concern in Tristan's eyes told Sadie he believed her. She would never be able to explain to him how much his instant belief in her meant. Even Connor hadn't always believed her words without question. The warmth and security of having someone truly on your side was a new feeling for her, and even her fear of the hooded figure could not pop the affectionate bubble of gratitude swelling in her chest.

Scanning the trees again, he said, "It looks like someone found us. We are being followed."

Setting her lips in a grim, determined line, Sadie glared a challenge at the trees. If the Redpath had found them, she would not let them endanger her friends again.

Chapter Sixteen

The Skeletal Moon

"What's that?" asked Airothane as a cool wind from the north ruffled his hair.

"What's what?" Sadie asked.

"It sounded like laughter." Airothane's eyes glazed over. "There are people ahead. Many miles still lie between us, but they are there."

"You're making it up," Sadie said exasperatedly.

"Actually, Airothane's right," Tristan chimed in. "We're close to Steepleton, a town in the sparsely populated region of Belland, known for the bells tolling in the steeples built by William Steepleton. I would imagine we will reach the first settlements by nightfall."

"Being good at geography doesn't mean he heard *laughter*," muttered Sadie.

"I also have exceptional hearing," bragged Airothane.

Sadie glowered at him.

"I want to get as close to the Dharlomin as possible tonight so we can find the mountain pass quickly tomorrow morning," said Tristan as he led the way along the Ilítanení, ignoring Sadie and Airothane's spat. "If all goes well, we'll be in Caris Nando in a few days' time."

Caris Nando. Sadie's stomach clenched and her heart accelerated. If Alldían offered her the opportunity to return home, would she take it?

Before coming to Carmelle, Sadie's desires had seemed so clear. They had defined shapes and labels. But Carmelle and the separation from her brother had muddled everything. The identifiable geometry of wants had unravelled, tangling into frayed webs she didn't recognize. She craved the adventures awaiting her in Carmelle, and though she feared the destruction her magic could cause, she still longed for it with a deep desire that hummed and smouldered in her veins. But she also wanted to break through the barrier erected between her and her brother; she loved the sense of belonging she found here, yet didn't want to abandon her brother. What did you do when you wanted two different paths so intensely at the same time? How do you proceed when you're the fulcrum of an existential dichotomy?

Sadie peered at the mountains looming above her, contemplating the glittering peach snow over roan red peaks as the sun began to set.

"How can the Dharlomin still have snow on them?" Sadie asked Tristan after a quick glance over her shoulder to ensure Haldin and Airothane still trailed behind out of earshot, immersed in their own conversation. "Or should I say how can they *already* have snow on them? After all, it's only—wait, what month are we in?"

"We are approaching the Autumn Equalizer, a time on Arwé when day and night become equal in length. If I recall Earth's months correctly, that would make it about halfway through September," Tristan informed her. "But the Dharlomin have snow on at least part of the mountains all year long. All mountains have their secrets."

Sadie mapped out the timeline in her head. She had first entered Carmelle at the end of July. Had she only been here for less than two months?

———— ❦ ————

They camped by the foot of the mountains in a small cave protecting them from torrential rain. Sitting by a fire, Sadie savoured the coziness of blazing flames warming her cold, tired muscles while rain hammered the ground outside. Thunder rumbled overhead, followed by a bolt of lightning illuminating every raindrop. All four companions turned to face the cave's entrance. Again, thunder clapped, and this time lightning illuminated a tall figure in a black hooded cloak, standing right outside the cave.

Sadie screamed.

Like lightning Tristan flashed to his feet, sword in hand. Haldin gripped his battle-axe with both hands.

"Show yourself, intruder!" Tristan demanded. "Or I'll gut you!"

Slowly the figure stepped into the firelight, an aura of power radiating from it.

"Don't be ridiculous, Tristan West!" the figure boomed, and they threw back their hood and cast off their cloak.

An older woman stood before them with long silver-laced white hair and mildly wrinkled dark brown skin. Lines of care intertwined with laughter lines branched from the corners of ice blue eyes. The front pieces of her waist-length hair were braided and tied back to keep the hair out of her face, and the high-collared ruby red mantle trimmed with gold she wore over robes the colour of her eyes framed her face.

"Tamlin!" Tristan exclaimed, and he sheathed his sword.

"*Who*?" Sadie asked, stunned Tristan knew this woman.

"Lane Tamlin," elaborated Tristan. "The oldest, wisest, and greatest wizard of this Age."

Sadie's mouth fell open.

"You forgot strong, ravishing, snarky, the light that eclipses the sun, a woman who loathes being ignored and who is certainly capable of introducing herself..." chided Tamlin.

Tristan's cheeks flushed the colour of nectarines.

"Put that axe away before somebody gets hurt—and it won't be me," Tamlin barked at Haldin. "And you!" she continued, turning to face Sadie. "Stop gaping at me, you look like a firefish!"

"B-but you're a wizard!" stammered Sadie. "Y-you can do magic!"

"You're a smart one," Tamlin commented dryly. "I can see why you keep her around, Tristan."

Sadie blushed scarlet, matching her dark red hair, and clamped her tongue between her teeth.

"What are you doing here?" Tristan asked Tamlin as she settled herself down cross-legged in the best spot by the fire.

"I had business to attend to in Carenthia. When I saw you there, I followed."

Tristan seemed satisfied with this explanation, but Sadie wasn't.

"If you're a friend of Tristan's, why didn't you present yourself to us sooner instead of following us?" she asked, anger lacing her voice. "Why frighten us and make us think we're in danger?"

"For amusement, naturally," said Tamlin without hesitation, "and because you could use a little scare to get you moving quicker. Most importantly because it gave me a chance to observe *you* without interference. The others I have met before or know of, but you are new to Carmelle, or I'm an ogre. And quite significant, unless my wisdom and magic have turned entirely to folly and wild fancies. You were not certain of me, but I was far less certain and a good deal more suspicious of you."

Turning to Tristan, she began inquiring after their adventures, leaving Sadie speechless.

Tristan told Tamlin they were in trouble with the Redpath because of Sadie. He gave no reason for why they had been in Carenthia, and to Sadie's relief Tamlin did not ask.

"Now we need to find a safe passage through the mountains to Caris Nando before the Redpath catch up," Tristan finished.

"Like any mountain range, the Dharlomin holds perils and hides secrets," said Tamlin, "but I know a path by Skeletal Moon Lake that will serve us well."

"Excellent!" exclaimed Airothane, an unsettling gleam of mischievous enthrallment glinting in his eyes.

Haldin's crestfallen face portrayed less enthusiasm, but he didn't dispute Tamlin's choice.

"Do I want to know why it's called *Skeletal* Moon Lake?" Sadie asked, looking from Airothane to Haldin.

"Oh, you'll find out," replied Tamlin rather ominously. "But that can wait until morning. Now is the time for sleep."

Tamlin did not lie down herself but watched and waited until the rest of them obeyed. Snuggled in her blanket by the warm embers of the fire, Sadie soon fell asleep.

Fog enveloped them the next morning, hanging low in the valley and shrouding the mountain in mystery. Sadie shivered and pulled the hood of her cloak up. Dark shapes loomed on all sides, resolving into boulders or tall trees when she drew level. The path became narrower and steadily steeper, and after many hours, the fog began to clear.

For the first half of the day, Sadie could concentrate on nothing but trying to control her laboured gasping and wheezing, and convincing her aching, fiery leg muscles to take one more step. Finally, as the sun began its descent, casting long black shadows on the rough cliff-faces behind them, Sadie's muscles adapted to the strenuous activity, and she fell into a steady albeit painful rhythm. They hugged the cliff-faces on their right as they climbed, avoiding proximity to the steep exposed cliff plummeting dizzily down on their left.

The sea of fog swirled among the trees below like eddies spiralling around sharp pillars of rock in the ocean. When the sky turned purple and the sun sank completely below the horizon line, Tamlin led them to a wider circular ledge with cliffs sheltering most of the circumference, and announced they would spend the night there. Sadie snagged the spot furthest from the edge and remained firmly planted there all night, hardly daring to sleep for fear she'd roll right over the cliff.

Deep purple and grey clouds returned in greater numbers the next morning, wreathing the mountain peaks like bruised crowns. Travelling in single file, the company started early and clambered along the steep path, occasionally slipping on loose pebbles. With each passing hour the path proved more perilous; chasms rent the rock and Sadie noted uneasily their unfathomable depths were lost in impenetrable blackness.

When they paused for a lunch break in the afternoon, Tamlin remained standing, gazing off to the west. Poised on the ledge of the path with the wind whipping her robes and white hair, she looked wise and venerable. Following her gaze, Sadie looked out at the rolling hills and flat plains separating the Dharlomin from Carenthia and the Ilítanení that joined with the Tolonení. She knew the Tolonení wound its way like a bejewelled ribbon to the Carenth-hild and the Tolotanteau beyond, but both were not visible from this distance.

Approaching her tentatively, Sadie asked in a breathless whisper, "What do you see?"

"A very inquisitive girl," Tamlin replied, glancing at her sideways. "But curiosity is not a crime if exercised with caution. I have good eyesight, but my eyes alone could not see as far as the Tolotanteau or Nethilya, for example, without an aid."

Sadie raised an eyebrow.

"I will show you," Tamlin decided, and she held up her right hand. A ring gleamed on her finger, a thick gold band branching into a nest of thinner gold bands in the centre. Nestled in this web of gold was a single pearl. To Sadie's surprise, Tamlin plucked the pearl from the ring as easily as if it had been attached by a frail spider's thread. Holding it aloft in her palm, Tamlin uttered a single word Sadie could not understand, but it elicited a strong tingling in her core. *Magic.* The pearl enlarged to the size of a crystal ball. Translucent with wispy silver smoke drifting across it, the delicate ball looked to be made of glass with only a hint of its old pearl sheen.

"Is that a crystal ball?" Sadie inquired in awe.

"No, at least not in the sense I imagine you're referring to, the kind that supposedly tells the future," said Tamlin with obvious contempt. "It is made of crystals found in Éaloth, but the magic is embedded in the crystal itself, and it's so rare only three exist in Carmelle. It is called an Avenéa, and it allows the beholder to see across great distances. It sees only what is right before it, like a magnifier. Only a wizard can control this powerful object. The stronger the wielder is with magic, the more detail they'll be able to see. If you lean closer and look through the Avenéa, I can direct the magic so you will see all that lies before us in closer detail."

Relief and disappointment vied for attention in Sadie's heart. The tension in her shoulders at having to reveal her powers and perform magic again melted away when Tamlin said she would direct it, but her shoulders slumped even further at not getting to discover her magical potential.

"I think I would like to see Nethilya," Sadie admitted.

Bending over the Avenéa, Sadie examined its depths. At first the view looked the same, but then the hills started moving rapidly beneath her as if she flew over them. Her chest swelled, a bubble of joy expanding until there was no room for fear or anxiety. She felt weightless, free, like an eagle soaring with the wind beneath its wings.

The Toloneni expanded beneath her as she glided over its swiftly flowing waters. Faster and faster the land sped by, until it came to a shuddering halt on the borders of Carenthia. The city sprawled before her with its bright houses, arenas, inns, and tents from the markets. At the mouth of the Tolonení stood the Ilíta-onon and Carenthonon, and beyond it the Carenth-hild and the vast Tolotanteau. Sadie even fancied she could make out a few waves.

Her breath hitched at the sight of Nethilya. Its turrets and towers shone like crystals and pearls once more, blinding against the dark sky.

Sadie sighed in content. "Just as beautiful as ever." Tearing her gaze away from Nethilya, she looked Tamlin in the eyes and said, "Thank you for showing this to me."

Tamlin waved away her thanks and continued her explanation of the Avenéa.

"The Avenéa helps with Elemental magic, as the crystal was grown from the earth," she continued. "It affects nature with only the smallest bit of magic applied. That's why it is both dangerous and highly useful." Lightning erupted out of the Avenéa and split a rock below, while a rainbow simultaneously arched from the Avenéa to paint the lands.

Sadie grinned.

An ear-splitting roar shook the mountains, accompanied by a bright flash of orange light from just below the ledge. On a rocky platform with moss dangling from its edges like a scraggly green beard was a dragon.

Sadie screamed.

The dragon did not even look up.

Green scales flashed, gold lightning crackling across its hide as it moved. Like the first dragon she had encountered, its underbelly was solid gold, as were its sharp talons. Its long neck boasted a red fringe and its eyes shone yellow. Crouched contentedly, it appeared to be sitting thoughtfully outside its doorstep.

"Why isn't the dragon trying to attack us?" Sadie whispered.

"It has no reason to," answered Tamlin. "We have done it no harm."

"So—so he doesn't know we're here?" Sadie asked, confused. "Even though I screamed?"

"Oh, he definitely knows we're here," Tamlin assured her with a small chuckle. "He is an old dragon of the ancient breed, and they are far smarter and more aware than most humans. But he is as good as dragons come. They're all the old strand in these mountains and have no desire to kill for the sake of killing. If we do him no harm, he has no reason to do us any. Ever since Vashi created his new breed of dragons, the old strand has become seriously misunderstood."

Watching a puff of smoke from its nostrils spiral into the cool alpine air like steam curling up from a hot mug of cocoa, Sadie reconsidered the dragon. Strength defined its powerful fore and hind legs, and an other-worldly beauty rippled across the emerald scales of its long thick neck as it tucked its head under an enormous wing.

When Tamlin and Sadie rejoined their companions, the group continued their ascent. The rocks became more jagged, and sinister shadows loomed as the sun set and twilight fell. An ebony cape cloaked the mountain's peak, a foreboding black summit swallowing the violet sky. Patches of snow dotted the path and roan red rock surrounding them, slippery and riddled with pockets of ice impossible to see in the waning light. The crunch of snow beneath her boots echoed in the still night air like breaking bones, and more than once Sadie had to seize the back of Tristan's pack as she slid and lost her balance, flailing.

"How far until Skeletal Moon Lake?" Sadie asked, trying to keep her voice steady as her foot slipped and an avalanche of pebbles cascaded into the yawning black maw below.

"Not far now," replied Tamlin, her voice light and cheerful. "About twenty minutes at this pace. The path will level out soon, we aren't going to the peak. There's a little mountain meadow nestled between peaks where the lake lies. We'll camp there for the night."

"And that's... safe?" Sadie couldn't stop herself from asking.

Tamlin chuckled softly. "With me it is."

When the path's steep incline flattened and they rounded the peak's shoulder, the full moon illuminated the alpine meadow and stole Sadie's breath. Patches of long silver grass swayed between ponds of snow. The perfectly circular frozen lake reflected the full moon, mirroring its pearly sheen, silver blots thinning into spindly webs, and speckled swaths of ivory.

An insatiable longing stole through Sadie, warming her blood and tugging at her core.

She had always been enamoured with the moon, but up here the pull magnified.

Became irresistible.

Heedless of her companions, Sadie glided over to the lake, eyes locked on its mirrored moon surface in fascination.

Red pebbles rimmed the lake, darker in the moonlight like clots of blood spilling from a greying corpse.

And jutting from beneath the thin layer of ice, grasping for the shore, was a hand.

The hand of a skeleton.

Shock gripped Sadie, holding her breath captive as she noticed bones protruding from the ice all along the lake's edge. Femurs tangled with broken feet, partial rib cages piled on pelvic bones, and half a skull leered up at her near her toes.

Behind her Airothane gasped, and for once, words failed him.

"What happened here?" Sadie whispered, her voice hoarse and throat dry.

"Dark magic," Tamlin replied, bringing up the rear and joining Sadie, Airothane, Tristan, and Haldin at the lake's edge. "Magic in Carmelle is based in four main Elements: Water, Earth, Air, and Fire. These are the good magics, the safe, predictable, and reliable magics that don't require additional sacrifices or harm because they are part of our inherited traits, of our evolution on Arwé. But there are some magics that cannot be wielded without suffering. Celestial magic—Moon, Stars, Void—used to be practised in Carmelle by some until it was banned by the Keepers for its brutality in the hands of those most tempted to harness its powers. Skeletal Moon Lake, once simply called Moon Lake, is the monument marking one of the darkest moments in magical history."

"Legend has it that Vashi practised Celestial magic exceedingly well, probably because he had no qualms sacrificing others for his own gains," said Tristan, taking up the tale. "Because of this lake's position and shape and the way it perfectly reflects the moon, it is the ideal location for harnessing Moon magic. With the help of some Armindís and other magic folk loyal to Vashi and interested in Celestial magic, they would capture innocent people and bring them here to kill them as a sacrifice to the Moon."

Sadie glanced up at the moon, its mysterious, entrancing beauty gnawing at her core. Why would the moon demand a sacrifice?

"When the Keepers discovered the atrocities Vashi and his followers had committed," added Tamlin, "they banned Celestial magic, believing it to be the dark side of Fire magic, as they are connected by light. Vashi was banned from Nirosula and stripped of his position as Keeper of Fire. They failed in capturing Vashi for his crimes, but they did put his followers on trial and found them guilty—and executed them. Some believe that is why the Dharlomin mountains are red, permanently stained with blood."

"The really creepy part," whispered Airothane, his eyes glued to the bones jutting out around the circumference of the lake like a crown of thorns, "is that because the lake is frozen for most of the year, the bodies have preserved much longer than is natural. During the brief few weeks at the peak of summer when the lake thaws, you can see the full mass of skeletons, and it's said some even still have flesh clinging to the bones."

Sadie took a hasty step back from the lake.

"Why were the bodies never buried once the Keepers discovered the carnage?" Sadie asked. "Why just leave them there?"

"Probably fear," answered Tamlin, but her furrowed brows held disturbed disapproval. "Fear of the unknown, of what repercussions might result from tampering with the sacrifices of Celestial magic. I also think the Keepers liked the idea of preserving the evident repercussions of wielding Celestial magic, as a reminder to those who might be tempted to try using it despite the ban."

All five of them gazed morosely at the lake in silence for a minute before Tamlin announced, "No use just standing here staring at it! Let's set up camp on that grassy patch sheltered by the peak."

But while Haldin and Airothane dropped quickly into a deep slumber accompanied by thunderous snores, Sadie remained wide awake, drinking in the pale silver moonlight. She felt like she needed to suppress her fascination with the moon—now she had been made aware of the dark, forbidden magics associated with it—but this need to control her impulses and rein in her heart's desire was too close to what she loathed about her life on Earth and her mother's unreasonable demands of her, and she couldn't help but resent it. She hadn't escaped one prison only to be trapped in another!

Too restless to stay still, Sadie rose silently and crept toward the lake.

"Sadie?" whispered Tristan. "Where are you going?"

He moved to follow her, but she said firmly, "I just need to stretch my legs, Tristan. I won't be long."

Tristan respected her request and did not follow. He lay back down, though she could still feel his eyes watching her.

Sitting a foot or two back from the border of bones, Sadie drew her knees to her chest and contemplated the sky-moon and the lake-moon, thinking of magic and fire and light.

"It's intriguing, isn't it?" Tamlin whispered behind her.

"How did you—" she spluttered. "I didn't hear you coming! And I should have! It echoes!"

"Magic is useful for many things," Tamlin said slyly.

"You used magic to get here?" Sadie stammered, confused. "But I didn't feel anything—I mean not that I would, but—what I meant to say is—oh, curses and 'cantations!'"

Tamlin chuckled. "I didn't use actual magic, no. I am far older than you think and powerful with magic, and my experience and strength influence stealth. Sadie, there's no need to curse your word fumble; I already know you have magic."

Sadie's eyes snapped to Lane Tamlin's in alarm.

"Did Tristan tell you?" Sadie whispered, dreading the answer.

"No," Tamlin assured her. "He's more trustworthy than you give him credit for. Tristan has told me nothing about you, nor do I believe he would even if I asked. Not without your consent first. Tristan and I are well acquainted, though he is a very closed person and does not readily reveal his true thoughts and feelings. The man has many secrets. Which is also why I know he would not share yours without your consent. He knows how precious and dangerous they can be."

"If Tristan didn't tell you... no one else knows..."

"You forget that I am a powerful wizard, Sadie, perhaps the most powerful in Carmelle. If someone near me has magic, especially if they channel that magic within a certain range, however inadvertently they might have done so—I know. I can sense it. In time, once you have harnessed your magical abilities and learned to wield them properly, you will be able to detect magic in others as well."

"I think I already can, a bit," Sadie stammered sheepishly, thinking of the strong surge of power she could sometimes sense emanating from Tamlin, a sensation connected to her core. "I think I can feel that you have magic. Not all the time, but sometimes I can sense this power about you in a way that's connected to my core. I don't really know how else to explain it."

Tamlin stared at her for a long time, until Sadie felt so uncomfortable she could no longer meet her piercing blue eyes and looked down at her shifty feet. Finally, Tamlin nodded slowly and muttered to herself, "Yes, yes. It is possible, of course." Then in a slightly louder and more confident voice she said, "Your magical gift is powerful, Sadie. You have potential. But caution is needed. A fire like the one you caused must not happen again."

"You know I caused it?" Sadie asked faintly.

"Naturally. Although I know it wasn't intentional, we must ensure it is not repeated. There's no need to be upset," Tamlin added, seeing Sadie's watery eyes. "Most magic folk make the same mistake before they are discovered and trained. I myself caused a tornado to sweep the plains of the Dharmaelian region as a little girl. Luckily that was before many people were living there so nobody was seriously injured. But you see how perilous magic can be? How easily it can go astray and cause destruction even with the best intentions? Magic can be fatal if used improperly. Let that be your first lesson."

"Lesson?" Sadie repeated. Fear burned the kindling of hope and longing in her chest.

"Of course! You didn't expect me to let you wander around untrained until you burned another house down, did you? All peoples with magic must be trained, preferably in Orinloth, the land of wizards. Training must commence in Caris Nando, now, though of course I do not know what Alldían has in store for you. But he knows the rules. Once he finds out you have magic, he knows he must turn you over to me, at least for a time."

The way she spoke as if Sadie had no choice in the matter irked her. She didn't want to resent Tamlin or her magic, but she would if they deprived her of her right to choose and be free.

"The question is," Tamlin continued in a low voice, "why weren't you identified earlier? Here in Carmelle, those with magic are usually identified quite young and brought to Orinloth for training. We have a pretty thorough system in place for finding people with magic, for we are dwindling in numbers and are eager to train new wizards. It was by pure luck and coincidence, or fate I suppose if you believe in that sort of idealism, that I was in the same city as you when you performed your first bit of magic."

Sadie didn't like where this was going. It led to questions she could not answer, not unless she revealed where she really came from; Tristan had insisted she mustn't tell anyone.

"There are many peculiarities about you," Tamlin continued in that same low, thoughtful voice. "First and foremost, there is your age. You must be around eighteen or nineteen. How is it that you only performed your first bit of magic now? For some with minimal magical abilities it could be understandable. But for one of your power... usually those of your ability are discovered and packed away to Orinloth by the time they are five."

Sadie had trouble processing this. *Five*? At five she wouldn't sit still for thirty seconds!

"I watched you, Sadie Sheldon," said Tamlin into the silence, watching her face closely. "I observed your behaviour, your moods, your interactions with the others. I watched for signs of magic as well, though I didn't expect to see any after the disaster of the first incident. Not if it truly was an accident and you felt guilty. The guilt shows you have compassion and empathy, and a good wizard needs both. The first time you use magic is a test in more than one way. Not only does it gauge your abilities, but it determines when you are ready to use that magic and in what manner it will serve you best. Most importantly, it tests your true character by your reaction to the event.

"Once I discovered you indeed felt remorse at causing others pain, I knew you could not be evil. You are a friend of Tristan's, whether he admits to such a label or not—I know how stubborn he can be when it comes to keeping his misery intact—so you could not be all bad, but you could not blame me for being suspicious. If she is not evil, I said to myself, then what secret does she carry so closely? It hangs over you like a stormy cloud."

Biting her lip, Sadie considered Tamlin. What would happen if Sadie told her she wasn't from Carmelle? Would Tamlin still want to train her in magic? Tristan clearly trusted Lane Tamlin. And if she was to learn magic from this woman, the truth would come out eventually. Maybe if she told her, Tamlin would be able to provide answers Tristan could not.

"I'm not from Carmelle," Sadie admitted. "I'm not from this world. I came from a more advanced world. A world where dragons and unicorns are fairy tales told to entertain children losing their imaginations and beginning not to believe in the magical land of Faerie. A world, ma'am, where there is no such thing as magic."

Tamlin said nothing, pinning Sadie with her penetrating blue eyes, waiting.

"I came here through a mirror two months ago," she continued. "My sister was getting married, and I was upset. Not because I didn't want her to marry but because I felt sorry for myself. Because I hated the world I was in and most of the people in it."

She felt the need to explain herself to Tamlin.

"My mother tried to force me to marry against my will. I felt trapped, so I ran away. And that's when I stumbled across the mirror, and Tristan. In Athatair, Tristan told me Alldían had sent him to bring me here for a purpose unknown to him. I was to be brought to Alldían as soon as I arrived, but because of the dragon we had to take the long way. I've been so angry and frustrated by my lack of choices here! Coming to Carmelle was supposed to be empowering, breaking out of the restricted mould of womanhood to find my own brand of heroism and give my life purpose. I wanted to make choices for myself instead of fitting into another person's agenda."

"So why didn't you?"

"I guess I felt like I didn't have any better options. That following Tristan was in my best interest at the time."

"That sounds like a decision made for yourself and not someone else to me," observed Tamlin. "You always have a choice, Sadie. Even if the choice is between the lesser of two evils. If you are choosing the right path for *you* then you are the catalyst of your own fate. I see no shortage of gumption in you, and no one will stop you, or question you, or doubt you because you are a woman here. Look at me! I am a woman, and the most powerful wizard in Carmelle. You don't have to choose between identities and labels, so always make the right choice for *you*. Now, when did you first realize you had magic?"

"I felt something peculiar in my core the moment I entered Carmelle, but at first I dismissed it as a side effect of transporting to a different world. When it persisted, I tried to keep it a secret but Tristan, possessing that uncanny way of reading people as he does, persuaded me to confide in him. It was he who first guessed I had magic. I refused to believe him at first. Now I know I have magic because of the fire, but that doesn't make things any clearer or easier. If anything, it only complicates them further."

Sadie thought of her brother, and her warring desires to see him again and learn magic. Maybe if she could open a portal without putting him in danger from the Redpath, she could travel between Earth and Arwé, and take turns visiting Connor and learning magic in Carmelle. Would Tamlin be able to help her with this in time? Sadie wasn't ready to ask her yet—what if she reacted like Tristan and thought tampering with portals when they were supposed to be closed was a bad idea? Or that Sadie's magical inexperience made her a liability to the portal's stability?

"Magic is never easy, and the lives of those who possess it are nothing if not complex," said Tamlin, nodding.

Sadie said nothing, staring at the ruby rocks beneath her feet.

"I will teach you magic, Sadie," Tamlin announced. "Then you can *decide* how you feel about it and *choose* what to do with your powers."

Sadie's eyes snapped to Tamlin's. Confidence and compassion shone in those light blue orbs.

Sadie's slow grin was euphoric. She would learn magic.

As they descended from Skeletal Moon Lake down the other side of the Dharlomin mountains the next afternoon, Sadie experienced a few near-fatal tumbles as she tripped over her own feet, staring at the open valley of long grass below instead of the tangled web of roots and rocks beneath her boots. The largest forest Sadie had ever seen swallowed the valley after a few miles, endless rows of thickly woven trees stretching in all directions. A thin morning mist clung to some of the trees.

"That," announced Tamlin, indicating the forest, "is Caris Nando."

An arrow of excitement shot through Sadie, and she thought she might throw up.

She was finally here.

Sadie followed the others into the valley. She ran down the hill and leapt up onto the red rock wall. Running water babbled to her left beyond the outlying arm of the mountain. Cutting through the ground below, a small river with foamy white waters like thick frothy lace flowed past. Following the line of the river back up the mountain, she saw it originated from a thin cascading waterfall leaping down the jutting rocks. From here the clear waterfall gleamed with a burnished metallic red, the dark secrets of the roan mountains leaking blood tears from an open wound.

"Dharvení," Tristan observed from beside her.

"Curses and 'cantations!" Sadie swore, clutching her heart. "How many times do I have to tell you to stop sneaking up on me like that?"

"I did not *sneak*, I merely followed you," Tristan corrected. "Is it my fault if you didn't notice?"

"Yes."

"Ha!" Tristan laughed. "I think Airothane here would disagree, wouldn't you?"

Sadie hadn't noticed Airothane standing beside Tristan.

"Of course I would," replied Airothane with a smug grin at Sadie. "It's not Tristan's fault you're hard of hearing."

Choosing to ignore Airothane, Sadie rounded on Tristan. "Oh, real mature *Sir West*, get the eleven-year-old to defend you. All the kid ever does is insult me and try to make me look stupid."

"Your pathetic life isn't worth insulting!" Airothane shouted hoarsely, and he stormed off to rejoin Haldin and Tamlin. Sadie could see them frowning at her, and Tristan shot her a disgusted look as he said, "Lighten up, Sadie, we were joking. Give Airothane a break."

Guilt pinched her heart, and her cheeks burned in shame.

For the rest of the day Airothane remained silent and sulky, determinedly looking anywhere but at Sadie.

When they made camp outside the forest that evening, Sadie looked over at Airothane. He sat apart from everyone else, staring gloomily into the fire. Making up her mind, Sadie sat beside him.

"How's it going?" she asked in a false cheery voice. Airothane didn't answer. He didn't even look at her. Picking up a stick, he speared it into the dirt and drew fierce circles with it. Sadie sighed. This was going to be harder than she thought.

"Look, Airothane, I think I owe you an explanation," Sadie began awkwardly. "I haven't been treating you well, and I'm sorry. Okay, I've been a total wench and hypocrite. I kept accusing you of being too young to know anything and yet I was the one acting like a child."

Airothane's stick paused, though he still did not look up.

"To tell you the truth, I think I sometimes envy you."

Airothane's narrowed incredulous eyes snapped to hers. "Envy me? That's nonsensical."

"Maybe so, but I do. I felt inadequate because someone much younger knew so much more about Carmelle and its people. Maybe if I had more knowledge of this world things wouldn't be so confusing and I wouldn't be so afraid."

Airothane's eyes widened. "This world? As opposed to a different world? Are you from a different world? Is that why you don't know Carmelle very well?"

Heart pounding in her ears, Sadie glanced at Tristan in panic, but he conversed with Haldin, unaware of her blunder. Tamlin's gaze fixed on the dark outside the campfire's light, but a small smile could be seen tugging the corner of her lips.

Sadie exhaled slowly, calming her heart. Her instincts told her she could trust the innocence in Airothane's wide eyes. Maybe she shouldn't be as closed as Tristan. Maybe it was time to trust her instincts and choose for herself.

She nodded, biting her lip.

Airothane recovered his dropped jaw quickly, squealing, "I knew it! I knew something wasn't adding up! Where are you from?"

"Earth. Do you know it?" When Airothane nodded eagerly, Sadie continued before the conversation took an inevitable tangent, "I didn't mean to hurt you. I was trying to make myself feel better, but I just feel worse. I disregarded your feelings and that was wrong of me. And you're far more intelligent than I was willing to give you credit for. Can you forgive me?"

Airothane stabbed the dirt in silence, and Sadie thought he would refuse to accept her apology. At last, he muttered, "I forgive you. I guess I was a bit of a prat myself."

Laughing in relief, Sadie extended her hand formally and said, "Friends, then?"

Airothane placed his small frail hand in hers and agreed with a nervous grin, "Friends."

Out of the corner of her eye, Sadie noticed Tamlin, Haldin, and Tristan watching them now with varying expressions of amusement. Sadie didn't care. This episode with Airothane epitomized immaturity, reminding her of childish grudges between her and Connor that evolved into adolescent banter. She wasn't perfect, and Airothane's grin was worth confiding in him and making amends.

Chapter Seventeen

Of Unicorns and Crystals

When deep golden rays of dawn streamed through the forest of Caris Nando the next morning, they revealed a border of bristly evergreens like a gate with knotted needles. Beyond this border, Sadie caught glimpses of ruby, chartreuse, and rust leaves—the first signs of fall. A gap in the evergreens' smooth silver trunks yawned before them, heavy with expectant silence. Beside her, Airothane balanced on the tips of his toes, trying to see through the curtain of needles without touching them, like a child attempting to discern the contents of a present without disturbing the wrappings.

Squaring her shoulders, Sadie marched to the gap and entered Caris Nando.

Half a dozen pairs of eyes halted her progress the moment she stepped across the border.

A small host of the ethereal beings she had once seen in Thomas Sheldon's book blocked the path. They embodied both the subtle beauty of a blossom in snow and a perilous mountain pass luring unwary travellers into the pretense of security. Pointed ears framed by braids peeked through long hair painted with strands of fractured gold sunlight. Two of their number dressed in fitted clothes instead of dark robes, holding long curved sage and cream bows in their hands and quivers full of white-feathered arrows on their backs. Antlers branched out from a few of their heads, some short and single-pronged like a young buck's, some tall and majestic and many-pronged like a noble stag's. Most of the antlered females had brown or white antlers, and the males' antlers were ebony. Wings also sprouted from the backs of a few, sweeping the ground with their golden, brown, and in the case of the males, dark green feathers. None of these Lantíés had both wings and antlers, and most had neither.

A man with waist-length bronze hair and robes of deep burgundy stepped forward.

"Welcome to Caris Nando," he said in a clear, lilting voice, "home of Alldían the Wise and the Lantíés of the North. We have been expecting you."

"Eldaron!" shouted Tristan behind her jovially.

"Tristan," Eldaron acknowledged with an incline of his head and a small formal bow of greeting, though it was personalized by a warm glow of happiness twinkling in his deep roan eyes. "*Nesta chai, ûmí-val.* Welcome home, my friend. You have been missed. Even the trees withered with sadness at your departure. Your coming will bring colour back to their leaves."

"It's good to be back," Tristan agreed, looking around at the leaves fluttering lazily down to thicken the carpet already blanketing the soft earth. "No matter how often I leave to journey in other lands, I can never find a place I love as much as this forest. Though I may be worlds away, my heart will always dwell here, under the eaves of this hauntingly beautiful wood."

"Haldin and Airothane of Dharmaelia, I presume," Eldaron continued, eyeing their Dharmaelian armour and sigils. "Sons of Peladorn King, our watchmen reported you accompanied Tristan. You are known to us, though we have not had the honour of meeting before. Friends of the Lantíés, you are welcome here in the ancient realm of Caris Nando."

Haldin gave a short bow from the waist and replied, "Thank you, Eldaron, we look forward to resting our weary wings in this eyrie of surpassing beauty and vitality. Already I feel exhaustion leaving my limbs. The very air of this wood pulses with life and seeps into the bones." He breathed in deeply, closed his eyes, and sighed with content. Airothane copied him, nostrils working fiercely to suck as much air into his lungs as possible.

Eldaron turned his gaze upon Sadie, but before he could say anything Tristan said, "This is Sadie Sheldon. She has come to see Alldían."

"Welcome, Miss Sheldon," said Eldaron with a slight bow and a warm smile. "I hope you enjoy your stay in Caris Nando."

"Thank you," murmured Sadie, gripping her skirt awkwardly, unsure if she should curtsy.

Turning to Tamlin, Eldaron bowed his head respectfully and spread his arms wide in welcome. "It is a great honour as always to welcome you into our lands Lane Tamlin, greatest of Wizards and long friend of Alldían the Wise."

To Sadie's surprise, Tamlin did not chide Eldaron for his needless formality. Instead, she bowed her head slightly in return and replied, "Thank you, Eldaron, but I fear the pleasure will be solely mine once more, as I am sure you will grow weary of my company ere the moon rises. I'm afraid I come bearing grave news. Or rather I have come across those who bear the bad news and am now caught up in their web of woe and must help unravel it. My true purpose in life seems to be unravelling riddles and keeping peace between all the races of Carmelle to sustain a united front against Vashi and his evils. As the tidings will tell, the web of discord has only tangled further. I fear it will be impossible to unravel without significant damage to the individual threads."

"Naturally I am the true bearer of this grave news, for I witnessed both events," said Tristan. "Ill news hovers darkly over me as ever. An unpleasant returning home gift to forever receive from me, I know."

At first Sadie did not understand Tristan's allusion to two events, but then understanding lurched violently in her stomach. The second event was the fire she had caused. The fire and the effect it would have on the Redpath. Dread washed over her like oily water, leaving a contaminated residue blemished with guilt. Even with all her endless brooding on her first use of magic, she hadn't comprehended the full repercussions. Not only had she ruined a nice couple's home and business and endangered dozens of lives, but the first time she used magic she might have inadvertently helped start a civil war.

"Whatever unpleasantness we receive from your tidings is overpowered by the joy of being reunited with you, Tristan," Eldaron assured Tristan kindly, and Sadie had the impression Eldaron was the closest thing Tristan had to a friend in Caris Nando. "Details of these evil tidings will have to wait until we are further into the forest. In these darkening days even the haven of Caris Nando may be unsafe to speak openly in. Even the wind who knows no barriers and may fly wherever she likes could catch the evil news and bear it to our enemies."

"But not intentionally," interjected Airothane. "Wind has been known to bear bad news, of course, but it is usually as a warning, not an opposing force."

"Airothane's a Windtalker," Haldin supplied by way of explanation.

The confusion arching Sadie's brow prompted Tristan to whisper in her ear, "Someone who can communicate with the wind, a rare gift allowing the wind to carry messages to him from long distances, and to send his own messages out upon her wings."

"Either way," said Tamlin. "We cannot put faith in the unknown. We must assume the Keepers will not encourage their elements to aid us in a civil war, and act accordingly. We must assume we are alone."

Grim faces met Tamlin's pronouncement, but no one disagreed as they followed Eldaron down the path and deeper into the forest of Caris Nando.

Caris Nando's beauty increased with every step Sadie took towards the heart of it. A canopy of colourful intertwining leaves formed a natural roof overhead. Leaves drifted lazily down upon their company, catching beams of sunlight like glowing fairies riding on their backs. Letting her imagination play, Sadie snatched at a leaf as it drifted tantalizingly past her face.

She jumped to catch another leaf floating just out of reach, and her delighted laugh echoed among the trees. Soon she had collected a few dozen leaves and began stringing them onto a vine, weaving an autumnal wreath. When Sadie plopped it on her head, she became an autumnal fairy. In her peripheral vision Sadie noticed Airothane following her in fascination, creating his own autumnal crown. He skipped and pranced, flapping his arms like wings, a little woodland fairy gallivanting in the wake of his queen.

It wasn't until they reached a cliff and a vision of seven-year-old Connor rolling down a hill after attempting to fly like a fairy flashed before her eyes that Sadie snapped out of her idyllic imagination and back to reality. Back to the gnawing hole in her chest left by Connor's absence.

Cascading over a mossy cliff face opposite their company, a waterfall pelted down to a small pool at the base. Clouds of misty silver droplets mingled with churning foamy waters like creamy snow. A noisy, swift river tripped over stones before tumbling around a bend and out of sight. Giant leaves from the ancient trees looming over the waterfall floated downstream, past a stretch of bank with knotted oak trees lining the edge of the velvety grass.

Sadie snapped her head back to the bank so fast she hurt her neck.

A flash of silver, a glance of pearly white velvet, a sparkle of iridescent crystal... could it be? Half concealed in thick dark green leaves, it was difficult for Sadie to be certain. A pointed spiral speared the velvety leaves.

A unicorn.

"Look!" Sadie exclaimed, flinging her arm with such wild exuberance she nearly knocked Airothane right off the cliff. "A unicorn! There's a unicorn down there!"

"Unicorns are indigenous to the forest of Caris Nando," Eldaron informed them.

"Wow, can I ride one?" Airothane asked immediately.

"No," answered Eldaron with an indulgent smile. "It would be considered a great insult to the unicorns if a human tried to ride one. Unicorns are wary of humans, but they trust us. We have even joined forces in battle and ridden out together, Lantíés on the bare backs of the unicorns."

"If they trust you, couldn't you get one to let me ride it?" Airothane persisted, somewhat impertinently in Sadie's opinion.

"Unicorns are their own masters," said Eldaron sternly. "We do not control them, simply maintain a close friendship with them."

"They're beautiful creatures," Haldin remarked, frowning at his brother pointedly.

Sadie's eyes fixated on the glint refracting off the unicorn's horn, flashing silver laced with gold in the deep beams of waning sunlight. Had Thomas Sheldon seen unicorns in Carmelle? Had he then perpetuated the mythologies featuring unicorns on Earth or tried to disprove Ole Worm's theory that all unicorn horns found on Earth were narwhal tusks? Sharp pain pricked Sadie's heart at the thought of Connor's disbelieving astonishment upon discovering one of his favourite mythological creatures was real.

"Indeed, unicorns are some of the fairest beings in Carmelle," Eldaron agreed, "but I must warn you, a unicorn feeling unsafe or provoked can be quite dangerous. No one in this company save Tamlin and Tristan should approach a unicorn unless a Lantíe is present."

"How come Tamlin and Tristan can go near them?" Airothane whined indignantly.

"Because," answered Tamlin in a dignified voice, "I have been around far longer than you might guess, and have the good fortune of sharing a special bond with the unicorns. One usually travels with me and is my closest friend and companion. Perhaps you shall meet her one day. As for Tristan, he was raised in Caris Nando and often counted among the Lantíés himself, even though he is obviously mortal. The unicorns have grown to trust him and will not harm him, though I believe I'm correct in saying he's not permitted to ride them."

"That would be correct," confirmed Tristan.

Sadie attempted to catch a glimpse of its tail, its mane, its hooves. Magic emanated from the entrancing creature, resonating within her. As the unicorn disappeared, a void opened in Sadie's core, leaving her strangely empty.

Night descended upon the forest, subtly changing the flora to a darker and richer hue. An enticing ocean of deep purples, blues, and rich silky blacks seeped into every vein of nature. Mesmerized, Sadie let the magic of this night-world wash over her in waves of content.

Until Airothane spoke.

"What do people on Earth use to get around?" he whispered. He had been bombarding Sadie with questions about Earth since she had confessed her origins to him last night, though he had at least refrained from asking questions when Lantíés were within earshot. Sadie had told Haldin after she told Airothane, knowing he'd blab to him anyway, but as far as she knew no one else outside their company save for Alldían knew she wasn't a native Carmellian.

"Do they ride horses like us? Use carriages and wagons? Do you even *have* horses on Earth?"

"Yes, we have horses on Earth, and we do use them to get around still. But we also have relatively new machines called automobiles, or motor cars. They're kind of like mechanical horseless carriages that use something called a motor to run on an oil-based fuel taken from the ground."

"Wow." Airothane's wide eyes glowed in the waning light.

Soon the darkness became too deep to see clearly, and the Lantíes produced lanterns from their packs. A soft orange glow suffused their dark glass panels, flickering like the waning light of fairies. Lantíes held aloft the lanterns by golden chains hooked through a copper dragon's head rearing from the triangular cap. Its scaly copper body draped over the golden prism top, its hind feet perched on the tainted glass and its long tail curling tightly around the imprisoned light. Eldaron's lantern differed from the rest. Capped with silver, the glass shone with a blended metallic silver and pearly sheen. A small metal fairy perched on the edge of the lantern's lid, and drops of pearls, marble, and molten silver trailed like fairy dust from its overhanging foot.

Sadie had no idea how long they walked in darkness, padding softly along the deftly woven carpet of moss and dead leaves. One moment she weaved between the ancient trees like an overgrown fairy amid floating orange and silver flames, and the next the company halted.

A giant waterfall cascaded before them, steeper and wider than the Setami waterfall where they had seen the unicorn. Glistening moonbeams braided the ribbons of water spilling swiftly over the edge, and winking stars shimmered in every water droplet.

"We have reached Éalindel, the Crystal Waterfall of the river Setami," Eldaron announced.

"Setami means *steady guard*," Tristan informed her, "named so because the west channel breaks from the main course a league or two northeast from here to wind past the doorstep of Sula-onon, the Moon Tower, and then flows steadily past the threshold of Alldían's Hall, the last natural defence for the heart of his kingdom."

"What are all the white flowers?" Airothane asked, pointing at the grass below their feet.

Sadie looked down and gasped. Haldin jumped back as though scalded.

Bursts of white flowers like solid snowflakes blossomed amid the long emerald blades of grass. Moonlight shone on their soft white petals, spread wide to drink in the cool night air. Like snowflakes, each flower was slightly unique, but they reminded Sadie of a cross between white roses and lilies. Haldin and Airothane had accidentally crushed a few with their heavy boots, sending a sweet fragrance of fresh, cold mountain water with a hint of coconut into the air. They blanketed the bank of the Setami on both sides of the river, winding their way like a path up to the foot of the Éalindel.

"The Lantíes bless the Setami's waters with the nalalíté flower as she flows out of Alldían's kingdom to reunite with the river's main flow on its journey to Tor Niro, the Silver Lake," Tristan explained. "Nalalíté means *snow petals*, and they only grow on the banks of the Setami and in Lothilya. The Lantíes pluck them for ceremonies in which symbols of honour, blessings, and grief are required. It's lucky you saw them for the first time at night," Tristan added, watching Sadie's reaction. "Nalalíté only open their petals in the light of the moon."

Sadie narrowed her eyes at the nalalíté by the waterfall's base. The more she gazed at them, the more she thought they looked like a definitive path.

"Why have we stopped here?" she asked Eldaron.

"The Éalindel holds many secrets, but none outside of Caris Nando are permitted to know her secrets unless Alldían wishes it so," answered Eldaron. "Tristan and Tamlin are already privy to them. We knew of Tristan's travelling companions from our watchmen before you arrived in Caris Nando, and Alldían informed me he wishes Sadie, Haldin, and Airothane to learn the secret of Éalindel. Thus, behold the Atha Onéa, the Cave of Crystals! Behind the Éalindel it dwells in secret, hidden by the powerful veil of her waters."

Eldaron pointed to the path of nalalíté, following it with his finger to where the last flowers nestled at the base of the cliff. "Those last nalalíté indicate the beginning of a stone path that leads behind the waterfall and into the Atha Onéa beyond. Follow me, and I will show you. We will rest in the Cave tonight."

Careful not to trample any of the flowers, Sadie and her friends followed Eldaron and the other Lantíés to the Éalindel, eager anticipation lining their faces. Tufts of moss and lichen vied for rule in the stone steps' deep cracks, making the stairs less conspicuous.

At the top, the steps evened out to create a narrow shelf behind the waterfall. Moonlight mingled with the crystalline glow of the white waterfall, dancing on the cliff like pale sunbeams shimmering on rocks resting on the ocean's floor.

Not everyone fit on the narrow ledge, so half a dozen Lantíés stood patiently on the steps while Eldaron ran his long fingers lightly over a section of smooth stone. Tracing the outline of a tall half-circle door, he brought his fingers back to the left side and paused.

"This is the entrance to the Atha Onéa," Eldaron announced. "Only Lantíés know the secrets of how to detect and trace the exact lines of the door, and the stone is enchanted so only a Lantíé's touch will open it."

Pressing the forefinger and middle finger of his left hand firmly against the spot his fingers had been covering, Eldaron stepped back and waited. A crescendo of nervous excitement rose in Sadie as she envisioned the mirror portal, and a thought ignited the stale corners of her mind: what if a portal existed here? Perhaps with her magic—using her magic still terrified her after the fire at the inn, yet if she could see Connor again—if she could find a crack in the magic hiding the closed portals, a chink wide enough to weave her magic through and apply a lifetime of practice imagining she was elsewhere...

She was good at creating something out of nothing.

The smooth stone cracked where Eldaron had traced the half-circle, forming a tall arching doorway. With a loud grinding noise, the newly formed door pushed into the cave and slid to one side, scraping against the rough stone floor as it revealed the Atha Onéa inch by inch.

As soon as the opening was wide enough, Sadie took a daring step into the darkness.

For a breathless moment the darkness pressed in around her, oppressive silence rushing in. Then light flared. Eldaron had uttered a word she didn't understand into the darkness, and a blue-white light ignited before them, flickering with spots of silver and black.

At first Sadie couldn't tell where the light came from. Ivory stalagmites thrust up from the glossy slate floor, and large ebony rocks interspersed between the stalagmites made the ground resemble a giant chessboard. Stalactites hung from the jagged cave roof, their surfaces sparkling an inky blue-black and coated with silver dust, sparkling like millions of minuscule stars in the midnight sky.

And the crystals. Clusters of crystals nestled in clumps between stalagmites, hung like chandeliers amid the stalactites, and sparkled against the black walls and boulders. Pointy and prismatic, their refracting light sent rainbows dancing over the awed, gaping faces of Sadie, Haldin, and Airothane.

In the centre of the Atha Onéa rose a crystal as tall as Sadie, lighting the cave with its brilliant iridescent glow. Beads of light emanated from its tip to the depths of the cave.

Eldaron led them down a narrow winding path between the stalagmites and crystals. The soft plunking of steadily dripping water echoed in Sadie's ears, and she could sense Airothane's excitement as he strained not to touch the crystals. Sadie understood. She longed to reach up and touch one of the mysterious stalactites glistening with silver like millions of minuscule stars.

The giant crystal stood in the middle of a small open space encircled by smaller crystals gleaming in the dim eerie blue light. An increasingly familiar tingling sensation somersaulted in her stomach as the crystal flickered with a sudden blaze of golden-orange light.

"Crystals are the great secret of the Atha Onéa," said Eldaron, gesturing to the crystal beside him. "They are rare and powerful, and therefore precious to the wizards and Lantíés who wish to strengthen their magic."

"But why hide them in a cave?" asked Sadie, pacing slowly around the crystal, examining it from all angles. "If wizards use them for magic, why should that be secret?"

"Because greed is an omnipresent flaw," answered Eldaron with a small, sad shake of his head. "We trusted, once. A price was paid."

"What price?" asked Airothane.

"Betrayal. Theft. Death," Tamlin answered grimly before Eldaron could. "An innocent Lantíé stripped of his generosity when humanity let him down."

"Brunea, an antlered and winged Lantíé of Caris Nando, brought a crystal home from Éaloth, the Land of Crystals, long ago and planted it among the trees by his home," Eldaron clarified. "No one knows how, but his one crystal became a whole garden. His generosity in sharing their beauty with everyone was repaid by accusations of him being a greedy *peryton*, and people attacked his home. It did not end well. His crystals were moved here and guarded by the ruler of Caris Nando."

Eldaron's lips had twisted in distaste as he spat out the word peryton, his eyes pained.

Sadie swallowed past an uncomfortable lump in her throat. She wanted to offer Eldaron words of sympathy for the way his people were treated but didn't know what to say. Guilt also fluttered in her stomach for being allowed to see the Atha Onéa. If they had such a painful history for the Lantíes, why did Alldían think her, Haldin, and Airothane worthy of seeing them? He had never even met any of them.

"I trust you will treat our secret with reverence and respect," Eldaron continued after a pause in which no one spoke. He looked at Haldin, Airothane, and Sadie in turn. "I know you will reveal it to no one."

Sadie nodded in unison with Airothane and Haldin, though the gesture felt feeble.

"Let us rest here for the night," Eldaron said to the group. "We will continue our journey at dawn. You are free to roam the cave, but do *not* touch any of the crystals. They are protected both by the best enchantments of wizards and Lantíes and their own power. You are warned."

Most of the company settled by the great crystal, preparing for sleep. Tamlin and Tristan sat at the furthest point from the great crystal. Haldin and Airothane wandered slowly down a different path, gazing awestruck at the crystals. Sadie plopped down beside Tristan and Tamlin.

While Tristan whetted his sword, Tamlin appeared to be lost in thought, gazing at the great crystal and idly twiddling her thumbs. Sadie thought she knew why Tamlin had chosen this resting spot. The great crystal called to her, tempting her to use her magic. For Tamlin, the greatest wizard of the Age, the temptation must be irresistible. Perhaps wizards were vulnerable to channelling magic in their sleep without realizing it. Sadie shuddered at the thought of starting another fire—this time in her sleep.

Sadie couldn't sleep that night. The company stretched out on the cool slate floor, cloaks wrapped tightly around them against the draft in the cave as Sadie lay awake fretting over her magic. Her core vibrated, magic coursing through her veins as it strained to reach the innocently winking crystals. The great crystal's beams burned her back, drawing her core towards it with enticing, overwhelming power. It took every ounce of concentration and defiance she could muster to ward off the power of the crystals.

Terror gripped her, squeezing her lungs with powerful claws.

She had already burnt down an inn, almost killing dozens of people. What if one of her friends got hurt this time? What if she destroyed the cave and all its precious crystals?

Unable to lay there waiting for her magic to consume her, Sadie rose silently from her spot beside Airothane. She eyed Tamlin's prone form, suspicious of the sleeping arrangements that conveniently allowed Tamlin to ensure Sadie didn't accidentally unleash her magic on the company as she slept. Sadie was probably being paranoid, but she was wary of coincidence.

Weaving her way between sleeping bodies, Sadie padded softly to the entrance.

Once outside, Sadie breathed deeply. The steady thundering of the waterfall pounded the fears of her magic away. She savoured the cool breeze of a dark starlit night playing across her face. The seductive heat of her magic felt less intense out here.

The night breathed enchantment again.

Stars winked overhead, reflected in the waters of the Setami river and twinkling in the cascading waterfall of secrets. Adventure awaited her... but where should she seek it?

Quivering with the anticipation of the unknown, Sadie closed her eyes to focus on her next path—and found herself swimming in the fiery currents of her core. Flaming threads crackled in a tangled ball of fire, the heat emanating from it unbearable and yet enticing. Sadie both feared those fiery threads and longed to pluck one from the tangled mass. An explosive spark burst from her core and burned a river of warm sunlight through her veins.

Snapping her eyes open, Sadie experienced a moment of heightened awareness and sharpened vision before the crackling spark in her mind fizzled and went out. Her heart sank at the same time she breathed a small sigh of relief. Everything seemed dull and lifeless in comparison to the fiery golden light that had suffused the veins of the leaves and trees around her.

Taking a few unsteady steps downstream, Sadie stumbled clumsily over her own feet. She felt disconcertingly susceptible to her magic's lure tonight.

As she rounded a bend lined with thick evergreens, a pearly silver tower loomed in the darkness with only the top rising above the wall of fir-tree sentries. A flat roof opened to the star-strewn sky, peculiar pillars spiralled upwards like thin reeds of a woodland crown, and an oddly shaped plank of white stone branched out from the roof like the prow of a ship.

An incandescent white light glistened in the corner of Sadie's eye.

Sadie scanned the line of trees, heart drumming in her chest.

A unicorn emerged from between the trees, its silver-white flanks glistening in the moonlight. Calm purpose gleamed in its black eyes.

Sadie took a few hesitant steps closer, not wanting to scare it, but needing proximity. With each step Sadie expected it to bolt, but it never flinched. The black pools of its eyes brimmed with intelligence, and Sadie had the impression the unicorn wanted to share its knowledge with her.

Before she could process this idea, the unicorn turned and trotted away. "Wait!"

She dashed after it, leaving a sweet aroma in her wake as she crushed a trail of white nalalíté. The unicorn cantered into the shadow of the trees, its luminous flanks reflecting the moonlight, allowing her to track it. Twigs snapped beneath her thudding feet. Branches tore her clothes and scratched her skin. Needles raked her face. But she was determined not to lose the unicorn.

Just when she thought her legs would collapse, she burst through the trees and windmilled her arms to catch her balance. Panting, Sadie slowly straightened, staring transfixed at the unicorn. A connection bridged the differences between them, embedding in her core and filling the hole she feared. Eldaron's warning about unicorns not tolerating humans echoed in her ear, but Sadie felt no fear.

Smooth and twisted into a long spiral, its horn tip gleamed like a sword in the moonlight. Slowly, she extended a shaking hand and placed it tentatively on the unicorn's forehead.

Whinnying softly, the unicorn pushed its muzzle into her palm, accepting her touch. Sadie's breath caught in her chest at its luxuriously smooth pearly skin. Burying her hand in its mane, she stroked the silky hair wonderingly.

After a small moment of connection, the unicorn galloped back into the shadows.

A familiar ache of loss gnawed at Sadie's core as she gazed at the place where the unicorn had disappeared, but the gaping hole had been mended. She would see the majestic creature again.

The unicorn had led her to the silver-white tower she had seen rising above the trees. The Setami river wound around it, so she guessed the tower must be the Sula-onon. White stone roots fanned out at the base like a monolithic splayed hand with naturally formed steps between them. The body of the tower resembled the trunk of a giant tree, and silver light flooded out of a leaf-shaped archway at its base.

Without hesitation, Sadie mounted the steps and passed through the archway.

Torch brackets jutted from the seamless white stone walls, the flames burning silver instead of orange. Sadie bounded up the tightly spiralling stairs like a character in *The Castle of Otranto*, barely noticing the doors leading off to other chambers. Emerging into a small circular room with a table bearing strange instruments, Sadie positioned a stool beneath a leaf-shaped handle on the ceiling's trap door.

Pulling the door open and ascending the steps lowered with it, she emerged onto the open rooftop. A pattern of ivory crystals encircled by a braided ivory ring embellished the sleek floor, and a few spiralling white pillars appeared to sway around the tower's oval-shaped circumference. No rails guarded the edge and the sheer drop over it.

Across from her, a narrow strip of stone connected the oval rooftop to a white quartz leaf-shaped platform, complete with intricate ivory veins. It looked weightless and fragile, like a dead leaf frosted white, still clinging desperately to the trunk of its sire.

Taking a deep breath, she stepped out onto the exposed leaf platform. A thrilling chill raised the hairs on her arms as she floated on the leaf like a cloud. Impulsively, she slipped off her boots and pattered to the tip of the leaf.

A soothing chill washed over her bare feet as she stood on the brink of the platform, curling her toes over the edge. Wind whipped the hair off her face and slapped her dress against her ankles, and Sadie closed her eyes, drinking it in.

Immediately the air shifted around her, as though the absence of sight illuminated the magic hidden in darkness' folds. She sensed *something* existing in the peripheries of the space just beyond the platform, a ripple through haze, a tangible yet transient slice of Otherness. Could she touch it if she reached far enough? Strands of magic crackled in her core. Maybe she could touch it with magic.

The intoxicating thought jarred her mind, and when she opened her eyes they alighted upon the full moon. Its opal surface mottled with silver spots and streaks screamed magic. The fiery strands of her core pulsed and writhed and lunged at the moon.

She must bring the moon closer. See its giant face right before hers, swallowing her vision until she could discover the mysteries of its contrasting whites and shadows. She must capture its light.

Her magic heaved and swelled within her, threatening to spill out of her core and flood her veins. Sadie could barely control it. The moon beckoned her.

Closing her eyes, she gave herself up to the magic.

Without thinking, Sadie seized a fistful of fiery threads from the crackling mass, plucking them from the tangled sphere with her mind. The loose magical strands throbbed and flooded her whole body in unbearable yet intoxicating heat.

The moon. Bring it closer. Capture its wondrous light.

"Sadie! What are you *doing*?"

Tristan's voice behind her. Sadie registered it dimly, but her magic's call was stronger.

She gathered the separated threads and cast them towards the moon like a net.

The night exploded.

Pearly-white light erupted from Sadie, radiating off her in waves, pulsating and slicing the night in blindingly bright circles. The dazzling force shattered the dark, fusing with the stars and blotting out the moon. Humming with power, her magic illuminated the night sky with such an explosive force the trees bent in half against its blast.

For half a minute Sadie unleashed her magic, her hair and dress buffeting madly. Then it abruptly collapsed in on itself, sucked from the air and overpowered by the night.

Darkness returned, deeper and denser than before. The moon shone with a dimmer light, the stars ceased twinkling, and even the silver Sula-onon dulled against the silky black canvas of the sky.

Teetering on the edge, Sadie heard Tristan's panicked shout before she pitched towards the darkness below.

Chapter Eighteen

Alldían the Wise

Dreams chased each other through Sadie's mind, swimming in autumnal coloured oceans and wandering among enormous trees. Deep chocolate brown eyes blinked down at her, shadowed in hints of layered secrets. Then powder blue eyes swayed in her vision, lingering and growing clearer.

When she could detect Tamlin's twinkle of amusement, Sadie knew her eyes were open.

"Yes, you are awake! This is not a dream!" boomed Tamlin. "One might mistake you for a wizard with your eyes open like that while you're still half asleep. Now that your brain has caught up with your body, you can sit up and tell me all about how you became a fool."

In truth, Sadie's brain had not quite caught up with her body. Groggy and breathless, her body ached as though pummelled by heavy fists, and her bleary eyes dragged back closed. Her pounding head felt compressed between a clamp, all cognitive functions squeezed out.

Where was Tristan? His absence nibbled at her heart in disappointment.

"I'm not a fool!" Sadie finally retorted, miffed.

"You certainly delight in their practices!" said Tamlin. "I know you can't think the magic you did on the Sula-onon wise. Using magic unaided when you haven't been trained is disastrous at the best of times. Which I explicitly *told* you, but apparently foolery runs stronger in your veins than I had anticipated..."

Sadie bolted upright and immediately regretted it as her head swam and vision blurred.

When Tamlin no longer had two heads, Sadie blurted, "I did magic? On the Sula-onon? But—but I tried so hard to hold it back! I..."

Sadie trailed off in horror, shutting her eyes against the truth as her memory flooded back. A leaf-shaped extension of the tower with no rails, an exceptionally bright and beautiful full moon and a burst of white-gold light blinding her, sucking all her energy as she collapsed to the ground...

She could feel Tamlin's eyes on her.

"You didn't do it on purpose then," Tamlin stated grimly. "You didn't know you were performing magic so strong it almost killed you?"

"Almost killed me?"

Tamlin leaned forward.

"Sadie, your magic is powerful. More powerful than I had guessed. What you did that night... I don't think anyone has done that level of magic without training in years. Certainly no one in this Age. You've been unconscious for a full day and a half."

Sadie's stomach dropped.

"You're lucky Tristan was there to catch you. Not only did you nearly kill yourself with magic directly, but you almost fell to your death anyway as a repercussion of such strong magic."

"Tristan saved me?"

"I guess he doesn't find you as annoying as I do," huffed Tamlin.

She paused. Her hesitancy disconcerted Sadie.

"Do you remember how you used your magic?" Tamlin asked, twirling a strand of her wavy hair distractedly.

"Well... I know it affected the light of the moon, or at least that was my intention. I think it might have just caused explosive destruction to the peaceful night air though."

"I believe you may have influenced light radiating from the moon, which is possible since light is separate from the moon, though it still should have been far too advanced without training. The bigger question is *why* you tried to use Celestial magic after I specifically told you by Skeletal Lake that it is forbidden—Dark Magic." Dangerous fury laced the sharp edge of Tamlin's voice and ignited her eyes between the dark spots of disappointment, though her tone remained calm. A chill electrified Sadie's body.

"I wasn't thinking, I didn't even remember Celestial magic in that moment. I never would have tried to do Dark Magic," Sadie stammered. "The crystals and the moon entranced me! I—wait, don't you need to make a sacrifice to wield Celestial magic?"

"What do you call this?!" Tamlin yelled in exasperation, indicating Sadie's depleted state. "I don't recall you passing out for over a day when you set fire to the inn!"

"Oh. Right," Sadie mumbled.

"First, I want to know *how* you used your magic. Where did you look for your magic, for instance? How did you summon it and release it from your body? Your first use of magic was cast without warning or intentional thought, but the second time requires thought. You are aware of your magic and are *choosing* to use it. The second use of magic is usually monitored by an instructor after the pupil has received guidance on how they should begin. I would like you to recall the process of using your magic, starting with the impulse. Try not to leave anything out. It may all be important. In fact, I consider it all exceedingly so."

Dredging up details from the corners of her mind like digging out shells embedded in sands of a murky pool, Sadie told Tamlin everything she could remember. She started with the unicorn leading her to the tower, and her fascination with the moon as she stood on the brink of the platform. Sadie kept her head bowed as she spoke, unable to look Tamlin in the eyes.

"I became overwhelmed with the desire to see the moon up close, to capture its light for my own," Sadie continued. "Seizing magic was easy. I had been fighting to keep it at bay all night. It waited right below the surface, so once I decided to use it… it took over. A fiery spherical core rose inside me, crackling strands of flame tangled together, and somehow I knew I must grasp those strands with my mind. I concentrated on separating strands from my core, and they came, gathering in my mind until I had a firm hold on them. And then…"

Sadie paused, glancing up to meet Tamlin's attentive, calculating eyes, though her thoughts remained veiled.

"I threw them out, casting them on the moon like a net. I hoped they would capture the moon's light and I could pull it to me like fish caught in a net. Obviously, that didn't work. I remember nothing after."

Tamlin remained silent for a long time, staring at Sadie with glazed eyes. Once Sadie caught her mouthing what might have been the word "fire" accompanied by a light sparking in her eyes, but she did not share her epiphany.

After three whole minutes of complete silence, Sadie could stand it no longer. She felt the need to justify herself to Tamlin, but she didn't know where to begin.

"I think the crystals loosened my hold on my magic, made me more susceptible to the lure of its power," Sadie blurted defensively, then shook her head. Blaming exterior forces, even magical ones, was futile. If her mind had been stronger and more trained, she would have resisted the pull of her magic, even under the influence of crystals.

Tamlin nodded absentmindedly. "Yes, yes, it certainly is possible you would not have lost control of your magic had the crystals not lured it to the surface."

"Do the crystals always have that effect on people with magic?" Sadie asked.

"Almost always, yes," answered Tamlin, "but the effect is strongest on those with greater magic. Most average wizards feel a tiny tug or tingling similar to the sensation felt when another magical person enters a room. The stronger your magic is, the harder it becomes to resist the impulse to release it. That's why I watched you closely in the cave, Miss Sheldon. I knew you would feel the pull of the great crystal quite keenly."

Sadie remembered Tamlin's subtle movements to distance herself from the crystals. As the most powerful wizard of the Age, her struggle must have been arduous.

"Sadie, nothing about your magical experiences thus far have been normal. You are exploring your magic for the first time at such a late age, you are attempting to figure out how to wield magic on your own after losing control, yielding to its beguiling power. I fear if we wait until you attend the wizarding school in Orinloth, your magic may control you. I cannot take that risk. Tomorrow, I will begin your magical training."

Sadie's stomach lurched as though she had stumbled at the edge of a cliff.

"Tomorrow?" she choked.

Half rising from the bed, Sadie started to object she would not be in Carmelle much longer now they had reached Alldían, but stopped at Tamlin's raised eyebrow, dropping her gaze to her burgundy satin sheets. She couldn't lie to herself any longer. She would not be returning to Earth in the near future.

Raising her eyes to meet Tamlin's again, Sadie repeated, "Tomorrow."

"Good. In the meantime, I must remind you how dangerous Celestial magic is. It was banned and labelled as Dark Magic for a reason. Do not dabble in it. Why don't you get dressed, and we can join the rest of our company to present ourselves to Alldían. I'll wait outside."

She indicated a rich navy blue velvet gown embroidered with gold draped over a chair opposite the bed. Tamlin swept from the room, pale blue robes and red mantle billowing.

Swinging her legs over the side of the intricately carved wooden bed, Sadie stood up and swayed as stars blurred her vision. Staving off a faint dizziness, she crossed over to the spindly maple chair and held up the gown.

As she slipped it over her head and watched it pool at her feet like a rippling navy lake, Sadie did her best to quell her growing nerves. She placed a half circlet wrought of twisted golden vines studded with leaves and delicate eight-petal flowers tentatively on her head. Long fine golden chains trailed from the back of the circlet, which Sadie braided into her plait.

Resting her hand on one of the wall's thick interlocking tree trunks, Sadie brushed aside a wisp of cascading ivy curtain to peek at the silent forest beyond her dwelling. Was it always this quiet here? Or did the trees mirror her own hesitancy, holding their breath against the life-altering moments to come? After all she had endured to reach Alldían, she didn't feel ready to meet him. To face her future. Looking up at the intertwined branches comprising her ceiling, netted with thick splashes of fire orange and ruby leaves, Sadie exhaled a deep sigh.

She could do this. She could stay in control.

Pushing open the door, Sadie nearly walked right into Tamlin's back.

"Ready?" Tamlin inquired.

Sadie squared her shoulders and said with much more confidence than she felt, "Yes, I'm ready to meet Alldían."

Craning her neck, Sadie gawked at the mammoth tree-pillars towering over the forest floor, marching in unstructured rows down an immeasurable hall, their leafy canopies invisible as they brushed against the sky. Autumn leaves floated languidly, suspended in time amidst the sun's rich rays slanting through the eaves of the forest. When the golden rays mated with the warm crimson and vermilion leaves on the ground they blazed a deep orange, illuminating the forest floor with a fiery glow. Tiny dust particles ensnared in the beams winked and glimmered like particles of magic.

"Get your head out of the clouds and watch your footing!" Tamlin barked, sounding far too much like her mother.

Sadie glanced down and retracted her foot before it could crush a giant toadstool fraternizing with a trees' roots. She kept her gaze low for a while, admiring small gardens boasting low, carved seats, stone fountains, and bursts of autumnal flowers.

As they approached Alldían's Hall the homes changed, now built on smoothly carved wooden platforms high in the trees. Some platforms bore long tables for dining, while others bore divans, cushions, and telescopes for stargazing. Soon the trees' vast roots splayed far from the homes nestled between them.

Passing through an archway of two enormous pine trees like watchful sentinels, Sadie and Tamlin rounded a bend and beheld a great hall erected around the tallest, thickest, and strongest tree in Caris Nando. Filling the entire little hollow, the tree rose from within the hall, its silver-grey trunk smooth until, craning her neck back as far as it would go, Sadie glimpsed a whole city of platforms and houses nestled among the branches.

"Is the hall crafted with magic?" Sadie asked, eyeing the walls of trees bent at an unnatural angle thirty feet from the ground to intertwine at the hall's peak and form a prism-shaped roof.

"If I said the trees just grew like that, would you believe me?" countered Tamlin.

"No."

"Then there's your answer. Although sometimes natural transformations are the most magical. Take Tristan here. His transformation from scruffy, unkempt vagabond to cleanly, respectable godson of a Lantian lord is nothing short of magical."

Spotting Tristan beside Eldaron, Haldin, and Airothane in front of the mahogany doors to Alldían's hall, Sadie's heart stuttered and she reigned her expansive grin into a small, secret smile pinching the corner of her lips.

"Why are you grinning?" Tristan demanded suspiciously when she reached him.

Raking her eyes over Tristan's clean chestnut hair, the embroidered silver thorny vines snaking up the sleeves of his emerald tunic, and the new sheathed sword belted at his side that changed his stance, Sadie replied, "I believe the appropriate greeting would be, 'Sadie, I'm so glad you're awake, we were so worried about you, how are you feeling?'"

"And I believe the first words out of your mouth should have been, 'Thank you Tristan for saving my life when my reckless folly was about to get me killed.'"

"There is that. But since we both know I'm grateful for you saving me from myself, and an outpouring of concern for my well-being from you would scare me more than console me, I'll skip over the awkward moment and ask you: is that your sword? The blade of a Swordmaster?"

Her eyes flicked between the emblem of a sword entwined with a thorny long-stemmed crimson rosebud stitched over his heart, and the closed rosebud pommel of his sword and wondered what it meant.

"Oh, yes, it is," replied Tristan, resting his hand on the pommel awkwardly.

The ebony sheath bore the same symbol of sword and closed rosebud branded in silver below the lip. Wrapped in burgundy leather, the long shaft branched into a silver vine-carved hilt. A single tear-drop shaped emerald nestled amid the vines at the hilt's centre. Sadie smiled wide.

"What? You're smiling again. Do I look ridiculous?" asked Tristan.

"Not at all. I'm grinning because I had an insane urge to steal a sword and march off to battle with you." Sadie laughed. "I rather crave battle sometimes."

Tristan raised his eyebrows. "Did that incident on the Sula-onon addle your brains?"

"Oh, Tristan, I took leave of my senses long ago."

Tristan stared at her.

Airothane laughed at Tristan's discomfort, and Sadie grinned at her young friend. His simple navy, velvet tunic and dark grey breeches complimented his clean, wavy wheat hair resting on his shoulders.

"What does the emblem on your chest mean?" Sadie asked Tristan. "It's on your scabbard as well. It's not *your* symbol, is it?"

Tristan shifted his feet, looking everywhere but at Sadie as he replied, "Er—yes, it is. It's my personal Swordmaster symbol. All Swordmasters have one; it's a way for us to identify each other and for others to identify us. Each Swordmaster's is unique, though all must include a sword and a flower of their own choosing. It becomes part of their identity."

Considering the image on Tristan's chest for a moment, Sadie said, "I like your choice of flower. The closed rosebud that has not yet bloomed. It fits you."

Tristan searched her eyes, probably looking for traces of mockery, but did not answer.

"When did you get your sword back?" she asked.

"Alldían restored it to me that first night when he healed you."

"Alldían healed me?"

"Of course. Alldían has great skill in healing. As I'm sure Tamlin has already impressed upon you, your *accident* was almost fatal. If Alldían had not been close at hand, the situation could have been much more serious."

Sadie gulped.

"Shall we enter the hall?" suggested Eldaron. "Alldían is expecting us."

Sadie followed behind the rest of the company as Eldaron threw back the heavy mahogany doors and they entered the hall of Alldían the Wise.

Immediately she searched for Alldían, but though she could spy a throne at the far end of the hall, the space was so vast she could not discern features of the figure sitting upon it. Still, her stomach swooped as she slowly closed the space between them, and though she drank in the hall's enchanting beauty, her eyes frequently flickered back to the throne.

Within a few steps, she could feel her heart expanding. Long and wide, the hall was lined with columns of living trees. A stone wall inlaid with vines and leaves separated the layers. Rising twenty feet before bending, the tree-pillars' upper branches snaked towards the ceiling's centre, a glass prism filling the space between their outstretched fingers. Fine gold filigree intersected the clear glass and outlined a single dark green leaf dangling by its stem from the northern tip of a new silver moon.

Sadie fingered the moon and leaf crystal bracelet on her wrist. If the symbol etched on the glass prism-ceiling above was associated with Alldían, maybe he really did send her the bracelet. She didn't know whether she would ask him about it yet, but her nerves mounted at the idea of meeting a man invested in guiding her future.

As though anticipating the anxiety those walking to meet the Lord of Caris Nando would feel, the hall's design sought to calm and soothe. Short stone columns topped with basins cupping small fires marched down the hall, making the wavy rays of Carmelle's sun symbol dance. Thin rays of slanting sunlight permeated the thicket of branches, bathing the ground in patches of gold. Splashes of mustard, ginger, carmine, and cinnamon-coloured leaves rained down like a medley of autumnal spices, tumbling through the air like sparks setting the hall on fire.

Beneath Sadie's feet soft moss blanketed the hall's floor, save for a tiled mosaic path like a still river illustrating natural wonders of Carmelle. In the centre of the hall, the path flowed into a mosaic of Carmelle's symbol. Beyond this circle, the path narrowed into a mosaic ribbon of Carmelle's history, depicting the knighting of warriors, crowning of kings, wars, treaties, discoveries, and art until it ended at the foot of Alldían's throne.

At the head of the hall loomed the base of the enormous tree, its massive roots twisting half a dozen feet above the ground like thick, contorted spider legs. Nestled between each vast root stood a dozen simple thrones, all carved elegantly of wood but adorned only with the symbol of each Lantian lord's house engraved just above where their heads would rest.

Halfway between these thrones, embedded between the two most immense roots of the great tree, sat Alldían's throne, raised slightly on a dais. Shaped like a tree, branches of leafy vines intertwined above the same moon and leaf symbol as on the glass ceiling, made of real jades and emeralds for the leaf, and veins of true silver foil for the moons.

Perched on this impressive throne was Alldían the Wise.

Sadie's chest constricted, and she unstuck her heavy tongue from the dry roof of her mouth.

Wearing open robes of deepest burgundy embroidered on cuffs and sleeves with gold, Alldían wore a dark brown floor-length tunic beneath the robes and a golden sash around his waist. A circlet of golden metal vines perched on his head around five-pronged ebony stag antlers, a single tear-drop ruby dripping onto his forehead. Straight dark coffee brown hair streaked with silver fell to the tips of his shoulder blades, though he showed no other signs of age save a few creases around the eyes and forehead. Dark green feathered wings sprouted from between his shoulder blades, resting open on either side of his throne. His deep sea-green eyes ensnared Sadie, dancing with shimmers of sapphire and bronze like the waves of an azure ocean caught in sunlight. Knowledge swam in the depths of those oceanic orbs. Knowledge of the joys and sorrows of present and past Ages. Wisdom born from first-hand experience sat upon his brow.

"My lord, I come before you in the company of your godson Tristan West and his travelling companions," announced Eldaron as they approached his throne.

A rapid crescendo of nerves mounted inside Sadie as the company bowed respectfully in unison. Alldían rose from his throne, smiling.

"Many moons have waxed and waned ere we parted last, Tristan, my son, and yet though we have been parted longer before, I feel your absence more keenly with each passing day," said Alldían, fixing Tristan with a warm, affectionate gaze. Tristan's face softened and his mouth twitched into a small smile of reciprocated affection. "Your presence in Caris Nando has been greatly missed, especially by me. As I expressed to you the first night of your arrival, my heart sings once more at the sight of you.

"Your council and friendship has been missed, Lane Tamlin," continued Alldían, shifting his gaze to Tamlin who inclined her head respectfully. "Long have I watched the moon and stars and listened for a whisper of your whereabouts, but both you and Tristan have remained out of sight or sound for quite some time. I shall be interested to hear where you have been and what you have been up to."

"You shall hear all in due course, Lord Alldían," assured Tamlin. "For now, let it suffice to say that we bring, as ever, grave news regarding the Redpath."

The lines on Alldían's face deepened and his smile faltered. "Grave news has reached me here as well, though the whispers have been hints and rumours rather than fact. More veritable information, however grave, shall be necessary to hear. We will speak of this in a moment. But first..."

Alldían turned his gaze upon Haldin and Airothane, and the lines smoothed. "Welcome Lord Haldin the Hawk and Lord Airothane Windtalker, sons of King Peladorn of Dharmaelia. I am so glad we have met at last. Word of your rare and special gift has spread even to our secluded lands here in Caris Nando, Airothane, and your unparalleled skill in battle and heroic deeds, Haldin, are well known throughout Carmelle. It is an honour to have you both as my guests. I hope we shall enjoy the comforts of Caris Nando together before you must depart."

Haldin and Airothane inclined their heads, and Haldin replied in his calm, confident manner, "All our lives we have heard tales of Alldían the Wise and his beautiful forest halls filled with song and lore, but legend cannot convey the wonder of reality. We would be honoured to remain as your guests for a brief spell before we journey back home to Dharmaelia."

Alldían locked eyes with Sadie, and the layers of flesh and bone guarding her soul stripped away.

She attempted to avert her gaze, but his eyes hooked hers, reeling her in. A gentle weight rested on her shoulders: Tristan's hands, lending her strength.

"Godfather, I'd like you to meet my travelling companion, Miss Sadie Sheldon."

Sadie wasn't sure what she expected him to say. An apology for bringing her here, an outright confession as to why she had been summoned. Instead, he simply said, "Sadie Sheldon. I'm pleased to meet you at last."

His empty words echoed in Sadie's numb brain.

That was it? This *wise* Lantíe planned to ignore the person he summoned through the portals between worlds?

His next words regarding the Redpath slid over her like contaminated water. Though not directed at her, they still left a foul taste on her tongue. Rushing blood thrummed in her ears.

She clutched her bracelet with a sudden movement she hoped would catch his attention, but his eyes didn't even flicker.

Only when Tristan mentioned the Redpath's attack on the inn because they thought Sadie a spy did Alldían glance her way again to offer her a platitude of, "That must have been frightening. I am sorry you had to endure such an attack."

Her stomach felt as hollow as his platitude.

This is what came from believing, for a moment, that she might be special. For letting herself think she might be on a hero's path. Heroes were not ignored.

Heroes also did not dabble in Dark Magic, even inadvertently.

Maybe when Alldían healed her and learned of her brush with Celestial magic he had changed his opinion of her. Maybe his wise mind cautioned him against her staying in Carmelle after all.

Maybe, just as her mother would have predicted, she had *almost* succeeded in having a purposeful life of heroic deeds, but her foolish fantasies had derailed her dreams once again.

Alldían would say he had been mistaken about her and help her return to Earth.

She would return to Connor. To her family. To her predetermined life at the Sheldon manor, walled in on all sides by prison bars she could no longer find a way to unlock.

And be left to ponder how she *almost* became the person she had longed to be her whole life but had been unable to escape the word that had always anchored her chains.

Almost.

Chapter Nineteen

A Wealth of Honour

Horns blared and bells clanged as Connor weaved through cars stopped at a light and crossed the street behind a dark green wooden streetcar, dodging puddles as he went. He expertly avoided the spray of a truck's wheel as it rolled through a deep puddle and leapt onto the opposite curb. He had left the rowdy Vaudeville trio of comical dancers in The Pantages Theatre to immerse himself in the orchestrated drama of the silent motion picture playing in the Rex Theatre across the street.

Connor had been theatre-hopping in Vancouver for the last two weeks while he waited for Pierre Curie's reply to his telegram, losing himself in an endless tidal wave of entertainment instead of roaming the same haunts Sadie had every day. His father had started berating him for shirking his responsibilities, beseeching him to stop wasting his time indulging in revelries like a vagrant child and grow up. But Connor could read the subtext. *Man up*, is what Roger truly meant.

"Isn't that what successful gentlemen business owners do?" Connor had challenged as he prepared to leave the house and his father's fresh reprimands behind that morning. The bitter bite in Connor's voice aimed to wound. "Commend each other on their fabricated virtues and make dubious drunken business deals in social settings without doing any actual work? I'm just practising for my future, Father."

He had stormed out of the house before his father could retaliate.

Hastings Street was the perfect place to drown in distractions. Theatres competed for space, crowded curbs, preening colourful signs, and endless strings of white lights, vying for the attention of passersby. Every step heralded a new sound of merrymaking. Raucous, indecent laughter blasted out of Vaudeville theatres; the grand epic swells of orchestras or the tinny plink of pianos assailed his ears as he passed cinemas; and soft, cheerful dinner music created a romantic ambience in restaurants. Heady scents of buttered popcorn, strong coffee, cigar smoke, freshly baked cinnamon buns, and exhaust fumes mingled in the air. Men and women dressed in their gaudiest clothes milled outside restaurants or hotels, debating about which form of entertainment they wanted to try next. And it lasted all day. He could spend an entire day losing himself among the crowds, one more sad soul seeking release in the song and dance of a showgirl, the jokes of a comedian, or the flickering figments of someone's dramatized life projected on a big screen.

The Hastings Great White Way it was called, and it lived up to its name. Rain misted down like silver confetti in the light of the streetlamps and thousands of white lights reflected in every window, every puddle, illuminating the street like a canvas of twinkling stars.

The irony of darkness consuming him among so much light was not lost on him.

But the loss of Sadie perpetuated the grief in his soul. If he didn't find a way to fill his heart's cavity soon, it would rot his soul beyond repair.

Connor bought a ticket at the booth before the curved entrance of the Rex Theatre. Opening the door, he heard the swell of violins accompanying a cello, but water leaking through a small hole in his boots made him look down. White lights reflected in the puddle, glowing like a cluster of fairies. At the edge of the puddle lay a soggy, half-torn piece of paper.

The reds and blues of the Union Jack flag against the winking white lights snagged his attention. They framed a soldier, stolid and impressive in his uniform as he proudly protected the honour of his nation. Above the image was the caption:

We Will Uphold the Gem of Liberty
"Glory is the Soldier's Prize,
The Soldier's Wealth is Honour"

Connor halted, mesmerized by the words, "The Soldier's Wealth is Honour." Not inescapable guilt over his family's monetary wealth and the unhappiness it had brought his sister, but a wealth of honour performing deeds to help save others from a horrible fate. Honour in defending the freedom and liberty of others, where he had failed in defending the freedoms his sister deserved among the rich.

Below the picture of the soldier were the words: "Shall we help to crush tyranny?"

Crush tyranny. Crush those who thought they could dictate someone's future because of what they were born into, those who would destroy others' lives to fit their own agenda—like what his parents did to Sadie—but he could do something to stop it. He could be useful for once.

He could continue uncovering the truth about Thomas Sheldon for his sister *and* help prevent others from suffering.

Connor checked the bottom of the flyer. An address was listed on Beatty Street not too far from the theatre for The British Columbia Regiment's recruiting office.

He looked back at the Rex theatre, glimpsing the stunning ivory and gold interior as a few people exited through the open door. Setting his lips in a determined line, he turned his back on the theatre, fished the flyer out of the puddle, and left the lights of the Great White Way behind.

Swaying gently on the swing with his arm coiled around the coarse rope, Connor picked morosely at the rope's frays and stared at Sadie's grave. A deep orange glow filtered through the wispy willow branches as the sun dipped below the horizon, a chilly breeze nipping at his ears. Dappled in golden-orange light, her tombstone emanated an innocent haunting beauty Sadie would appreciate, but its warm glow left Connor cold and hollow. He couldn't see the magic anymore. Sadie had taken it with her.

Grass rustled beyond the willow tree and slow, soft footsteps padded towards him. Mabel drew back the willow curtain and let it fall back gently behind her. Wispy tendrils of hair spilled around her face, escaped from the loose braid resting on her white lace dress. A brooch pinned to the throat of her high collar drew his attention to the dip between her collarbones, and he longed to plant a kiss there. Like him, she had grown up in the past few weeks. The announcement of the war had changed everyone. It thrust people into maturity, though Sadie's death had already been a catalyst for change in Connor. Mabel warmed his heart and quickened its pace, but even she could not entirely fill the void he floundered in.

"Tanaya told me I could find you here," offered Mabel quietly. Connor could feel her steady gaze, but he did not look up. Instead, he concentrated on the 'S' in Sadie's name etched into the tombstone. "She said you've been out here all day. I figured I'd try and persuade you to come inside for a bite to eat."

"I'm not hungry," Connor replied automatically. Chancing a glance at Mabel, he noticed hurt undulating in her eyes and tried to amend his coldness. "Look, Mabel, we need to talk. Do you want to sit down?"

Connor leapt off the swing and offered it to Mabel, who hesitated before wordlessly accepting.

"Sadie's death really—" His voice broke. He still could not speak a sentence containing the words *Sadie's death* without choking on them. Sensing his struggle, Mabel laid a comforting hand on his wrist. A warm surge of adrenaline coursed through him, and he gave her a weak smile. She did lend him strength, and he would miss that.

"Sadie's death devastated me." Mabel's hand slid into his and intertwined their fingers, squeezing encouragingly. "I feel empty, like I'm not the same person. I'm uncomfortable in my own skin, and I can't stand walking the same halls Sadie loathed. You have been my only anchor to sanity, and I don't want to leave you, but... I need to get out of here. I need something to take my mind off losing Sadie, but more importantly... I need to feel like I have a purpose. A reason for my existence other than shouldering the family business like my father wants. I need to act, fight for something. Believe in a cause, and hopefully find a way to believe in myself in the process."

Mabel's eyes pooled with tears. "You want to enlist in the army and fight in the war."

Her unwavering voice impressed Connor. Despite her watery eyes, she remained strong and in control. Looking deep into her eyes, he tried to convey the conflict tearing his heart at the thought of leaving her.

Mabel turned her head away. Connor placed his fingers gently under her chin, coaxing it upwards so she could see his sincerity.

"Believe me, Mabel. I care for you deeply and loathe having to leave you. But it's not fair to either of us if I keep existing as a mere shell, a sponge soaking up your love. I'm wrung out, dry of the love I could release back. I am lost. But if I go to war, I might find myself."

"Connor I don't..." Mabel trailed off. Connor knew she did not fully comprehend his reasoning. He needed Mabel to understand. He needed her to not hate him for his decision, otherwise he didn't know if he could go.

"Do you know why Sadie always loved fantasy and adventure stories?" Connor asked rhetorically. "Stories of good and evil pitted against each other? It's because the experiences of people in those stories force them to discover who they are and what they stand for. They're forced to choose between good and evil, and test that choice to their core. Life at the Sheldon residence is too mundane for me to prove anything to myself. I have nothing to react to, nothing to take a stand for except my feelings for you. But that proves nothing about my character except that I'm capable of earning the love and respect of the most amazing girl in the world. I want that to be enough Mabel, I do, but I need to take a stand for what I believe in."

Mabel's whole frame hunched as though attempting to shield herself from each word's blow.

"You have to understand, Mabel," Connor pleaded. "Before you, Sadie was my world. We did everything together..." A sob caught in his throat. Mabel did not interrupt him, a look of pity mingling with the pain. "I always prided myself on being daring and adventurous, defending justice in an epic yet honourable manner. Mischievous heroism, Sadie used to call it. This war is my chance to prove to myself I'm really that mischievous hero. That it's not a persona I adopted as Sadie's sidekick, but who I truly am on my own... without Sadie."

Mabel anchored his rambling with her eyes, and clasped Connor's hand, lifting it to her lips and kissing it softly. "I may not fully understand how you're feeling, but then how can I? I'm not the one who lost a most beloved sister. I cannot ask you to be any less than who you are, Connor. I suspected you might want to fight in the war as soon as it was declared. I just didn't think you would join this soon. I'm not going to be selfish and tell you to stay here. You should do what you feel you need to. I wish I could be useful as well. But I—I'm going to miss you."

Reaching out tenderly, Connor stroked her cheek. Trailing his fingers down her jawline, he traced the outline of her lips, pulled her close, and kissed her on the forehead.

"This is my opportunity, and I don't want to miss it. I don't want to wait until the war's over..." Connor murmured into her hair. "It will be okay..."

Cutlery clinked at the silent dinner table, the only sound at Sheldon family dinners now. No one spoke. No one mentioned the empty seat across from Connor, though everyone stole glances at it between bites. When Connor cleared his throat, his parents' and Tanaya's necks snapped up, wide startled eyes scanning the room for an imposter holding a gun before landing on Connor.

"Sorry," he apologized, his voice deadpan. "I wanted to let you know I've volunteered with the British Columbia Regiment and have been assigned to the 7th Battalion. I leave for training in Valcartier, Quebec in a few days."

Connor calmly watched jaws drop, forks go limp in trembling hands, and eyes slit in fury. He still had not entirely forgiven his family for closing every door to Sadie, and he wouldn't let them do the same to him. Sharing his plans was a courtesy, and not up for debate.

"But you're underage," protested Victoria. "They wouldn't let a seventeen-year-old enlist. You must be eighteen."

Connor shrugged. "I didn't have to show a birth certificate. Just filled out the attestation papers. Said I was eighteen. They didn't question it."

"You're a fool," Tanaya hissed. A single tear rolled down her cheek. "What makes you think that at seventeen you could do anything in the war but die?"

"Of course he'll die!" his mother wailed. Her hands shook and her voice cracked, the tears flowing freely. "How could you do this to your mother? After we just lost your sister! I can't lose another child, I can't. We'll tell them you're underage, show them your birth certificate."

"I used a fake surname," Connor admitted. "Avery. It'll make it harder for them to verify my age." *And I can leave the Sheldon name behind.*

"Well, they'll believe your father when he marches in there and sets things straight," Victoria huffed. "You can't do this, you don't have a choice. I won't let you."

"Is that what you told Sadie when she said she'd rather explore the rainforest than be forced into a high society marriage?" Connor countered, raised voice quivering.

His mother recoiled and blinked rapidly as though slapped.

Connor averted his eyes to his plate and set down his fork, unable to swallow past the shards of pain building at the back of his throat. He forced himself to take a deep breath, though his tightened chest squeezed his lungs. He wouldn't let his mother guilt him into staying.

"Say something, Roger!" Victoria pleaded.

But his father just stared wide-eyed at his only son for a moment longer, his face unreadable—then scraped his chair back and left the dining room without a word.

Connor watched him leave, heart sinking a little, but not surprised. His father never confronted his emotions. He would rather run away and hide from them.

Am I doing the same?

No. He wasn't his father. He wanted to grow, become the hero Sadie had always believed him to be. Find an outlet for his grief, not bottle it inside. Staying would mean running away from his grief. Becoming a soldier would force him to confront it.

He tried to ignore the doubt twisting and roiling in his stomach.

Their car screeched to a halt at a train station on their right. Connor was sandwiched between Tanaya and Mabel in the backseat, his parents in the front. Mabel clasped his hand tightly, squeezing his fingers as though afraid to let go. Connor worried he might never get to hold her hand again. When they parked the car, he kept his fingers laced with Mabel's. Slinging his rucksack over one shoulder, he led the way to the ticket booth to pick up his reserved ticket for the train departing at seven sharp. He had exactly ten minutes to say his goodbyes and board.

Connor turned to Tanaya first, shuffling his feet, hands shoved in his pockets. He fixed his gaze on her quivering chin so he didn't have to see the tears pooling in her eyes.

"You know, I thought you were mad at me after Sadie's death," Tanaya said. "That you had lumped me in alongside Mother as part of the problem. Whenever I tried to make eye contact, you walked away. I feared you'd yell at me if I tried to talk to you, and I couldn't face the rejection on top of losing Sadie. And then when you announced you had enlisted at dinner... I could feel nothing but bitter anger towards you at first. How incredibly selfish he is, I thought. Depriving Mother and Father of another child, and his sister of her only remaining sibling for a cause he's too young to fight for. But then I thought of Sadie, and realized I was being the selfish one. You're thinking of the greater good. Fighting for your country for those who can't fight for themselves. And maybe, for Sadie?"

Connor sniffed and nodded at his boots.

Tanaya's pitch climbed higher. "I think that's the bravest thing you've ever done."

Connor looked into her watery eyes, and she smiled through the tears wetting her lips.

"You're a true hero, Connor."

Connor gulped and pulled his sister into a hug, scrunching his burning eyes.

"Thank you," he whispered into her hair. Pulling back a little, he added, "Things will be better when I get back. I'll be a better brother to you. I promise."

"Just come back. The rest will follow."

Connor also had trouble looking his mother in the eye. She stood before him, dabbing her eyes with a handkerchief, and he didn't know how to feel. She reached for his cheek, and he had to resist the urge to flinch. She stroked his cheekbone tenderly.

"So young," she croaked. "My baby is still so young. I know all mothers wish their babies didn't have to go to war, but I wish—I just wish mine could go to war with love in his heart. Love for his family. His mother. Do you hate me, Connor? Ever since Sadie... you never talk to me."

Sighing, Connor bestowed a short but sincere hug on his mother. "I don't hate you, Mother. I wish things were different too, but I don't hate you. I don't wish to part with bitter feelings between us. I know you loved Sadie. And I know you love me—"

"I do love you," Victoria interjected fervently.

"Then that knowledge shall have to be enough for both of us. For now."

Connor kissed his mother's cheek and turned to his father. During the ride to the train station, Roger had remained silent. Connor wasn't sure if he would say anything even now. But surprise overwhelmed him when his father pulled him aside and gave him a heartfelt hug.

"I want you to know," his father began gruffly, his hand still clasping Connor's shoulder, "that I really do wish you luck in the war. You have always been strong-willed, and I respect that about you. I know Sadie's death has been indescribably hard for you—it has been for me too—and if this is what you think you need to do, well, I want to make sure you know I'm proud of you. I'm proud to call you my son."

Connor blinked away tears, not knowing what to say.

His father plowed on, unperturbed by his silence, determined to finish his planned speech.

"I love you, Connor." He stuttered a bit over the foreign phrase. "Please... please don't forget that."

Connor threw his arms around his father and whispered, "I love you, too". He tucked the moment in a pocket of his heart to carry with him.

Twining his fingers with Mabel's again, Connor led her to a spot away from his family. His nerves prickled painfully at the prospect of saying goodbye to Mabel. Her hand was so warm, her presence so comforting...

Was he the craziest man alive for leaving her? Forcing himself to remember why he had committed himself to the Canadian Forces and what this step in his life represented, Connor stroked her face with trembling fingers.

"You are my world, Mabel," Connor assured her, his voice quivering with emotion. "You don't try to grow up too fast, and your beauty reflects your soul. I'm the luckiest guy in the world to somehow have earned your mutual affection. Leaving you is the hardest..."

Connor faltered. Her entrancing sage eyes reflected a lantern's flame, and a deep warmth spread through him. His lips sought hers, slanting over them more insistingly than he had ever kissed her before. Mabel's surprised stiff lips melted into his and parted, their warm breaths mingling together. He slid a protective, cushioning hand behind her head and pulled her closer with the other.

Connor could have lost himself in this blissful kiss forever—but a train whistle pierced his euphoric bubble and reality pressed back in. He was a soldier now, and war did not wait for anyone. Connor slowed his kisses, gently tracing the shape of her lips with his, full of yearning but also saying goodbye. He pulled back a fraction, his fingers lingering around her cheekbones and earlobes as he rested his forehead against hers.

"I love you," he breathed in her ear.

"I love you, too," Mabel exhaled back. "Remember yourself out there, Connor. Remember what *you* want matters too."

Connor nodded and kissed her forehead one last time.

As the whistle blew again, Connor boarded the train and raced to find a window. Mabel stood a little apart from his family, tears streaming silently down her face as they all waved goodbye and blew kisses. Connor drank in the shadowy faces of his loved ones, his nose pressed against the cool glass until the train turned a bend and hid his past from view.

Almost a month later, Connor arrived in Britain after a brief training stint in Valcartier, Quebec. They had completed their journey across the Atlantic Ocean in the middle of October—the day after Sadie's birthday, in fact; she would have been nineteen. As they travelled from the ship's landing port to Salisbury Plain where he would continue his training, they passed through a town on All Hallows' Eve.

Trundling over cobblestone streets and squelching through puddles spotting the road, their truck wended its way through pedestrians and vehicles. A full harvest moon glowed orange through a web of bare branches, a bright blot against a clear sable sky. The deep yellow eyes of lit street lanterns and house windows followed their movement. Dead leaves crunched beneath hurried feet, and candy apple, toffee, and cinnamon aromas wafted out of the houses.

The full moon and spooky ambience of All Hallows' Eve fit the ominous mood of going to war. Horrors awaited him, but the eerie unknown intrigued him. He had heard some people in Ontario had started wearing costumes on All Hallows' Eve in the tradition of Scottish guisers, masking their faces to become someone else. Maybe Sadie was right, and truth did lie in fantasy and the imagination.

Connor was proud to be a soldier fighting for his country, because he believed he could help save innocent people like Sadie from a horrible fate, but wearing a soldier's uniform likened to wearing a costume at times. And maybe people loved the costume, not the intentions behind it. If he was honest with himself, Connor wasn't sure he could live up to the uniform. Live up to Sadie's expectations of him.

But the future beckoned. It was time to honour Sadie's memory and prove he could be the hero she always believed him to be.

It was time for war.

Chapter Twenty

Moonleaves, Mysteries, and the Magic of Midnight

The noon sun rose directly above the hollow as Sadie and her company ascended the path back to their quarters. As they approached a secluded garden marked by a large willow with long, wispy, trailing branches, Tristan tapped Sadie's arm and halted.

"Tamlin, why don't you go ahead with Haldin and Airothane, I want to show Sadie this garden," said Tristan. Sadie raised her eyebrows, though relief flooded her at the opportunity to talk to him. Tamlin raised a single eyebrow and smirked before continuing down the path, Haldin keeping pace with her after only a brief bemused hesitation. Airothane craned his neck over his bony shoulder as he trotted in Haldin's wake, not bothering to hide his curiosity.

As soon as their friends vanished around a bend, Tristan pulled back the curtain of willow branches and held them open for Sadie to pass through first. A vision of her own hand pulling back a willow-branch curtain on the Sheldon lawn to sit on her favourite secluded swing flashed before her eyes as she passed beneath the parted veil and entered the garden.

The willow tree's mighty trunk and dramatic firework explosion of branches comprised an entire wall of the garden. A hedge and double rows of birch trees with slender leaves burnished a deep gold comprised the other walls. Intermingled fallen autumnal leaves and flower petals blanketed the ground. A few carved wooden benches dotted the perimeter of the garden, and in the centre loomed a fountain with a broad-edged basin. A stone lyre mounted on a pedestal topped the fountain, four ribbons of water replacing the strings.

Time seemed suspended in this garden. Sadie could feel its halting force, an eternity held in each second. Sitting on the stone rim of the fountain, she trailed her fingers across the water like a paddle dragged through a lake, relishing the caressing coolness. Aware of Tristan's eyes on her, Sadie watched the rippling fountain even when he sat beside her. She waited for him to break the garden's slumbering tranquility.

"How're you feeling?" Tristan asked.

"You mean other than leaving a meeting with Alldían feeling more lost and emptier than ever instead of brooding over a plethora of answers, which is what you led me to expect? I don't even think he knew who I was."

"I thought that might be bothering you, which is why I made an albeit flimsy excuse to pull you aside." Pausing, Tristan sighed. "Look, Sadie, Alldían knew who you were right away. He knew you were the girl from his vision."

"How do you know? If my arrival was as important to Alldían as you made it seem, he would have acknowledged bringing me here and not treated me like everyone else in the company."

"I know your brains are probably still addled from your recent encounter with magic, but try not to be a fool if you can help it, Sadie," countered Tristan, anger crackling in his voice now.

"Excuse me?" challenged Sadie, getting to her feet. Water droplets dripped from her fingertips. "You have no right to call me a fool. You keep putting me in situations I'm completely unprepared for and expecting me to understand what's going on. How on earth would I know what to expect from Alldían?"

"I didn't think I needed to prepare you for every encounter with Carmellians beforehand. I didn't think Alldían not wanting to spill all his secrets the second he meets you in front of people who have nothing to do with his vision needed explanation. I thought you were a better judge of character. Clever enough to intuit the intentions behind the words. To know the most important messages hide in the unsaid," retorted Tristan, and the disappointment in his voice burned more than a scathing remark. "I guess I was wrong."

Warring waves of embarrassment and pleasure at his esteem of her clashed in her brain. Her cheeks heated, but she stiffened the stubborn clench of her jaw. "It's not unreasonable to expect a few words of what to expect when these lands, these people, and their customs are foreign to me."

"*These people* are not much different than the people on Earth, Sadie. Their clothing, appearances, customs, and beliefs all may be different, but the races of Arwé are no more eager to divulge their hard-earned secrets or risk the fate of their people than the humans of Earth would be. Maybe Lantíes have a harder time trusting than other races—I did already explain the prejudices against Lantíes because of their peryton origins to you. Alldían could say no more than a respectful greeting to you while Haldin, Airothane, and even other Lantíes were present."

"He doesn't even trust his own people?" Sadie asked. Her stomach dropped. If the depths of Lantian mistrust ran so deep, how could she trust Alldían?

Tristan pulled at the bridge of his nose and motioned for her to sit down again. Sadie hesitated, then perched at his side. Petty quarrelling would solve nothing.

"Caris Nando may appear like a safe secluded haven, but this is an illusion. You must not be deceived. The Lantíes are devoutly Ilyance in principles and ethics, and loyal to Alldían. But no race can claim every single one of its members are unequivocally pure of heart. There is always the risk of treasonous thoughts blackening a heart. Some may even be direct spies for Vashi, biding their time until they learn something of value. Fearing everyone in paranoia is not the answer. But abandoning wariness in the eager pursuit of truth is foolish. Alldían had to feign ignorance in the presence of those who do not know the truth. Didn't you feel the lance of his gaze as he searched your eyes and exposed your soul?"

Sadie shifted her weight uncomfortably.

"And don't forget, Alldían may want to be sure of your character before he decides to help fulfill his vision."

Sadie flinched at hearing Tristan confirm her fears.

Tristan noticed, and his brows drew together. "Acting upon any vision of the future is an enormous risk," he clarified. "Alldían's decision to bring you out of your world into Carmelle may drastically change Carmelle's fate. Only a fool would neglect to proceed with caution."

Sadie nodded but averted her eyes, her chest collapsing under the weight of her mistakes. Nervousness at speaking with Alldían and a new wariness for the hidden perils of Caris Nando amalgamated into a tight knot in the pit of her stomach.

Tristan eventually broke the silence again.

"So... how are you feeling? After your magic on the Sula-onon the other night."

"Honestly? A little shaken. Tamlin told me the power I wielded could have killed me."

Tristan held his inhalation for a minute before admitting, "For a moment, I thought you *were* dead. When I caught you as you started falling... I thought I was saving someone already lost. It scared me." His voice had fallen to a whisper.

Sadie searched his eyes. No trace of mockery or sarcasm glinted there. Nothing but somewhat surprised sincerity gazed back at her.

She grinned awkwardly. "Well, good. Scaring you is ever my sole intent. Though I suppose once again I do owe you thanks for saving my life. So, thank you."

"Anytime, tellurian." His genuine smile ignited his chocolate brown eyes with bronze sparks, like an errant spark reigniting a fire's dying embers.

Once more, that wily fickle trickster Time played tricks on the company. Slipping past in great dollops, time was a swollen tear brimming with peaceful dreamy moments, then splashing across the mind like paint flicked from a brush.

Enveloping her in its dark embrace, night stole over the mighty trees and leaf-strewn paths of Caris Nando, creating ominous shadows. Starlight twinkled upon the forest's canopy, but in this part of the Lantian kingdom the eaves grew too thick for starlight to penetrate through.

Tristan acted as their guide tonight, navigating the smooth paths for them with his keen eyesight. Sadie kept forgetting this was Tristan's home, the place he grew up and still dwelt when duty permitted. He appeared comfortable, but did he ever feel he didn't wholly belong? Where was his family? Why was Alldían Tristan's godfather?

Before Sadie could dwell on the answers further, Airothane fell into pace with her long strides, running on every alternate step to keep up as he began chattering like an angry squirrel.

Sadie gawked at Airothane, torn between exasperation and amusement. "Do you ever stop talking? Your ability to reel off thoughts without taking a breath is disturbing."

"Breathing is for the weak," said Airothane in such a contemptuous tone Sadie guffawed. With his scrawny arms swinging like wet noodles at his side and his frail, thin chest heaving with the effort of jogging beside Sadie, he looked like weakness personified.

Behind them, Haldin echoed Sadie's laugh. "Exaggeration is ever your shadow and friend, little brother. I wonder if all Windtalkers are as long-winded in speech as you."

"They're not," asserted Tamlin. "In fact, most are brooding and quiet, wandering in solitude, their voices growing hoarse with idle use. They converse with the wind in their minds, and seldom aloud to humans. Airothane rejoices so much in the sound of his own voice, it's a wonder he hears anything the wind says."

Airothane began spluttering a retort, but Tristan interrupted to announce, "We have reached the spot. Our feast is nigh."

They stood in the middle of the path they'd been following for the last fifteen minutes. A single lantern adorned the bole of a trunk nearby, but nothing else indicated a feast. Sadie had been expecting a grand feasting hall, not a rustic picnic on the path. They were to dine with Alldían, his closest kin, and fellow Lantian nobles for his customary ceremonial welcoming of guests—an honour that would have occurred sooner had Sadie been conscious.

"Er... are we eating on the ground?" Sadie asked.

"Of course not!" Airothane exclaimed confidently, though curiosity infused his voice and his eyes darted along the path as though a secret chamber might pop out of the ground.

"We have reached the steps leading to the platform in the trees where a feast, and Alldían, await," Tristan clarified. "Let us ascend and keep them waiting no longer."

As they walked around the tree with the lantern, Sadie noticed a smoothed wooden half circle like a mushroom embedded in the trunk. Peering up, she discerned similar shapes jutting out from the tree above.

Thousands of little lights flickered into existence. They spiralled around the trees, twinkling like hovering fireflies or luminescent pearls of dew.

Sadie floated among the stars.

The lights illuminated each step at the base where they connected to the trunk, ensuring the Lantíés knew where to place their feet as they ascended to the platforms above.

"Ladies first, tellurian," said Tristan with a mock bow.

Elbowing Tristan in the ribs as she passed him, Sadie lifted the hem of her dress and began to climb. Airothane leapt forward to follow her.

When they reached the point where branches diverged from the trunk, the platforms became more distinct. Shaped like different leaves, the platforms connected to one another in midair or hid in the uppermost branches like nests.

They emerged onto a large platform with a long, low wooden table running down the centre. An array of high-backed wooden chairs and raised cushions encircled the table. Lantian nobles already gathered there, some seated, some still standing in small clumps, talking softly.

Sitting at the far end of the table in an aspen chair was Alldían, now in robes of silver slashed with cream, glinting like a mantle of shimmering stars. On his right sat a younger Lantíé, still with the depths of many winters glinting in his ice blue eyes, but without the small lines of age upon his brow or the strands of silver in his hair like Alldían. His thick buttermilk hair cascaded in waves down his back to his waist, resting upon robes of deep blue trimmed with white like a stormy sea. He had neither wings nor antlers. Alldían and the younger Lantíé were deep in conversation as the company crested the platform but broke off abruptly after glancing at Sadie.

Sadie's cheeks burned, but her anger also sparked. Had Alldían been talking about her? She seethed at the idea of him discussing her with other Lantíés before even talking to her.

"Welcome, honoured guests," greeted Alldían, rising from his chair. "Tonight, we share a grand feast to formally welcome our guests to Caris Nando, and afterwards there will be music and song. Join me at the fore of the table, and we shall wet our lips with wine together."

Tristan sat upon Alldían's immediate left as his godson, while Tamlin received the honoured spot beside him. The rest of the guests filed in beside Tamlin, and Sadie found herself sandwiched between Tamlin and Haldin, with Airothane on the end.

As soon as everyone was seated, half a dozen Lantíés in robes of deep eggplant crossed lithely over a narrow connecting bridge, bearing covered silver platters in their hands. They placed themselves uniformly behind the seated guests, and at precisely the same moment set the platters down in the centre of the table and lifted the lids.

A pool of saliva gathered at the corner of her mouth at the sumptuous aroma wafting towards her. Since regaining consciousness, she had been ravenous.

Mountains of fruit in a darker palette of reds, purples, and greens balanced precariously; mounds of fluffy white grains, freshly baked loaves of bread, and salads of yellow, brown, and burgundy seeds and beans drizzled in aromatic sauces and spices constituted the earth-tone selection; and a plethora of colourful steamed vegetables were served in rows upon puffed brown grains like an edible garden.

When Sadie reached for a round, green fruit, the whole mountain of fruit cascaded down, rolling and bursting across the table like sweet little grenades. Sadie's company laughed as her cheeks burned, and she scrambled to help the Lantíés in eggplant robes pile the fruits again.

As Sadie began shovelling food into her mouth, a movement at the head of the table caught her eye. Leaning conspiratorially closer to Alldían so their heads almost touched, Tristan whispered in his ear, his eyes tightening. Tamlin subtly tilted her body and puckered her brows. The anonymous Lantíé on Alldían's right surreptitiously shifted an inch closer, a twinkle of knowledge flashing in his eyes like the sun sparking the ocean on a clear day.

Sadie paused with a forkful of speared carrots halfway to her mouth, staring at the group of conspirators. Catching sight of Sadie's expression, Haldin followed the piercing beam of her gaze.

"You know what they're discussing is serious, otherwise Duvandir wouldn't betray such blatant interest," Haldin stated, sounding unconcerned despite his fixated eyes.

"Duvandir?" Sadie repeated.

"The Lantíés on Alldían's right," clarified Haldin. "He is Alldían's only son and heir. Though I had not been formally introduced until I happened upon him yesterday, I have heard he is aloof except when something dark or dangerous is discussed."

"You're not wrong," chimed in Tamlin, and Haldin jumped a little, unaware Tamlin had been listening to him and eavesdropping on Tristan at the same time. She kept her voice low. "Duvandir loves intrigue and reads people better than his father. He usually prefers to observe rather than converse, so when he concentrates on serious discussions he can look quite sinister and brooding—and his prolonged absences from Caris Nando don't do his reputation any favours. But Tristan knows of Duvandir's skills and would never try to tell Alldían a secret when Duvandir is sitting right there. Whatever he's saying is meant for both of their ears. Just maybe not ours."

Sadie rubbed the back of her neck as she stole quick glances at Duvandir, dreading his slow, calculating eyes piercing hers. If Alldían's gaze made her feel exposed, how would she feel under the scrutiny of a Lantíé who could perceive *more* than Alldían?

A grunt of frustration blasted from Haldin's other side, and Sadie peered around him to find Airothane glaring at the conspirators with a mutinous scowl. His knuckles had turned white from the tight grip on his fork.

"Er...Airothane?" Sadie asked, alarmed by the ferocity of his expression. "You okay?"

"How they can have the nerve..." Airothane began, but apparently his anger rendered him speechless.

Haldin shook his head in indulgent exasperation.

"It's because they aren't including me," Haldin explained. "Airothane is very defensive of me." He returned to his food, losing interest in the conversation now that it was about him.

"It's outrageous, how could they not include Haldin in important discussions?" Airothane burst out in a whisper-shout that nonetheless carried a little. The conspirators did not look up though. "Do they not know who he *is*? He's the first-born son of King Peladorn, a prince of Dharmaelia! He's Haldin the Hawk, the greatest warrior in Dharmaelia! He is the most trusted and respected person other than the King among our people! And they won't even include him in their counsels? Do they think Dharmaelia scum undeserving of their respect? How can they—"

"Airothane, that is quite enough!" Haldin interjected in a low, non-negotiable voice. Airothane clamped his mouth shut.

For most of the feast, Sadie chatted with Haldin and Airothane about Dharmaelia. The brothers planted images in her head of vast, sweeping golden plains, epic sunsets of burnished gold and orange, and the stark jagged red peaks of the Dharlomin mountain range marching down to Dharmaelia. Though the brothers asked her about her own land, Sadie evaded answering as much as possible. Her feelings about Earth were too conflicted now to want to dwell on her homeland.

When the feast ended, the table was cleared and replaced with giant velvet throw cushions in deep burgundies, golds, and emeralds. Instantly, Sadie and Airothane engaged in a fierce scuffle over the nearest emerald cushion embroidered with silver unicorns. Sadie won and plopped the cushion down triumphantly behind two Lantíes snuggled together. Tristan sat beside her.

Anticipation ignited her veins as Sadie watched two Lantíes place their palms in slight indents in the tree's trunk. The outline of a perfect oval door separated from the trunk with a *crack* and swung forward on invisible hinges. Three harps perched on a bed of forest green velvet, their golden curves illuminating the dark hollow with a soft glow. Choosing the two tallest harps, the Lantíes carried them to a cleared space.

At first the duo played wordless ethereal music to swell the listeners' hearts and haunt the spaces between stars. When the sky deepened another shade and the stars crowded those haunted spaces, the Lantíes took turns singing along to the music, creating a story.

Immediately Sadie's mind was swept away. Rushing down roaring rivers, plunging down waterfalls, galloping with unicorns, flying with eagles, swimming with merpeople in the ocean, and wandering contently through garden mazes. The world was magical and enchanting.

Storytellers. There was no mistaking their alluring power.

Mouth agape, Sadie turned to find Tristan watching her, his face unreadable.

"Yes," he confirmed in response to Sadie's expression. "These two Lantíes are Storytellers like me. They are two of three Lantian Storytellers. The other lives in the southern Lantian dwelling of Lothilya. Though Storytellers normally perform alone, these two have mastered the art of telling a story together, weaving words and melody to create cohesion. Their prodigious skill and harmonious integration are beyond the skills of a human Storyteller."

No trace of envy marred Tristan's face. She respected his humility in regards to his skills.

Both a wonderful and terrible idea struck Sadie. Struggling to keep her voice even and casual, she asked, "Are you going to perform tonight?"

Tristan's eyes searched hers, and Sadie wondered if he detected her fear, despite her best efforts not to let her voice quaver.

"Yes," he affirmed quietly, not taking his eyes off her.

Sadie nodded, afraid of speaking lest she say something she'd regret. A clandestine part of her heart longed to be submerged in the worlds he created that resonated in her soul, sweeping her away more than the two Lantian Storytellers could. But knowing Tristan could ensnare her mind so easily still disconcerted her. With so much uncertainty and powerlessness governing her life, Sadie craved a bit of control. A bit of her mind she could keep to herself.

Tristan did not push the subject, but Sadie could tell it remained on his mind, and when the two Lantian Storytellers ceased to play, Tristan avoided Sadie's eyes as he retrieved the third and final harp. It was smaller than the others, with a crown carved like a fairy. Had Tristan chosen the fairy? It seemed a surprising choice, even a little childish. But then Sadie remembered the closed rosebud of Tristan's personalized Swordmaster emblem and reconsidered. A connection with innocence and a more haunting beauty coincided with the rosebud.

As Tristan seated himself before the guests, Sadie stiffened, bracing herself for the inevitable usurpation of her mind. And yet curiosity ebbed her anxiety. What kind of story would inspire Tristan tonight? What facet of history, what ancient legend, would he recall from the mists of forgotten memory?

The transition was seamless, fluid as one calm stream flowing uninterrupted into another. One moment she teetered on the precipice of a cliff, contemplating the foggy landscape below, and the next she plunged into the fog as it shifted into definable details.

Pale golden sunlight sliced through gaps between birch trees. Lily pads bearing blushing lilies floated to the surface of a pond. A soft breeze caressed the trees, rippling the water and fluttering the bright green leaves. Sadie swore the same breeze played across her cheeks.

A human in a green velvet dress appeared in the forest. She linked a path through the trees with her hands, her ebony plaited hair swaying with the motion as though in a dance.

Sadie noticed the shadow blotting sunlight on the moss before discerning its source. Crouched on the lower branch of a tree above the wandering girl perched a man all in black. The hilt of a dagger peeked from the lip of his boot, a sheathed rapier hung on his black belt, and a quiver full of black-and-red fletched arrows was slung over his back. He held a strung bow, ready for use. Only the symbol of a red flame stitched onto the back of his cloak and black leather gloves hinted at his identity.

Silently and stealthily as a leopard, the man drew an arrow and fit it to the string.

Although immersed in the story, this time Sadie could appreciate the narrative and admire Tristan's ability to create tension in the scene before letting the action unfold. Just before the man loosed his arrow, the woman whipped around and hurled a dagger at him. He toppled out of the tree. Burgundy blood stained his shirt and seeped into the moss around him, and the inch of blade still visible above his chest glinted in the golden sunlight. Sadie could taste the blood.

When the story ended, and the last image of a king lowering a crown onto the woman's head faded away, Sadie jolted back to the present with dizzying abruptness.

She had survived one of Tristan's stories without losing control of her mind.

But she couldn't do it again. As Tristan poised his fingers above the harp's strings once more, a desperate restlessness overwhelmed Sadie. Anxiety gripped her. Sweat beaded her forehead, and the crisp night air stifled her.

Standing to leave, Sadie accidentally kicked her cushion. It toppled Airothane, whose feeble frame was no match for the pillow's light weight. Cursing her clumsiness, Sadie's cheeks burned as she hurried across the platform, not daring to meet the eyes boring into her back. Guilt twanged her heartstrings, but she kept fleeing. She would explain to Tristan later and hope he did not hold it against her.

Thousands of tiny lights sprinkling the trees amid real twinkling stars evoked the wondrous impression that she walked through the spirals of the Milky Way. The thought soothed her anxiety, and a smile crept across her face.

Once she reached the bottom, Sadie paused, unsure where to go after only being conscious in Caris Nando for one day. Choosing a path at random, she skipped down it, her arms flapping like a bird about to take flight.

Sadie halted abruptly.

An army of trees faced her.

They loomed before her silently, their uniform trunks arrayed in perfect formation, rank upon rank fading into an eerie mist.

Hesitating, Sadie contemplated turning back. No lamps adorned these trees. Only the silver sheen of mist lit her way, and Sadie had serious qualms about trusting a mist tangled so intimately with such imposing trees.

A white light flashed between trees in her peripheral vision.

She whipped around. Nothing.

Squinting, Sadie stared at the swirling mists, trying to detect movement more tangible than condensed vapour.

A black hoof, a velvety white torso, and a long head tipped with a pearly twisted horn bobbing gracefully as it trotted forward out of a thick cloud of mist...

The same unicorn Sadie had followed to the Sula-onon approached her without hesitation this time and lowered its head into her outstretched palms. Sadie buried her head in its neck and tangled her fingers in its mane. Contentment and strength poured through her like molten fire. The unicorn nudged Sadie with its muzzle and turned back towards the mist. She kept one hand entwined in the unicorn's mane as the sea of low-lying fog swallowed them.

After ten minutes, a long stone building materialized before her. Leading Sadie through the opening, lit with a pale orange glow, the unicorn brought her inside a stable.

Unicorns rested on the soft mossy forest floor, eating grains and fruits from basins mounted around the perimeter of the open stalls, or drinking deeply from marble fountains and troughs. One by one Sadie visited the stalls, meeting their eyes and allowing them to search her soul. Her unicorn companion stayed behind her, sometimes placing its muzzle encouragingly in the small of her back. Its presence comforted Sadie. When they reached the furthest stall, the unicorn entered ahead of Sadie and drank deeply from a low trough. From its thicker consistency and silver swirls, Sadie guessed the liquid was *yenalin*, the drink Tristan had mentioned at Maeldré, the Golden Bowl by the Athatair.

"Unicorns certainly are magnificent creatures."

Sadie's heart stopped beating.

There, his silver-threaded hair glinting in the moonlight, his ebony antlers blending with shadows, and his hands tucked in his robes' sleeves, stood Alldían.

"Y-yes, they are," stammered Sadie. Avoiding his intimidating gaze, Sadie fastened her eyes upon the unicorn's swishing tail.

"He likes you," Alldían observed. "I have rarely seen anyone who can stroke a unicorn with such calm, natural affinity. The way you look him steadily in the eyes and instinctively comprehend his intentions—it is a connection nigh unheard of with humans."

Smiling guiltily at Sadie's narrowed eyes, Alldían answered her unspoken question: "I confess, I followed you from the feast and witnessed you greeting the unicorn. Also, I heard all about the unicorn leading you to the Sula-onon."

Silence stretched painfully as the expectation for Sadie to say something spiralled awkwardly, but she remained stubbornly silent and dour.

"In fact, the only other non-Lantíé I have seen connect with a unicorn in my lifetime is Tamlin. I don't know whether she has informed you, but she has a deep friendship with one unicorn. Not unlike the one you have formed with this fine creature here—" Alldían nodded to the unicorn behind Sadie, who kept one eye fastened upon Alldían as he drank, clearly aware he was being talked about— "and she and her unicorn friend, Khalí, often travel and battle together. I would not be surprised to see you engaging in similar endeavours with this unicorn one day. Once a connection is formed between an animal and human, it is not easily severed or forgotten by either party."

"I-I do feel a strong connection with him," Sadie admitted. "Like our souls are connected. But I'm not sure why he tolerates me. I'm nothing special. Not like Tamlin, a renowned wizard."

Alldían smiled knowingly. "No, you are not the same as Tamlin. But you are special, Sadie. You may not know it, but this unicorn certainly does. He has put his faith in you. You should do the same for him—and for yourself."

The unicorn nudged Sadie's back with his nose, and she blushed.

"Your connection with this unicorn is clear, but I must warn you unicorns act for their own purposes. I don't know why he brought you to the Sula-onon that night, but although unicorns often have great foresight, their purpose and desired ends may not be the same as yours."

Sadie caught her lower lip between her teeth. What could the unicorn have planned for her that did not coincide with her own purpose? "Does he have a name?" Sadie asked.

"We don't typically name unicorns unless a special bond is developed with one, and then the bonded person chooses the name. They are not horses, trained to come when we call. If we want to use something other than pronouns or speak to them directly, we use the term *míval*, which means 'friend' in Tavé."

Míval. A beautiful term, but not quite right for her bond with him. She would think on it.

"And now," Alldían continued in a more cheerful voice, "would you be so obliging as to accompany me on a walk, Sadie? There is more I wish to discuss."

Sadie's stomach fluttered, but she slowly detached herself from the unicorn's side and followed Alldían out of the stable and along a path, heading north.

"Your magic appears to be strong, Sadie, especially for a human not from Carmelle," Alldían began as the path curved around close-knit trees. "I have heard of both your inadvertent exertions of magic. I knew you were special and would affect our world, but I must admit even I did not suspect you would affect it so profoundly so quickly!"

Sadie ducked her head, thankful the filtered moonlight didn't quite illuminate her burning cheeks.

"A civil war started and two near-death experiences! I never expected anything more exciting than a run-in with some bragûl or a tussle with an innkeeper on your journey here with Tristan!" He seemed to consider the shattering of his expectations a treat.

"I know Tamlin has discussed your magic with you already, and she is the right person to do so, but I do have some information to share. Answers to questions I know you have."

Sadie waited for a moment, but when Alldían did not elaborate, she ventured to ask a question that had been building inside her since she had discovered her magic: "Did you know I would have magic before you brought me here?"

Alldían glanced at her face before returning his gaze fixedly ahead, as though re-examining an image imprinted in the darkness. "No, I did not know for certain you would have magic. I knew you were special, and we needed you but... Sadie, this topic is the primary reason I sought you out tonight, and we will discuss it more, but let me ask you first: why did you antagonize Griswald in the streets of Carenthia the day you first used your magic?"

Sadie considered his question. She could have a terrible temper, and Griswald's arrogance and ignorance had frustrated her into action—which had been her explanation to Tristan at the time—but it went deeper.

"Where I come from, Griswalds are not uncommon. They believe we can only thrive through progress and advancement, obsessed with making life easier, often at the expense of the natural world. Their ambition spawns greed and power-hungry lust so blinding even their family become pawns in their game of advancement," Sadie replied bitterly. "Ugly black smoke permeates city air, hovering above the horizon line. Machines create detachment and disillusion between people and nature. As soon as I came to Carmelle I felt the difference: magic sparks in every aspect of this world."

Sadie waited for her mother's exasperated reprimands at her impassioned speech to echo out of Alldían's mouth, but he stayed silent, watching her patiently. She shook her head and continued.

"I'm not saying this world doesn't have its problems. Every world with interacting species can never be entirely at peace. You can't force sentient beings to think the same, nor should you. But for Griswald to proceed down a path I know will bring discord to a world with such wonder… I lost control. To escape one world and find another headed down the same path angered and depressed me. Are the inhabitants of every world doomed to the same fate? I've only been here a few months, and already I've fallen in love with Carmelle and want to defend and preserve it. To be honest, I feel more at home here than I ever did in my world."

Sadie thought she detected triumph in Alldían's eyes at her last words. "I am touched and pleased to hear you care about Carmelle, Sadie. Your beliefs regarding her best interests coincide with mine. Though I agree with you regarding Griswald's arrogance and flawed designs for improvement, I do not believe progress carries the negative connotations you seem to associate with it. Progress is not a stagnant word by definition. The results of progress are multifaceted, and progress in our world could have different meanings and repercussions than in yours. Besides, you don't know it will be negative long-term in your world. Even if change seems bad at first, there is no need to despair until all hope and love are abandoned."

Seeing the wisdom in this, Sadie could think of no response, but defiance still gripped her heart. Griswald was arrogant, power-hungry, and greedy, and even if other Redpath members had better intentions, Sadie knew Griswald had his own agenda.

As though listening to her thoughts, Alldían added, "Griswald is not a man you want to anger. Stand up to him, but he is a man who does not forgive, or forget. I caution you not to underestimate Griswald. He has no magic or special gifts, but he is vengeful, cunning, and ruthless, and those can be just as powerful weapons."

"You talk as though Griswald is still alive," Sadie observed. "But Griswald is dead, sir. He perished in that fire. He was trapped by the flames, there was a giant gaping hole too wide for him to jump across... there's no way he could have survived."

"Ah yes, forgive me. A grammatical error. The Redpath, however, will still want revenge. The dragon guarding the Gap of Talarí was sent by the Redpath, which means they are willing to use fatal force to achieve their ends regardless of who it affects. I fear a civil war is inevitable. Us Ilyance will not tolerate control of our freedoms. Too many Redpaths joined because of the opportunities for power over others. Now that Griswald is gone, the other members will be competing to fill his position as leader, which means they will try to prove their power by being the one to find and kill you."

An uneasy tingle prickled the back of her neck at the similarities between the Ilyance fighting for their freedoms against those craving power, and the power struggle between her and her mom over Sadie's freedoms.

Fractals of ice fanned out from her heart as she thought of the danger she now put everyone she cared about in. The Redpath had her targeted, and their aim may not waver even if she crossed through a portal into another world. What if she remained their sighted target, and her family got caught in the crosshairs?

"And now," Alldían continued, "to explain my purpose in bringing you to Carmelle."

A chill of foreboding stole over Sadie as she looked into Alldían's deep, oceanic eyes. She had waited for this moment since spinning through the mirror into Carmelle, but Sadie wasn't sure she wanted to hear his explanation now. What if she had been brought here for a purpose she couldn't fulfill? What if she was stuck in Carmelle forever? And maybe even worse... What if she *could* go home now?

Alldían stopped walking and extracted something from the folds of his robes. A small metallic click followed a hum, and light flared from a thin disc resting in his palm. Wrought like a full moon with a leaf suspended between the tips of a quarter-moon, the disc featured real leaves clustered in the centre like a closed flower bulb waiting to bloom.

When Alldían held it in the path of a moonbeam, the leaves slowly unfolded. Silver moonlight filtered through their veins and pooled at the centre, forming a sphere of opaque pearly light. Sadie held her breath. The sphere glowed brighter and rose an inch or two above the leaves, illuminating Alldían's face. A gasp escaped Sadie when Alldían let go of the disc. Instead of obeying gravity and falling to the earth, it rose in the air a foot or two.

Magic. Magic to interrogate her? Her nerves elevated instead of alleviating, though she tried not to let it show on her face.

"What's that?" Sadie asked, struggling to keep the awe out of her voice.

"A moonleaf light," Alldían explained. "The trapped moonlight in the metal disc fuels the moonleaves crowning it on top, which in turn open to soak up new moonbeams and produce a portable sphere of moonlight. Under the right circumstances, moonleaves can both capture the light of the moon and serve as prophetic aids. In fact, it was through the power of moonleaves that I first saw you and knew I must bring you to Carmelle."

Sadie looked at Alldían expectantly.

"Yes, Sadie," Alldían continued quietly. "You were brought here because in my chambers I have a moonleaf tree and a pool, and through the networking of certain moonleaves and the plucking of others to cast in the pool below, I can see visions in the pool of things to come. I saw you. Here, in Carmelle. The images are not to be interpreted as exact prophecies. They are only portents of significant future happenings, flashes of what someone may do or be if their path is set that way. Sometimes the setting of their path needs a helping hand. I'm afraid that is what I took the liberty of doing with you."

Already aware of the liberties he had taken, Sadie stomach still ached as though punched hearing it said aloud. She fingered her moon and leaf bracelet. She was certain he had sent it, but she wasn't ready to confront him about it. What difference would it make anyway? Even without the bracelet, he had manipulated her into coming to Carmelle. The bracelet was just one more piece of evidence in uncovering a known truth. She already didn't trust him.

"I would like to offer a small redeeming factor in my defence," Alldían continued, eyeing her discomfort with a small grimace. "I instructed Tristan not to encourage you to walk through the mirror unless he thought you might be happy to leave your world for an adventure in another. You see, moonleaf magic is tricky because the moon has both a light and dark side, so every vision the moonleaves show is double-sided. The moonleaves show you the light side, even if the deeds it shows are evil, but there is always the unknown shadow side. The vision only showed *part* of your potential in Carmelle. Moonleaf magic stems from Celestial magic. My ancestors, the perytons, had a special connection with Celestial magic, so I sometimes act based on my instincts connected to those peryton roots. But it is always a risk. Lantíes don't fear Celestial magic the same way most races of Carmelle do. We still use it in tools like moonleaf lights and visions, as long as we aren't wielding the magic. But trusting Celestial magic is always a risk."

Sadie eyed the moonleaf light with new wariness, wondering if her magic would be drawn to it.

"Perception also plays a big role," Alldían continued. "I may have wanted to see someone who could help our world, and therefore interpreted your images as helpful to Carmelle, when in fact they could be detrimental if your personality is altered because your new path departs too greatly from your personal dreams. In short, I hoped to steer you to Carmelle, but exercised caution to ensure your happiness here. A small comfort, I know, but…"

He spread his hands wide as if to say *here's the smidgen of thought I designated to considering your well-being*. Take it or leave it. Sadie would leave it. He only considered her feelings to ensure his scheme worked. He had played her like a pawn in a crude game of chess. Even her mother's schemes had always at least been transparent and predictable. It was difficult to feel anything towards Alldían but furious indignation. Could he really be so selfish?

Of course, he could, she answered herself. Since entering Caris Nando, he had already chosen to share the guarded Lantian secret of the Atha Onéa with her just so he could test Sadie's character and magic. He had risked her life and others' to serve his own agenda.

"Let me guess, you won't tell me the nature of these visions, or what exactly I'm supposed to do to help Carmelle?" Sadie fired at him.

Alldían considered her accusing gaze before speaking.

"I did not bring you here to fight a civil war between the Redpath and the Ilyance. I believe you are integral to the inevitable war against Vashi, which I feel will come much sooner than anyone anticipates. His minions are spreading destruction and chaos already. Some attacks are subtle, some more active skirmishes, but there is no doubt they have dramatically increased."

Alldían paused. "I could tell you more specifics—how the images unfolded, where they took place, what exactly you were doing in them—but I want you to be the one to decide how much you want to hear. I am willing to divulge more but allow me to remind you that sometimes knowing less about your future is better. Especially from a vision that is only half the story. It may allow you more freedom of mind and power of choice. Your choices will always define your future, rather than your future defining your choices, Sadie."

Fixing her eyes on the levitating sphere of moonlight to avoid looking at Alldían's face, Sadie contemplated what she really wanted. Dark shadows veiled moonleaf visions, only showing half the story. Alldían had chosen to act on the unknown, on a half truth. But half truths could be more dangerous.

Believing she might have a destiny to fulfill was one thing, but knowing the specifics was another. It seemed ridiculous to place so much faith in something ultimately still unknown. Alldían admitted the moonleaf images could change depending on individual choice and extraneous circumstances. So, wasn't it better to remain in the unknown? This way events wouldn't feel anticlimactic. For better or worse, she wanted everything in her life to be experienced in the moment.

She refused to let the unknown play on her fears until she came to believe she had control over her future.

Controlling her future could never be anything more than an illusion. She knew that now.

Sadie's brow furrowed as a thought occurred to her.

"How do you know I'm the girl you saw in the moonleaf images? A girl with red hair and green eyes... that could be *anyone*, in any world. How did you know I was the right one? Was my name branded across my forehead? Are you sure you have the right person, even now?"

"I knew you would ask this question," Alldían conceded with a knowing grin Sadie found patronizing. "The secrets of moonleaf prophecies are well-guarded by the Lantíés. The plant is unique to these woods and only Lantíés can divine their secrets. Moonleaves also trace the trajectory of the subject's life. I saw images of your house, your family, your city—and there are even more specific signs if one knows how to interpret them. I did not doubt who the images pertained to before I sought you, and your deeds in Carmelle have only proven I was right. Consider your magic, the effects you've had on people's lives, and the civil war you accelerated into motion! Not to mention your professed sense of belonging and love for Carmelle. Do you doubt you were meant to be here?"

Sadie couldn't honestly deny her connection to Carmelle, so she said nothing.

"I know this is a heavy burden for you to bear, Sadie," Alldían said in a soft, soothing voice. "It's not easy for anyone to shoulder more responsibility, especially not in this magnitude, and I know you must feel bitter. If I can help spare these bitter feelings, please let me know."

Fuming, Sadie started pacing, fists clenched. Of course she was bitter! Some old stag-man with wings had decided to dictate her future, and when she finally met him for answers, he enhanced her feeling of being a pawn by admitting his motives for keeping her happy were born from a desire to prevent her straying from the hero path, not compassion. He didn't care about the painful and confusing realization that right now she wasn't even sure if she wanted to go home. Everyone used her for their own agenda: Tamlin, Alldían... even Tristan!

She had grown to trust Tristan and accept he was duty-bound. He had suggested answers would be revealed when she talked to Alldían. But this meeting left her empty and cold. Alldían had told her nothing beyond what she could guess and others had hinted at. Had Tristan truly believed Alldían held more answers, or did he have his own plans? Did the friendship she thought they were building mean nothing to him?

"You can help by telling me why Tristan is such an insufferable, backstabbing ass! You don't turn another person's life upside down just because someone tells you to! Grow a conscience! How could he not know what he did was wrong?"

"Because he believed he was doing the right thing," Alldían interjected. His voice held a grave and, for the first time during their conversation, wary edge.

"You *told* him it was right!" Sadie exploded. "He allowed you to deceive and control him just as you deceived and controlled me! He chose to ignore the obvious immoralities and risk my happiness anyway!"

"Tristan had more reasons than what I told him, Sadie," Alldían explained, sighing deeply. "I wasn't going to tell you because it's not my place, but for the sake of protecting Tristan's character I feel I must. Tristan is not from Carmelle, Sadie. He's from your world."

Sadie froze. Shards of ice shattered her thoughts. Tristan's biggest deceit should have angered her, but it didn't. Calm washed over her instead. She was no better than Tristan. She accused him of judging her prematurely, and yet she had done the same to him. He had never mentioned he was from Carmelle. She had just assumed.

He knew her world. He knew better than anyone what she must be going through. The wonder mixed with guilt, the overwhelming desire to belong in a world she loved as an outsider, the strange gifts manifesting within her never able to come to fruition in her world... He knew it all. Sadie's heart ached, wishing he had shared his true origins with her from the start. The need for more information splintered the ice in her brain and allowed her to face Alldían.

He watched her, waiting for a reaction.

"When did—why did he—" Sadie spluttered. Diminishing fury collided with increasing confusion and stuck in her throat, but Alldían seemed to understand.

"Tristan was very young when he came to Carmelle. He came through the same mirror portal as you, though the how and why is something I will let Tristan confide. He was the first human from your world to come to Carmelle since your ancestor Thomas Sheldon. At first he did not show extraordinary gifts, which I wondered at, since people usually come here from another world because they have a unique purpose to fill or a gift they can only use in Carmelle. Eventually we discovered his gift as a Storyteller, and he has been important to the wars in Carmelle since his youth. He was raised here in Caris Nando under my personal care and is a kindred spirit dear to my heart. I entrusted the mission of transferring you to Carmelle to Tristan, both because I trust him explicitly and because he is the only Carmellian with intimate knowledge of your world and its people. Though your world has changed since Tristan left it, he could still evaluate your life circumstances and make an informed and impromptu decision better than any native Carmellians. You see, Tristan acted because he assessed the situation and truly thought helping you find the portal was the right choice based on your behaviour and his knowledge of your world and its people."

Despite drinking in every word, Sadie only swallowed one idea: Alldían could not tell her how and why Tristan came to Carmelle. She needed to know.

"Wait..." Sadie began hesitantly, dread prickling the nape of her neck. "How come Tristan never went back to his—my world? *Can* you get back to my world once you're here? Or did Tristan lie, and I'm stuck here forever?"

"Tristan is not stuck here, Sadie," Alldían clarified. "He chose to stay in Carmelle. He liked it better than his old world. He felt more at home here than he ever did in your world. Even at such a young age, he knew where he belonged."

Sadie tried to ignore the tingling in her arms, goosebumps rising at the familiar statement.

"Normally, you are never confined to one world. You'd realize this if you weren't overwhelmed with information. Your own ancestor, Thomas Sheldon, returned to your world after his adventures here. Tristan told me you read his book. There are exceptions of course. Some people are inextricably bound to Carmelle. But these exceptions are rare. As long as the portals remain open, those who come to Carmelle can always leave again."

"Then why—"

"There are times when the portals close and no one can re-open them until the portal deems the time right. Portals have their own magic. They close when they sense immense danger for both worlds, such as large-scale wars, and will not re-open until those dangers have passed. I would theorize your world and Carmelle are both about to be in a state of massive war. Which supports my prediction that civil war with the Redpath is not the only war Carmelle will fight soon. The mirror will re-open when it is safe again to pass between worlds, and then you will be more than welcome to return to your world and leave Carmelle as Thomas did before you. No one will stop you. But in the meantime, I'm afraid you are stuck in Carmelle. The portals are the only gateway between worlds, and they seem to have closed right behind you.

"In fact," Alldían added, perhaps noticing Sadie's downcast eyes, "you may say the mirror waited for you to pass through to Carmelle before closing, bringing you here for a purpose. There is no doubt in my mind, Sadie. You were meant to do great things in Carmelle."

Sadie's chest ached. She had wished desperately for a purpose, to be part of something bigger than herself and shake off the heavy manacles of obscurity. Relief flooded her veins to hear Alldían confirm she was meant for greatness, and yet a thread loosened in her heart, a tear that fear and self-doubt poured into. For the first time in her life, an authority figure looked at her with confidence and pride in her powerful potential, and not just as a woman but an equal human with the power to change the world... but disappointment gnawed at her heart.

The emptiness of solitude stung.

Chapter Twenty-One

Tor Niro

Sadie sat on a cushioned window seat in the main library of Caris Nando, intermittently gazing at the rain and thumbing through a book. No sounds existed other than thrumming rain, muffled shuffling of boots against packed earth, and the occasional crackling of thick parchment paper as someone turned a page. There were no rushed footsteps, no panicked voices, no dire warnings or portentous declarations of destiny. No pressure, no tension, no fear. No conflict of truths upon which one was expected to smile. Just rain pattering against the window, carving tracks across the glass like tears on a cheek. Soothing, comforting... perfect. The rain eroded problems from her mind, washing them away like pebbles caught in a stream's current, clearing her mind of debris.

Sadie was here with Haldin and Airothane as part of their obligatory tour of the inner Caris Nando city, Tristan acting as their guide. His many duties meant he was not always available to show them around, but he had insisted upon coming to the library. Sadie had avoided being with Tristan alone since her talk with Alldían, but his past loomed in her mind like a sleeping dragon. A tangible mystery perched on a pile of treasure, alluring yet terrifying when her subconscious padded too close.

Collected for over a millennium by scholars throughout Carmelle, the books were arrayed on log shelves with vines twining around them.

Trees dotted the stone walls at regular intervals. Vaulted ceilings, supporting pillars, and tall ornately framed windows featuring the occasional stained-glass artistry reminded her of Gothic architecture. Tristan had explained that what was once a cozy private library for the Lord of Caris Nando had been added to over the years in odd or perpendicular ways, lending a labyrinthine effect to the network of bookshelves and rooms.

At first, Sadie's enchantment with the library had erased her problems. Leather bound and embroidered on the spines, the books' hand-painted covers and embossed designs complimented the handwritten scripts on heavy parchment paper of inconsistent cuts. Thick scrolls coated in dust mingled with pristine scrolls tipped with tasselled golden rods stacked on shelves. The scent of old, musty books permeated the air.

But the closer Sadie examined the titles, the more her excitement ebbed. So many books explored war and its impact on individuals and nations. Conflict was a commonality every race in every world shared, and for most worlds, war became a cyclical habit. Greed, envy, power, anger, mistreatment, tyranny, racism, fear, clashes of morals and principles—these were typical reasons for war, but Sadie thought there was more to it.

Conflict arose when two or more unique individuals clashed over their differences. Sadie believed differences were assets, not detriments to society. But what made conflict escalate into war? Sadie thought about what Alldían had told her about two possible wars on the horizon for Carmelle. A civil war and... How would the war against Vashi be classified? He was a tyrant with huge forces at his back, but it wasn't a war of nations. It was a war against one man's arrogance and deranged sadism. A war of pluralism versus individualism. A glance at the book titles showed Sadie countless books on Vashi as a threat to Carmelle's peace. Sadie knew Vashi had been thwarted but never defeated, which begged the question: *could* he be defeated? She made a mental note to find out. Malevolence of that magnitude could not be allowed to reign or there was no hope for Carmelle. And the antagonism between the Ilyance and the Redpath would be futile because Carmelle would be doomed no matter what it collectively believed in.

Running her fingertips lightly over the spines, Sadie had come across a title that froze her fingers and snagged her heart: *The Evolution of Earth: Understanding the Histories and Peoples That Differentiate My Native World From Carmelle* by Thomas Sheldon.

Thomas Sheldon had written a book about her world for the people of Carmelle. This was the sister-book to the one sitting in the Sheldon library.

She had come full circle since first picking up *Adventures in Carmelle* a few months ago. This book was the bookend to her adventures thus far, the mark of a new beginning. Until the portals opened again, she was no longer a temporary guest in Carmelle, but a resident intimately connected to this world.

The thought electrified her spine with equal fear and exhilaration.

Sliding the book from its shelf, Sadie had brought it to the window seat without a word. Finding Thomas Sheldon's other book was a profound and slightly poignant moment she did not feel like sharing. She wanted to know how Thomas perceived their world, and what he deemed important to relay to Carmellians.

As Sadie skimmed through pages for subject headings and highlights, she discovered her suspicions were correct: war dominated Thomas' account, staining her world's history like blood. Divisions of regions, race, and classification of species were recorded in a cyclical pattern, inferring antagonism dictated order and structure in her world. Alldían's guess must be right: time's wheel had turned, and war waited to wrap her world in its deadly embrace again.

Staring at a page headed "Religious Wars", Sadie recalled Tamlin's words about how the Keepers would react to a civil war: *"We must not put faith in the unknown. We must assume we are alone."*

Maybe Tristan was right. Maybe Alldían placing his faith in Sadie enough to gamble with the unknown and bring her to Carmelle *was* a courageous act. Alldían had chosen to accept his prophecy as truth, had acted on his faith in the unknown; Sadie had chosen to confront the unknown with her intuition rather than act in accordance with a predestined path. It was a subtle difference, but she was beginning to appreciate the unknown's subtle ambiguities.

Drumming harder against the windows, the rain pounded the confusion from her head, massaging out the worried wrinkles in her mind. Book still open on her lap, she closed her eyes and let the rain soothe her tumultuous thoughts.

"Religious Wars?" a voice inquired in her ear. "Religious Wars! Plural! What a ridiculous thing to have a war over. If I didn't happen to know Thomas was reputedly one of the most honest men in Carmelle, I'd swear he made half the stuff in his book up."

Sadie's eyes flew open.

Tristan looked at her with his crooked sly grin, ready to engage in one of their banter sessions. Sadie's blood boiled at the blatant lie. She clenched her jaw, gritting her teeth against the charade. He was from her world. Whether he believed the wars were ridiculous or not was irrelevant. Was he ashamed to be from the same world as her? Did he not see the bonding opportunity from their shared experiences of coming to Carmelle from Earth?

The smirk slid from Tristan's face at her narrowed eyes and scowl.

Sadie slammed Thomas' book shut, tucked it under her arm, and stormed off.

A few hours later, Sadie trailed the hem of Tamlin's ice blue cloak as it slithered behind her over jumbled roots and rocks. Tamlin hadn't shared their destination when she plucked Sadie from the tour group like a lizard flicking out its tongue to snatch a fly, just said they had urgent business.

Old trees bled into moss-covered thickets, and smoky tendrils of mist swirled around her like weightless clouds. Dew settled in her skin and she shivered, wrapping her cloak more tightly around herself. After about twenty minutes of downhill descent, during which Sadie's chief concern was not tripping over Tamlin's billowing cloak, the path emerged from dense forest into a small opening marked by an enormous rock.

"Are we climbing this boulder?" Sadie asked Tamlin.

"She speaks!" Tamlin gasped in mock astonishment. "Yes, Miss Sheldon, we are climbing this rock, though not beyond, unless you fancy a swim."

Before Sadie could comment, Tamlin leapt up the rock in graceful bounds. Following much more clumsily and cautiously, Sadie joined her at the top and looked around.

Her mouth fell open.

An ice-blue lake tinted grey lay before her in the middle of the forest, rippling in the light breeze. The rock they stood on dropped into a cliff below her feet, though a steep descent to the water's edge was still possible. Mist hung low around the peripheries. Bordered by rocky ledges and close-knit trees curling their roots into the cool water, this clandestine misted lake seeped magic—but the opposite shore's sublimity stole her breath.

Craggy cliffs towered over the water, jagged and treacherous, their grey faces stained with orange and brown striations reflected in the lake below. Ice and sprays of snow frosted its upper ledges, glittering with refracted light from a narrow waterfall cascading down the centre cliff-face.

"This," Tamlin announced, "is Tor Niro, the Silver Lake. The icy blue, glacier-fed daylight tinge is beautiful, but night is when it's truly magical. Millions of stars bloom in the ebony sky like a field of floating nalalíté flowers, clustered so thickly it feels as though you could leap from one galaxy to another. Constellations sidle up to planets, and shooting stars race across the sky. The lake shines silver with reflected stars and the moonlit cliff, and the waterfall showers down like a sprinkle of shooting stars."

Sadie stared at Tamlin. She had never heard her speak with such reverence for nature—especially the night sky, which brimmed with potential for the Dark Magic she cautioned so strongly against. Tamlin gazed raptly at the water, her eyes glazed as though seeing a memory reflected on its surface, and for the first time Sadie beheld Tamlin not as the most powerful wizard in Carmelle, but as a woman with a complex past.

"It's curious, isn't it, how some of the most magical things in this world are completely untouched by magic," Tamlin mused in a whisper, as though she had forgotten Sadie's presence. In a louder voice she added, "Nature can always perform more outstanding magic than you or I ever could, Sadie. Remember that."

"Is that why you brought me here? To learn the magic of nature? Because that is one lesson I don't need. I'm well aware of nature's magical powers... and how nature can affect my magic," Sadie added bitterly, thinking of the incident with the moon's captivating beauty on the Sula-onon. As much as she craved the nighttime Tor Niro celestial paradise Tamlin described, she also feared it. The warmth of her desire fought against the icy grip of her terror.

"Not at all," answered Tamlin, tearing her eyes away from the lake to look at Sadie. "Though it does coincide nicely with why I brought you to one of the most magical places in Caris Nando for your first lesson. You need to learn how to control your magic and use it when *you* want to instead of letting it use you. I will begin today by showing you the first step of controlling your magic, which requires no magic but strength of mind. The art of meditation. Mastering your thoughts and emotions so you can tap the magic within."

Sadie flinched. *Meditating*? Relief at starting her magical training warred with a stronger desire to skip to performing magical spells.

"Take a seat, Miss Sheldon, and close your eyes."

Sadie obeyed, sitting cross-legged, her generous skirt fanning out around her.

When she closed her eyes, her first thought was *this will never work*. Lack of vision heightened her other senses. The distant waterfall roared in her ears like thunder clashing with howling wind. Cawing crows, chattering squirrels, and shuffling foxes shattered the forest's quiet tranquility. A cacophony of snapping twigs, swaying branches, and lapping water assailed her, and Tamlin's breathing mingled with her own sounded like the obnoxious snorting of a winded horse. Still, she kept her eyes screwed shut, determined not to give up before Tamlin even issued her first instruction.

"Relax your eyes," Tamlin's voice instructed in her ear.

Sadie jumped and snapped her eyes open.

Tamlin heaved an exasperated sigh, and Sadie snapped her eyes closed again. "Lesson one," admonished Tamlin, "Never let outside voices disturb your mind's peace. They are not your concern. Nothing exists but you, the essence of you. Everything else is exterior, viewed through the veil of an alternate reality. When you hear another voice, you don't need to block it out or ignore it. Let it slide through your subconscious, registering in—but not disturbing—your mind. When you have mastered the art of meditation, you will be able to carry on a conversation and perform magic without disturbing the equilibrium of your mind. Wizards often engage in duels and battles and other aggressive magic, and they must be able to assume meditative control to harness and employ their magic under stressful conditions. Learning to control your mind and magic amidst chaos is integral."

Though she understood the need to overcome startling, unexpected voices, Sadie found not knowing what the voice was doing while her eyes were closed disturbing. She braced herself for the shock of hearing a voice again.

"Stop screwing up your face like that," chided Tamlin. "You look constipated. Relax every muscle. Let your eyelid rest on the ridge below... unclench your jaw, loosen your cheeks, smooth out the furrows in your brow... and breathe, slowly and deeply. Inhale... and exhale. Feel the rush of oxygen to your brain... feel and hear the expansion and collapse of your lungs, the beat of your heart..."

This is ridiculous. She bit back a laugh at her comical deep breathing. The exaggerated rise and fall of her chest hurt her back, and her thudding heart and rushing air from her lungs flooded her ears as though she was drowning. Still, she kept her eyes closed.

"Now, things will disturb you at first—noises from the forest, itchy body parts, stiff limbs—but you must push these things aside. As cliche as it sounds, you must be one with your surroundings and yet apart from them. When you feel an itch, concentrate on soothing and erasing it with your mind, and eventually you will. You must let go of your thoughts and feelings, and concentrate hard on nothing. Or if you must concentrate on something, try picking an object to focus on. Drive every thought and feeling into that object, feeding it with the excess contents of your mind until nothing exists but you and this object. This will also be good practice for later in your magical training, because you focus your magic in the same way."

Sadie picked an object at random—the necklace she wore—and held every detail in her mind's eye. A fly buzzed in her ear. She pictured it zooming around her head—and the image of her necklace broke. She summoned the necklace back, but this time the lake gently lapping against the rock penetrated her mind, and Sadie pictured the necklace floating away on the water.

Maybe her image wasn't strong enough. She pictured a rock, firm and solid. Her left elbow itched. Fighting the impulse to scratch, Sadie struggled to keep her face smooth as she concentrated on the rock, attempting to bully her mind into believing she wasn't itchy. She imagined rubbing her elbow on the rock, which seemed to help a bit. A bird sang somewhere in the distance. The waterfall hummed steadily in the background. The lake rippled quietly against the cliff. A fish splashed nearby. The wind whistled a soft lullaby in her ear... The forest played a quiet, soothing song for her, and her mind drifted, the image of the rock fading as she was swept away...

A gunshot rang in her ears and Sadie jolted back to reality, shaking the reverberations from her groggy mind. Her eyes flew open in time to see a trail of greenish smoke floating away across the water. She whipped her head around like a confused puppy, looking for the source of the explosion, until she spotted Tamlin standing behind her.

"Did you do that?"

"You fell asleep."

"I did not! I was just in deep meditation, which you disturbed—"

"You were snoring," interrupted Tamlin, evidently amused. "Not to worry, perfectly natural for a beginner. Wilfred Windemere—wonderful wizard, very gifted in magic concerning natural weather phenomena—fell asleep 429 times before he mastered the art of meditation! Try again, Miss Sheldon. Perhaps concentrate on a different image this time. Do not force the object upon your mind. Close your eyes, and let the object come to you."

Taking a few calming breaths, Sadie tried again. It took her five more times of falling asleep before she finally made progress. Closing her eyes, Sadie wiped her mind blank, letting it go dark. Her mind was an unlit dungeon. A boundless obsidian void between stars. From this vacuous darkness a single sphere of blue flame flickered into existence. The dome of fire shifted and shivered, tasting the darkness experimentally. This image was different. Part of her soul.

Slowly, one by one, she fed thoughts and aches and itches into the fiery orb. Nothing existed outside of this flame. She basked in its warmth and took comfort in its subtle flickers, like an encouraging wink from a friend. The flame's dome swelled as she fed all distractions into it. Only the sound of her breathing disturbed the peace. Sadie tried to feed it to the flame as well, coaxing it to a quieter level. Her lungs constricted but that struggle was outside the flame, and she fed it to the flame as well. Her breathing became ragged, but she pushed on, determined to channel all physical symptoms out of her mind...

And then Tristan appeared in place of the cool sphere of flame. Tristan pretending to be baffled by Earth like it was a foreign world. Tristan apologizing for not telling her about his Storytelling abilities or Swordmaster title while withholding a greater secret that could have bridged the gap between them. A life preserver he could have thrown her as she drowned in the politics, magic, and uncertainty of a new world—

"Sadie! Sadie!"

Tamlin's panicked voice bellowed in her ears. Her shoulders were shaken and—

Her eyes snapped open and beheld intense icy blue eyes treading water against the currents of anxiety and anger. She blinked. Tamlin's eyes narrowed into slits, face livid.

"What in Bren's name do you think you're playing at?" Tamlin roared, irate. "I said to calm your breathing, not stop it altogether! You almost killed yourself! Only *you* could find a way to make meditation dangerous, killing yourself through the most peaceful action ever!"

Sadie exhaled a deep, shuddering gasp. Immediately she began coughing, sucking oxygen in huge gulps until it burned her lungs. Her vision blurred, head swimming as she tried to focus, but still Tristan's face burned across her mind, the daggers of his deception piercing her with betrayal. She tripped over her dress as she stumbled to her feet.

"Where do you think you're going?" hissed Tamlin as Sadie lurched across the rock. Unable to dwell on Tamlin's anger, Sadie took another steadying breath—and ran.

Chapter Twenty-Two

Playing with Fire

A frigid breeze brushed Sadie's groggy eyes open, and a snowflake floated through her cracked-open window. Leaping out of bed without remembering to throw back the covers, Sadie tripped over her blankets and landed in a tangled heap on the floor with a loud *thump*. When she finally managed to disentangle her limbs from her blankets, she drew back the lace curtain and gasped through a euphoric grin. A thick blanket of snow glittered softly in the rising sun, its pillowed folds fresh and undisturbed. Icicles decorated roofs and windowsills like jagged crystals. Snow slid off heavily laden branches, sprinkling the ground like icing sugar sifted over a cake. The world had gone silent. Tranquility reigned.

And then silence exploded into cacophony. Sadie's door slammed open, and feet thundered across her floor as a small figure streaked past, knocking Sadie to the floor again. A high voice shrieked, "Snow! Snow! Snooowww! Did you see it, Sadie? Have you been outside yet? We get tons of snow in Dharmaelia, it's my favourite time of year! Except in the fall when the wheat fields turn gold. We're further south than Caris Nando though, so I bet they get more snow than we do! Let's go explore! Are you ready yet? Come on!"

Sadie glowered at Airothane from the floor, her backside throbbing from landing on it twice in a minute. "You ruin everything," she muttered bitterly.

"Airothane doesn't know the meaning of moderation," came a deeper voice from the doorway. Haldin stood there with a mingled look of apologetic empathy and amusement. "When he's excited he not only can't contain it, but he has to show it twice as intensely as anyone else. And he does love snow. Ask my father how many injuries he has received as a side effect of Airothane's enthusiasm."

Airothane stuck his tongue out at his older brother. "So, are you coming, Sadie? Get dressed, let's go!"

Sadie ignored him, grumbling as she got gingerly to her feet.

"Tristan and a few Lantíes are in the practice field for their morning weapons training session," Haldin informed her with an unwarranted knowing smile. "We could go watch."

Sadie knew Tristan and some of the Lantíes practised with their weapons every morning, but she had been avoiding Tristan since her discussion with Alldían. She *was* curious to see Tristan's skill with a blade. Maybe she could observe without interacting much with Tristan.

"Okay, sounds good. I'll meet you boys outside," she replied as she gathered clothes.

Five minutes later, Sadie emerged wearing a heavy wool dress in deep green trimmed with gold, and an emerald cloak lined with black fur. Black wool mittens protected her hands, and her hood was pulled up over her wavy hair. She smiled at the satisfying crunch of snow beneath her boots and her breath puffing out in spirals. Did snow hold real magic?

"What took so long?" demanded Airothane. Without waiting for Sadie's answer, he bounded off into the snow like a deer. His extra layers of thick tunics and cloaks made him look like a normal-sized boy for once. Haldin wore fur-trimmed clothes embroidered with gold and bronze, his cloak clasped with a medallion featuring a golden hawk.

"Are you planning on practising too?" Sadie asked Haldin, indicating the axe at his side.

"I may," he replied indifferently. "Sometimes I join in if they have odd numbers and someone needs a sparring partner, but I don't like to be presumptuous."

"Even though they said he could the first time he showed up outside the enclosure to watch," Airothane shouted from around the bend. "Haldin's too modest, he refuses to admit he has as much skill with that axe as Tristan and the Lantíes do with their swords and bows. He thinks he's unworthy to practice with them everyday."

"Sometimes I loathe his enhanced Windtalker hearing," Haldin admitted, sighing.

"I heard that!" echoed Airothane's voice on the wind.

"My little brother does not understand that appearance and reality are two different things. Though it is true I have sparred with Tristan and the others, it is only because they go easy on me. I have seen them fight each other, and know I only slow them down. They always best me in every duel without much strain. Besides, even if I appear to be calm and in control, that is mostly illusion. I know how to master my emotions while fighting. I may be considered a good warrior in Dharmaelia, but I am no Swordmaster."

Though Sadie knew Airothane exaggerated, she also guessed Haldin's humility stemmed from real insecurities of inferiority. Maybe he didn't realize his full skill. She suspected Haldin's sparring with Tristan and the Lantíes was somewhere in between the two brothers' assessments.

"Do you enjoy the snow as much as Airothane?"

"Almost." Haldin laughed, though a solemn sadness tinged his tone and flecked his eyes. "I have seen twenty-seven winters, but not all have been magical. Some are marked with deep sorrow and loss, and others... others are remembered with disappointment and regret. I do love the snow though, and winters in Dharmaelia can be quite magical. The plains transform into a white sea, and the snow-capped peaks bordering our lands are breathtaking. My father's hall is always decorated with wheat-wreaths prepared in the fall and sprigs of holly, and there is a day of feasts and celebration at the Winter Solstice. Everyone in the kingdom is given leave from their regular duties to enjoy the snow and relax by the blazing fires in the hall's hearths. The hall is cozy and warm, and my father generously lets his people frequent the hall at all hours. Everyone is brought together by the cold, and it is a time of merrymaking... Though of course when many humans are in an enclosed space for a prolonged period of time..."

Haldin trailed off, and his angular jaw tightened.

"What kind of sorrow and loss do you mean?" Sadie blurted, then cringed.

But Haldin did not appear offended. He paused, forehead creasing before answering, "My mother died one winter, for example. Arianna was her name."

"I'm sorry, Haldin," Sadie whispered.

Haldin did not answer. When they reached the practice arena relief flooded Sadie, until she noticed the battles raging beyond the fence. Her jaw dropped.

Chaos reigned. Blurred shapes skated past, snow spraying like ocean-side geysers, and the cacophony of steel clanging and arrows thwacking echoed over the snowy grounds like a thunderstorm. Sadie did not know where to look first. Their transitions from one fluid stance to another looked as natural as exhaling. They parried and reposed back and forth, lunging and feinting and swiping and stabbing in a rapid, rhythmic dance.

The duelling duos danced around each other, wielding mostly slender longswords or slightly curved cutlasses, but at least two pairs fought with rapiers and quarterstaffs, and one pair duelled with broadswords. Beyond the duellers, warriors practised lunges, cuts, and dagger techniques on their own or with partners. Archers aimed at long distance targets and hit the bullseye every time. Most trainees were Lantíés, but Tristan must've been there somewhere...

And then she spotted him. Employing a complex and speedy cut against a Lantian woman about his same height and weight, Tristan wielded his longsword near the fence to Sadie's left. Sadie had never seen his face so intent and yet serene. His sword was an extension of his arm, blurring as he launched a merciless attack, gracefully changing stances as he forced his opponent to retreat. Slowly the pair inched their way towards Haldin, Airothane, and Sadie. As they drew level, Tristan changed tactics and spun, knocking the Lantíé's sword out of her hand and hooking her knees so she landed flat on her back. He rested the tip of his sword over her heart in victory. Reaching out his sword-free hand, Tristan hauled her to her feet, shook her hand genially, and they parted ways.

Airothane and Haldin applauded. Tristan looked up in surprise to see them standing there.

"Truly a pleasure to watch, as always," Haldin complimented, shaking Tristan's hand.

"Thank you, Haldin, that means a lot coming from you," Tristan replied. His guarded eyes locked on Sadie's.

"I see why you are a Swordmaster," she said, trying to keep the bitter coldness out of her voice. She didn't entirely succeed as she eyed the light sheen of sweat glistening on his forehead and raised an eyebrow at his super-human athleticism.

The corner of her mouth quirked wryly as a terrifying, yet exhilarating, idea occurred to her. "Could you teach me how to swordfight?"

"Teach you?" Tristan repeated, flustered. "I—I, well, I guess I could... that is, if you're up for everything it demands... I mean, it's not an easy skill to acquire, and takes tons of practice to—"

Tristan actually looked at Haldin for an answer.

Sadie refrained from kicking his shins.

"I say go for it," Haldin commented, grinning at Sadie. "She's not asking to become a Swordmaster. And she's feisty. She could do quite well with a blade."

Sadie beamed at Haldin.

"All right then," Tristan acquiesced. An evil grin tugged at his lips. "Ready to take on a Swordmaster, tellurian?"

"Are you ready to lose to a tellurian?" Sadie countered. She threw back her hood, shook out her long wavy tresses and climbed over the fence, landing gracefully—for once—in front of Tristan, their faces inches apart.

Sadie slit her eyes into sword tips and glared a challenge at Tristan. His eyes danced as he cautioned, "Your stubborn defiance will serve you well in this arena, but don't let it define you. Let's begin."

Over the next few weeks, Sadie worked hard at her magic with Tamlin, and improved with each lesson. After two or three weeks, Sadie struck the balance between her meditation fire-orb consuming everything and absorbing the extraneous so only the essentials remained. She could now hold the flame-bubble in her mind for an hour, letting it sear away all thought and emotion—and this, according to Tamlin, meant she was ready to advance to the next phase of her magical training.

The first step was to find her magical core while in her meditative state. Concentrating on the subtle wave of the fire-dome's edges, Sadie was then instructed to look inside herself and find what she had glimpsed that night on the Sula-onon.

But no guaranteed specific method to view a tangle of magical threads inside your body existed. "It's an instinctual process, unique to every wizard," Tamlin informed her. "An emotional feeling resonating in your soul. Imagine sliding down the veins and tubes in your chest, settling somewhere between your heart and stomach. While concentrating on the flame, feel for your magic, and eventually you will see your tangled web of magical strands."

"Could you be more vague?" Sadie grumbled.

Tamlin puffed air out of the corner of her mouth like a tetchy dragon.

"Each wizard's magical veins are different colours," Tamlin offered in measured tones of ebbing patience. "Personality and the type of magic in which they excel help determine the colour. Mine are a light cerulean. Regardless of individual thread colour, once a wizard's magical core is untangled and controlled, it will look like a smooth, glassy orb, individual threads no longer distinguishable. Once you learn the function of each flow and how to separate them, you can extract threads from the smooth orb and unleash them to use your magic."

Though Sadie followed Tamlin's instructions, it took a few sessions to find her core on her own. Tamlin made her try it alone at first, but by the third session she offered to help.

"Are you kidding?" Sadie demanded. "You could have shown me from the beginning but decided to make me look foolish instead?"

"I had to, it's important for you to connect to your soul on your own," Tamlin explained. "It's better to learn the technique beforehand so it'll be easier to summon after. All I'll show you now is where your core is, how to envision getting there, and what it looks like."

Tamlin put her hand on Sadie's shoulder, closed her eyes, and seamlessly melded her mind with Sadie's. The flame vanished as she plunged into her mind's depths, like finding a hidden underwater cave during a deep-sea dive. Tamlin's presence felt intrusive and Sadie fought the impulse to terminate Tamlin's disconcerting control. When they reached Sadie's core, a bright vermilion glow emanated from Sadie's magical threads. Blazing heat radiated off the forked flame-tongues lashing out from her core. Sporadic crackles of magic rippled through her threads, eliciting enticing sparks she longed to seize and unleash to taste the world with voracious tongues. Without thinking, Sadie concentrated on the blue sphere of flame amid a sea of darkness, and the desire to latch onto her magic vanished. Her core became a background image. Bright and strong, but controlled.

"Good!" Tamlin yelled, beaming. "Well done, Sadie! See why it's important to do this in steps? You were able to master the force of your magic on the first try! You'll be able to find your core and access your magic safely in no time!"

By the end of their next lesson, Sadie could summon her magical core and keep it under control quicker than blinking, causing Tamlin to pronounce, "Now you're ready to learn the different magical flows and how to use them in the correct, safe amounts!"

On a cold December morning at Tor Niro, Sadie finally started practising unleashing her magic. Sitting on an icy rock, her fingers white and numb, she watched her breath billow thick puffs of steam. Over the last few weeks, the weather had progressed from chilly November rain washing away first snowfalls to frigid and icy but dry, and Sadie had fallen in love with the forest of Caris Nando all over again. Frost glittered on grass and dusted branches every morning, the sun shone coldly on a palette of pale slate and cerulean, and the air tasted like snow.

Sadie listened as Tamlin explained how to detect different flows of magic and what they were used for. "Only a small set of about two dozen different flows exist," lectured Tamlin, "but each flow has a plethora of different uses and combinations. Training properly at a school will be essential to fully utilize your magical abilities, but for now I will teach you the four major flows from which all other flows derived: Earth, Air, Fire, and Water."

Sadie wiggled her tingling fingers in anticipation.

"Since your first use of magic was starting a fire, I'm going to presume Fire is your strongest element, so that's the flow I will show you first."

Tamlin placed her hand on Sadie's shoulder and melded her mind with Sadie's. Directing both of them to her core, Sadie focused on the tangled mess of fiery strands.

"The elements are the basis of all magic," Tamlin explained. "All magical energy flows from the natural world around us. This is why people with magic tend to have a strong connection to nature. We have the same energy and harness its flows as magic. Some elements of nature possess magic different from ours because their energy, anatomy, and cognitive powers vary. The Elemental flows reside at the centre of your magical core. To reach them, we will have to unravel your core's tangled strands. Here they are."

Using her own magic, Tamlin highlighted the flows in different colours, making them glow brighter so Sadie could distinguish them more easily. The fire strand gleamed red, the water blue, the earth green, and the air white.

They spent the next half hour untangling her core, Sadie extracting threads and organizing them into Elemental groups with her mind under Tamlin's guidance, until they reached four threads knotted together. The fire strand was already almost untangled from the other three. After they untangled the Elemental threads, Sadie twined them together under Tamlin's instruction. This new construction would form the nucleus of the smooth orb core she aimed for.

When Sadie had completed the oval-shaped weave of the Elemental nucleus, Tamlin announced she could learn how to extract threads from the main flows to externalize her magic.

"When you want to use one of the four Elemental flows, you must summon the image of the oval pattern and extract the imprint of the specific flow you desire by seizing it and casting it like a fishing net. You are ensnaring something with the web of your magic like you did on the Sula-onon. Some types of magic require incantations and spells, but most basic magic using one Elemental thread at a time requires no words or incantations. Direct it by envisioning the result in your head, and when you release your magic it will obey your wishes. However, this only works if you use your magic in a manner inherent to each element. For example, you can only command the fire flow by thought alone if you ask it to start a fire or otherwise transform through heat."

Tamlin released her shoulder and broke the connection of their minds.

"As I mentioned before, it would probably be wise to start with fire," Tamlin continued. "Why don't you try something now?"

"Okay..." Sadie replied slowly, unsure of what to attempt. The waterfall cascading from the cliffs caught her eye.

Closing her eyes, Sadie envisioned the blue flame then pictured her core, connecting to her soul—and there it was, the newly formed Elemental pattern. The fire strand burned orange and a thread extricated itself without her beckoning, floating towards her. Seizing it instinctively with her mind, Sadie cast it out, willing it to leave her body and attach to the waterfall.

When she opened her eyes, her mouth fell open.

A waterfall of molten lava poured over the cliffs. A river of flames billowed over the ledge, greedily licking the rock face with forked tongues tinted blue, heat radiating off it so intensely Sadie could feel it from across the lake. Whatever minimal vegetation had grown in the crags of the cliff was now scorched. The waterfall of flames she had seen in the land the portal had first tried to take her to swam to the forefront of her mind.

Her brain numbed, unable to comprehend her success, let alone stop it.

Tamlin also gaped at the fiery waterfall for a moment before Sadie felt her release magic. Instantly, the lava-like flow transformed back into the old waterfall.

Tamlin turned to face Sadie, her eyes intent, inquisitive, and even—unless Sadie imagined it—a little troubled. After a pause, Tamlin said, "That was most impressive, Sadie. I did not expect... Alldían was right about you. You do indeed appear to possess great power."

Sadie gripped her arm, flattening the raised hairs at Tamlin's words. She forced a trickle of saliva to moisten the parched sands of her desert tongue. If her potential power seemed so disturbing to Alldían and Tamlin, did she even want it?

She had always craved the freedom and power to control her life, but she had failed to consider freedom and power might control *her*. She was no longer certain she had the strength to take the reins and tame the wild forces within.

Chapter Twenty-Three

The Dimensional Tree

When the light filtering in through Sadie's open window dimmed with the setting sun, Tamlin poked her head in to inform Sadie her presence was requested in Alldían's personal garden.

"Alldían wants to see me?" Sadie repeated blankly.

"Is there an echo in here? Yes, I believe that's what I said, Sadie. Honestly, I've met toadstools faster than you," Tamlin replied, rolling her eyes.

Sadie's mind accelerated into turmoil again. What did Alldían want with her now? Did he not tell her everything the night of the welcome feast even though he promised he would?

Following Tamlin out of their living quarters into a golden sun-stained forest, Sadie barely heeded their direction until a heavy black iron gate wrought to fit perfectly between two huge oak trees jarred Sadie out of her stupor.

No guards stood at the gate, and Sadie did not see a keyhole. Tamlin's eyes narrowed, and she murmured a few words of incantation Sadie did not understand. The gate clanged open, slowly creaking inwards.

Did this meeting have something to do with Tristan? Had he told Alldían Sadie was avoiding him and acting distant? Tamlin led her through the garden, but the exquisite statues, fountains, and trees faded to the peripheries as an image of tickling Tristan's throat with a dagger until he confessed his true origins dominated her mind.

"Wipe that wicked grin off your face, Sadie, the leaves are withering with fright at the sight of you. And lay off the self-indulgence glazing your eyes, you look possessed." Tamlin's admonition wiped the vision from Sadie's mind and the smile from her face. Her eyes slid back into focus and latched onto a thick curtain of ivy.

"We're here," Tamlin added.

"Er... here where? All I see is a wall of vines."

"That's because you're as blind as a bat and as dim as a troll," Tamlin replied smoothly. "Try pulling the vines back. Like a curtain."

Sadie glowered at her. "Why don't *you* do it?"

"Because I'm not coming with you. I have better things to do. Besides," Tamlin added, her mouth twitching, "Alldían requested you proceed from this point alone."

Tamlin's ominous tone was not unusual, but Sadie's stomach still sank.

"Why do we have to be alone?"

There was no answer.

"Lane? Why—" But Tamlin was no longer there.

Sighing, she yanked back the curtain of ivy, a determined fire sizzling her veins.

After her first few determined steps, however, Sadie's feet faltered. Towering before her, its enormous branches unfurled like giant wings with splayed fingers, was the most magnificent cherry tree Sadie had ever seen. With a thick trunk layered in deep, gnarled chocolate brown bark, the cherry tree compensated for its modest height in breadth. Huge flowers blanketed the tree like a cloak despite the winter season, blooming in its own eternal spring. The pale pink blossoms clustered together in clumps.

It was a tree thriving with life while everything else withered.

Sadie noticed several pools grouped in a wide circle between the tree's giant roots. The pools looked natural, flawed in shape and size continuity.

Standing before the tree and pools, his robes a pale silvery blue reflecting the clouds, was Alldían. He gestured for Sadie to join him at the nearest pool. Her stomach fluttered as she stepped into the shadow of the cherry tree.

"Hello, Sadie. Welcome to my personal garden and home of Telwé Unvar, the Dimensional Tree, and The Seven Pools. I have requested your presence here today so I can show you some of the aspects we discussed a few weeks ago."

"What do you mean by 'show' me the aspects of our discussion?" Sadie asked, examining the tree. It didn't look like the moonleaf tree Alldían had used for his vision of her.

"Telwé Unvar holds keys to all the worlds. It's how we know other worlds exist and in what ways they relate to ours. It's also a tool for glimpsing what transpires in these worlds. Each cluster of flowers represents a different timeline of worlds, or worlds that exist on the same parallel. There are many worlds out there, in our universe and others. And each world belongs to a cluster of parallel worlds. Arwé and Earth are parallel worlds. We exist on the same timeline, and our species, customs, and morals are similar. You could go to any world on your parallel and find familiar elements and ideologies, as well as some differences. Before you came to Arwé, you had heard of unicorns and dragons, even if you had never seen them existing in your world, am I correct?"

Sadie nodded slowly.

"That's because someone in your world had either been to a parallel world and then written about it like Thomas, or creatures like unicorns and dragons entered your world through portals before the portals were controlled and were sighted. Writers and Storytellers can also feel a connection to a parallel world and be inspired by it without going there. Some people are more naturally attuned to the existence of other worlds, people who believe in fairy tales and exercise their imaginations. They believe 'muses' inspire them, when in reality they detect a connection flowing between the two worlds. Carmelle is a sister-world to your world, but there are many other parallel worlds connected to ours. In fact, ours is the largest cluster, spanning over three great branches! Even I have not been able to glimpse them all."

"How did this tree get here?" Sadie asked. "How is it you are privy to the knowledge it has to offer, and the rest of Carmelle is not?"

"Nobody knows for sure how this tree got here. It was here before Lantíés evolved, and we discovered its function. I suppose we were lucky to discover it first and become keepers of its knowledge. It is not a burden we bear lightly, nor a gift we take for granted. Only the current leader of Caris Nando is permitted to see and use Telwé Unvar when they see fit. People outside of Caris Nando may ask to view it of course," Alldían added, perhaps to appease her accusatory glower, "but only the leader of Caris Nando can grant permission. A tree as powerful as this could be used for evil purposes. It leaves other worlds open to vulnerability if we can learn about them without their knowledge of our omniscient voyeurism. Each leader of Caris Nando takes an oath not to use this tree or the Seven Pools for harmful purposes."

Sadie snorted at the irony of unfair voyeurism when a vision had instigated Alldían's interest in her.

"Though there are many parallel worlds connected to ours, we know the most about yours," Alldían continued, ignoring her snort. "Members of your world are so closely connected with our own they affect events in Carmelle. In some cases, people find they are more 'meant' for another world than their own and decide to stay if they get the opportunity."

A thousand questions chased each other around Sadie's mind. "Can you get to any parallel world from any world on the same parallel? Are there portals to every one of Arwé's parallel worlds here?"

"I believe so, yes," Alldían replied ambiguously, "but that is only my personal theory, and not proven fact. I know of twelve different portals in Carmelle leading to parallel worlds, including yours, but there are over five-score parallel worlds to ours, and portals can come in forms we may not suspect or be able to discover. We did not know about all twelve portals at once. Each portal was discovered at a different time, so in theory, portals could continue to be discovered in the future. There could even be portals on Nirosula, Land of the Keepers, but since Carmellians don't go to Nirosula, we would never be able to use them. The same is true of your world. The only difference is your world has no system for tracking parallel worlds, as they have not yet acknowledged them as such."

A fleeting thought of sharing the discovery of parallel worlds with the scientific community on Earth entered Sadie's mind, but it trickled back out like cupped water. No one would take a *woman's* discovery seriously anyway, not until it was backed by a reputable man. Clenching her jaw, she asked, "Can people from worlds on one parallel ever get into worlds on another parallel?"

"It has happened only twice in history, and evidence suggests it can only happen under special circumstances to special people. Though I have not met anyone who has been to a world on a different parallel, I have been granted the opportunity to glimpse them through this tree. I use the Seven Pools at the base of Telwé Unvar," Alldían explained. "I pluck a petal from the flower representing the world I want to see, then drop the petal in one of the corresponding pools. The petal infuses the pool with the properties of that world, triggering the pool to function like a mirror, reflecting real images happening in real time in the world you have chosen. Normally, the Pool can identify the seeker's desire, sorting through billions of possible images so it shows ones relevant to the inquirer, but the seeker can direct them as well. For example, if I wanted to track someone—like if I wanted to see what you were doing in your world before you came here—I could command the Pool to show me images of them."

Sadie's eyes latched onto a Pool and did not let go. *Connor*. Voice quivering, Sadie asked, "If so few are permitted to use the Tree, why show me?"

"Because understanding is essential to your happiness here," replied Alldían gently. "Your body is in Arwé, maybe even your heart. But a piece of your heart will always be on Earth. Few in Carmelle have such personal stakes in other worlds. Others might seek this tree for knowledge or power or political gain. But when *you* look in the Pools, you will see the missing piece of your heart, and that is worth protecting."

The empty shard of her heart throbbed. Her longing grew palpable. She didn't care if Alldían's words were weighted with any sincerity. She *needed* to see her brother.

"Allow me to demonstrate," Alldían requested, turning his back on Sadie and stepping towards Telwé Unvar. He plucked a petal from a left-hand branch and gestured for Sadie to join him.

Alldían handed her the petal. "Here, drop the petal in this pool to see glimpses of what has occurred in your world since you left. I know you must miss it, or miss some of the people."

Accepting the petal silently, Sadie hesitated with her hand poised over the still reflective surface of the pool, heart racing so fast it rattled her chest and dizzied her mind. She wanted to see her brother's face again more than anything—but what if seeing him hooked her back into her old life? What if the image made her regret coming to Carmelle? Could she ever live with herself if gaining control of her own life meant losing a connection to her brother's?

Like an exhale, she let the petal fall. Circular rings rippled out upon impact, but a few seconds passed before anything happened.

An image spread rapidly outwards from the petal until it covered the whole surface.

A barren wasteland devoid of human life and colour rippled across the pool. A few lone trees dotted the horizon, their lifeless brown and sickly yellow leaves sparse as fall decayed into winter. Hazy grey fumes choked the air and hovered over the wasteland, blanketing it in despair. Sadie wasn't sure where the symbiotic chain of desolation began, nor could she see the hope of its end. Brambles, churned mud, and bracken from bushes long stripped of their vegetation riddled the land. Tendrils of smoke spiralled into the air from holes in the pockmarked landscape. On the peripheries of the pool, deeper gorges gouged the earth, stretching in one long man-made line as far as she could see. In the distance, shapes of battered buildings loomed over the landscape, forming a small village. The location was unfamiliar; Sadie wondered what part of her world it was in.

For a few seconds the scene stayed perfectly still, only a few wispy smoke tendrils trailing in the air. No animals moved, not even a bird.

Then chaos erupted.

Muffled booming artillery and rapid-fire gunshots emanated from the pool, reverberating in Sadie's shocked ears. Cannons exploded, fountains of dirt sprayed up, and men spilled out of one of the trenches, labouring across the wasteland, avoiding shells and bullets. Everywhere, bodies buckled, collapsing into the mud where they were trod on by soldiers rushing forward. Sadie cringed at severed limbs and eyes gouged by flying shrapnel. A chorus of blood-curdling shrieks, moans, and bellows of pain harmonized with the baritone barrage.

The image abruptly switched to the village and buildings smashed to smithereens. Soldiers flew between debris piles, seeking refuge from single shots and rapid fire from an unidentifiable source. Squinting, she peered at the wreckage and spotted them: hiding behind smashed windows and exposed columns on the buildings' upper floors were a handful of snipers and two huge rapid-fire guns mounted on stands, operated by a few soldiers each. Men caught out in the open for a second too long were shot down instantly without mercy. Thick, glutinous blood sprayed everywhere. A man pursued by rapid-fire bullets leapt behind a dead horse for cover; bullets peppered the horse's belly, spewing forth its intestines. The image changed again.

This time two armies faced each other on a field next to a canal, one side with their backs to the canal, defending it. Glittering in the faint sunlight piercing through grey clouds was the ocean, a few ships waiting just offshore to aid one of the armies. A torpedo raced through the water towards one of the ships—and fizzled out.

And then the image changed once more. Sweeping over a sea of white tents pitched in neat rows on an open plain in the shadow of rolling hills, the vision focused on a few groups of soldiers just outside the maze of tents. They marched, practised shooting, or worked on their bayonet techniques. Muffled shouts of command came from the man standing before the marching troops. Gunfire crackled amid the scraping, spine-tingling clash of metal on metal as the trainees with bayonets practised close-range combat. The pool narrowed on a man's back in the group with rifles. Wearing the military uniform of a soldier-in-training, he was tall but lanky, still growing into his muscles. Something about his stance and frame seemed familiar to Sadie. The rifle kicked slightly in his hands as he pulled the trigger and hit his target two hundred yards away. As his comrades hurried to congratulate him, the man turned around.

Sadie's stomach plummeted to her toes.

Brown hair swept casually away from hazel eyes. A face not quite relinquishing the roundness of youth to the angular jawlines of men.

Connor's face in the pool shimmered.

But it was not the Connor she remembered. His eyes no longer glinted with receptive warmth or mischief. They were cold and hollow, full of unmasked sorrow and pain. He shook hands with the men congratulating him and allowed his mouth to slide into a half-grin, like he was pleased being perceived lethal, but it did not reach his eyes. His face looked gaunt, the hollows beneath his eyes shadowed in dark purple half-circles that made her cringe.

And he was in military uniform.

Her seventeen-year-old brother had joined the Canadian Army...

Connor had become a soldier in the most destructive-looking war in her world.

Sadie's heart forgot how to beat.

Chapter Twenty-Four

Becoming a Soldier

"Left! Left! Left, Right, Left! Gauche! Gauche! Gauche, Droit, Gauche!"

The bellows of the Sergeant at the head of the marching column rang in Connor's ears, even from his position near the back of the line. Barking out orders with a growl in his throat, the Sergeant's face glowed red and spit flew from beneath his neat moustache, spraying the unfortunate first two rows. Connor had been inclined to laugh the first time spittle tangled in Sergeant Higgins' moustache, but that impulse had vanished when his friend, Will, in the front row, had snorted and received such an upbraiding he started to cry. Connor soon learned Sergeant Higgins took his position seriously and would tolerate nothing that compromised his authority or showed disrespect. Connor was not afraid of Higgins—more merciless officers higher in the ranks deserved his fear more—but he was not foolish enough to deliberately provoke him either.

Marching was becoming routine, his feet falling into a more natural rhythm with each step. *Left, two, three, right, two, three, pivot, two, three, halt!* Patterns formed in his head as he acquired this new skill that bred discipline and comforting structure. The repetition, monotony, and order helped Connor calm the chaotic storm raging in his mind. Though it may be a futile exercise designed to stroke the egos of the soldiers as they marched to the pompous tune of an officer's shouts and whistles while on parade for civilians, marching was the epitome of structure and the rhythm of it brought Connor peace.

Peace to counteract his paralyzing fears.

Fear of Thomas Sheldon's book—the book he had brought to keep a piece of Sadie in his pocket and provide comfort in times of strife had already dug a painful wound in his mind like a shard of glass. Every passage reminded him of the life Sadie never got to live. Of her unfulfilled dreams. Of unmet promises. Of questions left unanswered.

But most of all, he feared the thoughts waiting for him in the dark corners of his mind. Sleep held no respite, for his dreams always morphed into nightmares. The darkness and silence of night stripped his identity away, leaving a vulnerable shell of disconnected images and feelings. Mired in confusion, lost in a quagmire of disgust with himself when his dreams ended and morning dawned, he was left to piece himself together again. Each new sunrise he rebuilt and recreated his identity, recalling everything that defined him until he was at least the semblance of someone he recognized.

The patterns, the rhythms, the constant physical and mental strain of rigorous training exercises—he clung to them to retain whatever sanity remained. The army gave him a sense of purpose, and he gave himself up to it wholeheartedly.

One thing he did not fear was the war. Though men at least twice his age showed trepidation in their eyes when they had left camp in Quebec for further training overseas, Connor let their tales of how nasty war could be from their first-hand experiences in the Boer War, or from stories they'd heard about the mass deaths in the American Civil War over fifty years ago, roll off him. He didn't care much about his fate. Even a slow, agonizing death could not compare to the pain he endured from Sadie's. Death might even be a relief.

At the shouted command of Higgins, Connor shifted the Ross rifle to his other arm and cradled it upright, the tip resting on his shoulder. He had grown attached to his rifle. Despite the weapons he now carried still feeling awkward, like they did not quite belong in his hands, they also instilled a sense of purpose Connor relished. The pain and exhaustion from weapons training allowed him no time to grieve Sadie. Maybe he would be so drained during the war, he wouldn't even dream at all.

When Connor had fired his first shot with the Ross rifle, everything changed. Loading the clip with bullets and hearing the satisfying click as he snapped it back into place; the series of methodical clicks as he pulled back the bolt; the calculating click of the trigger as he took aim and pulled; the resounding *crack* and fizzling as the bullet exploded towards the target, and the immense satisfaction at seeing he had hit the mark on his first try... Connor had found sanctuary in each step and grew to love the rifle. With the rifle nothing could touch him, not even dreams or the skewed thoughts of his own warped mind. When he gripped the rifle, nothing else existed.

Another weapon, however, gave Connor equal joy and pain to see: the sword. It reminded him of Sadie and her stories of ancient wars, recalling the days when people fought with chivalry and honour for a cause they cared intimately about. But no intimacy forged a connection with this war for Connor. He had become a cog in a machine, often forgetting the machine's purpose, but finding satisfaction in knowing without all its parts, the machine wouldn't function.

The sword represented a lost art of warfare, where mental and physical skill bred heroes in the face of evil. Of course, Connor and his fellow low-rank infantry men would never use a sword in this war. Only the officers wore them at their hips, and Connor suspected they were merely decorative. But he wouldn't use a sword if he could. Though he was finding purpose and solace in becoming a soldier, he wasn't sure he wanted to be the hero. He just wanted to *be*.

"Heading for target practice?" Will asked after Higgins released them from marching.

"I don't know… I thought about catching up on some reading during our free period."

"Reading? Come on, man, you read that book like it holds the secrets of winning this war," complained Will.

Connor shrugged uncomfortably. He had been scouring Thomas' book for answers every spare moment he had, determined to uncover something to help assuage the guilt curdling his stomach. But everything he read became fuel for his nightmares.

"I suppose I could always use the extra practice…" replied Connor slowly.

"Let's be honest; it's *me* who needs the practice," said Will. "You can give me pointers. Share the secrets of your success."

"What are you talking about?" asked Connor.

Will chuckled, but when Connor didn't join him he frowned. "Are you serious? You're the best shot in this camp! Or at least the best among the new recruits. You really don't see it?"

Will's incredulous face held no traces of mockery.

Connor wondered if his preoccupation with Sadie had prevented him from becoming his best self out in the world.

Maybe it was time to take a break from the Sheldon mystery. Maybe then his grief wouldn't be so all-consuming.

"All right. I'll come."

Will whooped and clapped his hands together.

As they trudged between tents, wending their way to the target practice area, Connor said, "Hey, Will. Would you like to borrow a book?"

If the book was still in his possession, he couldn't resist perusing it.

Will laughed. "A favour for a favour. Sure, buddy, I got your back."

A weight lifted from Connor's shoulders.

Rain lashed against the tent. Howling wind rattled the canvas with incessant, tumultuous force. Connor loved storms, but he could do without the endless mud that never dried. He and Sadie used to sneak into each other's rooms or the library and tell scary stories, or re-enact an epic battle scene, to reflect the battle between the elements outside. They would sneak to the kitchen, make hot chocolate, and gather everything toasted over a fire. Piling it in their arms, they would snuggle up in blankets as they told stories. To Connor, storms meant comfort. While his fellow soldiers moaned and groaned about the noise of the storm and the water steadily dripping through the leaky tent, Connor latched on to the memories of comfort.

Hunched over a candle burning low and dripping with wax, he sat at a splintery wooden table near the tent's entrance, paper spread out before him and a pen in hand. The storm had inspired him to write a letter to Mabel. Before he left, he promised her he would write as often as he could, and he already missed her.

Closing his eyes, Connor held onto the memory of Mabel's warmth as rain hammered and thunder rolled ominously outside. Restless frustration gnawed at his mind at the delay here on Salisbury Plain in England before he could fight. What if the war ended before he could join the fight? It had already been three months since war had been declared—how much longer could it last?

"Private Avery," intoned a voice from the open tent flaps, startling Connor at the sound of the fake surname he'd adopted to hide his age. "Letter for you."

Connor held out his hand eagerly, anticipating another letter from Mabel, but it was from his father. When he slit it open, he discovered a letter with a note attached. The note read:

This letter arrived for you. Don't worry, I was the one to receive it, and I thought it best not to inform your mother of its existence.

Nervous tingles radiated down his arms and his stomach swooped as he remembered the telegram he had sent Pierre Curie a few months ago. Heart fluttering, he read the telegram.

Dear Connor,
I regret to inform you that Pierre Curie died eight years ago. Thomas Sheldon was a good friend of my husband's. Pierre and I always found his theories fascinating, both scientific and literary, and were shocked by his sudden death. I would be happy to receive more correspondence from you if you have questions. And, of course, if you're ever in France, you are always welcome to visit.
Marie Curie

Hope trickled into the crevices of his punctured heart. He would be in France soon, fighting in the war.

Maybe Marie Curie could help him piece together more of the Thomas Sheldon puzzle. What did she mean by his scientific theories? If they tied into his literary theories, maybe that alluded to his book. And if something in his book about Carmelle connected to modern science on Earth, maybe he knew vital information that advanced important science here. Knowledge like that could be powerful, an advantage many would seek. A weapon, in the wrong hands.

A weapon some might even kill for.

"Hey, Connor, you got that book?" Will asked, poking his head around the tent flap.

Reaching into his rucksack, Connor clasped the spine—and paused. What if a clue about Thomas' scientific theories lay in those pages? Something he could ask Marie Curie about in his next letter? Slowly, he released his grip and let the book fall back to the bottom of the bag.

"Actually, I think I'm going to hold onto it for now."

"You sure?"

Connor nodded. His interest in Thomas Sheldon no longer tied solely into protecting Sadie's legacy. He had questioned the unknown, and the unknown had answered. His instincts had been validated. Something wasn't right, and he wanted to know why. Thomas was his ancestor too, and understanding more about him might help him better understand himself.

"It's a part of me, but not all of me. I promise I'll show up for the stuff that matters more now," Connor assured Will.

It was time to trust his instincts and believe in himself. He could uncover the truth Sadie had sought, the truth of their ancestor's death, and maybe Sadie's, without it consuming him.

Perhaps this mystery had been his to solve all along.

Chapter Twenty-Five

The Rhetoric of Revenge

Blood dripped from the knife in his slackened grip, drops splattering the snow outside his tent where he had dragged the deer after killing it to be prepared for cooking. A small red pool stained the white flakes between his grimy boots, marring the pristine purity with its dark, glutinous globs. Deluged in hot sticky blood cooling and congealing fast in the frigid night air, the knife weighed light in his scarred hand despite the heavy ornate handle, as though itching to be used again. His taut muscles tensed against the struggle to resist the knife's restless command to kill. Fabius Griswald allowed nothing to control him, least of all such base desires as killing for fun. Logic governed his brain. If there was no reason, no purpose to his actions, then he simply did not execute them. But he was under no illusion logic prevailed throughout mankind, and therefore approached logic with caution. The Sheldon girl, for example. There had been no logic to her actions. She had rejected the boundaries of logic he attempted to impose on her, and his failure to reason she might not draw the same conclusions had resulted in the worst pain...

Griswald clamped down on that thought, biting his tongue. He must not think of the pain, or the girl. Not quite yet. He would gain nothing by dwelling on the past. The future was the way, the key. The Sheldon girl was a problem of the present, but also a stepping stone to the greater vision of the future. It did not matter what tools he used to get there. Griswald banished the girl from his mind, gaining composure.

He fastened his eyes on the mangled carcass just beyond the stained snow. Dull, black-pronged hooves jutted out at unnatural angles, snow and ice clinging to the short, coarse hair. Blood soaked the velvety brown coat, matting the fur as it dried. Yet even in death, the deer managed to exude nobility and majesty. His antlers were enormous, boasting five tines each.

Griswald had been required to kill more times than he could count, whether it was because he needed food and therefore logic dictated an animal had to die, or because a human tried to thwart his plans and their deaths became necessary for the plan to succeed. Every death he instigated was in service of a greater purpose, so he never experienced remorse. There was no point feeling guilty about the pattern logic and reasoning weaved together. A man could drive himself mad trying to defy logic. Look at those fools, the Ilyance, who attempted to defy change and progress! Evolution and progression were natural and healthy.

But every time he had to kill, he could not stop himself from looking at the victim's eyes, glazed over in unseeing death. The sight disturbed him. To him, their eyes held more emotion than they had in life. Reproach, remorse, despair, acceptance, pain, release, shock, regret—a myriad of contradictory emotions flooded him in sickening waves through their blank eyes.

Tearing his eyes away from the buck, Griswald barely concealed a shudder as he began drying off the blade with deliberate strokes. No point in letting blood or snow ruin his best hunting knife. Griswald was a practical man, and he never wasted anything. Hide, antlers, meat—he intended to use every part of this animal, and he had mandated his soldiers not waste any of their own catches. When he had a five hundred strong army to feed, clothe, and equip, he needed all the material he could scrape together.

Sheathing the knife, Griswald looked around. Tomorrow the Redpath would have to camp beneath the shelter of trees without attracting Lantian attention, but for tonight he allowed his troops to remain out in the open. Many of them foolishly believed in superstitions about the Lantíés' power connected to their pointy-horned ancestors and were scared to enter the forest. After what they had just endured—well, Griswald didn't think spooking them would be effective tonight. Griswald was betting every-thing on this plan, so it needed to succeed. He had rolled the dice for the first time in his life, but only because the stakes were so high. He was not a gambling man, but sometimes gambling was the only logical choice.

Bursts of orange flames danced in the distance, marking campfires around which five-hundred Redpath members huddled. Did any of them have regrets? Beyond the fires loomed the Dharlomin mountains, their snow-capped peaks glistening in the moonlight, their red-stone shoulders black in the blanketing gloom of night. Though imposing and impreg-nable in appearance, the facade of fortitude masked a secret.

The smell of roasting venison permeated the camp. Soldiers huddled together, intent on stoking fires, turning a spit, or chugging back mug after mug of strong ale. But nobody spoke much. Horrified exhaustion silenced them, and they exchanged blank stares like mindless machines. New re-cruits populated the camp, not yet used to fighting for a cause instead of a nation. It was an important distinction most Redpath members did not fully understand until they gained experience.

As Captain and Commander of this Redpath contingent, Griswald sat before the muddy white folds of the largest tent. Standing just outside the orange glow of the largest fire were two other men. One wore a uniform similar in all but rank to Griswald, the gold cog pin on his cloak marking him as an officer, and the other oozed extravagance.

Wearing robes of deep plum with wide, trailing sleeves, his close-cropped ebony hair matched his black beard gelled into a crispy, fine point as though dipped in wet ink. One tiny gold hoop pierced his right earlobe, rings with enormous gemstones adorned his long, knobby fingers, and a silky black eyepatch in the shape of an upside-down triangle covered one eye. Griswald thought the man's pomp and gaudiness arrogant and foolish, but his ostentatious appearance did not reflect his dangerous nature. Rahkkar Tarquin Morshade was the one man in the camp who made Griswald wary.

He had witnessed first-hand how lethal Rahkkar was capable of being. Unpredictable and impossible to read, Griswald questioned his true intentions. Why had he agreed to be the Redpath's mage? Did he believe in their cause and the values they stood for, or did he have an ulterior motive? Griswald was inclined to think it was the latter. A powerful mage did not submit to civilian command unless there was something in it for them. Maybe the Redpath's leader, Hargrim, had struck a deal with the mage. Whatever the case, Griswald remained distrustful of wizards because their magic defied logic. If they embodied illogical practices, how could their actions and thought processes reflect logical or consistent patterns? And if his views put him in the minority even among other wizards, Griswald must keep both eyes open around the mage.

As soon as Griswald gave him his attention, Officer Wenhart, the young officer accompanying Rahkkar, began relaying his report. As Wenhart talked, Griswald gutted the buck methodically, the busy work of his hands belying the acute attention with which he listened. He found it useful to feign aloofness with his officers; it prevented suffering from swollen heads.

"We have enough food to satiate the soldiers, Captain," Wenhart reported in clipped tones. "It has all been distributed to the designated campfires. The troops have been allotted an extra measure of potent *wenaf* as you commanded, and I must say it has already brightened their spirits. A watch has been set around the camp's perimeter, and the scouts I sent out earlier should be back any moment, sir. Their orders are to come straight to you to make their reports."

At last, Griswald thought with heated fervour. *At last, I'm about to get some answers.*

"Be sure they do," Griswald growled, keeping emotion out of his voice. He needed those answers—it was the whole point of their venture last night, the reason Skeletal Moon Lake glistened with fresh blood—but he was not about to let anyone know of his personal vendetta, his blind loathing for that girl. He would have his revenge. He always did, in the end.

When Wenhart did not continue his report, Griswald turned to the magician. "And what news have you for me, Master Morshade? Are all the fires still invisible? You know how crucial invisibility is to the plan."

All the mages of Rahkkar's level were addressed with the title 'Master.' Griswald did not know specifics of magical education or wizarding levels—to him it was all just magic to be contemptuous yet wary of—but he did know mages, more than wizards, were known for their battle-magic talents. Griswald respected Morshade for his battle-savvy, but he still studied the mage's eyes for flashes of betrayal.

"I understand," Rahkkar replied smoothly, unruffled. "I assure you every fire continues to be invisible to anyone not part of the Redpath army. Acts of secrecy and stealth are my specialty, Griswald. You have no need for fear."

"Fear," Griswald snorted. "Don't be a fool. Fear is for those who accept failure, a foreign idea to me. You best remember the dangers of a man without fear, Rahkkar. Thus far you have served the Redpath well, and for that I thank you. I shall always be indebted to you for saving my life, even if you were just following orders. Just know that if you fail to bring us to Caris Nando and the Lantíes undetected we will face the full might of a Lantian army, and then my life would not have been worth saving. Now, do you have anything new to report to me or can we get this infernal healing thing over with?"

"No news tonight, Griswald," Rahkkar intoned softly. His tone suggested Griswald had crossed a line, so he submitted to his wound treatment without uttering a single complaint.

Gruesome, raw burns scabbed over with thick, bumpy pink-and-black scars marred most of his body. Bone threatened to protrude from the charred flesh of his right cheek. His mangled appearance reminded him of his folly and encouraged his men to follow his lead in sympathy and vengeance. Griswald had allowed the mage to rid the burns of infection, lessen the unsightly black char, and lighten the reddest, oozing raw flesh. Bumps and cracks pimpled the burnt flesh, bubbling as though still boiling from the heat of fire.

Griswald would never forgive Sadie Sheldon for the excruciating pain she had caused him. Not only had she left him deformed and near death, but she had humiliated and belittled him with her escape. Though he would have no peace of mind until he had killed her himself, Griswald had to admit her escape and decimation of a high-ranking captain had propelled the Redpath into action more effectively than his frequent efforts had achieved. He had been goading them into an act of war for over a year, claiming now was the time to assert their position as a superior organization while the Ilyance remained passive. But the pacifists of their council had hesitated and debated over such a bold move. Shock and horror at Griswald's near-fatal experience had been a catalyst, like a stone dropped in calm waters. Every single member now cried for vengeance against Sadie and the Ilyance she represented. They were compliant in his hands, and Griswald took full advantage of their blind submission.

Little violence had been necessary for the first part of their quest. They could not question anyone in Carenthia without risking Ilyance spies discovering he was still alive. They had questioned a few villagers in Belland, and some of them had required persuading, but when it became clear none had seen Sadie's company, they resorted to darker means to gain the information they needed.

For the first time in over seventy years, Dark Magic had been performed at Skeletal Moon Lake by Rahkkar Morshade.

Human sacrifices had been made for the moon. Ancient bones of past sacrifices had been resurrected and fed to the fires of Morshade's Dark Magic. And eventually, the moon had shared her secrets.

Scouts had been sent to Caris Nando the moment they emerged on the other side of the Dharlomin, ordered to slip past the Lantian sentinels and confirm the moon's tidings.

Interrupted in his reverie by the first returning scouts, Griswald signalled for Rahkkar to pause healing. When the scouts had all assembled he said, "Tell me."

One by one, the scouts relayed their information. Griswald learned Sadie had indeed taken up residence by Alldían's Hall, confirming the necessity of luring her away from Alldían's protection. They also reported confirmed sightings of the Swordmaster Tristan West, and Haldin and his younger brother, Airothane, both princes of Dharmaelia. Griswald knew Tristan was Alldían's pet and would not be duped in familiar territory, but one of her other companions could bait his trap. A companion who, if they believed their homeland was in trouble, would do anything to ensure her safety. A companion who mattered enough to the Ilyance alliance that they'd want to honour them. Fight for them. By the end of the scouts' report, Griswald had formed a plan. He scrutinized the trees calculatingly, then nodded to himself. All he needed now was bait to catch the bait...

"Officer Wenhart," Griswald growled. "Bring me the lowest ranking, least worthy soldier in your unit. I have a special job for them."

Hiding his puzzlement, Wenhart inclined his head and left at once. When he returned, a scrawny young man trotted behind him, pockmarks blemishing his face. He kept stumbling in the dark, and when they halted just inside the firelight, he wrung his sweaty hands, glancing from Wenhart to Griswald with panicked eyes.

"What's your name?" Griswald barked at the nervous man.

"S-Simon," he stuttered.

"Well, Simon. You have the honour of serving the Redpath in a very special way."

Rahkkar stepped into the firelight. Griswald signalled for him to begin.

The mage's lip curled. Simon writhed, eyes rolling back in his head.

He did not stutter once as he screamed.

Echoes of screams pressed against Sadie's skull, building pressure in her ears and popping in the corners of her mind. She curled her stomach around the nausea billowing from her core. Lifting her eyes to the stars as though pulled by an invisible string, Sadie squinted at the blurry specks of white light—then shuttered her eyelids again.

No. If this was Celestial magic beckoning her, she wanted no part of it.

Her head ached, the pressure behind her eyes increasing—

A vision burst to life behind her scrunched eyelids. A man with harrowing eyes burning vindictively in a mangled face. He was hunched on the peripheries of a campfire, his face half in shadow, smirking at something on the ground near his feet. The screams echoed louder in Sadie's head, reverberating and rattling until she realized—

They were *her* screams.

And she didn't know if they would ever stop.

Griswald's sneering, mangled face had marred her vision.

And now everyone she loved was in danger.

Chapter Twenty-Six

Truths Between Stars

Fingering feathers of ice clinging to delicate snowy petals sparkling in the cold dawn sunlight, Sadie closed her eyes and let the sounds of rushing water from the Éalindel wash away the nightmares still tainting her mind.

She had set out for the Setami river a few hours after midnight, giving up on a sleep marred by visions of Connor shot down mercilessly in fields mingled with flashes of Griswald's mutilated sneer. Sitting among the nalalíté she had sunk into a numb stupor, unable to feel anything unless it was despair. She slumped listless, like a marionette waiting for someone else to control the strings.

When the incessant freezing mist of the steady pummelling waterfall had pounded all thoughts from her head, she followed the river downstream.

Emerging from the woods into the clearing of the Sula-onon, she warily eyed the tower protruding from the earth like the bone of an ancient creature. If Tristan had not caught her when she fell that night, she would have died… just like Connor soon could fighting in a war. A wave of pain and grief threatened to engulf Sadie. She raced to the tower. For a few brief, glorious minutes, thoughts of Connor catapulted out of Sadie's mind as she concentrated on the exertion of running up the steps, trying to stop her legs from buckling. Sweat poured down her temples and dangled off her nose, but she pushed herself to keep running. She relished the physical pain, and though her lungs burned and legs ached, the ghost of a smile crept across her face.

Emerging onto the tower's summit, Sadie choked on a chilly breeze freezing her burning lungs. Clawing at a stitch in her side, she stumbled over to the leaf-shaped extension, careful to stay far away from the ledge. Could she use her magic to fly? Ever since she had read *Peter and Wendy*, a book about a boy who refused to grow up and could fly like a bird, Sadie had dreamed of soaring freely above the land. She would sprint across the lawn with her arms spread wide like wings, or jump off the veranda steps with her arms flapping furiously, and Connor—

Her fond memory of their playful antics transformed instantaneously to depression over the foolish imminent danger he had put himself in. Slowly, Sadie lowered herself to the platform and sat cross-legged on the cool stone, staring at the crown of trees.

Why had her brother joined the army? Make-believe swordplay in their youth did not equate becoming a soldier. Those images from the Pool of desolated battlefields and grisly, merciless deaths lingered in the peripheries of her vision. The sounds of rapid-fire bullets peppered her brain. If he thought he was seeking adventure, he was being horribly naïve.

A bitter tang coated Sadie's tongue, and her throat burned. *She* had been horribly naïve. For most of her life she had craved battle. The idea of brandishing a sword and besting someone in combat had seemed so satisfying. A chance to prove she was more than a trinket in a frilly dress. She had been so obsessed with the heroics of battle and triumphing over evil that she had failed to realize the dark side of that desire. In her imagination, her foes had always been monstrous, evil incarnate that she would feel no qualms killing. But what if the monsters were regular people like her brother, trying to defend their own homes and families? What if the lies they'd been fed by greater powers made them feel like they had no choice?

Would she still be willing to kill them? And if so... what did that say about her?

Her skin itched, and bile rose in her throat. She felt unclean. Tainted by the uncertainty of her convictions.

What had Alldían been thinking? A vision of her in Carmelle meant nothing. Right now, she was more likely to destroy Carmelle, not save it. She had been unsure about returning to Earth because of how much she loved Carmelle, but maybe she *should* return if given the opportunity. Maybe she would do less damage there. She berated Tristan for his lies when she betrayed herself with far worse ones. Tristan told lies to evade his past; she lied to pretend she had some control over her future.

As her mother would say, it was time to stop playing pretend.

Sadie winced as an appalling thought sliced through her mind like a knife. Had her absence spurned Connor's decision to leave? Connor believed her dead, if Sadie's dream soon after entering Carmelle was true. His face, distorted in pain and sorrow as he knelt before her grave swam before her eyes, and she blinked. Could he have sought refuge in a war to deal with his grief? Was it her fault Connor had become a soldier?

Tears trickled silently down Sadie's cheeks, following a well-worn path. Coming to Carmelle was the tangible manifestation of a dream for Sadie, and yet her presence here had engendered nothing but grief for everyone both in Carmelle and her home world. Maybe her quest to find magic in the mundane meant stealing magic from other lives, sacrificing their happiness and power of choice so she could exert her own.

Whether she stayed in Carmelle or returned to Earth, she seemed fated for failure.

Sadie left her perch atop the Sula-onon when evening fell, fearing the moon's captivation. When she re-entered the heart of Caris Nando, she realized nobody had bothered trying to find her.

Perhaps everyone had concluded she was more of a hindrance than a help. Maybe her mother had been right all along. She wasn't a strong female version of Odysseus. She wasn't a hero at all. Just a naïve girl trying to create a reality that did not exist, oblivious to who she hurt along the way. She didn't deserve this world or her magic.

Terror gripped her at the thought of vanishing into obscurity. Of the bleak, yawning empty promise of normalcy. Of becoming another faceless woman destined to fade into the shadows of men and never shine. Never leave her mark. Never shake the foundations of the earth and roar above the cacophonous din of ceaseless oblivion.

And yet...

Sometimes dreams morph into nightmares and awaken to reality.

Every step she took towards escaping obscurity and fulfilling a heroic destiny shadowed her soul in darkness. Every step hurt someone she cared for. If proving her worth meant diminishing others', then maybe her only course of action was to surrender. Cease fighting the nightmare. Let it consume her.

Embrace obscurity, and find peace in it.

Sadie sat on her bed, a book about a legendary pirate who once roamed the Tolotanteau and stole a Lantian king's entire treasure trove, along with his precious daughter, propped on her knees. But her mind kept drifting back to her brother. Connor was her only connection to Earth, the only person who had never attached conditions to his love. Losing him would be like losing part of herself, losing almost eighteen years of her life. What if she had to return to her old world without her brother?

A quiet knock marred the silence. Sadie ignored it.

The knock came again, louder, and more insistent.

"Who is it?"

"It's Airothane."

"Go away," she replied automatically.

"Sadie, please, I want to talk to you, no one has seen you all day and—"

"GO AWAY," Sadie repeated.

"I'm not going anywhere until you open this door, so—"

"Oh, fine, get in here then, I'm not getting up—"

Airothane was in before Sadie could finish her sentence. He attempted a look of stern disapproval, but it was compromised by a smile twitching at the corners of his mouth.

Sadie returned to her book.

Airothane coughed deliberately.

Sadie flipped a page.

Airothane shuffled his feet and coughed louder.

Sadie immersed herself in a bloody account of the pirate murdering his first mate.

Airothane kicked a chair then cursed, hopping on his bruised foot.

Sadie marvelled at the amount of spurting blood decapitation produces.

"Er—Sadie?"

Sadie took one look at Airothane's concerned face and knew he would never betray her trust. He may be nosy and annoying, but his desire to help her was sincere.

"Why are you so upset? Do you want to tell me about it?"

Putting her book on the bed, Sadie admitted, "I'm worried about my brother. He's fighting in a war on Earth, and he's only seventeen... I'm scared he'll die, and I'm powerless to stop it."

"Oh," said Airothane, confusion rippling across his honey sea eyes, and Sadie remembered he was a prince from a warring nation where children were probably born with swords in their hands.

"I know you probably don't understand," Sadie hastened to explain. "War is a way of life for Dharmaelians. Skill in battle and death fighting for your people bring honour. I love reading about ancient civilizations on Earth, like the Trojans, who glorified battle, and have always longed to fight for a cause I believe in. But I also know taking a life can't be as glorious or romanticized as the books make it seem."

"It's not," Airothane assured her. "Dharmaelians fight because we *have* to, not because we want to. Fighting is in our culture because our land is right next to Vasmorloth. Vashi's minions attack us constantly, so it's fight or be slaughtered and allow other Carmellians to be slaughtered. Should we let them murder innocent people instead? Should we not defend the land we were born and raised in? Believe me, every soldier's dream is to stop going to war. But some things are worth fighting for. That's why I'm so proud of my brother. His deeds in battle aren't great because he wants fame and glory, but because he fights for justice and protecting what he cares about. Our convictions give us power."

Sadie's heart swelled at the sage words coming from such a young mind.

"I wish I could be certain what my brother is fighting for is worth it," said Sadie. "Warfare and weaponry on Earth have changed. Close combat with swords is becoming a thing of the past. Weapons called guns and cannons have been part of warfare for a while now to allow soldiers to kill quicker from a distance. But the visions of this new war on Earth, visions Alldían showed me..." She paused and shook her head. "Something felt different about them. They terrified me. I fear the desolation, the long line of huge gouges in the bullet-riddled earth. I don't remember hearing about war transforming the land quite that much. The speed of some of those guns... I keep thinking about how many people could die before they even had a chance to draw their own weapons with guns that fast. How impersonal it would feel, and less chivalrous. And the war seemed to be on so many fronts; the scale looked different than anything I have read or heard about before. I can't shake the feeling that honour will be much more difficult to come by in this war, especially if your motivations are muddled."

"Why do you think your brother's motivations are muddled?" asked Airothane.

"I fear he believes I'm dead and made a rash decision to enter this war from grief."

"There are lots of reasons people go to war," Airothane replied, his tiny arms swinging back and forth like a pendulum as he spoke, reminding Sadie of how young and impulsive he still was. "Even if they die for that reason, it doesn't mean it was the wrong decision for them."

"I know, but..." Sadie sighed, trailing off. How could she explain her gnawing guilt, the vision she'd had of Connor by her grave, or the way things were for her and Connor in their world? The relentless weight compressing her lungs and chewing on her intestines at the thought of her brother dying on a battlefield without her seeing him again and apologizing for leaving him. Or even worse, her never even being able to find his body to mourn him if she did return to Earth.

"I understand losing your only connection to your world would make you devastated," Airothane assured her, showing a level of perception she had not been able to express even to herself. "My friendship with my best friend, Wulfric, could never compare to my bond with Haldin. But maybe there's a different way to think about this. You found yourself in an unfamiliar world, and your brother found himself in a world unfamiliar to him without you. A war is taking place in your world, and war is certainly brewing here in Carmelle. Maybe your brother was meant to fight in that war, and you were meant to fight in Carmelle's. War changes people, but it doesn't always have to be for the worse. Big wars in two parallel worlds at once—I'm sure that means something."

Sadie could think of nothing to say. Whether her and her brother were meant to fight in these wars or not, Airothane was right that it didn't have to change them for the worse. Even if he had been influenced by her actions, Connor alone had made a choice for his life. Sadie still had the power to do the same. They had lost each other, but they weren't *lost*.

The unknown path just made the self more known.

Airothane leaned over and gave her a quick hug before darting out of the room.

"Thank you, Airothane!" Sadie called after him.

The next day Airothane greeted her with annoyingly knowing looks every time she furrowed her brow, as though she could only have one problem at a time. Restless jitters bounced her legs and twitched her fingers. Despite her talk with Airothane, the unclean feeling crawled up her spine.

Sadie waited until stars sprang into view against a navy sky and then sneaked into the woods. She needed to mull over everything Airothane had said, and she knew the perfect place to do it. Her lantern glowed brightly, and bioluminescent flowers shone in the moonlight. Her midnight blue cloak slithered over leaves behind her and shadowed her face with its hood, and moonlight glinted off the pearl-studded ultramarine belt girded over her silver dress.

The hollows in her chest filled and her breath hitched, knowing what that meant. A pearly-white gleam streaked through the trees. A moment later her unicorn strode majestically out of the forest, tossing his mane as he greeted her like an old friend. He nuzzled her neck as she ran her fingers through his mane and stroked his horn.

"I missed you," Sadie cooed, and he whinnied softly. Continuing down the path with the unicorn walking beside her, Sadie wrapped her hand in his warm mane. The distance until they reached Tor Niro Lake flew by with her friend at her side, and soon she clambered up the giant rock. A dark silhouette greeted her, outlined by the full moon. Someone had usurped her spot.

Sadie froze. She recognized the tall figure with his short ponytail.

Tristan.

Sadie deliberated turning back, but she had missed Tristan. Sitting next to him, she drew her knees up to her chest and folded her arms around them. He continued gazing at the stars, though she knew he was aware of her presence. It was impossible to sneak up on Tristan.

"As you know," Tristan commented, still examining the stars, "most Carmellians fear the stars, loathing the constant reminder of the terrible horrors inflicted on them by those who wielded Celestial magic before and may be tempted to do so again. Astronomy used to be a popular field of study in Carmelle before the Celestial magic deaths increased dramatical-ly. After Celestial magic was banned, astronomical studies died off. Folk feared their scientific studies would be deemed Celestial magic, and some even went so far as to destroy their instruments of observation and models. The bravest scholars continued their studies in secret though, so some advancements have still been made in the last century. Some, like Tamlin and Alldían, who are educated in the knowledge of other worlds, know the extent of Earth's astronomical discoveries, and verifiable facts about a network of planets and stars burning immeasurable distances away helps alleviate their fears of Celestial magic. And others believe Celestial magic is the fodder of gossips and elders trying to scare the next generations into good behaviour, and the stars bear no inherent evil."

Sadie studied Tristan's face closely, remembering Skeleton Lake and the Sula-onon, and the moon's enticing pull on her magic. "What do you believe?"

"I believe power alone does not equate to evil," Tristan replied slowly, considering his words. "A person's intentions are always part of the equa-tion. I'm not saying Dark Magic doesn't exist. But just because something *can* lead to evil, does not mean it is the root of it. Ingested alone, nalalíté flowers are harmless, beneficial even, but when mixed with the ruby pollen of the rare sapphire and crimson suléa flowers, they create one of the deadliest poisons in Carmelle. All I feel when I look at the stars is solace and hope."

A person's intentions are always part of the equation. She certainly never intended to hurt anyone. Maybe she had enough light to combat the darkness inside her. Sadie smiled, the fluttering nerves in her stomach settling. "Me too."

"I also know Earth and Carmelle have the same constellations, with different names, which shows our worlds are not so different." Tristan looked sideways at her. "Perhaps that's why Earth and Carmelle are poised for synchronized wars. The two worlds are more connected than we think—and you and your brother are more connected than you think."

Sadie stared at him, heart thrashing against her throat. Alldían could've informed him of the congruent wars, but no one knew she'd been thinking about her brother lately except...

"That little traitor!" Sadie cried, fire burning in her chest. "He blabbed to you, didn't he? I knew I was stupid to trust him, I—"

"Airothane did not tell me anything, Sadie," Tristan reassured her. "You were right to trust him. I overheard your conversation. I was returning to my quarters and your window was open a crack, and I heard you two talking. I admit I listened in. You wouldn't tell me what bothered you, so when I realized what you were talking about... I had been thinking you were upset with me for something to do with my Storytelling. You walked out after my first song at the welcoming feast and have been cold towards me ever since. I-I'm sorry for listening."

Tristan trapped her eyes in the sincerity warming his, and her initial surge of fury ebbed. She probably would have done the same.

"Thank you for the apology, Tristan. I'm sorry that's what you had been thinking. It wasn't to do with your Storytelling at all; I love your Storytelling gift, I truly do. You're a wonderful Storyteller. I just get scared by the way your stories sweep my mind away, leaving me vulnerable. The feeling of having no control over my mind unnerves me. I do trust you though, I want you to know that. I'm trying to work on accepting I can't control everything. There's a difference between having choices and always needing to be in control. I'm starting to realize I don't need to do the latter to still have the former. Vulnerability is okay sometimes."

Tristan's whole body visibly relaxed, his shoulders slumping and his hands dropping from where they had been clutching his knees. "I'm glad you trust me, Sadie. I trust you too."

"Besides, I don't want to become my mother," Sadie joked.

"No, couldn't think of anything worse," Tristan agreed with a small chuckle.

They shared a smile, but Sadie's faded quickly at what she had to tell Tristan next. "Alldían took me to Telwé Unvar and the Seven Pools, and I saw my world at war. It was... terrible. Death and destruction reigned everywhere I looked, lands laid waste by guns and cannons and fire, steam rising from pockmarked stretches of shell-ridden earth... Soldiers shattered to pieces... and then Connor firing rifles at camp, ready for his body to be mercilessly mutilated..."

Sadie trailed off, unable to continue. Her eyes watered but she blinked back the tears as she focused on the stars reflected in the lake.

Tristan found her hand and squeezed it briefly, lending her strength and support, before letting go.

A translucent silvery sheen illuminated every facet of the lake, glinting like a layer of magic dust in the moonlight. Stars dusted the inky black dome overhead, so numerous and clear the sky looked crowded, like someone had dumped a huge vat of silver glitter across it. Pine needles glinted like metallic daggers. The waterfall flowed like molten silver, sparkling with pearly diamonds in the light of the winking stars. The lake mirrored it all.

"It's like another world, isn't it?" whispered Tristan. "A parallel dimension with a more magical Tor Níro. I know magic has its drawbacks, but I've always preferred the surreal over the ordinary."

Sadie raised an eyebrow.

"I know, I know." Tristan's hollow laugh echoed across the lake. "How very optimistic of me. But sometimes it's okay to make a different reality for yourself. It's okay to like it in Carmelle better than your old world."

Tristan fixed Sadie with a grim smile. "You don't have to feel guilty for loving this world because Connor is still in the world you hated, fighting in a war. It is not wrong to choose one reality over another. I know it's not easy to leave your world behind knowing someone you care about deeply can't exist in the same reality you do—trust me, I do—but you must remember Carmelle and Earth are not estranged. You are not as disconnected from him as you think."

For a moment Sadie latched her gaze onto the pupils of Tristan's eyes, an anchor amidst the chocolate brown current of his irises. How did he know exactly what she was thinking? She wished he would confess he was from her world. His secret was like a moat between them, creating a distance she could not cross until he lowered the drawbridge.

But she refrained from asking him to lower the bridge. Pressing him to allow her in would only make him withdraw further.

"I like your way of looking at it," Sadie admitted. "I do love Carmelle, and I know Connor fighting is not my fault, not really. Airothane helped me see that. Connor has the power to make his own decisions, just like I do. I just miss him."

"I know," Tristan whispered.

"Aren't you supposed to be throwing some sort of snide comment my way now?" Sadie asked to break the sudden silence. "Isn't that how we work? If you don't mock me, how will I know you care? You're always up to no good."

"That's why you keep me around," Tristan replied with a sly grin Sadie returned.

"You know, I used to banter with Connor all the time. We constantly plotted ways to cross lines, so bantering became how we conversed. It's different with you though," she added thoughtfully. "Connor and I bantered as an act of defiance—with you it's natural, like I can be myself and a character from stories all at the same time."

Before Tristan could respond, a loud snort erupted between their ears, followed by an impatient hoof stamp. They both wheeled around to find the unicorn. Sadie's cheeks flushed. She had forgotten him.

"Has he been here the whole time?" Tristan asked warily.

"Yes. He found me on my way here and joined me. I wasn't expecting you to be here though, so when I saw you I forgot about him... sorry, boy," she added to the unicorn.

"Unicorns do not take kindly to being ignored. I'm surprised he hasn't nipped or pushed us into the lake. Is he the same one who led you to the Sula-onon?"

"Yes. He keeps finding me, though I'm not sure why. I feel more complete when he's around. Like there's a connection between our souls."

After a brief pause, Tristan confessed, "I've always been envious of Tamlin's connection to her unicorn. Unicorns tolerate me better than most humans, but normally one would never stay this close to me."

"Maybe he's trying to protect me," Sadie teased, "You *are* kind of scary looking."

"Unicorns are very perceptive," Tristan agreed, smirking. "Maybe you should give him a name. You can't keep calling him *boy*, he'll start to get offended."

"What do you name a unicorn?"

"Whatever you want. Xavier, Storm, Snowstar, Chai—"

"Chai?" Sadie repeated, a smile tugging at her lips. "Like the tea?"

"There's a tea called chai?"

"It's the most delicious tea with hints of cinnamon and ginger spices..." Sadie's mouth watered wistfully.

"Right, well, I meant like the word for 'home' in Tavé," clarified Tristan.

"Okay, but also, the tea," repeated Sadie.

Tristan rolled his eyes.

"He certainly makes me feel at home," Sadie conceded. She looked up at the unicorn to see its reaction. "What do you think? Do you like the name Chai?"

The unicorn whinnied, tossing his mane, and stamping his hooves.

"Chai it is then!" cried Sadie, and she hugged Chai's knees.

Shooting stars bridged the silence that followed.

Tristan watched the arc of their bridges, then extended one of his own. "I'm not from Carmelle, Sadie."

Sadie froze and did not speak.

"I know you're going to think I lied to you, but although I avoided mentioning it, I technically never lied. I never said I was from Carmelle. I don't know why I didn't tell you—fear of recounting my past probably, and of judgment, but I know now I should have said something sooner for your sake. I'm from your world, Sadie. I was born close to you, in fact. That's why I knew how to work the mirror, and how to find you. I came through the same mirror to Carmelle when I was six.

"I remember everything from my life on Earth so clearly. But like your Earth memories, they are not very pleasant. I just thought you should know..."

He trailed off, and for the first time since Sadie had met him, he looked vulnerable.

Instantly, Sadie decided not to deceive him.

"Thank you for telling me, Tristan," she said quietly and sincerely. "I know that must have been difficult for you. I must confess, Alldían told me where you are from the night of the welcoming feast. I was upset at your role in my transference here, so he informed me of your past to protect your character. I would have preferred to hear it from you first, but now I finally feel like I'm getting to know the real Tristan."

Tristan's jaw clenched. Sadie couldn't tell if he was mad at her, Alldían, or himself.

"What made you decide to tell me?" Sadie asked.

Tristan peered at the stars again before replying, "It became too difficult to hide it from you. That day I commented on Thomas Sheldon's book and the religious wars in your—our—world, and you stormed off... I knew I had to tell you soon. And then hearing about your brother..."

"I didn't come here tonight to talk to you. This is my favourite place in Caris Nando, and I come here often at night to think and clear my head. But as soon as you arrived, I knew now was the time to tell you."

"So... how did you come to Carmelle then, and why?" Sadie probed, curiosity burning inside her.

"I didn't come from a privileged family like you. My family was poor. I know my mother loved me, but I mostly felt like a burden instead of a blessing to my parents. We lived in the slums of Vancouver among the dregs of society. I never really got to be a child," Tristan mused. "I witnessed far too many things a child should never see. I never experienced innocence or felt carefree with no responsibilities. My father beat me and my mom, though she still idolized him and submitted to his every whim. It wasn't until the night they died that I realized the depth of their abuse. I became full of hatred for everyone in our world, regardless of class."

"What happened?" Sadie whispered, her voice raspy and broken.

Tristan's whole body stiffened, and Sadie feared she had pushed him too far.

"There was an accident." He spoke barely above a whisper, his knuckles white where they gripped his knees. "My parents frequently visited a friend on his boat down by the docks where my father worked. One night a gang of men sneaked on the boat while we were below deck having dinner. Nobody heard them coming. By the time we realized something was wrong, the smoke already choked us and flames blocked the exit. I was the only one small enough to fit through the tiny hatch..."

Sadie's hand flew to her mouth, her eyes wide. Tristan's voice did not quite break, but his hands shook slightly.

"They died that night, and I became an orphan. I was only five. I was sent to an orphanage not too far from the Sheldon manor. On the opposite end of the woods bordering the manor, in fact."

"I know that orphanage! You were so close to my home! I can't believe..." She trailed off into shocked silence. She could not comprehend the proximity of their backgrounds. All this time they'd had more in common than Sadie had ever dreamed.

"I know," Tristan replied. "I could not believe it at first when Alldían asked me to return to almost the exact same place I intentionally left seventeen years ago. I was sure Alldían had misinterpreted his vision. I won't lie: going back was one of the most painful experiences of my life. Barely a year after my parents died, I ran away from the orphanage, tired of enduring the abuse and wretched conditions. I ran into the woods and found the mirror."

Sadie had been so preoccupied with her own problems and bitter at Tristan for not confiding in her that she hadn't stopped to consider how coming back through the mirror to his home world would have made him feel.

"Tristan, I owe you an apology." Sadie's voice was laced with desperate sincerity as she followed the lines of pain etched in his forehead and the corners of his eyes. "I shut you out after Alldían told me of your past. I felt betrayed by the apparent lack of trust you had in me and our friendship. But I think it was also easier to blame you for all my problems and insecurities instead of facing my mistakes."

Nerves needled her stomach, and Sadie exhaled deeply to soothe them.

"I took my life on Earth for granted. I had a family, I was privileged in so many ways, but I couldn't escape the prison of my own mind. I felt so... heavy. Like chains weighed me down. I couldn't shake them off. I came to loathe the word 'almost' because of how often my mother used it to describe my shortcomings. I got anxious and restless, breaking out in cold sweats and feeling dizzy and faint. Like the sharp pain pressing against my chest would squeeze me out of existence every time the black hole of an impending marriage and life I didn't want threatened to swallow me. I feared becoming obsolete more than anything, and it stirred a sorrow so deep it pulled me down with its own crushing gravity. I couldn't see the light ahead. But the present wasn't as dim as I thought. I know now that accepting who I am and caring about the people around me means I never have to fear obscurity."

Tristan reached for her hand and squeezed gently. "It's okay, Sadie. I get it. I understood your frustration and longing to escape. It's good you know your life was privileged, but that doesn't cancel your pain or make it less real. No one should have to feel their existence is not superfluous. We were both prisoners of that world in different ways. But here, we are free."

Turning to look Sadie in the eyes again, Tristan grinned. Relief and content rippled across his eyes, like clouds parting after a storm. Sadie couldn't help but return his smile. Beneath the swirls of his chocolate brown eyes a warmth smouldered, making Sadie feel safe and content. She tucked that feeling securely in a pocket of her heart.

Tristan was right. She did feel freer in this world, but there was more to it. Maybe true freedom wasn't becoming a strong heroine in the tradition of male heroes she read about in her favourite stories. Maybe true freedom lay in accepting every facet of herself, including flaws. She didn't need to carry this burden of guilt about things she couldn't control. She couldn't control Connor's decisions. She couldn't control Griswald's actions, if her brief vision did indeed mean he was still alive and potentially seeking revenge. All she could do was control her own actions. Her fears of becoming obsolete. She could be present in the moment with the person who accepted her for exactly who she was.

"You know, because I left Earth at such a young age, I never had the opportunity for education there," Tristan said after a few minutes of silence. "I always loved gazing at the stars, both before and during my time at the orphanage, but never knew their names. What's that one called in our old world?" He pointed at a ladle-shaped formation.

"The Big Dipper. Part of the Ursa Major constellation," Sadie replied with a grin, ready for the new game.

"And that one?" Tristan asked, indicating a formation resembling a hunter.

"Orion. And that huge cluster of stars like a swath of glittery paint is the Milky Way."

"Such different names..." Tristan mused. "Thank you, Sadie," he added, a multitude of unsaid things coating his words.

"Thank *you*, Tristan."

Chapter Twenty-Seven

When the Hawk Flies

Swordplay training with Tristan felt different this morning. Sadie's heart was lighter, her focus less intense, and a smile accompanied every lunge. Unpacking her guilt and relinquishing her unyielding grasp on control felt so freeing. She felt ready to take on the world.

Sadie unleashed a vicious cut at Tristan's throat just as a voice shouted, "Tristan!"

Tristan had been meeting Sadie's cut with a lazy parry but turned his head at the sound of his name. Sadie seized her advantage and lunged at his middle. With a triumphant yell, she stabbed him in the liver with the point of her wooden blade. Tristan grunted as Sadie laughed.

"That doesn't count," he wheezed. "You cheated."

"Oh, don't be a baby," she chided. "At least be mature enough to admit your defeats."

Tristan admitted no such thing as he met a Lantian messenger at the fence. The man's voice was low and urgent as he relayed a message from Alldían, and Tristan sighed as he informed Sadie he had been summoned to Alldían's hall and must cut their practice short.

"Can I come with you?" Sadie asked.

The messenger pursed his lips, and Tristan hesitated.

"Please?" she pressed. "I won't get in the way, I don't even have to hear what Alldían has to tell you. I can just wander around the hall. I'd love to see it again in closer detail."

"I guess it would be all right," Tristan conceded. "Alldían didn't specify coming alone."

As Sadie trudged beside Tristan through the fresh snow, she reflected on the improvement of her swordsmanship. Now she could parry, lunge, and cut in the eight basic positions. After a few sessions, Tamlin had come to the practice field. As she watched Sadie practise her lunges, she had informed them channelling magic through weapons was possible.

"Can I learn?" Sadie had asked, her sword tip pointed at Tamlin.

Tamlin had considered her for a moment before saying, "I would not have brought it up otherwise. However, you must improve with your weapon of choice first before you are able to learn more than just the theory."

Sadie hoped she had improved enough to learn channelling magic with her sword soon.

She rounded a corner and Alldían's Hall greeted them in the hollow below, the slanted branches of the roof buried in sparkling snow. Snow and frost also covered the bare tree trunks comprising the wall, and though a path had been cleared to the front of the Hall, icicles thicker than her arm framed the double doors.

"They're enchanted to not fall," Tristan told her, seeing her eyeing them warily.

Sadie followed him beneath the icicles and into the hall.

With the stone wall separating the inner tree-wall from the elements, the bare branches and trunks were devoid of snow. The flames at the top of the pillars lining the aisle burned an icy blue now, emanating a soft, wintry glow. Frozen patterns spiralled across the glass prism ceiling, shooting out like fireworks. Frost crackled under her boots like crunching bones as they marched up the otherwise silent hall.

When they reached the line of thrones, she bowed in unison with Tristan to Alldían and the assembled Lantian lords low. Behind these lords loomed the base of the greatest tree in Caris Nando, its smooth silver bark flecked with white frost like an old man's hoary beard.

A frazzled Lantíe stood before the lords as well. His eyes shifted sporadically beneath his disarrayed hair as though expecting an attack, and his tensed muscles looked prepared to spring into action.

"You summoned me, godfather?" Tristan asked, his eyes wandering to the nervous Lantíe and back.

"Should I go amuse myself at the other end of the hall?" Sadie asked Alldían. Eyeing the serious faces of the Lantian lords, she added, "Or… wait outside for Tristan, perhaps?"

Alldían smiled. "That won't be necessary, Sadie. I'm glad you're here. Beryl has brought news from the Mínando watchmen on our western borders," Alldían continued, gesturing to the nervous Lantíe and addressing both Sadie and Tristan. "A few nights ago, they heard strange noises coming from the Dharlomin, like the echoes of screams. It could have been the mountains creaking and groaning under so much snow, or the shriek of a particularly ferocious wind as such noises are not uncommon in the winter. Perhaps it was an avalanche. Nevertheless, the noises unsettled the guards and they felt it prudent to inform me and decide whether it should be investigated. The other Lantian lords deem further action unnecessary. What do you think?"

"Maybe it was only an avalanche or trees exploding from the frigid air," Tristan replied slowly, eyeing the watchman again, "but it couldn't hurt to send scouts out, just in case."

Alldían looked pleased, but the other lords frowned or pursed their lips. Though the watchman gave Tristan a grateful look, he also appeared eager to smooth the lords' disgruntled faces.

"If I may suggest," Beryl started, but the hall doors banged open, cutting Beryl off.

Striding up the hall with composed purpose was another Lantian watchman, followed closely by Tamlin, Haldin, and Airothane. Sadie and the others watched in frozen silence as the newcomers drew nearer. This watchman appeared more composed than Beryl, save a sheen of sweat beading on his spotless forehead. Tamlin's eyes looked troubled, and Haldin's expressed both worry and restlessness.

"My lords," the new watchman said as soon as he drew level with Sadie and Tristan, inclining his head first to Alldían and then the others. "I bring strange tidings from the western borders. This morning, the Mínando found a man wandering aimlessly around the western entrance. They tried hailing him in our usual custom, but he either did not hear or would not answer. A few of us drew close enough to see his face, and... something ailed him. He acted like a madman. He winced or flinched any time we got near, and high, keening wails punctured the incessant muttering under his breath. He lashed out violently then cowered in fear. He shouted 'Dharmaelia!' and raved adamantly about the nation needing aid. We all believed something terrible must have happened there, at first. But his slips in and out of coherent speech suggested it unwise to panic at the words of a madman. I must admit he was the sanest while raving about Dharmaelia, though. We agreed to inform you at once."

Sadie glanced at Haldin and Airothane's anxious faces. No one spoke for a full minute.

Then Alldían calmly asked, "Where is he now, Marius?"

"Several of the Mínando are guarding him," replied Marius. "He was very... reluctant to move. We thought it best not to push him."

"We must go to him!" Airothane insisted, his high voice shrill. Sadie's heart pinched hearing his anguish. "We have to learn what is happening in Dharmaelia so we can help them!"

"Don't be hasty, child," said one of the shorter Lantian lords. "People whose minds have been altered cannot be trusted to ramble facts. We must discuss this and proceed with caution."

"Certainly, we must not allow haste to brand us fools," conceded Haldin, "but Dharmaelia is my land, and I cannot sit idly by while her people may be suffering. Airothane speaks without thinking, but his instincts are true to the Dharmaelian spirit. Mad or not, there's a reason the man spoke of Dharmaelia. Maybe he heard of trouble there, or maybe he's from Dharmaelia and his malady is he irrationally fears its demise. Or perhaps he is not acting alone, and someone wishes us to think Dharmaelia in trouble. Either way, as prince of that land it is my duty to investigate any potential threat to our kingdom and its people. I will go see this man and question him."

Sadie admired the confident set of Haldin's jaw and the challenge in his eyes inviting the Lantíe to contradict him. One of the Lantian lords opened his mouth, but Haldin cut him off.

"You may send whoever you wish with me to ensure my safety or analyze the man's answers. I would not object to some company."

"I'll go—" volunteered Airothane, but Haldin interjected with an emphatic, "*No.*"

Airothane scowled and hunched his tiny shoulders. Haldin did not look at his younger brother, but a small smile of pride tugged at his lips.

"Marius, will you consent to accompanying Haldin?" Alldían asked the watchman. "You can show him where the man is. You may bring other Mínando with you, but keep the numbers limited. After Haldin questions him, bring him here to be cared for if you can. Whatever you do, don't hurt him. If he cannot be brought here peacefully, please do not force him."

Marius nodded his consent and Haldin appeared satisfied, but the back of Sadie's neck prickled. She wasn't sure why, but she feared all was not as it seemed.

"Let me go with you," Tristan volunteered as everyone began dispersing. "One more pair of eyes to watch everyone's backs cannot go amiss."

"No!" chorused Airothane, Haldin, and Alldían at once. They all looked at each other, surprised.

Haldin broke the silence first. "I appreciate your concern, Tristan, but I don't think it's necessary to tear you away from your duties to defend me when I am perfectly capable of defending myself."

"I didn't mean to suggest—"

"I too would prefer you to remain here, Tristan," Alldían interjected quietly but firmly.

Tristan eyed their unrelenting faces before shrugging in defeat. As they passed Haldin on their way out of the hall, Sadie saw Tristan rest his hand on Haldin's arm and warn in a low voice, "Do not underestimate the dangers of a madman, Haldin. I know you are no fool and will tread carefully, but I implore you to exercise extra caution. I don't know what I fear, but I cannot shake this mantle of uneasiness. Promise me you will approach this man warily."

Haldin studied Tristan for a moment, then clapped him on the shoulder companionably. "You're a good man, and a good friend. I'm lucky to have you in my life. Do not fear. Dharmaelians are not as hot-headed and war-hungry as many seem to think. I know how to exercise caution. I will not walk into a trap."

Sadie stared after his retreating back, her own mantle of unease lightening a little. Haldin was a great warrior with a wealth of experience. He would be fine.

Griswald adjusted his grip on the pommel of the sword girded at his waist but did not take his eyes off the narrow gap in the trees across from him. Laughter echoed through the forest, sounding unnatural in the silence suffocating the woods, and the men around him shifted their feet in anticipation. Rahkkar Morshade's eyes narrowed at the innocent gaiety, but then his lips twitched into a sly smirk. They had no idea what awaited them.

At least it would be quicker than the poor souls at Skeletal Moon Lake. Quicker even than the torture they put Simon through. They were showing mercy, really.

The drawn-out screams of those they had sacrificed at Skeletal Moon Lake echoed in Griswald's head, and he shuddered. He wasn't immune to the suffering of others. He did not derive pleasure from inflicting pain. Rahkkar was the sadistic one, not him. He was a man who recognized potential and possibility, and wasn't afraid to dirty his hands trying to bring visions of a brighter future to fruition. Everyone had to sacrifice part of themselves to better their personal lives, but when you were trying to better the whole world, sometimes the sacrifices you had to make affected other people's lives as well. Griswald had drawn this logical conclusion long ago, and it resolved his conviction—but didn't make the screams any easier to endure.

A keening wail pierced the air, and Griswald glanced at Simon. His gangly arms spasmed at his side as he paced along the outskirts of the woods between the Redpaths hiding—cloaked in Rahkkar's invisibility spell—and the gap in the trees across from them. Simon kept wincing and cowering at the Lantian guards flanking him on either side, and an involuntary tic throbbed below his greasy hair. Though the exact spells used to torture Simon were not known to Griswald, the writhing contortions of his body, blood trickling from his ears, nose, and mouth, and the way he clutched his head as he screamed told Griswald the poor lad's mind would never be the same. He sympathized with the young soldier but didn't dwell on his fate too much. If they could quell the dissenting voices of the Ilyance and advance some of the Redpath designs for the mechanization of Carmellian tools and natural resources, then Simon's sacrifice for a cause he believed in would be worth it.

And if Simon's sacrifice also helped exact revenge in Griswald's personal vendetta against Sadie Sheldon—well, Griswald would lose even less sleep over the means needed to achieve that end.

Sounds of crunching snow grew louder, and a minute later the two men the Redpath had been waiting for stepped out onto a barren blanket of snow stained gold in the late afternoon sun: one Lantian guard, and Haldin, the man they had been trying to lure. Griswald recognized Haldin by his Dharmaelian clothing and the long wavy wheat-coloured hair their spies had described. Immediately the duo headed towards Simon and the Lantian guards. Twin expressions of relief bloomed on the two Lantian guards' faces as they spotted Haldin and the Lantíe drawing near.

"Thank goodness Alldían allowed you to come to us right away," gasped out one of the Lantíe. "He's getting worse. We were just going to—"

"Dharmaelia..." Simon's fervent whisper cut the Lantíe off. Everyone froze. His intense, feverish eyes fixated on Haldin, and he wrung his hands together. *Good*, thought Griswald. The seeds Rahkkar had planted worked. Simon had to concentrate hard on forcing the muscles of his lolling tongue to formulate words.

Haldin leaned closer, concern wrinkling his forehead.

"Dharmaelia!" Simon gasped, and the single cry spent all his energy.

In Griswald's peripheral vision, Rahkkar raised his hand and closed his fist.

Speeding whistles jarred the silent woods before five simultaneous *thwacks* were followed by the muffled thuds of four bodies keeling over in the snow.

Haldin alone remained standing. Slowly, he looked down at the arrow impaling his chest. A dark crimson stain flowered around the arrow shaft, black against his tunic. Staggering, Haldin drew sharp, ragged breaths. Griswald frowned at the bowmen. One of them must have missed the mark with Haldin. An inexcusable mistake, since he was the primary target.

But then why was Rahkkar smiling?

Haldin swivelled his head and hips, scanning the trees. Rahkkar waved his arm and brandished his purple sleeve.

Was Rahkkar purposefully retracting part of the invisibility spell to reveal his sleeve?

Haldin staggered a few unsteady steps forward in Rahkkar's direction.

A second arrow pierced Haldin's chest, right above the first.

What was Rahkkar playing at? They had discussed killing Haldin, not playing with him.

When Haldin began shuffling through the snow towards them again, Griswald took a step forward and reached for Rahkkar, trying to get his attention without speaking and revealing their location further. The invisibility spell cloaked image, not sound. Rahkkar must have been healing Haldin a little between each blow for him to still be standing and moving. He toyed with the Dharmaelian, but Griswald didn't like the risk that posed. Underestimating your enemies was dangerous and foolish. A clean kill was always better. Why couldn't Rahkkar ever follow orders exactly without adding his own sick twist?

But Rahkkar shook Griswald off and signalled for a third arrow to be loosed.

It hit Haldin just as he slithered his axe free of his belt loop.

He sank to his knees, finally overwhelmed.

Thinking Haldin finally dead, Griswald opened his mouth to bark an order—then shut it again as he noticed the blood on Haldin's chest congealing and crusting over. Haldin breathed deeply, then coughed uncontrollably as excessive oxygen saturated his damaged lungs.

Rahkkar had healed him again. *Why?*

The woods cupped an eerie silence in twined branches. Griswald's neck hairs stood erect.

"Who are you?" Haldin bellowed in their vague direction, echoing among the trees. "*Where* are you? Show yourselves, you cowards! Stop hiding in the trees like children while you kill innocent men! Where is your honour? Fight me face to face, you swine!"

"Perhaps you're right, son of Peladorn," mused Rahkkar in his slick voice, walking forward a few paces. Griswald's jaw dropped, sure the mage had just exited the invisibility barrier entirely. Amused malice glinted from his good eye, and he sneered complacently. "Perhaps a show of bravery is required before death. I've never advocated for honour when facing death; what good does it do the victim, really? But if you think it necessary, why not allow you this small freedom? It changes nothing for me. So go ahead Haldin, son of Peladorn. Prince of Dharmaelia. The Hawk to your people. Here I am. Strike me."

Any fool could see Rahkkar baited Haldin. Griswald did not think Haldin a fool, but he did think Haldin smart enough to know Rahkkar would kill him regardless of whether he sprung his trap or not, and therefore may as well try defending himself instead of awaiting more arrows.

Sure enough, Haldin stepped forward, axe raised.

Nothing happened.

Haldin closed the distance between them slowly, but Rahkkar sneered, amused by his hesitancy and caution.

Griswald only noticed the soldiers breaking rank a second before they charged. Haldin jerked his head away as the tip of a blade stabbed where his throat had just been. Swinging his axe upwards into his assassin's groin, Haldin pivoted on his heel and dealt the next attacker an instant kill blow to his heart. Slitting the man's abdomen to free his axe blade from his ribs, Haldin used the momentum to swing the axe behind him, catching the next soldier in the thigh. The man screamed and dropped his sword. Haldin smashed his skull with his gauntleted fist, yanked his axe free, and lopped the soldier's head off.

Nostrils flaring, hands clenching and unclenching, pulse leaping rapidly in his throat, Griswald yanked a bow and arrow from a soldier's hands and drew the fletching back to his cheek. Rahkkar had gone too far. Redpath soldiers should not be dying to stroke his ego. He would kill Haldin himself, and end this.

Just as he tried to release the arrow, his arms and legs froze. He tried to move them, lower the arrow or take a step, but he had become a human ice sculpture. Even his lips had been frozen shut. Griswald glared at Rahkkar, irate he would dare hold him with magic.

Haldin spun to face his next attackers. Eight men and women brandishing swords rushed at him from different angles.

Dropping down from a tree where they had been hiding like falcons waiting to swoop down on prey, two Lantíés attacked four of the soldiers rushing Haldin. One killed two of the soldiers before a third stabbed him in the heart. The other Lantíé killed one soldier before an arrow impaled his gut. He keeled over, clutching his stomach.

When the remaining four soldiers drew near enough, Haldin stepped quickly to his left, placing the other soldiers behind the far left one, and swung his axe in an elegant, graceful curve, slicing through the first man's midriff. Pivoting sharply to avoid the second soldier's sword thrust and throw her off balance, he caught her in the spine with the opposite blade of his double-bladed axe. In less than a minute, all four soldiers sprawled in the snow, staining the white flakes red.

As Haldin yanked his axe from the last soldier's throat, unfazed by the blood bubbling out of his severed esophagus, a knife blade pressed against his throat from behind. A second man sprinted towards him, sword raised.

Acting faster than Griswald thought possible, Haldin stomped on the inner toes of the soldier holding him from behind, thrust a sharp elbow into his gut, squeezed his wrist until his knife grip slackened, then threw his head back into the man's face, breaking his nose. Haldin hefted his axe to adjust his grip, then threw it at his oncoming opponent.

As his axe split the man's skull with a squelching thud, the next arrows came.

Thwack.

Thwack.

Thwack.

Haldin had no time to shield himself. Three arrows clustered around his left lung. He collapsed to his knees, his eyes sliding out of focus.

"You see, honour makes no difference in the end," Rahkkar said conversationally, as though demonstrating a lesson for a wayward pupil.

Haldin responded with a gurgling moan.

"I'm sorry, I didn't catch that."

Rahkkar gestured idly with his hand, and Haldin's eyes slid back into focus. Healed again.

"What kind of sick, twisted lunatic are you?" growled Haldin, echoing Griswald's thoughts. "*Who* are you? Why are you here?"

"I don't think you're in a position to ask those questions," replied the mage with a small smile. "Did you enjoy your chance at honour, Prince?"

"You have shown no honour here," Haldin spat. "Unleashing hidden assassins upon me is not honourable. Nor is sending others to fight your battles instead of fighting me yourself."

"Oh, I disagree. You are a renowned warrior, Haldin the Hawk. Your reputation necessitated killing through ambush. You just killed nine of my soldiers despite their advantage of surprise and numbers. I always say it is dishonourable not to use all the assets at your disposal to vanquish your enemy. You may be a formidable warrior with your axe, but are you a match for cunning tactics? It would appear not."

"So why revive me?" demanded Haldin. "Why not let me die of arrow wounds?"

"Because, Haldin," the mage replied in a low voice, a sinister glint sparking in his eye. "There is great power and magic in the number three."

Haldin lunged desperately for Rahkkar's throat with his bare hands.

He was too late.

The next set of three arrows hit him directly in the heart.

As blood pooled across the sunset pink snow beneath Haldin's inert body, Griswald felt his limbs and lips thaw, freed from Rahkkar's spell. He stalked over to Master Morshade, a vein throbbing in his temple.

"I don't know who you think you are, wizard, but *I* give the orders in this company," Griswald growled at Rahkkar. "I said to kill him, not play with him. You killed nine Redpath soldiers for no reason other than satiating your own vindictive pleasures!"

"Isn't that what you're doing? Killing innocent Redpath soldiers for your own revenge against the Sheldon girl?" whispered Rahkkar calmly, a dangerous bite to his words.

Griswald recoiled as though slapped. "That's different. She's a spy for the Ilyance, working to overthrow the Redpath. She's an enemy to us all. And in the end, she is naught but a tool to instigate a war and unlock a greater prize for our organization's goals. We are following orders from Hargrim himself. If you don't agree with the head of the Redpath's orders, that's for you to take up with him. But in the meantime, you follow my orders, or you'll suffer the consequences of insubordination when we return."

"Yes, *sir*." Rahkkar hissed, his smirk still pasted on through his gritted teeth.

"And don't you *dare* touch me with your filthy magic again," Griswald threatened in a low, icy voice, leaning close. "Or I won't wait for Hargrim. I'll gut you myself and teach you a lesson on what *real* pain is."

"What do we do with this antlered mutant?" a Redpath soldier asked, kicking the wounded Lantíé with his boot. The Lantíé groaned.

"Leave him," Griswald instructed after a pause. "He'll die soon enough. Let him suffer for his interference."

And we need him to deliver a message, thought Griswald, a sneer coiling his lips. Time to lure the big prize in with their new bait. So far, their plan was working perfectly.

Chapter Twenty-Eight

A Tear of Flame

Holding the sword away from her body, Sadie closed her eyes and inhaled deeply. Her magical core filled her vision, the orange fire strand gleaming brightest among the four knotted elements. A fire spark detached from her core and flew towards her subtle reach. The fire strands waited at her fingertips now without thought. Concentrating on the sword, Sadie seized a tiny tester speck and willed a flame to latch onto the sword.

She screamed, dropping the sword in the snow.

Steam rose from the sizzling, scalding blade.

Sadie plunged her burnt hand in the snow, gritting her teeth and cursing. Tamlin had warned her not to try magic with a weapon yet because she didn't believe Sadie understood the theory, but Sadie had convinced herself Tamlin was being over-cautious.

A burned hand was less than she deserved for such foolhardiness.

She wasn't sure what she had expected to happen. Flames shooting out of the sword's tip to light up the dark evening sky, or a shower of sparks erupting from her blade when it clashed against her opponent's weapon. Or maybe—

A powerful ache assailed her magical core. It felt... black. Streaks of oily black stained her mind, mired in palpable evil. Dread crept through her veins, branching from her core and tingling her spine.

Something had happened. Something unspeakably bad. Yanking the cooled sword from the snow, Sadie hurried towards Alldían's hall.

When Sadie entered Alldían's hall, Tamlin already stood by Alldían's throne, speaking urgently in a low voice. Sadie guessed the dark look on Tamlin's face meant she'd felt something similar. Appraising the look on Sadie's face, Tamlin said to Alldían, "She knows."

Hurried footsteps pounded behind Sadie, and a few seconds later Tristan and Airothane stood beside her.

"Well," said Tristan, breaking the silence. "I see we have interrupted something. Might it be regarding Haldin? We overheard the Lantíes conversing in the communal eating hall, and they're worried, which made me think perhaps I missed something this morning."

Alldían appeared calm and congenial, but Sadie noticed lines of concern creasing the corners of his eyes.

"You did not miss anything, godson, but it would appear your fears are not unfounded. Tamlin has just reported a grave vision she had, and she believes it's related to Haldin."

"Not a vision, exactly," corrected Tamlin. "I have not seen Haldin or Marius or the madman, but I can sense magic from a long range, provided it is not cloaked by the wizard performing the magic—in this case, Dark Magic. Its evil presence forms in my mind as a black cloud, and I can sense the malice behind it. Isn't that right, Sadie?"

Tristan's head snapped towards Sadie, his eyes piercing. "You saw this black magic too?"

Sadie nodded. "That's why I came here. To see if Alldían might know what it meant."

"And you sensed this black magic was performed on Haldin?" Airothane asked in a trembling whisper.

"I did not sense anything about Haldin at all, at least not in the magical sense," replied Tamlin. "But my considerable mental acuity coupled with my belief these things usually aren't coincidental, and my unfortunate habit of jumping to the worst conclusion first, leads me to strongly suspect it might have something to do with his mission. Of course, this does not mean he was directly affected himself."

"What do we do about this ominous feeling you and Sadie shared?" asked Tristan.

Sadie and Tristan both looked from Tamlin to Alldían expectantly. Before either could answer, the muffled bang of doors slamming open echoed behind them, followed by the clatter of galloping hooves. A unicorn charged in, narrowly avoiding a collision with Airothane as it skidded to a graceful halt.

Though the unicorn's sides heaved, he proudly snorted and tossed his mane as though challenging Alldían to demand why he had stampeded into his hall. Barely clinging to the unicorn's bare back, his back hunched to cradle a bloody hand clutching his stomach and his mouth contorted in pain, was a Lantian dressed in the Mínando garb. His long pale blond hair matted around his sweaty face, and his ice blue eyes radiated urgency and fear.

Alldían vacated his throne and took a few concerned steps forward. "What has happened, Efarin? Are you all right?"

Tamlin rushed over and put her hand on Efarin's stomach. The bleeding stopped, and his ragged breathing eased a little.

"Thank you, Tamlin," he gasped. "I'm afraid I bear grave news. My fellow sentries, Marius, and Haldin—" But Efarin broke off abruptly as he spotted Airothane. "Perhaps we should discuss this in private."

Airothane's face had gone so white it was almost translucent, his shoulders hunched as though warding off a blow. Yet though his hands shook, and his wobbly knees looked ready to buckle, he raised his quivering chin and said in a steady voice, "If something has happened to my brother, I want to know. In fact, I demand to know. I am a prince of Dharmaelia, and I have a right to hear my brother's fate."

Everyone looked to Efarin except Sadie, who kept her eyes locked on Airothane. His pale cheekbones popped from his clenched jaw, braced to hear the inevitable bad news.

Efarin hesitated, then delivered his message in one exhalation as though the news was a heavy burden he needed to release.

"I come from the northwest border where the madman was spotted. Haldin and Marius joined two other Mínando. I know not whether they got any information from the madman. Naldor and I arrived after the action had started. The bodies of all three Mínando and the madman were sprawled lifelessly in the snow, arrows protruding from their hearts. Haldin was alive when we first arrived—he is not now. Haldin the Hawk, son of Peladorn, is dead."

Airothane's knees buckled. Sadie caught him before his head hit the floor. Cradling him in her arms, she hugged him fiercely to her chest as she blinked away the tears threatening to spill onto her cheeks and swallowed the shards of glass scraping her throat. Airothane had been there for her when she needed him. Now it was her turn to be his rock in such a devastating storm.

Instead of wailing or crying out, he scrunched his face in silent sobs, tears cascading down his cheeks and soaking Sadie's sleeve as he rocked back and forth against the pain. Sadie did not try to stopper his grief with soothing words. She let the pain leak from him like a sieve. She knew how dangerous bottling misery could be. He clung to her encircling arms, and Sadie squeezed gently, lending him comfort and strength.

Alldían, Tristan, Tamlin, and Efarin watched Airothane's grief through glazed eyes, Haldin's death swirling between them like the bitter aftertaste of blood in saliva. A single tear escaped Tristan's eye and trickled down his cheek. Efarin quietly dismounted the unicorn and stroked its muzzle.

"How did he die?" asked Alldían after a moment.

Efarin's voice croaked as he recounted Haldin's death. Sadie locked her arms around Airothane as he explained how the arrows impaling Haldin's chest had not killed him immediately. He had even defeated nine soldiers who had charged him. Efarin and Naldor had tried to help, but there were too many. Naldor perished, and Efarin had been wounded. A man with dark hair and purple robes had talked with Haldin, but Efarin had been fighting to maintain consciousness and did not hear most of their conversation. It seemed obvious to Efarin this was the man in charge, ordering the soldiers to attack Haldin and fire the arrows. But Sadie remembered her vision of Griswald and wasn't so sure. Efarin recounted how Haldin had been hit by more arrows after defeating some of the soldiers, and this time they had found his heart, and he died.

"He died a warrior's death worthy of the Hawk," concluded Efarin, glancing at Airothane. "Few people could have vanquished so many of their enemies with arrows piercing their bodies. I have a special bond with the unicorns. They sensed my distress and came to my aid, consenting to let me ride Moonstar here to reach you quicker."

"You say these men were soldiers," said Tristan, frowning. "Did you recognize their uniforms?"

"I did," replied Efarin gravely. "They were Redpath soldiers."

"This news is troubling on many levels," said Tamlin after a profound silence. "Who were they targeting with this attack? Did they attack Haldin because he's the prince of Dharmaelia and the madman's ravings about Dharmaelia carried some validity? If so, what are the Redpath's plans concerning Dharmaelia?"

"I'd like to know how many soldiers there are, and how they got to the borders of Caris Nando undetected," added Tristan.

"Who is this man in the purple robes?" asked Sadie. "And, most importantly, if they *were* targeting Haldin, how did they know he was here?"

"How indeed?" echoed Alldían. "And what is to be done about it?"

"We have to retrieve my brother's body!" Airothane choked out, hiccuping through his sobs. "We can't just leave him there! H-he needs a p-proper f-funeral."

"We will properly honour your brother, Airothane," Tristan assured him soothingly. "We need to retrieve the bodies of all who fell in this attack, and honour all properly. But caution is necessary. Even if they were only after Haldin, I don't believe the danger is over. They may know Efarin didn't die and escaped, in which case they'll be expecting people to come for the bodies. I fear the immediate retrieval of the bodies might mean another attack. There can't be too many soldiers if the Lantian watchmen never spotted them, but we must avoid falling into a trap."

Sadie watched red mottle Airothane's crestfallen cheeks at the idea of his brother's body freezing in the snow and becoming carrion for scavenging beasts.

"What if we approach the bodies in an unexpected way?" she asked, not taking her eyes off Airothane. "Like from a different direction or vantage point? Is that possible?"

"The bodies are situated between sparse border trees and open fields of white. The Redpath will see us coming from all directions," replied Efarin. "I suggest sending a small contingent to approach from the forest among the trees instead of along the path to the Caris Nando entrance and then across open ground. We can take cover behind the trees for as long as possible and thus perhaps sneak up on them from behind and take them by surprise."

"And yet whoever goes should be prepared for a fight. If they do spot us, we don't want to be ridiculously outnumbered," said Tristan. "Feigning innocence and reasoning with them may work since they probably won't know us and may truly seek no further confrontation now Haldin is dead. But we cannot count on that."

"They must be prepared for a fight, but I do not want to send an army. I know war with the Redpath seems inevitable, but I would rather not start it on my doorstep," said Alldían.

"I will go," volunteered Tamlin. "It's clear magic is involved, and I should be there to counteract any magic used against the Lantíes."

"I'll go as well," said Tristan. "A Swordmaster may be needed, and I would like to ensure the bodies are safely returned."

"I'm coming too!" announced Airothane fiercely, but Alldían, Tamlin, and Tristan all shook their heads simultaneously.

"You can't go, Airothane," Sadie replied before anyone else could. "You're too young and much too valuable. You are also a prince of Dharmaelia, and you must survive to deliver this news to your father and uphold your brother's honour. I'll go in your place. It's the least I can do after the kindness and acceptance your brother showed me."

Airothane seemed incapable of smiling, but the gratitude shining in his watery eyes spoke louder than words. Tristan frowned at Sadie, though he refrained from commenting.

"I agree the three of you should go," acquiesced Alldían. "Efarin, please lead them to Haldin's body and gather two score of our best warriors, ensuring they are heavily armed but still able to move quickly and silently through the forest, and transport the bodies back. You will all leave together at sunrise."

"Yes, Lord Alldían," intoned Efarin with a respectful bow.

They exited the hall to prepare for their departure, Sadie's arm around Airothane's bony, narrow shoulders. Plans formed in her mind as a mangled Griswald flashed before her eyes once more.

She had no intention of waiting until sunrise to depart with her friends.

Though the subtle crunch of snow beneath her boots sounded quiet even to her own ears, Sadie's heart pounded with each step. Frost coated her braid like sprinkled icing sugar, and she had to keep blinking to stop the ice from freezing her lashes. Silence pressed down on her in the still darkness, but she knew she could not give in to its compelling call to be broken. She needed her companions to stay asleep until sunrise.

Instead of sleep, she had been plagued by tear-blurred visions of Haldin's maimed body.

She needed a head start. She needed to go to Haldin's body alone.

The moment she'd felt Dark Magic she'd known, and Airothane's plea had cemented it.

No one else could accompany her to Haldin's body because this wasn't about Haldin.

This was about Griswald's vendetta against her.

Sadie didn't believe in coincidence. She didn't know the man in the purple robes, but she did know her vision of an alive Griswald and the taint of Dark Magic in her core were connected. If Griswald was complicit in the attack on Haldin, then it was because of her. She didn't know if his interest in Dharmaelia or Haldin was because of a Redpath agenda, but he had risked innocent people to avenge his bruised ego after their first encounter, so if he had survived the Crowned Sun Inn fire, then he would want revenge against her again.

Haldin might have died for being her friend. She could not let another friend risk their life for her.

Until she could find a portal and open it, Connor's fate was beyond her control, but she could choose to fix her mistakes and save her friends. If retrieving Haldin's body was a trap, she didn't want anyone else to suffer. It was *her* responsibility. *Her* mistake that had inspired vengeance in Griswald. *Her* rash tongue and misconceptions of a hero.

While selecting a breastplate to wear over her dress the night before, she had realized she'd been no different than Griswald during the fateful moment on the street in Carenthia. He and the Redpath sought a better world free of their perceived problems. Sadie had also endeavoured to find a better world and escape her problems. The difference was that her vision involved preserving magic and enhancing her power of choice, whereas Griswald's meant technological advancements to increase his power over others. Yet they had both failed to recognize change needed to be *internal* first before the world could follow suit and change for the better.

All her life Sadie had run from her fears, convinced if she could prove her worth like the heroes in the stories she loved, she would find the key to life's magic. She wouldn't be forced into an arranged marriage, she wouldn't have to endure the stares, whispers, and berating jibes of high society because of her fiery spirit, progressive views, and imaginative whimsy marking her as a social pariah. She wouldn't feel so small and insignificant and obsolete. She would slay the dragons of her depression and find peace.

But she had been wrong.

Being a hero wasn't about proving her worth to others, it was about proving it to herself.

She had thought heroism would give her strength and combat the powerlessness she felt as a woman on Earth, but what she had failed to realize was the heroes she aspired to be were men portraying idealized male qualities. She didn't need to conform to male ideals of strength to be a strong woman. She *was* a strong woman already. And the strength of womanhood was multifaceted.

There was strength in her boundless imagination. Her capacity for love without borders. Her loyal protectiveness of those she cared about. Her love of literature and the deep well of contentment it filled inside her. Her fight to tread water against the waves of depression and anxiety weighing her down, even on days that left her gasping for air. She didn't always need to be the strongest or most powerful to be a hero. She just needed to be herself, because she was already enough.

As she flitted from tree to tree like a less graceful snowshoe hare evading a predator, Sadie reflected on how changing Earth's perceptions of female strength could not come before she changed her own. She needed to embrace her loud, adventurous strengths, but also listen to the quiet ones. Elevate them so their voices could be heard too. Because sometimes the quiet strengths screamed the loudest.

No more running from her fear. No more shrinking away from her doubts and insecurities. She thought she understood now why Connor had decided to go to war. Not because of naivety or grandiose thoughts about perceived heroism, but because telling himself the same repetitive lies and expecting his flaws to go away was lunacy. Only when he stopped running and confronted them could he truly find purpose in his life.

She couldn't control what others thought or feared about her flaws, so it was time to embrace them. Confront the lies the dark corners of her mind whispered to her and hold accountability for her mistakes.

Starting with amending her mistake with Griswald.

Golden sunlight slanted through the trees, creating checkered shadows against the ground's white canvas. Patches of sunlit snow sparkled like clusters of winking stars against a blanched sky.

As she approached the last line of trees Sadie slowed her movements, holding her breath and placing her hands gently on the rough bark of a tree to peer out at the open plain.

There, lying in the snow with his limbs spread wide as though about to make a snow angel, was Haldin. Lantian and Redpath bodies lay heaped around him. Though he was still about twenty feet to her right, Sadie could see his open, glassy eyes and mottled blue and white face framed with frozen strawberry blond locks. She blinked away tears and bit the inside of her lip so hard she drew blood.

A black taint infiltrated her mind like the oily residue of a poisonous slug. Dark magic had occurred here. A deathly silence, potent and suffocating, strangled the scene like a noose. No living thing moved in the clearing. There were no Redpath soldiers ready to trap her. No man in a purple robe waiting for her. No Griswald.

Maybe she had been overreacting. Maybe nothing awaited them in this clearing but lifeless bodies. Perhaps Griswald truly had perished in that fire, and the vision of his mangled face had been nothing more than her guilty subconscious haunting her.

Whether a trap awaited her or not, there was only one way forward. Now was the time to prove to herself she was more than her fears. Cast off the weight of worthlessness and choose to challenge the misconceptions about her. About her capabilities as a woman. About her grasp on reality simply because she dared to dream. *She* knew she was worthy, just the way she was, and she would allow no one to steal that self-assertion from her, not even Griswald.

It was time to choose her own destiny, even if she must spring a trap to save her friends but not herself.

Taking a deep breath, Sadie removed her hand from the tree and lifted her foot to step out into the open.

Her cloak's clasp dug into her throat as she was yanked back by her hood, but before she could scream a callused hand clamped over her mouth and she was spun around.

Warm chocolate brown eyes locked on hers, and her breath hitched. *Tristan.*

As she spiralled down the whirlpool of deep concern in his eyes, her heart sank, and a pit hollowed her stomach. He wasn't supposed to be here.

Tristan's wide eyes hooked hers with fearful fervour, and she couldn't look away. She could feel the slight tremble in his heaving chest beneath her fingertips, hear the hoarseness in his ragged breathing.

"Why, Sadie?" he whispered. "Why did you come alone?"

"If it's a trap, it's because of me," Sadie whispered back, her voice pleading. Breaking. "I don't think the Redpath were after Haldin or Dharmaelia, I think this is about Griswald and his personal vendetta against me—"

"Griswald's dead, and even if he isn't, his choices and actions are not your fault. You have to stop blaming yourself for everything that goes wrong—"

"*No*, you don't get it," Sadie interrupted, insistent. "I have made too many mistakes, and I need to stop running from them. I need to stop running from myself and face this threat alone. I know people think I'm a weak woman with a flighty imagination, but I *am* capable, Tristan. I have strength too. I can't let any more of my friends or family suffer for me. I can't."

Tristan's thin lips quirked at one corner, but his tone was serious when he said, "I get it, I really do. Your strength makes you one of the most capable people I know. I have always believed in you, Sadie. But in your determination to control your choices, I think you're forgetting other people make their own choices too. What you choose for them may not be what they choose for themselves. Whatever the Redpath's intentions, Haldin didn't choose to come here for you. He chose to come for himself, and for Dharmaelia. Just like your brother didn't choose to enter a war because of you. We chose to come here because Haldin is our friend too, and we believe in preserving the power in Carmelle's natural resources instead of letting the Redpath abuse them.

"Grant others the same power of choice you desire for yourself. Remember, our choices are strengthened by the people who care for us, and by our compassion for them. People care about you, Sadie. *I* care about you. It's great to recognize your self-worth and want to change. But you don't have to change alone."

Sadie shared a trembling smile with Tristan's suddenly blurry face through watery eyes.

"Thank you," she whispered.

"It's so quiet," whispered Efarin from her left, startling her into breaking eye contact with Tristan. She hadn't noticed the rest of the company arrive. How had they travelled so quickly?

"Too quiet," muttered Tamlin, peering around Tristan's shoulder. She leaned against a tree, looking ready to keel over with her eyelids drooping heavily. Had she not slept well? Or were these after-effects of significant magic? "I don't like it. Why would they have left their soldiers instead of burying them?"

"It's definitely a trap," said Tristan. "So how do we retrieve the bodies?"

Nobody answered for a minute.

Sadie thought something moved in her peripheral vision, but when she turned to look, all she saw was a tree.

"Could we float them to us with magic?" suggested Sadie.

"That would still reveal our location. The Redpath could follow their floating bodies," observed Tristan.

This time the tree definitely flickered.

"Uh... Did anyone else see that?" Sadie asked.

"See what?" Tamlin asked distractedly.

"Maybe if we..." Efarin began, but stopped abruptly, staring at a tree. "Did that tree just—"

The trees vanished. Stripped of the forest's protection and exposed on all sides, they found themselves standing in the open surrounded by hundreds of small stumps. The trees bordering Caris Nando had been cut down and replaced by an illusion.

An undulating battle cry echoed across the open plain, and the remaining forest beyond the stumps came alive. A cacophony of discordant sounds exploded the air. Trees swayed and creaked against the onslaught of movement. Coniferous needles rained on the snow as bodies brushed past them. Boots pounded thunderously against the snow, crunching like splintering bones.

Redpath soldiers charged their contingent, rolling out of the trees toward their exposed little group like a rogue wave swelling and breaking upon the sand.

The battle had begun.

Pain and nausea assailed Sadie, so intense she projectile vomited in the snow. Clutching her stomach and gasping for air, Sadie's wild eyes searched for a knife embedded in her gut but found none. Tristan bent over her in concern, a protective hand on her shoulder. The epiphany catapulted into her brain, and her vision blurred in dizziness. Magic. Magic on a scale she had never thought possible.

Tamlin. Where was Tamlin?

She glimpsed powder blue robes and a deep red mantle by the forest's edge. Lane Tamlin faced a man with slick black hair, a pointed black beard and short moustache, and deep purple robes. Sadie's stomach flipped and she swallowed before it could heave again.

The man in the purple robes was a mage.

And he was locked in a duel with Tamlin.

The strength of their magic was staggering. Sadie couldn't see the flows, but she could *feel* them, like a weight in her stomach vibrating her core, and the intensity and complexity of the weaves was formidable. They radiated power.

Some of the spells had no visible effects, but most did, and the damage left Sadie in awe. Gouges cut through the snow to the layers of frozen dirt beneath the grass, and chunks of mud, rock and ice scabbed the scarred earth. Broken branches littered the snow from the wizards hurtling them at each other like javelins, and the mage's robes were soaked as though Tamlin had tried to drown him.

Even as Sadie watched, the ground rumbled and shook like an earthquake and then split open beneath Tamlin's feet with a resounding *crack* like lightning. Calmly, Tamlin sidestepped to her right as the earth crumbled into a deep chasm where her feet had just been. As the chasm widened,

Tamlin stepped forward to rest her foot in midair as though perched on an invisible step. To Sadie's astonishment she began climbing, the air forming solid steps for her. As she stepped, ropes flew from her hands and wrapped themselves around the mage, pinning his arms. The mage smirked, but his smirk slid into open-mouthed revulsion as the ropes became snakes and wriggled towards his face, fangs bared.

Tristan tugged on Sadie's arm, trying to get her to stand up and move. Her eyes snapped back to her immediate surroundings, and she screamed.

A sharp blade thrust towards her heart.

Tristan's boot kicked the sword out of her attacker's hand before it impaled her. Without pausing, Tristan slammed the heavy pommel of his sword into the man's face, breaking his nose with a *crunch*. Whirling smoothly to face his attackers from the front, he fought three off at once.

Tristan's sword blurred in his hands as he executed intricate and elegant footwork. He did not stumble or hesitate, but flowed from position to position with such apparent ease that Sadie gaped as he incapacitated those three opponents in mere seconds. Tristan and the sword were one, and it was impossible to say which was more dangerous.

Angry with herself for being so useless, Sadie leapt to her feet and drew her sword from its sheath. A man with shaggy hair and an un-kempt beard charged towards her, and Sadie frantically tried to remember everything Tristan had taught her. He swung his sword at her head in a wide arc, and Sadie ducked. The force of his swing ruffled her hair, but his momentum carried him too far and he swayed, off balance. Instinctively, Sadie thrust her sword under his outstretched arm and stabbed at his kidney. With a cry of pain, he dropped to his knees, gasping.

Sadie stared at him. She should wound him further so he couldn't kill her when her back was turned, but she couldn't stomach stabbing him coldly while he knelt at her feet.

Before she could decide, Tristan decided for her. He pivoted, smashed the man's skull with the butt of his sword, then turned to engage a new attacker.

"Curses and 'cantations," muttered Sadie. She felt like a weak burden to Tristan. Steely determination ignited her heart's embers.

Fire! Of course! Sadie had almost forgotten her own magic. She closed her eyes.

With one calming breath the blue flame-orb in the void was there, and in the next breath she could see her magical core, its tangled ball of threads glowing brightly. She opened her eyes to find two men nearly upon her. Without pausing to think, she seized strands of fire and hurled them at the soldiers. They burst into flame.

Their terrified shrieks pierced the roar of flames, and everyone in their vicinity paused fighting to watch.

One soldier staggered, slipped, and thudded onto the snow.

The flames consuming him fizzled out, smoke billowing from his clothing.

Catching on, the other man dropped to the snow, rolling until all flames had been smothered. They lay there moaning in pain, letting the freezing snow soothe their burning skin.

When the flames ceased the fighting resumed, but now the soldiers seemed a bit warier around her. Tristan noticed. Grabbing Sadie's hand, they ran towards the woods.

"Are you mad?" Sadie shrieked as they ran. "Why are you taking us back to where *more* Redpaths wait to kill us?"

"Remind me to teach you tactical warfare one day," he shouted back. "When you're outnumbered like we are, you don't want to be exposed in the open where they can surround you and cut off all escape. The trees offer cover and the advantages of stealth and obstacles, giving the outnumbered a fighting chance. I don't know how many soldiers they have yet, but I can see enough that I know we don't want to be surrounded."

Sadie scanned the battlefield and flinched. Every single Lantian soldier was engaged in battle or dead, and those still fighting duelled three or four Redpaths at once. There were too many. As Sadie had the thought, more marched out of the trees, appearing from nowhere as though crossing an invisible barrier. They formed an intimidating, impenetrable line, their weapons held at the ready, elbows and shields touching. Their precision, rigidity, and expressionless faces radiated cold menace.

Sadie estimated there were at least a few hundred against maybe thirty of them now.

As Tristan led her towards this unyielding force of fatality, Sadie knew she would die. But this knowledge did not deluge her in despair. It ignited her fury. Fire seared her bones and bubbled her blood, and a deep logic-defying loathing for these soldiers twisted her gut.

Who did the Redpath think they were? Was she about to die at the hands of imbeciles whose twisted vision of the world fuelled their ignorant beliefs about improving it and made them justify killing innocent people for no other reason than their views and visions differed from theirs? Her rage at their inevitable triumph pulsed in her throat until fear vacated her heart. She needed to show them they were not invincible.

Redpaths attacked as they crashed into the forest, and Sadie did not hold back. Unlike Tristan, her methods held no grace, no flow between the different cuts and parries. Her strokes were clumsy and reactive, but she managed to fend off the few who made it past Tristan.

At first Tristan gripped her hand tightly. Whether he wanted to keep her close so he could defend her or keep her from doing something stupid in her fey mood she couldn't tell, but she shook him off quickly. She needed both hands to fight, even if he did not.

Time became meaningless. She fought until her rage ebbed into exhaustion. Occasionally Sadie launched a magical attack, unleashing billowing clouds of flames at her opponents like a dragon, but magic consumed far more energy than swordplay—she also worried about accidentally setting Tristan on fire as he danced between her and their opponents.

The radius of her fire-cloud was large and incapacitated many Redpaths which helped buy time and gave Tristan a quick second to breathe to reassess their situation when she had enough breath to warn him, but she didn't always have that luxury. Tristan's graceful fighting style became more sporadic and desperate as the Redpath closed in, but he still managed to step with quick feet and maim with precision, ensuring Sadie did not fight more soldiers than she could handle.

Sadie blocked sword-thrusts with increasingly heavy arms. Pain lanced her muscles, and she knew soon they would refuse to cooperate. Panting heavily, her throat burning, she shivered at the sweat beading all over her body. Her eyes burned from lack of sleep.

Crushing weight pushed her arm down as she tried to lift her sword to prepare for her next opponent, but her muscles wouldn't cooperate. She couldn't lift it. A raw scream of frustration tore her throat. She looked up to see who would deal her death blow, but no Redpaths were in her immediate vicinity. She had a brief respite to realize they stood near the border of the forest, yet still in the open. The Lantíes and Tristan's fighting skills were exceptional, but even they could not vanquish such overwhelming odds. Sadie counted no more than a dozen Lantíes still standing, and as she watched, Redpaths herded them together, slowly driving them further into the open like cattle.

The end was near.

She wondered if Airothane would mourn her or resent her for not returning Haldin's body.

And then she had an idea.

Sadie closed her eyes, and her magical core greeted her. The fire element burned bright orange, ready and eager to be wielded at her command, but she ignored it. Instead, she focused her energy on the white tangle of air threads. It was an element she knew little about and had hardly worked with. Earth was the only other element that yielded any results. Blocking out the cacophony of battle, Sadie concentrated all her energy on untangling one strand of air. Slowly, it unravelled and extricated itself from her jumbled core. As it floated free, Sadie wrapped a thought around it, branding it with one word she focused on with all her strength: HELP.

It was a foolish idea. Even if Airothane could hear her plea as a Windtalker, he was miles away and no help could be sent on time.

She released her message upon the wind anyway in desperation.

Redpaths pressed together, advancing but not attacking, forcing Sadie and Tristan to retreat from the hope of tree cover along with the remaining Lantíés.

Hot fury infused Sadie's tired limbs. Beside her, Tristan's battle cry echoed the angry despair burning her veins as he lunged at the thick line of bodies pushing them back. But the Redpath soldiers proved insurmountable, the soldiers appearing to multiply like a hydra every time one fell. A few Lantíés in better positions broke free and raced towards the trees.

That's when the arrows started flying.

In less than thirty seconds the escaping Lantíés were killed, grey-fletched arrows protruding from their chests.

Sadie spotted their slayer instantly. Her gaze narrowed in on him as he stepped out from behind a tree.

She froze, barely noticing the Redpath soldiers pushing her back with ease.

Griswald.

Alive.

Beside her, Tristan still fought the soldiers, oblivious to Griswald's presence. But it was over for her. Haldin needn't have died. Griswald just wanted to lure her out from Alldían's protection to exact his revenge.

The last nine Lantíés joined them, and the Redpath encircled them. They were trapped.

Leaning her back against the others', Sadie noticed Efarin had been corralled with them. A bloody gash slashed his cheek, matching another slash matting the hair near his temple, but otherwise he seemed okay.

"Where's Tamlin?" asked Sadie.

"Still battling that mage," said Tristan. The tightness in his voice drew Sadie's eyes to his, and her breath caught. A promise to defend her burned through the acceptance of certain death in his eyes. Though she knew she exasperated and annoyed him at times, and it had taken a long time for her to fully trust him, Tristan had come to mean so much to her. His friendship anchored her, his presence a steady light guiding her through a new world. He made her laugh. He listened when she cried and didn't dismiss her emotions as invalid. He reflected on life with her and encouraged her to be herself. The thought of him dying hollowed her aching heart, crushing her lungs until she couldn't breathe. She studied the bridge of his long nose, the small crease at the corner of his eyes.

Pain lanced up her left arm as a blade swiped across it. Her knees buckled, but despair wadded her throat and stifled her cry. Tristan immediately decapitated the soldier who had broken rank, but Sadie barely noticed him fall. Her numb brain was drained of energy. Halfheartedly, she reached for her magic—and couldn't find her core.

Sadie's neck snapped backwards as a gauntleted hand backhanded her across the face. Spots blurred her vision, and something warm and sticky trickled sluggishly past her eye. She touched it numbly, her fingers coming away with blood.

Griswald loomed over her.

His repulsive face was almost unrecognizable; half his features had been melted away. Bone peeked through patches of flesh where his right eyebrow had been, and yellow scabs caked the rest of his raw face.

Tristan tried to lunge at Griswald, but a dozen Redpath soldiers immediately trained their weapons on him, ready to kill Tristan or die themselves to save Griswald.

Sadie could feel satisfaction radiating off Griswald like a bad stench. His smirk sickened her.

"I have dreamed of this moment for a long time," he said.

"Original," retorted Sadie with a bitter sneer. "You'd think after brooding on your revenge so long you would have come up with more than a tired cliche. I hope you weren't expecting that to impress me."

Griswald's face contorted, but he quickly replaced irate fury with a casual smirk. "About to die, and you still have the gall to sass me. Still so immature. So ignorant. Almost not worth wasting my time coming after you. But I never forgive, and I never forget. I couldn't let you get away with almost killing me. Luck saved you then, but it will not save you now. Was the defiance you grated me with and the fire you started in Carenthia worth these Lantíés and your friends dying for? Was it worth your life?"

"You bastard," spat Sadie. "How can you think setting you on fire and disrespecting you is worth killing innocent people and starting a civil war?"

"You *are* ignorant. Civil war was inevitable. Plans were already in motion. But this way, it's the Ilyance's fault. You messed up, and now your friends and their backwards ways will suffer the consequences. But first, I get my revenge."

Griswald's eye glinted as he casually reached back to his quiver. Tristan shifted his grip on his sword, ready to die shielding her. She couldn't let that happen. She had to stall him for as long as possible.

"How did you find me? How did you get here without the Lantian watchmen noticing?"

Griswald grinned through his gruesome exposed flesh. "As if I would tell you, a spy for the enemy. It wasn't difficult tracking you through the mountains and Skeletal Moon Lake. A fair few gave their lives to reveal the rest." A disturbing smile lifted his cracked lips.

Sadie's gut iced over. Griswald's mage must have used dark Celestial magic to track her here. It wouldn't have mattered what she'd done or where she'd gone to hide. Griswald would have found her. Unless, perhaps, she'd managed to open a portal back to Earth. How many lives would have been saved if she hadn't abandoned her original purpose of finding a way to open a portal? If she hadn't questioned whether she even wanted to return? She had told herself she could be saving lives on Earth by not risking the Redpath following her through the portal, but it had just been an excuse. She had no way of knowing for sure if tracking her through a portal was possible. She had been so eager to feel heroic, she had forgotten the most heroic deed of all: being willing to sacrifice her own happiness to save others.

War cries and thundering hooves erupted in the distance. Griswald stopped to look.

Two hundred Lantian soldiers thundered towards them on horseback, charging from the southern border of Caris Nando toward the Redpath's rear flanks.

"About, face!" Griswald hollered to his army, spittle flying from the craters of his mangled face.

The Redpath soldiers obeyed Griswald, turning as one to face the Lantian cavalry.

The cavalry broke upon the Redpath army like a wave, towering over them as it crested, then knocking the first line of defence off their feet to tumble and churn beneath the horses' hooves like kicked up sand. Spears and arrows catapulted into the Redpath's inner ranks, impaling soldiers as they forced a path through the middle to the surrounded Ilyance contingent. Whether hacked down like harvested wheat or bowled over by stampeding horses, the Redpath army were no match for the cavalry. They scattered, fleeing the massacre.

Sadie sighed in relief as the circle surrounding them broke. They were no longer alone.

"*I é Telwé!*" one of the Lantíé on horseback shouted.

The Lantíés in their contingent ran along the path the cavalry had carved to the trees.

"Come on!" Tristan yelled to Sadie.

But Sadie's eyes hooked on Griswald's crooked smirk as he watched the retreating Lantíés.

Tristan grabbed Sadie's hand and pulled, but before she had stumbled more than a few steps forward, he froze.

The trees moved again.

Not just flickering.

They had come alive.

No... those aren't trees.

Enormous feet with gnarled, splayed toes like roots. Thick wooden legs with knotted skin or armour like bark. Long, twisted arms, thinner branches twining like tendons. Wide hands with crooked twig-like fingers. Faces roughly hewn with jagged gashes for eyes, noses, and mouths. Some heads fanned out like intricate branch crowns, some were topped with shaggy moss and lichen, and some bore horns like battle helmets. A crescent crest even grew on top of one head, a plume of witch's hair lichen trailing from the rear tip. They were all different, and all equally terrifying.

But they weren't trees. Between gaps of branch and twig, at the joints of shoulders and knees and elbows, even through the hollows of their eyes, wheels and cogs and gears turned. Metal pieces welded together, fitted in precise patterns, whirring and spinning to create mechanical movement. Plates of metal patched their bodies and skulls, and some even had whole metal forearms or feet.

At the centre of each of their bark-plated chests, a jewel rested in an intricately woven nest. Amber, emerald, ruby, opal, jade, amethyst, topaz, quartz—each of the two dozen creatures had a different gemstone, and every stone infused wood and metal with the same coloured glow like blood coursing through veins.

Though made of wood, fashioned like trees, and bedecked with a jewel, there was no mistaking it: these were machines.

Through the fog of her shocked brain, a word coaxed from the recesses of her mind surfaced. A word for a little wooden figure at a fair, a puppet with no strings, moving with a network of connecting gears and wheels: *automaton.*

Automaton trees. Powered by *magic.*

Sadie could feel the magic exuding from the stones in their chests.

The tree-automatons bellowed like a roaring forge and charged the Lantian cavalry. Some carried giant clubs, double-bladed axes, or hammers, but they didn't need them. Each swipe of their gnarled fists sent Lantíes and horses flying like dandelion fuzz. The thud of their enormous feet shook the earth and rattled Sadie's teeth.

Griswald's grin was maniacal.

An automaton thundered towards Sadie and Tristan, flattening everything in its path. Tristan readied himself, but a sword would be useless against an enormous machine. Grasping a few strands of fire magic, Sadie quickly wove them into a ball and hurled it at the automaton.

The ball of fire catapulted at the automaton and hit its thigh, igniting the wooden part of the machine in flames. The automaton screeched at the annoyance but kept running.

Sadie's next fireball hit the centre of its chest where an amethyst gleamed. The amethyst exploded, raining shards of purple stone mingled with sharp slivers of wood and metal down upon Redpaths and Lantíes alike as the tree-automaton collapsed.

"Nice one!" Tristan shouted. Sadie's grin quickly slid from her face as three more automatons changed course and charged.

Sadie hurled another fireball at one of the oncoming automatons and hit it mid-torso but missed the gemstone. The automaton stumbled and fell from the fiery force now blazing in its face, but it wasn't destroyed. She was knocked off her feet by a Redpath soldier ramming into her as she took aim at another one. Tristan impaled the soldier with his sword, but the Redpath had been spurred on by the powerful automatons at their back, and Sadie could barely keep her sword in front of her to parry the renewed attacks.

And the automatons kept charging.

Nerves clogged her throat and cascaded through her chest as Sadie desperately seized any small amount of fire magic she could handle while sword-fighting harder than ever, and threw it out at the automatons, hoping to slow them down. Arms and legs caught fire, but none were destroyed, only enraged.

As automatons and Redpath soldiers closed in around her, exhaustion and hopelessness clung to her limbs and drowned her heart like sticky sap. She had been defeated, after all she had endured since coming to Carmelle. Alldían, Tamlin, and Tristan had believed she was special, but they had been wrong. She was not destined to help them, only cripple them. She had failed them, and now the Ilyance's best chance of stemming the poisonous Redpath tide was ruined.

Searching the battlefield, Sadie spotted Tamlin send a swirling blizzard of huge, jagged icicles hurtling at the mage. The mage conjured a wall of stone to break the ice—then vanished. Tamlin slowly backed away, her head swivelling from side to side like a spooked owl. Sadie's heart thrashed against her chest and pounded in her ears. Where had the mage gone?

Tamlin's mouth opened in surprise before she clutched her side where a knife hilt protruded. Her hand came away coated in blood. An invisible force pushed her chest, and she flew backwards through the air, landing a few metres away with a deafening thud. Her white hair tangled across her umber face. She didn't stir.

"No!" Sadie cried.

The mage reappeared leering over her body in the snow, his chest heaving. When she didn't move or retaliate, he looked directly at Sadie.

The heinous hook of his sneer promised death for her next.

Sadie welcomed it.

Lane Tamlin, the woman who had taught her not just about magic but about her inner power as a woman, had died.

Tristan would probably die next.

And it was all her fault.

The people she cared about most in Carmelle were about to pay for her stupid pride and rash anger.

A single fat tear crowded the corner of her eye and trickled down her cheek.

Her tear pooled at the tip of her chin, then dropped.

It stopped in midair, halfway to the muddy snow, suspended as though dangling at the end of a string. As though invisible hands cupped it. As though it was made of glass.

It grew.

Slowly, it enlarged to the size of a small coin. Pear-shaped. Incandescent.

Peering closer, her lips parted in shock, Sadie discerned movement in the tear. A tiny flicker. A pinprick of orange light.

A perfect little flame danced in the centre of the tear, ablaze in a bubble of water.

Sadie thought of the foes surrounding her.

Slowly, the tear of flame floated towards the battling Redpath soldiers and automatons.

Time caught up with her magic, and the tear landed with a soft *splash* in a patch of mud peeking through the trampled snow at the soldiers' feet.

The world exploded.

Chapter Twenty-Nine

Flawed Logic

The explosion's backlash blasted Sadie off her feet. She landed hard beside her companions, numbly watching waves of snow and ice, layered with chunks of frozen mud and rocks, spray Redpath soldiers amid clouds of billowing fire.

Struggling to gain control of her lungs, Sadie scrambled to her feet and gaped at the desolation before her.

The entire Redpath force in front of her—about one hundred and fifty men and women and ten automatons—had been blasted off their feet. A low, agonizing chorus of moans hung in the air like the deep notes of a tuba. Her stomach heaved at the sight of the maimed corpses that had received the full force of the blast.

Flesh hung in bloody, serrated strips, and bits of cloth matted against burnt flesh and bone, congealed with fresh blood. Lopped limbs littered the landscape, staining the snow deep red. Pools of blood blossomed in bold, disturbingly beautiful patterns against the white snow, merging into a ruby lake. The air smelled of burnt flesh, charred bone, and rotten fluids. The metallic aroma of blood was so potent she could taste it on her tongue. Automaton parts dotted the charred earth between bodies. Bits of metal twisted and melted by the explosion's heat, cogs and wheels spinning beneath severed tree-limbs, fragments of colourful gemstones glinting in the mud, their magic gone. The explosion had even reached the forest, setting the front line of trees ablaze. Flames licked the pine needles greedily, and dark charcoal smoke ballooned into the air like a distress signal.

The Lantíes looked both confused and expectant as they searched for the source of the explosion, probably looking for Tamlin. Those who knew Sadie had magic probably thought her incapable of that kind of power. Tristan, however, gaped at her. He knew. He was also the only one to keep his head. He spared her one last calculating glance before shouting, "Run!" and leading the way over maimed bodies towards the forest.

It didn't take long for the Redpath soldiers to recover. Before the remaining Ilyance had gone more than a couple dozen meters, the Redpaths caught up with them and engaged in battle again.

Sadie trailed behind a little, looking over her shoulder at Tamlin's body. Exhaustion rattled her aching bones and pulled at her heavy limbs. The magic required for the explosion had drained her energy. Is that what had happened to Tamlin? When she looked in front of her again, Griswald and the mage stood there, blocking her path to rejoin the Ilyance.

"Where do you think you're going?"

Griswald's every syllable quivered with loathing.

"How'd you do that?" the mage hissed. Did a tinge of fear mar his unctuous voice?

"As if I would tell you," replied Sadie, echoing Griswald.

"Then I guess we have no further use for you," said the mage. Pressing an amber stone on one of the many gemstone rings he wore on his fingers, the mage fixed unblinking eyes on Sadie. An automaton with an amber gemstone in its chest turned and started lumbering over.

Sadie's heart sank. She tried to connect with her core, to grasp a fire strand, but it slipped through her mind's fingers like water cupped in her hands.

"Hold on," instructed Griswald unexpectedly.

The mage and Sadie both pinned him with looks of incredulity.

"Hold on for what?" the mage demanded. "Isn't this the girl you have been dying to kill?"

"Sometimes our greatest enemies can become our allies," answered Griswald. His voice was quiet. Thoughtful. Sadie didn't like the way he appraised her like a prize.

"Your ally?" the mage repeated. He looked between Sadie and Griswald, his eyes narrowing to dangerous slits. "I see."

His last two words lingered between them like a threat. A poised sword ready to strike.

The automaton did not stop its advance.

"I said, *hold on*, Rahkkar" Griswald commanded, venom dripping from his tongue. The heat of his glare could melt steel. "Remember your deal with Hargrim."

Rahkkar's face blanched. He lifted his arm in an exaggeratedly slow movement to press the amber ring and halt the automaton. As he did so, his sleeve slid down his arm a little to reveal a bracelet encrusted with more linked gems. Hairs rose on Sadie's arm, and she touched the crystal moon and leaf bracelet on her wrist.

Griswald noticed. His eyes widened then narrowed in quick succession. The moisture evaporated from Sadie's mouth. Violent nauseous fluttering launched from her stomach past her accelerated heart to her dry throat. He recognized her bracelet.

She stumbled back a step, but her weak knees buckled, and it took all her strength to remain standing. Retreating was not an option.

Griswald let the palpable tension fester for a moment before taking a step towards Sadie and elaborating. "We could use your talent in the Redpath organization. That explosion... I've never seen such mass destruction. Think of the implications. The possibilities. With the right progressive minds to collaborate with, you could solidify your name in the history books forever."

"Are you seriously trying to recruit my loyalties after pursuing me halfway across Carmelle to kill me, and murdering dozens of innocent lives in the process?"

"I am a logical man. If an opportunity arises, I seize it. Redpath advancement supersedes personal grudges. I remember the desire in your eyes when I mentioned purpose at our first encounter in Carenthia. You denied yourself the purpose you crave then. I'm offering you another chance to make a difference. To be part of something greater than yourself."

"Those were the naïve dreams of a girl trying to be anyone but herself," replied Sadie, her voice thick with emotion. She tried to grasp for a strand of fire magic and failed. "And even then, I never would have been wooed by the promise of mass destruction. Those are your warped and twisted dreams, not mine. Why would I want to contribute to the types of advancements that are killing my family? I warned you before you would regret your perceived purpose. I don't plan on sharing the same regrets."

"Yes, you keep speaking as though you have knowledge of Carmelle's future," observed Griswald slowly. His eyes flickered to her bracelet. "Or is it knowledge of another world you possess?"

Sadie couldn't breathe. Her lungs felt flattened, but her pounding heart rushed in her ears, drowning out all sounds of battle. Her eyes locked on the sinister glint in Griswald's calm stare. She forced her lungs to exhale.

"I don't know what you're talking about," she whispered.

"Oh, I think you do," said Griswald, his tone bloated with quiet menace as he took another step closer. "Your knowledge of industrialization doesn't come secondhand from Ilyance filth. You've seen it yourself firsthand. You're from Earth."

Sadie didn't bother denying it. She lacked the strength to maintain a non-beneficial lie.

"I don't know why you think advancements on Earth are killing your family, but if you're worried about them that much... Why don't you show me?"

Griswald's tone was light, but Rahkkar's neck snapped in his direction, fixing Griswald with a searing glare from his one eye.

"Commander, I do not think this advisable, we are under strict orders not to share our knowledge of—" Rahkkar began, but Griswald cut him off.

"Circumstances change, Master Morshade. They will understand. Do it."

Rahkkar hesitated, eyeing Sadie warily. Whether threatened by her or merely distrustful, it was clear the mage wanted to arm Sadie with as little knowledge as possible.

"NOW!" barked Griswald, spittle flying from the vibrations of his mangled skin.

Cheeks burning a mottled crimson, Rahkkar gritted his teeth but clutched something in a pocket of his robes, raised a hand, and closed his eyes.

The air shimmered and rippled, a veil between the Seen and Unseen fluttering invitingly.

Tears blurred Sadie's vision. This couldn't be happening.

The ripples spiralled into an image. A sweeping lawn blanketed in snow. Frosted bare willow tree branches framing an abandoned wooden swing. She could just make out a giant festive wreath on the door of the manor beyond the willow tree.

A portal in the middle of battle. A portal to take her home.

"How did you know?" she whispered in disbelief. Beads of water kissed her lips, the salty taste of sorrow lingering on her tongue. How had they known where she lived?

"Did *you* send me this?" she asked, her voice cracking as she held up her bracelet.

"No," said Griswald, "but now I know who you are. If you're missing your family, why don't you show me the destruction your advancements are causing, and then I will let you return to your family. No tricks. No lies or betrayal. Convince me the Redpath's plans are detrimental, and the fighting will stop. Your Ilyance friends will be safe, and you can be reunited with your family in peace."

Pain lanced her chest, so acute she pressed a hand to her heart. *Connor.* She could see Connor again. Find solace in his hugs, the quirk of his mischievous grin. The palpable ache wracking her heart beckoned faint strands of magic to stumble weakly from her core and stretch towards the portal. She was so close. The guilt of leaving him behind, of selfishly abandoning him in the naïve pursuit of her daydreams would be assuaged.

But what about Carmelle?

The world she had fallen in love with, where she had found a sense of belonging and self-acceptance for who she truly was. What about the people she had grown to care about?

Sadie glanced at Tristan, fighting so desperately he had finally lost track of her.

She didn't know how to choose who to leave behind. Which part of her soul should remain empty. But it didn't matter; Griswald's promise was empty. He might leave her in peace with her family, and he may even cease fighting the Ilyance—for now. But he would not leave Earth or Arwé alone. He would do whatever it took to advance his own agenda. He would kill people on Earth, cause death and destruction on disastrous scales if need be, to obtain the technology he needed. He would bring it back to Arwé and apply that technology to Carmelle. Tristan and the Ilyance had deduced the Redpath wanted control of the portals, and of other worlds. If that was true, her family wouldn't be safe anyway. There would be a new war to fight, and Connor would never come home.

Choosing a path diverging from her brother's hurt more than her numb brain could comprehend, but the aching hollows of her heart could not belie her certainty this was the right decision.

Griswald was wrong. She was already part of something greater than herself. She had a foot in both worlds, and she needed to defend them, not hand the enemy the key to their demise.

"Well?" Griswald prompted. "Are you ready to end this fight and fulfill a greater purpose?"

"*Almost*," Sadie whispered.

She took a step away from the portal.

"I'm sorry, Connor."

She stepped back again.

A ruby and blue blur hurtled past Sadie and knocked Rahkkar off his feet, breaking his connection with the portal. The shimmering window to her yard fizzled—and vanished.

The portal had closed.

Wild white hair swept across the woman's ruby mantle and light blue robes as she pinned Rahkkar with her knees, cold determination glinting in her ice-blue eyes.

Skin tingling, Sadie let loose a strangled gasp around the breath caught in her chest.

Tamlin.

Before Rahkkar could react, Tamlin conjured a long dagger from thin air, gripped the hilt with both hands, and plunged the sharp steel into the mage's chest.

Rahkkar's ragged gasp ended in a gurgling moan, and his one widened eye ceased to blink as his body stiffened.

Tamlin heaved herself off his corpse, drawing deep, rattling, winded breaths.

"You killed Rahkkar Morshade," Griswald stated, stunned.

"Would you like to be reunited?" Tamlin threatened.

Griswald took a few hasty steps backwards.

A clamorous screeching and whirring rent the air. The remaining tree-automatons started malfunctioning without Rahkkar alive, the gemstones in their chests flickering. The amber stone on the one Rahkkar had tried to sic on Sadie cracked and fractured, the lustre fading. Slowly, it keeled over.

Lantíes and Redpaths alike screamed as they scrambled to get out of the way.

Tamlin swore and raced towards the falling automatons, throwing her hands out as she ran to start working spells.

Griswald slowly turned to face Sadie. He pulled an arrow from his quiver and nocked it.

Sadie summoned the void and cobalt flame dome, and they embraced her eagerly.

Shards of frigid ice fractured Griswald's manic eyes. They held no emotion—only death.

Seizing a fire strand, Sadie envisioned a bolt of flame, and an arrow of fire appeared before her, hovering at eye level, pointed at Griswald.

"Kill me then," Griswald growled. "Kill me like your mentor killed Morshade."

"I don't want to kill you," said Sadie. "You deserve retribution for the deaths you caused, but I derive no pleasure in taking life. You can still choose to use your position of power for good. Help the other Redpath members see advancement through control will only lead to suffering. Carmelle's natural resources, the magic infused in its environment, the very lives of its peoples will be threatened. The efficient systems you envision will require sacrifices. Poisonous chemicals choking the lands you love, trees and cultural landmarks torn down to make way for industrialization, lives lost in dangerous labours and experiments. What starts as innocent improvements in medicine and reduction of physical labour turns into a contest of power. Who can discover more powerful and deadly weapons and use them against their adversaries first. Your ideal world will turn on you, and you'll be at its mercy. Is that really what you want? Is that what the other Redpaths want?"

Sadie gestured to a small group of Redpath soldiers who had started to come to Griswald's aid but paused when they heard her speech. They looked between Sadie and Griswald uncertainly, doubt seeping into their battle-hardened eyes.

"The story doesn't always have to be the same," Sadie continued, aware her words had hooked the Redpaths. She remembered the daydream she'd had in her bedroom back on Earth, the vision of armies on the cusp of battle and the bard's jaded views on cyclical human conflict. "You can be the change. You can't all think the same; that's not human nature. I'm sure most of you are feeling conflicted emotions right now. Those emotions are valid. Your views are valid. You can change the story, right now."

"Be quiet!" Griswald screeched, and his high-pitched voice sounded unhinged. "Why would I take the word of an insipid *woman* like you? I know how they treat women on Earth. Your opinion has zero weight. I'm sure you came to Carmelle thinking you'd adopt some agency, make a name for yourself performing deeds you never could in your world, but you're *nothing*. You'll always be nothing, and I'll make sure you die in obscurity the way you deserve."

Griswald drew back his nocked arrow to his mangled cheek.

Cold sweat beaded Sadie's trembling body, her rapid breathing painful in her squeezed chest, but she pushed down the swelling panic. She caught sight of Tristan running towards her in her peripheral vision, and her breathing eased. Her chest loosened.

"I don't need my name to be remembered," she said softly, calm washing over her. "My brother will remember me in my world. Tristan will remember me here. I can never die in obscurity if I'm remembered in the hearts of those who matter to me most."

Griswald snarled, took aim, and released his arrow at Sadie's heart.

Never taking her eyes off Griswald's face, Sadie released her fire bolt and dove sideways.

Sound ceased as she drowned in the void between a second and eternity, holding her breath as she landed hard, eyes still locked on Griswald.

Griswald's arrow whistled over her head, missing her by a few feet.

Her fire arrow found its mark. A small circle of golden-orange light flared over Griswald's heart for a moment then dimmed, the only sign of the magic that had killed him.

Sadie could not breathe past the fist gripping her lungs as she stared at his blank, unseeing eyes. She forced herself to turn away.

Movement blurred. Noises muffled. Swaying where she stood, Sadie fixated on a spot of blood against the snow. Moments later a pair of strong arms wrapped her in a hug, crushing her body against his. She inhaled the mingled scent of sweat, blood, and a faint hint of cinnamon.

"It's over now, Sadie," Tristan whispered in her ear. "It's all over."

She didn't bother correcting him. For her, it had only just begun.

Chapter Thirty

It Tolls for Thee

Heady scents of gingerbread, eggnog, and peppermint wafted tantalizingly through the YMCA dance hall of Sutton Veny, a village where they had taken a few days' leave. The decadent perfume warmed Connor's insides, like sipping steaming, rich hot chocolate. Wreaths of evergreen boughs festooned with holly, big red velvet bows, and gold and silver bells decorated the hall, along with the occasional strategically placed cluster of white mistletoe berries. Strings of green and red paper chains draped across the ceiling, and the far corner boasted a huge Christmas tree decorated with candles, strings of popcorn, and an eclectic assortment of coloured baubles. A quartet of musicians encouraged couples to brave the dance floor where they soon forgot to be awkwardly embarrassed and lost themselves to the infectious rhythms of holiday songs.

Connor leaned against the wall by the refreshment table, a glass of eggnog in one hand and a ginger molasses cookie in the other. He had already eaten five cookies and a heaping plate of sausage rolls, and he had downed three full glasses of eggnog before Corporal Cunningham spiked it. He had no desire to get drunk like some of his comrades, so he held his glass of eggnog and cookie in front of him as a shield against hopeful girls. The other men not dancing hunched by the food table joking and admiring the girls basking in the soft golden glow of the Christmas tree.

Connor had already been approached by several women asking him to dance with varying degrees of boldness, but he had politely refused each one, much to the amusement of his sniggering buddies. Will chided him for his stubborn melancholy on Christmas Eve, but he felt it would be dishonourable to Mabel if he danced with another girl. He only cared to dance with her anyway. He missed the elegant bounce of her long wavy golden hair as they waltzed around the Sheldon manor ballroom, the feel of her waist beneath his clumsy hands, the sparkle of her sage eyes reflecting the moon as her warm hand twined with his.

"You only live once!" Will reminded him yet again as a brunette smiled at him. "I'm not saying to forget Mabel, but it's just a dance. These girls are so pretty, don't you get lonely out here? Look, even that twat Corporal Cunningham found a girl!"

Will cocked his head in the direction of Cunningham, who approached with a girl's arm looped demurely through his.

"What's the matter Private Avery, too chaste to show a girl a good time?" Cunningham taunted. "Or maybe you just don't know *how...*"

He whacked Connor's shoulder hard with his own as he passed and chuckled.

"Why didn't you stand up to him?" Will asked, glaring daggers at Cunningham's back as he led the girl out of the hall.

"He's not worth the extra push-ups in the morning," replied Connor, shaking his head. The truth was he didn't notice if the girls were pretty or not. They weren't Mabel.

"I'm going for a smoke," he announced to Will. Without waiting for objections, Connor exited the dance hall by the back door into the cold December air.

The dance hall snuggled up to a little park, so Connor decided to go sit on one of the benches illuminated by the golden glow of a lamppost.

Darkness settled between the lampposts like an opaque fog. Snow dusted the grass and lampposts, and slow, lazy flakes floated in the lamplight. Puffs of smoke escaped from his lips before he even pulled out a cigarette. He could discern the shape of two people huddled together on the grass just outside the lamplight further down the path. He hoped it wasn't Cunningham and that girl. The last thing he needed was for the Corporal to goad him into trouble.

Pulling a cigarette and lighter from his jacket pocket, Connor lit it and took a long drag. A wave of calm washed over him immediately, and he sank back against the hard, cold bench.

Smoking was a habit he had only indulged in recently. Most of his fellow soldiers smoked, bonding over a shared desire to calm their frayed nerves. Their facade of tough invincibility and confidence masked their fear of imminent death. They would kill people, their friends would get killed, and they might die themselves. The inevitability haunted them all. Sadie's death had already burned a hole in his heart. So he smoked, and it helped chase away death's lurking shadow.

Shifting slightly on the bench, he gazed listlessly at the colourful Christmas lights looped around trees and above storefronts on the street behind him. At the end of the block stood an old brick Catholic church with a tall steeple. As he looked, the big church bell began to clang, ringing in the midnight hour. It was Christmas Day. Through the open, welcoming doors, a melodious choir sang their midnight mass hymns. Connor's feelings about God and religion were mixed after Sadie's death, but listening to their uplifted voices singing in harmony, he felt peace for the first time that Christmas season.

And then that peace shattered.

A scream ripped through the night, then cut off with a loud *smack!*

Connor whipped his head towards the sound, and noticed the two figures he had seen further down the path were no longer visible.

Sprinting down the path, he searched the bushes frantically. Scuffling and muffled cries emanated from behind a bush to his left. Without pausing to plan, Connor darted behind the bush.

Corporal Cunningham pinned the girl he had left the dance with against a tree. One hand clamped over her mouth, her eyes wide and terrified above it. The other hand was raised to strike.

Before Cunningham noticed him, Connor kicked him hard in the kidneys and shoved him off the girl. They rolled in the snow, wrestling to gain control. Cunningham was bigger, stronger, and older than him, but his adrenaline surged and a white-hot rage blinded him. The corporal had been abusing this girl. All he could think about was Sadie being abducted by a man in the woods and murdered.

He may not have been able to stop what happened to his sister, but he sure as hell would stop this.

Somehow Connor managed to pin Cunningham, and started punching every inch of him he could reach. But the corporal was too strong. He heaved Connor off him. Staggering, Connor turned to launch another attack—and found himself staring into the mouth of a pistol.

"Shit."

Out of the corner of Connor's eye, he noticed the girl had run away while Cunningham was distracted, but now Connor was alone.

Death had found him again.

Sadie.

"No!" he shouted. A raging fire coursed through him as he knocked the gun out of Cunningham's hand, caught it with his other hand, and aimed.

Connor had become a very good shot. He never missed.

The bullet embedded in Cunningham's shoulder.

His upper body twisted back, and he fell, gripping his shoulder in shock.

It was the advantage Connor needed.

He ran, gun still in hand so Cunningham couldn't shoot him in the back. But before he passed the first bench the corporal was on him again, trying to choke him with his uninjured arm. Connor twisted and whacked him in the temple with the gun. Cunningham staggered, tripped, and hit his head with a sickening *crunch* on the bench's metal armrest. His body crumpled to the ground.

Blood poured from his head, creating a ruby red halo in the snow.

Corporal Cunningham was dead.

The church bell tolled in the distance, and the mingling music of the dance's band and angelic choir greeted the new Christmas morning with joyful fervour.

Connor stared down at the dead soldier.

"Shit, shit, *shit!*" came Will's voice as he ran up to Connor, taking in Cunningham's prone, bloody body. "What the hell happened here? I came to look for you and see Cunningham choking you, and you whacking him with your gun and then… the bench…"

Will floundered, gaping at Connor with wide, shocked eyes.

"He was hitting that girl, dragging her into the woods," Connor whispered, his throat grating. "I couldn't let him. My sister…"

Connor couldn't voice the rest, but Will's look of horror told him he understood. Though Connor had told Will his sister had died recently, he hadn't shared how.

"It's all right," Will said after a moment, studying the ground as though answers were written there. "I saw Cunningham attacking you, I saw him hit the bench. You never dealt the killing blow. I even saw the girl running away when I first came out. Defending someone's honour is the kind of soldier you are, Connor. We all know it. I'll vouch for you, and everything will be fine."

Connor nodded numbly, patting Will on the shoulder to convey his gratitude. He no longer had Sadie, but he wasn't alone. He could defend her honour by figuring out exactly how Thomas Sheldon had died and why, and if his death was linked to hers. And he could defend his country's honour. He had strength enough for both.

Though he had not dealt the final killing blow, Connor had defended that girl against the predatory Cunningham like he would defend his nation against those preying upon her.

He was a true soldier now, in name and spirit.

There was no turning back.

Chapter Thirty-One

The Next Adventure

The sky wept for Haldin during his funeral.

Thick snow crowded the air like crystallized tears, but Sadie barely noticed the flakes stinging her face and settling in her hair as she listened to a Lantian female singing a funeral dirge. Her lilting, melancholy voice transcended the keening mourners, and yet the two sounds complimented each other, their echoes mingling in the clearing. Sadie knew the pyre they had built for Haldin was in honour of his Dharmaelian customs. Tristan had informed her the Lantíés of Caris Nando did not cremate their dead, as their immortality allowed them to bury their fewer dead in graves amid the roots of trees. The burial was a celebration of life with music and Storytellers, and their decomposing bodies would then nourish the trees and reciprocate the gifts nature gave them in life. Though the bodies of the Lantíés who had perished in battle rested atop their own pyres so they could honour all who fought at the same time, they would not burn them. Their burials would occur after Haldin's cremation.

The tallest pyre in the middle was reserved for Haldin. Grouped around the base of his pyre were Airothane, Tristan, Alldían, Tamlin, and Sadie.

As Haldin's bier arrived and the men bearing it began climbing wooden ladders hooked to the sides to place Haldin's body on top, Sadie's chest constricted. His long strawberry blond hair had been combed and arranged around his face; he had been washed clean of blood and grime and dressed in his Dharmaelian armour; and his eyes had been gently closed so he looked as though he slumbered peacefully. Folded in his hands was his axe, Ilígon, cleaned of blood and rust. Nalalíté flowers encircled his whole body, carefully placed by Lantíés as a blessing and mark of honour. But this peaceful image did not comfort Sadie.

Once the bier had been secured atop the pyre, Airothane climbed the ladder and Tristan followed carrying a bundle of personal effects. One by one he handed Airothane Dharmaelian coins, knives, and the other personal items Haldin had brought with him on his quest. Sadie glimpsed a few decorative hawk feathers among the collection. A few honorary tokens such as a shield with the Dharmaelian crest made for the occasion were placed last. Airothane bent and kissed his brother's forehead, whispering something in his ear. Even from the ground Sadie could see the tears cascading down Airothane's cheeks.

Tamlin passed a lit torch to Tristan, but when he reached to ignite the straw and dry kindling around Haldin, Airothane's tiny arm shot out. Hesitating only a moment, Tristan handed the torch to Airothane. Sadie's heartstrings twanged at the determined look in Airothane's eyes as he performed his duty as a prince of Dharmaelia and respectful brother. He lingered a moment after the fire was lit to drink in the features of his brother's face one last time before descending the ladder and rejoining them at the pyre's base.

While Sadie watched the flames lick Haldin's body and followed the plume of eddying smoke fighting through the snowflakes and trees to the overcast sky, a plethora of emotions assaulted her. Grief, despair, confusion, anger, and guilt warred in her head. Airothane's tiny hand slid into hers and squeezed her fingers hard. A few minutes later Tristan's large, callused hand clasped her other hand, twining his fingers through hers with comforting pressure, lending her the strength Airothane borrowed.

Through the roaring flames, the hauntingly beautiful keening notes of the Lantian woman singing in Tavé rose, and a single tear rolled down Sadie's cheek.

After the funeral, Sadie wandered to the Éalindel, hoping the rhythmic roaring of the pounding waterfall would wash away her tumultuous thoughts. When she stepped out of the trees onto the open bank of the Setami, however, a half-frozen waterfall greeted her. Instead of deafening rushing water, a slow trickle across splintering ice tickled her ears. Though she had been here a month ago, the Éalindel's stunning transformation left her breathless.

Snow buried the nalalité flowers, and patterns of shaved ice spotted the partially frozen river. Plumes of frothy water from the waterfall's base had frozen into jagged pillars of interlaced ice, forming a frozen cone with clandestine crevices. Even in the sunless daylight the frozen cone emulated a pearly silver-blue glow like moonbeams caught in an icy web, lighting its frosted halls from within like hundreds of tiny glowing wintry fairies.

Deep content ached in her soul, profound to the point of poignant. It was a feeling bigger than herself, more powerful than she could contain, a feeling to convince her of her soul's existence. It was the same profound happiness she felt when looking at the stars, the ocean, or a sunset.

"It doesn't seem right to experience content in the wake of sorrow, does it?"

Sadie didn't take her eyes off the waterfall at the sound of Tristan's voice as he joined her silent vigil. She had not heard him approach, but she was beyond reacting to surprises.

"You know, your habit of following me borders on creepy sometimes."

"Sorry. I wanted to make sure you were all right."

In spite of herself, Sadie smiled. "I know, Tristan. I'm happy you're here."

Neither of them said anything for a few minutes. Sadie held out her palm to catch snowflakes despite her numb fingers, concentrating on the unique patterns spiralling into her hand. They were all so different with distinct personalities. The soldiers who died on both the Ilyance and Redpath sides were not as innocent as the snowflakes gathering in her palm, but she couldn't help making the correlation. The soldiers had their own individual dreams, fears, and aspirations. If Griswald hadn't intervened, maybe some of them would have heeded her words and laid down their weapons to change the story.

And what about Griswald? Now that he was gone—now she had killed him—she realized she knew nothing about him. Did he have a family? Was he the pinnacle of another person's world? Or was he alone, never truly loved by anyone, not even his soldiers?

Maybe the bard in her vision had been right, and stories were always the same. But while that may be true for the themes and events of a story, Sadie had seen how people could have different reactions to the same event. Griswald and Rahkkar Morshade, Sadie and Tristan and Tamlin—they all responded to the same events differently, which showed it was people's unique individual strengths and emotional responses that defined each story. Her unique emotional blueprint was valid and could not be replicated. A strength with the power to change her story.

Above all, Sadie thought of Haldin. Ever since their first meeting in the halls of Nethilya, he had been a pillar of strength, confident without arrogance, reserved but brimming with love and a passion for the life he shared with those he trusted. She had grown to count on him as a constant in her tumultuous life in Carmelle, and the loss of him punctured her heart.

"It wasn't your fault Haldin died," Tristan whispered.

A tear escaped Sadie's eye and rolled off her cheek into her palm, melting the snowflakes nestled there. Once again, Tristan had known her thoughts a second before they formed in her mind, and his vocalization of her guilt released her tears. She couldn't answer him.

"Haldin was a good friend of mine," Tristan elaborated. "We fought together in Dharmaelia, and he always accepted and understood me. He was a loyal comrade, but his loyalties weren't restricted to his friends and family. He was loyal to the Ilyance and what they stand for, and sought ways to thwart the Redpath. Above all, he was loyal to Dharmaelia. Dharmaelia was part of him as much as his blood and bones, and he would do anything, including lay down his life, to defend her."

Sadie shuffled snow around with her boot, and accidentally touched Tristan's boot. She kept her foot there, resting against his.

"Haldin thought his land was in trouble because of the madman's ravings," Tristan continued when she didn't speak. "We may never know if Dharmaelia was in danger from the Redpath at that time, but I believe the Redpath do want to target Dharmaelia eventually as a solid Ilyance nation they think easier to eradicate than the Lantíés. In any case, Haldin believed he was dying to protect the thing closest to his heart. He went for Dharmaelia, not for you. Griswald was responsible for Haldin's death, not you. And, thanks to you, Haldin's death was avenged."

Sadie snorted in self-deprecating laughter. "And yet somehow that doesn't console me."

"It's difficult to process the first time you take a life," Tristan agreed. "Even if it was necessary for self-defence or saving someone you love. You still feel like a murderer. I felt the same way the first time I killed someone in battle. I questioned whether I was any better than the evil murderers of the world. A lot of people believe killing means you're soulless regardless of the circumstances."

Sadie chanced a glance at Tristan. He watched the waterfall, the space between his brows scrunching together. Sadie liked how seriously he contemplated morality. How he wasn't quick to claim perfection, but truly questioned his motives and actions.

"And what do you think?" she whispered, holding her breath expectantly.

"Maybe they're right," mused Tristan, "but I wonder how you know you have a soul if you close yourself off to recognizing the difference between good and evil, and judging when an act of violence is sometimes necessary. If I don't stand up for my principles and what I believe in, then how can I say anything defines my soul? I prefer using words to stand up for my beliefs and do so as often as possible. Maybe one day Arwé will be a world in which fighting is never necessary, and battles are an archaic barbaric notion of the past. I hope it will be. I fight to eradicate the evil that will allow it to be so."

"I'm sure the Redpath would say the same," remarked Sadie dryly. "Why is your definition of evil, your beliefs, better than theirs?"

Tristan's tight-lipped grin exuded grim irony. "I wish I could answer humankind's greatest unsolved mystery, the source of most conflict, but I can't. I just have to trust my instincts. The voice telling me the things that ache in my soul and whisper of feelings greater than myself are worth defending. Carmelle's natural wonders give me that feeling. I'd rather avoid killing if possible, but when you're attacked and it's a choice between killing someone to survive and defend the pieces of your soul or die and have everything you love die with you... well, it becomes easier to justify at least. Honestly, you never get used to the bloodstains on your hands, but sometimes it is a necessary evil in order to prevent the greater evil alternative."

Sadie sighed, hunching her shoulders against the depletion numbing her body, and held her head between her hands.

"I guess I naively thought I'd feel fulfilled or satisfied if I defeated an evil enemy, like in the epic stories of good versus evil," replied Sadie in a quiet voice. "I've always dreamed of fighting in battles, of wielding a sword or brandishing a bow as I marched with my fellow soldiers, cutting down my enemies like a farmer slicing through wheat with a scythe. I craved the sense of purpose I thought it would bring. Battles were black and white; you killed your enemies because you had to, because it was morally correct to oppose something threatening your world and those you love. But... the lines have blurred, my moral compass faded to grey. My dream came true, and I embarked on the greatest adventure of my life, feeling like I have a greater purpose every day, but the cost of my new magical reality is proving more difficult to bear."

"It's good to feel compassion about death," said Tristan. "Death is a powerful and random force, and those who don't respect it will soon succumb to evil. But you can't let it consume you, either. The despair would drown you, Sadie. Not even Alldían knows what the future holds. There is always hope."

"So what am I supposed to do?"

"You mourn Haldin by remembering him as the brave, selfless, and loyal person he was. You spend time with your friends who care about you. And day by day, as time works its healing magic, you will learn to forgive yourself for Griswald's death, and hopefully come to see the good in your brave deed. You are already a hero to the Lantíes and the rest of us for vanquishing a tyrant like Griswald. And you shed the weight of the word 'almost.'"

Sadie lifted her head and met Tristan's eyes, heartbeat skittering erratically. There were no walls up, no hint of mockery. Just sincerity, compassion, and warmth.

"It has become a marker of your virtues, not your shortcomings," he continued. "You *almost* gave in to despair when all hope seemed lost in the battle, but you didn't. You *almost* helped Griswald further his agenda and show him the advancements he wanted in the portal, but you didn't. You *almost* killed him without giving him a chance at redemption, but you didn't. At every encounter with *almost*, you're choosing to not let the shards of doubt and insecurity embedded in your heart cripple the instinct that points your moral compass towards good. You're not *almost* enough, Sadie. You always have been enough."

A weight lifted from her chest, and she laughed at its sudden lightness despite the tears welling in her eyes. She had never appreciated his friendship more than in that moment.

"Thank you, Tristan."

"Oh, and Sadie," he added with a crooked grin. "Merry Christmas."

A slow grin warmed Sadie's face.

Christmas passed and the new year dawned, and Sadie found herself trying to escape encounters where people treated her like a hero for dealing the final blow against Griswald. She found herself seeking out Airothane's company often, for though he was grateful for her avenging her brother's death, he still thought of his brother as the hero more than Sadie.

Well, and himself.

"It's lucky my Windtalking talent is so powerful, otherwise you all would be dead right now," Airothane bragged for the umpteenth time as Sadie, Tristan, Airothane, and Tamlin huddled around the warmth of a fire in Tamlin's room. "I heard Sadie's plea for help, and I didn't even wait to ask Alldían's permission. He had told me earlier that morning he was preparing to welcome back a Lantian cavalry he had sent on an expedition months ago, though he didn't know which day they would arrive. I listened and sure enough I heard hooves thundering on the wind. None of them were Windtalkers, so I tried projecting my voice onto the wind, shouting out a message for the wind to carry to whoever may have been more attuned to listen—and it worked! They heard my message and galloped to your rescue!"

"Yes, we are all very grateful for your talents," Tamlin agreed, indulging Airothane with her fourth grateful smile in the last two days. Sadie thought that must be a record for her.

"Ninaya, the Keeper of Air, must have decided to take sides," insisted Airothane.

"The Keepers don't take sides," Tristan intoned automatically.

"Then how do you explain the cavalry hearing my voice on the wind over thundering hooves when there was no Windtalker?" Airothane challenged.

"Your incredible talent?" Tristan replied dryly.

"I still think it's a stretch, even for my talent," mumbled Airothane churlishly, crossing his arms. "It was really nice of you to think of me, and have faith I could help," Airothane added to Sadie in a quiet, more sheepish voice.

Warmth blossomed in her heart. Every time Airothane let his vulnerability shine through his bravado, her affection and protectiveness for her young friend increased. "I knew I could count on you to be every bit the hero your brother was," replied Sadie.

Airothane blushed, but his smile lit up his whole face.

"At least we captured enough Redpaths for some to stand trial," said Tristan. "Maybe it will warn those who escaped to proceed with caution."

"Doubtful, but one can hope," said Tamlin. "I'm still surprised Rahkkar Morshade worked for the Redpath, and somehow discovered an undetectable, invisible cloaking magic capable of concealing five hundred soldiers and their tree-automatons. I don't remember him showing such an affinity for Air magic at Orinloth, but I guess Dark Magic will change a lot about a person. Like the ability to create a portal, for example. No one has done that in hundreds of years. I don't want to know what sacrifices he must have made with Celestial magic to learn that."

"Or why he wanted to learn to open portals in the first place," Sadie added, failing to keep the bitterness out of her voice.

Tamlin gave Sadie a sharp, calculating look. "Yes, why indeed…"

Guilt still plagued Sadie about Connor and the portal, but though she longed to lift the burden from her chest, she didn't tell anyone the full story. She had told Tamlin, Tristan, and Alldían that Griswald had been trying to convince her to show him advancements on Earth that he could use for the Redpath, but she left out his offer to return her home to her family. It felt too personal, and she still questioned whether she had made the right decision. Choosing not to walk through that portal felt like losing her brother all over again, a wound as fresh and painful as losing Haldin. She felt like she had betrayed him twice; first by choosing to walk through the mirror without him and then choosing to turn her back on him again to stop the Redpath's agenda. She wondered if Connor would ever forgive her.

Rahkkar had been able to open a portal. Tamlin thought he had done it with Dark Magic, but what if there was a way to open one without using Celestial magic? Sadie would not give up trying to see her brother again. She *would* find the answers.

Near the end of February, when the snow started melting a bit and walking through the forest became easier, Alldían intercepted Sadie on her way back from swordplay training with Tristan.

"Sadie, I wanted to talk to you," said Alldían. A few Lantíes mingling nearby paused their conversation and stared at Sadie and Alldían together. Sadie looked away, colour creeping up her cheeks. Though she had tried to ignore it, the Lantíes treated her with a mix of respect and admiration now. At first it bothered her to gain fame for killing, but as Tristan had predicted, she did eventually begin to recognize the necessity in what she had done. She was no longer the girl who gave in to despair because her parents dictated her fate, but that didn't mean she was comfortable with being an object of fascination to the Lantíés now.

"Er… why don't we walk and talk," suggested Alldían.

Falling in line with Alldían, Sadie asked as they walked, "Where are we going?"

"I thought you might want to visit the Seven Pools again. I thought after seeing your world through the portal Rahkkar conjured, and losing Haldin… well, I thought you might be thinking about home more and want to see it."

Her heart fluttered at the thought of seeing her brother again, but Alldían's mention of Rahkkar inspired another thought that blotted her excitement.

"Did you send me this?" Sadie asked, holding up her wrist where she still wore the crystal moon and leaf bracelet.

Alldían examined it closely, then shook his head. "I'm afraid not. I've never seen that bracelet before, although I see why you might think it was from me. Where did you get it?"

Pinching a crescent moon crystal between her fingers, Sadie watched Alldían's face closely as she said, "On Earth. I received an anonymous package, and it burned my wrist when I stood in front of the mirror portal, contemplating whether I should go through. When it burned, the image changed, and I saw Thomas Sheldon…"

Nothing. No eyebrow raise, no widening eyes, no gasp or smile or sneer of satisfaction. Alldían betrayed no emotion as he asked, "And does it still burn?"

"No," Sadie answered flatly, turning away from his unreadable face in frustration. She had been so sure Alldían sent it—did his denial mean he had sent it with duplicitous intentions and didn't want to admit it? Or was his denial sincere, and someone else had sent it?

"Well, it may be benign now then. I have no idea who sent it or why, but it sounds like it was enchanted, and at least tried to control you. I'm not sure I would advise continuing to wear it, just in case the spell can be reignited," cautioned Alldían.

Sadie had considered taking it off many times for the same reason, but it hadn't burned again once since entering Carmelle. And though it may seem silly, she had received the bracelet in her home. In her mind, it linked the two worlds of her heart, and provided comfort.

When she reached Telwé Unvar, Alldían gave her privacy as she knelt in the shallow snow at the base of a Pool. Plucking a petal from the eternal flower buds on the Tree's branches, she let it float gently down to kiss the pool's surface. The Pools had been impervious to the winter's icy touch, their mirror-like surfaces smooth and clear. As ripples bubbled from the petal, an image took shape and focused.

Men in uniform bustled around white tents and barracks, shoving clothing and personal items into bags, and labelling their trunks and suitcases. She spotted Connor sitting on his bed, his packed bag beside him, shining his boots methodically. She wondered what he thought about. Was he scared about the prospect of killing? Soon he would be far more intimate with the idea of taking a life than her. Did he ever think about her? Did he miss her too? She couldn't bear the idea of losing her connection with him.

Eventually the image in the pool darkened, breaking her hungry gaze. She continued staring at the empty pool, letting the snow soak her dress.

Sadie sensed Tamlin's magical core before hearing her approach. She crouched on her heels beside Sadie.

"Alldían told me I could find you here. I wanted to talk about your future in Carmelle."

"Okay," replied Sadie warily.

"I think it's time for you to move on from Caris Nando, and frankly I think you feel it too. There's nothing keeping you here, and I strongly feel it's time for you to receive proper magical training. In Orinloth, you'll learn to harness and use your magic to the best of your ability, guided by the best teachers—and myself, for I must return to Orinloth as well. You have already performed more complex magic than many senior students, so imagine what you could accomplish with some schooling. Frankly it would be too dangerous for you *not* to go, and you owe it to yourself to explore your potential."

Sadie knew her departure from Caris Nando was imminent and her training at Orinloth inevitable. Lately a restless energy stirred in her veins. Tamlin was right: she was a liability without proper training. Her experiences with Griswald had made that abundantly clear. Maybe she could find answers about portals in Orinloth and discover a way to open one to Connor.

"When would we go?"

"In just over a week, around the beginning of March. The snow should be compact enough by then to travel, and I would like to arrive by mid or late March.""Can I have tonight to think about it and let you know by tomorrow?"

Tamlin smiled and patted her shoulder. "Of course."

That night, Sadie rode Chai for the first time, an exhilarating experience. She suspected she might find Tristan at Tor Niro, his favourite spot in Caris Nando, and she wanted to talk to him. Racing through the trees on Chai's bare back with his crystal horn gleaming in the moonlight and her cloak streaming behind her, she felt more alive than before the battle.

It was a clear night, and when she burst through the trees and leapt up onto their lookout rock, startling Tristan, the stars glittered like billions of brightly lit candles. A dusting of constellations consumed every inch of the charcoal canvas, and shooting stars fell in abundance. Her problems always melted to trivial insignificance under the majesty of the stars.

"What're you doing here?" asked Tristan breathlessly, sitting back down.

"I figured it was my turn to follow you." She sat next to him, drawing her cloak close.

"Oh."

Tristan's hands gripped his knees, and a sadness Sadie wasn't sure she understood dulled his eyes. He seemed lost, anxious, and depressed at the same time.

"I wanted to talk to you about Orinloth," explained Sadie, suddenly unsure of herself. "You know more about me than anyone here. How would you feel about me going to Orinloth with Tamlin?"

"I don't think there's even a question," he replied. "You need to go to Orinloth. It's why you were brought to Carmelle. There's nothing keeping you here. But you already knew that."

He was right. Her feet itched to follow Tamlin, but she had needed to hear Tristan's acquiescence. She hadn't missed the bitter bite chewing his words though when he said nothing kept her here. And then it dawned on her.

"What will you do?" she asked in nervous alarm.

"I can't come with you, Sadie." Sadness laced his voice. "I need to stay in Caris Nando while this Redpath business is sorted. The battle was won, but civil war has just begun. I'm needed here and maybe in other cities and towns to help against the Redpath's oppression. By now they have chosen a new leader and are regrouping. We need to stop them before they grow too strong. Our duties have diverged, but we must stay true to them."

Sadie didn't try to hide the tears pooling in her eyes. Tristan had become her best friend. He had been there for her throughout their journey in Carmelle, even when they had disliked each other. He had supported her through discovering her magic, had defended her against the Redpath, and had saved her from falling off the Sula-onon. She trusted him. She would miss their easy banter, but more importantly she would miss *him*. Impulsively, she leaned over and hugged him, burying her head in his chest. She breathed in his scent, that faint hint of cinnamon.

Tristan hesitated with his arms sticking out awkwardly before wrapping them around her gently. They stayed like that for a long time, Sadie crying silently against his chest.

Eventually she whispered, "I'll feel so lost without you."

Tristan laughed, a deep thrumming rumble in his chest.

"You know, tellurian, I might just feel a little lost confusion without you as well. My verbal sparring skills will certainly rust."

Sadie laughed as they broke apart, wiping her eyes. "You're my best friend, you know."

His smile was so genuine she thought his eyes even sparkled, though that could have been reflecting starlight.

"Likewise. I'm going to miss you, Sadie."

"I'll miss you too, Tristan."

"But you know, this isn't goodbye. We'll see each other again, soon I'm sure. Orinloth is not too far from Caris Nando. I could visit you. In fact, I often have to go there on business for Alldían or to train swordsmen. They have a swordsmanship school there, and as a Swordmaster I must instruct at least one class a year. So do not despair, tellurian. You will have my charming, brilliant, talented self back in your life again far sooner than you wish, I'm sure."

Sadie sighed in exaggerated sarcasm. "That's what I was afraid of."

The week before their departure passed in a blur of packing and councils with Alldían and Tamlin about the best routes to take and Redpath contingents to avoid. Sadie tried to spend as much time with Chai as possible, dreading the moment she would have to part from him. Tamlin explained their souls were inextricably linked now, so they would see each other again, but unicorns were an independent nomadic race and never stayed with their human soulmates exclusively. When they needed each other, they would find each other no matter what.

The day before their departure, Airothane approached her while she and Tamlin were in her room, checking her bag for the umpteenth time.

Without preamble, he announced, "I've decided I'm coming with you. My bags are already packed. There's nothing for me here either. I need to return to Dharmaelia, but I cannot travel there alone, and I would like to see Orinloth first. My father has replied to my letter informing him of Haldin's death now, so delaying my return for a few months longer won't make much difference."

Sadie gaped at Airothane then turned to Tamlin with a frown. She could tell his speech had been rehearsed, and he had that stubborn set to his jaw, but Sadie couldn't help thinking King Peladorn would want his son back under his wing soon to keep him safe and have him mourn with the rest of the family. She suspected Airothane might not be ready to return to the home where memories of Haldin would haunt him everywhere he turned.

To her surprise, Tamlin agreed with Airothane.

"I think it would be a wise course for you right now too, Airothane," she said. "I will most likely be able to accompany you to Dharmaelia after a time at Orinloth."

Airothane beamed at this, his whole face lighting up more than Sadie had seen since Haldin's death. "It's settled then! Sadie?"

"I would love for you to come with me to Orinloth, Airothane," Sadie replied, finding that she meant it with her whole heart.

Pale golden rays of wintry sunlight suffused the clearing before Alldían's Hall the next morning, bathing the three travellers in a hopeful light. Alldían and Tristan had come to see them off. Tristan wore the tunic with his personal emblem of a sword wrapped in a rosebud stem and his favourite forest green cloak, while Alldían wore heavy robes of deep burgundy. Sadie shouldered a backpack over her long black travelling cloak and midnight blue travelling dress. The snow beneath her feet was light and compact, perfect for walking. Excitement tingled through her veins. She was about to embark on another adventure.

Their goodbyes to Alldían and Tristan were brief after spending so much time together during the week.

"It was an absolute pleasure to meet you, Sadie, and to have you stay in Caris Nando," Alldían told her, shaking her hand. "You will be missed. I will be in touch, and we will see each other again soon. I know you will do well in Orinloth, and I have no doubt you will one day be a great sorceress. Take care, Sadie."

"Thank you for everything, Alldían," Sadie replied. "I look forward to our next meeting."

Tristan tried to envelope her in a short hug, but Sadie found herself lingering, unable to let him go. The ghost of regret already haunted her heart at the prospect of leaving him behind. Why must she always leave the people she cared for most?

"I'll miss you," she whispered.

Tristan's shoulders sagged, and he melted into the hug. "I'll miss you too, tellurian. Although you *are* kind of exhausting. Maybe I'll finally get some rest. Just try not to start any more civil wars, all right?"

Sadie punched his arm. "Try to work on your jokes while I'm gone, they're a little clunky," she teased.

Tristan grinned. "What jokes?"

"Well, I hate to break up... whatever this is, but we should get going before I have to hear more of it," said Tamlin. "Come, Sadie, Airothane. Let us begin our courtship with adventure."

And with an ecstatic grin, Sadie took the first step into her next adventure.

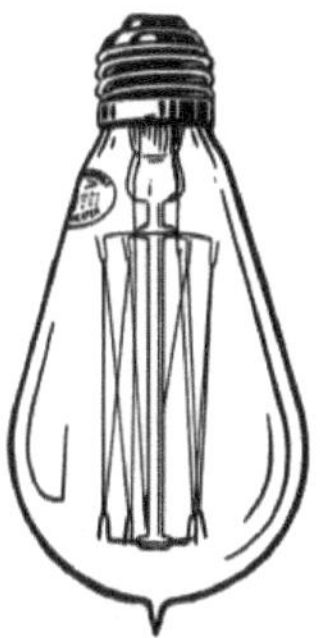

Epilogue

North Sea, near Ypres, Belgium

Wind buffeted Therius' frail frame, threatening to unbalance his stance atop one of the small hills bordering the coastline. Sitting to lower his centre of gravity, he grabbed a fistful of the tall grass needling his thighs with one hand and his pendant with the other. Stars canopied the sky, fewer in number than the stars he remembered in Carmelle, but bright enough for his purpose tonight.

Concentrating on the brightest star, Therius pressed the clear, diamond-like stone in the middle of the metal flame pendant and closed his eyes.

When he could no longer hear waves crashing against the sandy beach, he opened them.

The stars had dimmed. All except the bright star he had concentrated on, which shone brighter than the moon.

"Can you see me, Master?" Therius asked the star.

"I see you, Therius," a voice said in his head. "Report."

"I have news related to Pierre Curie," Therius hastened to explain. "Or rather, his wife, Marie. Pursuing the connection he made between crystals and electricity was worthwhile, no thanks to that insufferable Thomas Sheldon. His work in piezoelectricity proved essential for our purposes, and now we have this."

Therius pulled a piezoelectric compensator out of his robe pocket. The round, brass base glinted in the starlight, but it was the piezo crystal clamped between delicate brass braces that seemed to pull most of the remaining starlight in, glowing brightly. A beautiful, if simple, device.

"Of course, we know now we need something more powerful. A shame Pierre caught me stealing his compensator. If I didn't have to push him in front of that carriage, his research may have produced something more powerful for us," continued Therius. "But now I have learned his wife Marie continues their research in radioactivity, and the elements they discovered with the help of this compensator. She may be the key to unlocking the full potential of the piezoelectrometer. And who knows... it may be possible to weaponize the radioactive elements she studies now."

"Yes, I agree she is worth pursuing," the voice mused. "Find her and learn more. Be wary. The youngest Sheldon, Connor, now fights in their war, and I have heard him talking of Thomas' book. I even heard him mention the Curies. He may be seeking answers. Do not let him obtain them."

Fiddling with his pendant, Therius watched the waves furl over. A couple walked hand in hand further down the beach, sharing a romantic moment as though battles hadn't raged only a few miles from here. Therius shook his head. "I don't pretend to understand their war or what they're fighting for, but it does seem to be keeping them occupied. I can't imagine a soldier getting leave for a jaunt to France, but I'll keep an eye on the Sheldon boy."

"Don't disappoint me, Therius," the voice warned in his head, and pressure built behind his eyes and in his ears. A reminder that even a world away, his Master could still reach him here. "Griswald failed me in

Carmelle; the Sheldon girl killed him. She's proving capable, like I thought she'd be. Though Griswald was a fool, he had his moments. Getting Morshade to show her that fake portal so she thinks it's possible to make one was one of his more cunning moments. I need our plans on Earth to work. You have always been my most loyal servant. Do not give me a reason to doubt you now."

Despite the threat, Therius' chest swelled with pride. "Griswald was a vengeance-blinded fool, and he got what he deserved. I disposed of Thomas Sheldon for you, obtained Pierre Curie's discovery, and got the model automaton through the Stonehenge portal for you before it closed. I even delivered the bracelet to the Sheldon girl to ensure she came to Carmelle—"

"Even though she didn't come directly to me, as planned," interrupted the voice.

"No, her stubbornness has wrinkled our plans a few times. But she is there. I did my job. I have not failed you yet; I will not start now."

"See that you don't. That which was given to you can be taken away," warned the voice. Therius' throat constricted, his muscles and bones weakened, and looking down at his hands, he shuddered at the rapidly returning wrinkles and spots.

"Time is a gift you were given, but only if you serve your purpose. Do not squander it, or you'll find yourself out of time. For good."

"Yes, thank you, Master, I am grateful," Therius intoned, bowing at the waist while still sitting. "What will become of the Sheldon girl now, Master?"

"Many who serve me are far more capable than Griswald," the voice replied. "She will be in Orinloth shortly, where one of my most loyal followers resides. She will fulfill her fate soon."

Glossary

Armindí (AR-MIN-DEE): Immortal race evolved from lightning birds. They are a nomadic people, dabbling in witchcraft.

Arwé (AR-WAY): Parallel world to Earth with magical properties.

Athatair (ATHA-TAIR): The cave system below the Calessar. Means 'caves of learning' in Tavé.

Atha Onéa (ATHA O-NAY-AH): Located in Caris Nando behind the Éalindel. Means 'cave of crystals' in Tavé.

Avenéa (AV-UH-NAY-AH): Crystal ball that allows you to see across great distances.

Belland: Region between Carenthia and the Dharlomin mountains.

Calessar (KAL-ESS-AR): Hills in the region of Melloth. Means 'jewel hills' in Tavé.

Carenth-hild (KA-RENTH-HILD): Bay by the city of Carenthia, meaning 'sunset bay' in Tavé.

Carenthia (KA-RENTH-EE-AH): Oldest non-Lantian city in Carmelle. Means 'sunset city' in Tavé.

Carenthonon (KA-RENTH-OH-NUN): One of the towers on either side of the Tolonení where it meets the Carenth-hild. It means 'sunset tower' in Tavé.

Caris Nando (KARE-IS NAN-DOH): Forest region of the northern Lantíes. Means 'ancient forest' in Tavé.

Carmelle (KAR-MEL): Continent in the Northwestern Hemisphere of Arwé. Means 'sun leaf' in Tavé.

Colour Seer: Can see colour auras that foretell a person's future emotions.

Dharlomin (DAR-LOH-MIN): Mountain range separating Carenthia from Caris Nando. Means 'red mountains' in Tavé.

Dharmaelia (DAR-MAY-LEE-AH): City west of the Zorlomin. Means 'red-gold city' in Tavé.

Éalindel (AY-AH-LIN-DEL): Waterfall hiding the Atha Onéa. Means 'crystal waterfall' in Tavé.

Éaloth (AY-AH-LOTH): Region in the northeast of Carmelle. Means 'crystal land' in Tavé.

Edgewater: Small logging town on the west coast of Carmelle.

Fírneth Lomin: Mountain range between the Melloth region and Lothilya. Means 'jagged crown mountains' in Tavé.

Froríz (FRO-REES): Northern ice fields of Carmelle.

Harthoné Orin (HAR-THO-NAY OR-IN): War that marked the defeat of Vashi and the end of the First Age. Translates to 'War of the Wizards' in Tavé because it took place in Orinloth, land of the wizards.

Helgur (HELL-GER): Small town nestled in the Calessar, in the Melloth region.

Ilígon (ILL-EE-GON): Name of Haldin's axe. Also known as 'Slasher'.

Ilíta-onon (ILL-EE-TAH OH-NUN): One of the towers on either side of the where it meets the Carenth-hild. It means 'white tower' in Tavé.

Ilyance (ILL-EE-ANCE): The alliance of Carmellians who believe the natural wonders of Carmelle should be preserved, not industrialized.

Kai-Nalu (KYE-NAH-LOO): Southern isles of Carmelle.

Keepers: The four oldest beings in Arwé, immortals imbibed with Elemental magic at the core of their being. They protect the elements of Air, Water, Earth, and Fire, from which their powers derive.

Lantíé (LAWN-TEE-AY): Immortal race of beings evolved from perytons. Some have wings and/or antlers.

Lenia (LEN-EE-AH): City east of the Gap of Talarí under Carenthia's rule. Known as a central trading post between different cities and regions of Carmelle.

Lothilya (LOTH-ILL-YAH): Coastal region of the western Lantíes. Mean 'fair land' in Tavé.

Maeldré (MAIL-DRAY): Bowl-shaped crater in Melloth that fills with golden light when the sun hits it at the right angle. It marks the end of the Sacred Lands. Originally called Teardhí (TEER-DEE), or the Seeker's Well, until it was drained of *yenalin*.

Melbeth (MEL-BETH): Gate into the region of Melloth, the Sacred Lands. Means 'sacred gate' in Tavé.

Melloth (MELL-OTH): Region between the Gap of Talarí and the Tolotanteau coast known as the 'Sacred Lands'.

Mínando (MEE-NAN-DOH): The name of the guards who watch over Caris Nando and protect its borders, reporting to Alldían. Means 'forest guard' in Tavé.

Moonleaf: A leaf that can both capture the light of the moon and serve as prophetic aids.

Nalalíté (NAH-LA-LEE-TAY): A white flower reminiscent of a hybrid lily and rose that Lantíes use for ceremonies of honour, grief, or blessings. Their petals open only in moonlight.

Nethilya (NETH-ILL-YAH): Palace of Carenthia where the King and Queen live. Means 'fair crown' in Tavé.

Nirosula (NEER-OH-SOO-LA): The continent on which the Keepers live.

Orinloth (OR-IN-LOTH): Region of Carmelle where most wizards and mages dwell.

Redpath: The alliance of Carmellians who believe Carmelle's natural resources need to be used to advance inventions and progress industries. Also known as 'New Alliance'.

Setami (SUH-TAW-MEE): River that flows from the Dharlomin through Caris Nando, branching off to wind around the Sula-onon tower before joining the main course again. It means 'steady guard' in Tavé.

Seven Pools: Pools below Telwé Unvar that can be used with the tree's petals to see into other worlds.

Skeletal Moon Lake: Formerly known as 'Moon Lake', this lake was the site of Dark Magic and now has the skeletons of sacrificed people frozen beneath the ice.

Steepleton: One of the small towns in Belland. Named after William Steepleton, who built the first steeple and bell in Belland.

Storm Kelpie: Human-like race with blue skin. They live in underwater caves among the Yena Aisis. They have retractable kelp wings that help propel them through the water and can create storms. They use poetry to challenge sailors passing through their waters.

Storyteller: A person who can recall stories from the past and weave them into magical songs.

Sula-onon (SOO-LA-OH-NUN): A lone tower in Caris Nando, meaning 'moon tower' in Tavé.

Suléa (SOO-LAY-AH): A rare sapphire and crimson flower. Its red pollen can have healing powers and be used in rubies.

Swordmaster: The title given to those in the highest tier of swordsman-ship. Rigorous testing is done before the title is bestowed on an individual.

Talarí, Gap of (TAH-LAR-EE): The gap between the Dharlomin and Fírneth Lomin mountain ranges. Talarí means 'dreams' in Tavé.

Talarí, river (TAH-LAR-EE): A river that descends from the Dharlomin at the Gap of Talarí and flows out into the farmlands of Tamarack.

Tamarack (TA-MAH-RAK): A small town between the Gap of Talarí and Lenia, surrounded by farmland.

Tavé (TAH-VAY): Oldest language of Carmelle, still spoken by people throughout the continent, but especially the Lantíes, for whom it is their first language.

Telwé Unvar (TEL-WAY UHN-VAR): The Dimensional Tree. Located in Caris Nando and controlled by the current Lord of Caris Nando. It is a giant tree, with each pink blossom representing a world. Petals can be plucked and dropped in one of the Seven Pools to view that world.

Tolonení (TOW-LOW-NEN-EE): The largest river in Carmelle, flowing from the Tor Stella Lalíté lake to the Tolotanteau.

Tolotanteau (TOW-LOW-TAN-TOW): The ocean off the west coast of Carmelle, which translates to 'the great sea' in Tavé.

Vasmorloth (VAS-MORE-LOTH): Region east of the Zorlomin. Means 'dark fire land' in Tavé. Vashi's stronghold is here.

Voita (VOY-TAH): Forest south of Carenthia where it is eerily quiet and rumoured to hold monsters.

Vulnek (VOHL-NEK): A collar designed to track and deliver increasing levels of pain the further the wearer gets from its master.

Wenaf (WHEN-AF): A strong alcoholic drink.

Windtalker: A person with enhanced hearing who can send and receive messages on the wind.

Yenalin (YEN-AH-LIN): Clear liquid with reviving qualities, mostly consumed by immortals and unicorns. Means 'star water' in Tavé.

Zorlomin (ZOR-LOW-MIN): The mountain range between Dharmaelia and Vasmorloth. Means 'black mountains' in Tavé.

Cast List

Lenia

Therius (THARE-EE-US): Servant of Vashi who kills Thomas Sheldon and becomes trapped on Earth.

Earth

Connor Sheldon: Heir to the Sheldon fortune and brother to Tanaya and Sadie.

Derek Spencer: Dances with Sadie at the ball and appears as her beau at Tanaya's wedding.

Henry: Marries Tanaya Sheldon.

Higgins, Sergeant: Sergeant in charge of Connor's unit.

Mabel (MAY-BULL): Connor Sheldon's girlfriend.

Margaret: Maid at the Sheldon manor.

Roger Sheldon: Sadie's father.

Sadie Sheldon: Middle child of Roger and Victoria Sheldon.

Tanaya Sheldon: Older sister to Sadie and Connor.

Thomas Sheldon: Sadie's great-grandfather, and author of the book *Adventures in Carmelle*.

Victoria Sheldon: Sadie's mother.

Will: Connor's best friend in the army.

Helgur

Ahmeric (AH-MER-IK): Young boy who Sadie helps save from the dragon attack on Helgur.

Edgewater

Arcturius Mauve, Enchanter (ARK-TOOR-EE-US MOHV): Enchanter entertaining at The Whispering Wind Inn.

Davin Ellwood: Oldest Ellwood son.

Dinah (DYE-NAH): The innkeeper James' daughter.

Ethan Ellwood: Second oldest Ellwood son.

Igino Ellwood (IH-GEE-NO): Logger, married to Marianina.

James: Innkeeper of The Whispering Wind Inn.

Maddie Ellwood: Youngest Ellwood daughter.

Marianina Ellwood (MARY-AH-NEE-NA): Cook at The Whispering Wind Inn, married to Igino.

Carenthia

Cassador, Prince (KASS-AH-DOOR): Son of King Vindor and Queen Morgaine. Prince of Carenthia. Ilyance.

Fabius Griswald, Commander (FAB-EE-US GRIZ-WAWLD): Commander of the Redpath Carenthian Company. Second-in-command to Master Hargrim.

Hargrim, Master (HAR-GRIM): Leader of the Redpath.

Morgaine, Queen (MORE-GANE): Queen of Carenthia. Redpath.

Phil: Innkeeper of The Crowned Sun Inn.

Tacitus, Lord (TAH-SI-TUS): Loremaster of Carenthia.

Vindor, King (VIN-DOOR): King of Carenthia. Ilyance.

Wenhart, Officer (WEHN-HART): Officer in Griswald's Redpath contingent.

<u>Keepers</u>

Bren: Keeper of Earth element. Immortal. Strongest Earth magic in Arwé.

Lin: Keeper of Water element. Immortal. Strongest Water magic in Arwé.

Ninaya (NIN-AY-AH): Keeper of Air element. Immortal. Strongest Air magic in Arwé.

Vashi (VAH-SHEE): Keeper of Fire element. Immortal. Strongest Fire magic in Arwé. Cast out of Nirosula and banished to Vasmorloth in Carmelle by the other Keepers for using dark, forbidden Celestial magic to gain power.

<u>Dharmaelia</u>

Airothane (AIR-OH-THANE): Second oldest Prince of Dharmaelia. Younger brother to Haldin. Son of King Peladorn. Windtalker.

Haldin (HAL-DIN): Oldest Prince of Dharmaelia and heir to the Dharmaelian throne. Son of King Peladorn. Known as Haldin the Hawk to his people, Wielder of Ilígon.

Peladorn, King (PELL-AH-DORN): King of Dharmaelia. Haldin and Airothane's father.

<u>Orinloth</u>

Lane Tamlin: Wizard originally from region around Dharmaelia. Most powerful wizard of the Second Age.

Rahkkar Tarquin Morshade (RAH-KAR TAR-KIN MORE-SHADE): Mage practicing Dark Magic. Works for Griswald and the Redpaths.

Caris Nando

Alldían (ALL-DEE-AWN): Lantíé. Lord of Caris Nando. Also known as Alldían the Wise for his prophetic talents. Tristan's godfather.

Beryl (BARE-ILL): Lantíé. Mínando watchman of Caris Nando.

Brunea (BROO-NAY-AH): Lantíé of Caris Nando. Planted the crystals in the Atha Onéa after people tried to steal the crystals he brought back from Éaloth.

Chai: Sadie's bonded unicorn.

Duvandir (DOO-VAN-DEER): Lantíé. Alldían's son.

Eberon, Lord (EH-BER-ON): Lantíé. Lord of Lothilya.

Efarin (EH-FAR-IN): Lantíé. Mínando watchman of Caris Nando.

Eldaron (ELL-DER-ON): Lantíé of Caris Nando. Tristan's friend.

Tristan West: Human. Godson of Alldían. Storyteller and Swordmaster.

Creature Guide

Bragûl (BRAH-GOOL): Black wispy creatures with jagged teeth, clawed fingers, and yellow or red eyes. Created by Vashi to fight for him.

Dragons: There are inherently good dragons, the most ancient ones, and there are evil dragons created by Vashi to do his bidding.

Lightning Birds: Huge black and white birds that summon thunder and lightning with their wings. The Armindí evolved from them and can still shapeshift into them. Non-evolved lightning birds still exist, and are loyal to the Armindí, even letting some ride on them.

Mermaids: Live in the Tolotanteau.

Perytons (PARE-IH-TUHNS): Stags with feathered wings like eagles. Both males and females have antlers. Prey on humans from parallel worlds. When they consume a soul, their shadow echoes that soul. A peryton's shadow can also foreshadow their next victim. Lantíes evolved from perytons.

Sun dragons: Celestial creatures inherently bonded to the sun. They dwell in Nirosula, and use dragon fire to enhance sunsets.

Unicorns: Noble creatures with no allegiance to people, though they live among the Lantíes of Caris Nando and tolerate them more than other races. Can bond with people and let the bonded ride them, but it's rare.

Wyrms (WERMS): Sea serpents who roam the Tolotanteau. They are the natural enemy of mermaids and can secrete an oil to paralyze its victims. But wyrms can act like guardians for storm kelpies.

Author's Note

Thank you for reading *A Spark From Embers*. If this is your first immersion into the world of Arwé, I hope it has inspired you to read the rest of the series.

I know time is precious and leaving reviews can be daunting, but I would be ever so grateful and honoured if you would consider leaving a review on Goodreads or Amazon. Other than purchasing a book, leaving a review or rating helps support an author, and will help other readers find the book and decide whether they want to read it. And I of course value and appreciate your feedback.

If you are already subscribed to my newsletter, thank you so much for subscribing! You can look forward to exclusive access to future novellas and updates on the world of Arwé soon. If you purchased a paperback copy of this book and are not yet subscribed to my newsletter, I encourage you to consider subscribing through my website at www.kayleaprime.com. Through my newsletter, you will be privy to monthly writing updates, first announcements about upcoming books and cover reveals, ARC opportunities, and other exclusive content. You'll even receive a FREE exclusive ebook of my prequel novella, *A Ballad of Hate and Hope*.

You can also find me across most social media platforms under the handle @kayleaprime.

Thank you again for your support!

-Kaylea Prime

Acknowledgements

How to properly acknowledge something that has lived in your soul for almost twenty years? My commitment to the world of Arwé, to these characters, to this story, has been longer than my commitment to my husband, or to anything else in my life. It sparked my imagination as a teenager, and stuck with me through eight years of university, getting married, having kids, and becoming a librarian. I grew as a person with this story, loved and lost with this story, traveled with this story, moved around the province with this story, and still it clutched at my heart and never let go. Of course, I wasn't working on *A Spark From Embers* consistently throughout those twenty years. I took breaks, sometimes years at a time, as life's adventures demanded I put it aside for a bit. But it has always been there with me, tucked in a corner of my mind, even if I just thought about it while I looked out over the ocean or scribbled ideas in the margins of my notebooks during lectures.

Twenty years is a long time for a story to marinate, and just like me, it evolved and grew and changed so much that much of it is unrecognizable from those first drafts. But the most amazing part about this prolonged labour of love to me is that no matter how much I changed, and my characters changed, no matter how long I neglected them while dealing with everything else life threw at me, they were still always waiting there for me to come back to them. I have seen them at their best and at their worst, and they have stuck with me through my highs and lows as well. I feel like I know them better than myself sometimes. They have so much of me in them, and so much of what I have learned and observed over twenty years.

But those characters would still remain in my head only if not for a plethora of people who have supported me through the years.

I must start these acknowledgements at the beginning, with the people who were there for me first. Who nurtured and celebrated my love of writing and stories. Who, from my toddler days, let me carry a book around with me everywhere like a security blanket. Who let me bounce ideas off them and helped me turn my room into a writer's retreat as a teen. Who encouraged me to never give up my dream, and believed in me even when I didn't. Thank you to my family, who I know will always be in my corner. My mom Sylvia, who taught me the meaning of unconditional love and always knows how to buoy my spirits when I'm down on myself. My dad Ron, who was the very first person to read the very first draft of *A Spark From Embers* (other than my teacher – we'll get to that in a second). My sisters Candace and Tamara, who became my first beta readers to suffer through my first draft (and somehow refrain from cringing to my face), and who are still my biggest champions.

If my parents and sisters are the roots of my support system, my husband Sid is the enriching soil, the sturdy stalk, and even the leaves branching from the stalk. Nourishing my passion for writing, always making sure I can find the time and motivation to keep my dream alive and strong, supporting my story in every way so it can grow and flourish. Alpha reader, mapmaker, tech troubleshooter, business consultant, therapist, fact-checker, fellow stargazer and dreamer – he does anything and everything he can to support me. You are my anchor, my guiding star, my soulmate.

Of course, even the richest soil is not enough alone for a flower to blossom. Jade and Eralyn, my amazing children, you are my sun and rain. The refreshing rain that cleanses my spirit, the bright beams of sunlight that warm my heart. You inspire me to be a better person, to show you the power of manifesting your dreams. I hope this book inspires you to follow your own dreams one day. And I hope Sadie helps empower you as well.

My critique partner and amazing friend Bethany. What can I say? Your support has been invaluable. I am the luckiest writer in the world to have befriended you and earned your trust. I am so happy I was brave enough to reach out to you and start our CP relationship, because now I don't know what I would do without you. Your advice and insights on my story and writing are so spot on and appreciated, and your own amazing writing inspires me every time I have the honour of reading it. I love that a true friendship has grown between us and would be lost without our email threads comparing writing woes and life adventures. I'm excited to help each other through the next stages of publishing our series!

To my developmental editor Talena, who helped shape this story into the final version it is today and who really seemed to understand my vision and how to bring it to life, I am so grateful for your invaluable insight. To my copyeditor Kayla, who polished this story so it would shine. To fellow author Deryn Collier, who helped hone the first chapter during her Writer-in-Residence period at TNRL and gave me the confidence to read an excerpt of my book aloud for the first time. And to my betas and every stage of the many, many drafts this book went through, thank you so much for providing the insight and advice I needed when I was too close to the story and couldn't see where to improve it anymore.

To my cover designer Timea at Fantastical Ink. Thank you for bringing my vision to life in such a breathtaking way! I could not be happier with how well it reflects my story and fulfills my cover dreams.

A huge thank you to Alyson and the other brave readers of some of my earliest drafts. My writing has improved *drastically* since some of the versions you read, but you read it anyway and supported me and offered advice that helped shape the final story.

Because this story has been with me since grade 12, I would also be amiss if I didn't thank two of my high school teachers. My English teacher Mr.

Murray for being the first teacher to give me confidence in my writing skills and encourage me to challenge myself. And Mr. Baker, my Gr. 12 Writing teacher, who introduced me to NaNoWriMo, and who was actually probably the very first reader of the first 50k words of the first draft of *A Spark From Embers* (and who was very encouraging despite how much I cringe when I read that first draft now!). Teachers never get enough credit, but you have not been forgotten, and I'm so grateful for the support you showed a budding teenage writer.

To everyone else who has supported me over the years, whether it was in person or as part of writing groups and social media communities, thank you so much for helping this writer's dream come true. I never truly found my voice as a writer until I started interacting with more writers in these communities and learned all the ways I could hone my craft, and for that I'm so grateful. I continue to learn and grow and improve as a writer because of you!

And lastly, thank you to every reader who picked up this book and gave it a chance. You will never know how much it means to even be able to say that I *have* readers. My dream since childhood is coming true, and it's all because you took a chance on Sadie, Connor – and me.

About the Author

Kaylea Prime is the author of the fantasy series, *Tears of Flame*. She is also a librarian with a passion for planning epic programs that immerse kids and teens into their favourite literary worlds. When she's not writing or working as a librarian, she can be found exploring the beautiful wilderness around her home in Clearwater, British Columbia, with her two kids, husband, and two golden retrievers.

@kayleaprime
www.kayleaprime.com

www.ingramcontent.com/pod-product-compliance
Lightning Source LLC
Chambersburg PA
CBHW051425190726
48289CB00001B/59